Your Closest Friend

KAREN PERRY

PENGUIN BOOKS

PENGUIN BOOKS

UK | USA | Canada | Ireland | Australia
India | New Zealand | South Africa

Penguin Books is part of the Penguin Random House group of companies
whose addresses can be found at global.penguinrandomhouse.com.

First published 2018
001

Copyright © Karen Perry, 2018

Set in 12.5/14.75 pt Garamond MT Std
Typeset by Jouve (UK), Milton Keynes
Printed and bound in Great Britain by Clays Ltd, Elcograf S.p.A.

A CIP catalogue record for this book is available from the British Library

PAPERBACK ISBN: 978–1–405–93665–1

www.greenpenguin.co.uk

Penguin Random House is committed to a
sustainable future for our business, our readers
and our planet. This book is made from Forest
Stewardship Council® certified paper.

PENGUIN BOOKS

Your Closest Friend

Praise for Karen Perry

'Builds to an incredibly tense finale – before delivering an amazing final twist. Riveting stuff' *Sunday Mirror*

'Like *Gone Girl* . . . it's the most gripping thing I've read for ages' *Evening Standard*

'Stunning' Simon Mayo Radio 2 Book Club

'Truly remarkable . . . Grips your heart from the first pages and simply never lets go' Jeffery Deaver

'This tense, unpredictable novel blends a thriller with an intimate family story to produce a most compelling read' John Boyne

'A twist-filled page-turner' *Closer*

'Both as a crime novel and an emotional journey, it's gripping stuff' Tana French

'Full of intrigue and incident and keeps us guessing until the very last tragic page' Liz Nugent

'An unputdownable novel . . . leading to a stunning conclusion you won't see coming' Michelle Richmond

ABOUT THE AUTHOR

Karen Perry is the *Sunday Times* bestselling author of *Can You Keep a Secret?*, *Girl Unknown*, *Only We Know* and *The Boy That Never Was*, which was selected for the Simon Mayo Radio 2 Book Club. She lives in Dublin with her family.

PART ONE

I.

Cara

It's his eyes that grab my attention. Not the gun. Eyes like a doll's: dark and malevolently blank.

Other details follow – the meagre scruff of beard skirting his young face, grey jeans and hoodie, a knife in his belt. These things register in a fleeting, abstract way as I walk towards the Tube station, my head still zinging with cocktails and revelations, the thrill of the illicit. The night is hot and clammy, a faintly faecal odour emanating from the drains masked somewhat by petrol fumes and cigarette smoke.

When I see the gun in his hands, my first thought is: *That thing's not real.* Clunky and oversized, it seems an exaggeration of a weapon, like a toy, or one of those guns they give you when playing Quasar or Splatoon. The word *terror* doesn't enter my head, even though the whole city has been on high alert all summer. Perhaps I am drunker than I realize, but when I see him prowling the street, his eyes sweeping for targets, I have the thought that this is a game – a stag party involving teams, some kind of jokey hunt that has spilled out on to the streets of Shoreditch. It's the start of the bank holiday weekend and I don't feel threatened yet. I'm too focused on my own misdemeanour – the person I've spent the past couple of hours with and how I'm going to explain it; how I'm going to cover it up. Sorrow is a long way off. I am giddy with alcohol and with the headiness of my encounter and all that trickles from it.

The air is split by the sound of screaming. My eyes dart across the street to a couple: professionals casually dressed for a Friday night date, kids probably at home with the babysitter. The woman is clutching at her partner, almost pushing him into a shop doorway as she recoils, face contorting with terror. The sound the gun makes seems too small for such an outlandish weapon – a firecracker, a sharply snapped branch.

It is not in any way like a game now. The woman crumples to the ground and the realization comes over me swiftly: I am witnessing a killing. Her companion reaches for her while looking up, his mouth open with the shock of an ending, the sweetness of the evening, his love, his whole life, already over. A bullet to the head and he is gone.

The street fills with panic. Screaming, feet pound the pavement, all of us running now. In the distance, an approaching siren whines. Everywhere swarms with movement, the crack of gunfire unleashed with abandon, limbs flailing, the wounded attempting to stagger away, flashes of blood on summer clothing, garish and visceral in its horror. I trip over a kerbstone and drop my bag, hands and knees on the asphalt, my breath high and light in my chest as I try to regain my footing. And it's as I right myself that I see him: a second assailant coming in the other direction. He wears khaki fatigues, and heavy boots, and he walks with a military strut, plunging his knife with an air of detachment like he is stabbing pillows, not flesh and blood. His eyes lock on me now – those same doll's eyes, glassy and unmoved, enmity in his blank stare.

My thoughts slow, and what returns to me now is a sensory memory of Mabel in my arms when she was a baby and I'd lift her from the cot – that instant when her soft, fragrant little body would meet with my chest – the familiarity of it coming over me in a way that is painful, knowing it's going to be snatched away. And with it comes a rush of feeling: angry indignation because I'm nowhere near ready for this, rage because so much of my life is yet unlived. *You fucker*, I think with spitting venom as my executioner closes in, the blade of his knife dull with blood. And that is when I feel it: the sharp grip around my upper arm like a claw. A hard tug and I am falling backwards towards a voice in the darkness.

'Get in!' someone hisses, and I stumble back over a threshold, the hand still pulling at me, so hard it hurts.

We are scrambling up a stairway now, feet clattering over metal steps. How many of us are there? Three? Four? Is he coming after us? Up ahead, tiny red lights blink and dance through the darkness, and it takes me a moment to realize they are lights in the soles of trainers, like the shoes I bought for Mabel in Clarks. I have no idea where we are going as I charge up the flight of stairs after the others, my heart clamouring with fear, not knowing if this is a path to safety or if we are barrelling headlong towards our own slaughter.

'In here!' the voice says.

A doorway appears, fluorescent light beyond, and I hurry after the others, the door closing shut behind me, my breathing wild in my chest, three of us listening, an uneasy triumvirate, each face caught in a rictus of fear.

Strip lighting on the ceiling gives off a sibilant hum.

Somewhere beyond this building there are whining sirens, screams, chaos, the crackling of firearms, but in here there is hushed silence and frightened eyes. A man and a woman and me, trapped in a room with a buzzing fridge, towers of bottled water and canned soft drinks, a table and some stacked chairs, empty hooks on the walls. There is a lingering odour of cigarette smoke, undercut by the hospital smell of detergent.

'We should go,' the man whispers urgently, and the girl shoots him a fierce look, puts her finger to her own lips to silence him.

Her face is small and triangular, like a cat's. Short, cropped hair that has been bleached yellow-white, the colour of sour milk. She is smaller than the man, smaller than me, and she looks young – not much more than twenty.

The man mops his hand over his face and shuffles from one side of the room to the other. I wish he would stand still so that I can listen, so that I can think. His trainers squeak on the linoleum floor and I look down and see large orange sports shoes, their logo emblazoned in red, lights winking in the soles – the same lights I'd noticed on the stairs. I have a sudden flash of him trying these shoes on for the first time, admiring them in the shop mirror, and the thought makes me feel sad somehow. I bet he never thought he would be walking them into a situation like this.

'Stay still, Neil, for fuck's sake,' the girl hisses. 'You're making me nervous.'

Her accent has an American inflection. I also realize that these two know each other, yet I can tell they are not a couple. Like the girl, Neil looks to be in his early twenties. Tall and heavy-set with hair that is probably reddish

6

but looks blond under the fluorescent bulbs. His clothing, like hers, is nondescript – jeans and a white shirt. The words 'Team PRET' embroidered on the back of his shirt point to their connection. These two work together, and we are standing in the storeroom of whatever Pret store they work in. It's only now that I notice, with a fresh plunge of panic, that the room has no windows. The only way out is the door we came in.

'This doesn't feel right,' Neil says, and beyond the skittish nerves in his voice there is something else: movement in the corridor outside.

'Quiet!' I hiss, and we all freeze.

Blood pounds in my ears, and I see a small pulmonary throb in Neil's neck, sweat beading on his upper lip. The girl says nothing, her angular features and tight mouth pulled taut in concentration. She is standing close to me and as we strain for a sound beyond the door, my eyes take in the white iPhone earbuds emerging from the neck of her shirt, dark circles under her eyes and a rash of tiny spots at the corner of her mouth. The three of us strain to hear a sound beyond the door, and when it comes again – a faint dropping sound, like a pebble falling on to wood – she moves quickly to the doorway, and reaches for the light switch, plunging us into a new darkness.

I have never experienced fear like this – not in my adult life. Fear that is pure and whole and occupies the body completely like some kind of parasitic invasion. Outside on the street, facing the killer, what I had felt was rage. But in here, trapped in this room, terror comes for me. I am rigid with it. Overhead, a blue glow fills the space where the fluorescent bulb had hummed. This ghostly memory of light redoubles the shivery fear I feel. In the darkness, we strain to hear a sound, poised on a terrifying threshold.

Neil moves and the lights of his shoes flicker briefly. From outside comes the sound of engines gunning, wheels screeching, but the night-filled streets seem suddenly distant. This room, our collective breathing, the furious throb of regret that has started inside me, seem to occupy a different plane, far from everything familiar, everything safe.

Run. Hide. Tell.

All summer long it's been drilled into us. At work, we've conducted rehearsed emergency evacuations. Our building is a potential target for terrorism, and I have attended seminars and training courses to learn how I should react in various situations of danger.

But now that I am here, in this room, hiding, while murder takes place on the street outside, I do not feel safe. I feel trapped. I can't escape the suspicion that we are sitting ducks.

'We should go.' There is heat in Neil's urgent whisper.

'No,' the girl says firmly.

I look in the direction of her voice, and all at once her face is there, lit by the glow of her iPhone.

'What are you doing?'

'We need to tell someone where we are,' she says. Her voice, although lowered, is firm and calm.

'They might hear you!' I whisper.

She ignores me and I watch her thumbs flying over the screen. There's at least ten years between us, yet she seems the authoritative one.

As she taps out her message, I remember my bag – how

I dropped it on the street. My phone, wallet, keys, Oyster card – everything gone.

'Shit,' the girl says in her deadpan tone. 'No fucking reception.'

The glow from the screen fades, and the darkness feels cloying, claustrophobic.

'We have to get out of here,' Neil says, his voice punched with the jittery panic I feel.

'No way,' she replies.

'I'm not standing around here, waiting for them to come and butcher me! We should run!'

'Maybe he's right,' I say, my instincts thrown off kilter. 'Is there another way out?'

'The only other way is through the shop, and that's shuttered. If you go back down on to the street, you could get killed.'

'They were moving,' I say. 'If they haven't already been shot by the police, they'll have moved on to another street.'

'You don't know how many of them could be out there.'

'What if one of them has a bomb?' Neil counters. 'For all we know they might have explosives strapped to themselves and we should be evacuating this building right now, not waiting to be blown up.' His voice rises with frustration.

'The police advice is to hide until it's safe.'

'But at some point, some fuckhead is going to realize the next big way to terrorize people is to hunt them down in their hiding places.'

I feel a movement of air past me, and Neil is at the door.

'Don't,' she warns him.

But he mutters, 'I'll take my chances. You two can do what you want.'

He flings the door wide, and I feel a new surge of panic at the prospect of him leaving. All my feminist principles take flight, and I find myself scared at the thought of being deserted by this man. Two women alone in a room. What chance will we have should one of those crazed attackers come up here? As Neil heads for the stairwell, I am suddenly sure that if I stay here, I will die. I have to take my chance now while there is still a chance to take. The door is closing and I can hear Neil's feet in his big orange trainers clattering down the stairs, and something propels me to push open the door and follow, nerves pinging all over my body. But before I even reach the first step, I feel the pincer grip around my shoulder again, tugging me back.

'No,' she says firmly. 'Let him go if he wants. We have to stay. We have to wait until it's safe.'

Her voice is low, throaty, surprisingly deep for one so young. I feel myself straining after Neil – the exit is so close. I can't hear his footsteps any more, and the darkness of the stairway seems vaguely threatening. From somewhere outside, I can hear breaking glass and I shrink from it now.

'Trust me,' she says, her voice softer. 'We'll wait together.'

At the top of the stairs, there's an Emergency Exit sign. The light from it casts her face in a green glow, and her eyes seem melancholy, pleading.

All of a sudden, I start to cry. Fat, hot tears burn my eyes, and I turn from her and head into the room, finding the wall and sliding down so that I'm sitting with my knees pulled up, the heels of my hands pressing into my eye sockets. *Mabel*, I think, picturing my little girl asleep in bed, and fervently wishing I hadn't been so stupid, so selfish and reckless, that I hadn't made the decision I did.

The light snaps on and I look up.

The girl shrugs. 'Less scary this way.'

'But if someone sees the light –'

'They won't. No one's going to come up here.'

'But Neil –'

'If Neil gets to safety, he'll tell some cop where we are and they'll come get us when it's safe. If he doesn't get to safety, well . . . then, I guess we made the right decision.'

Her voice seems to hold the shrug, and she seems more relaxed now, even though her shoulders are high with tension as she lopes across the small room to free a can of Coca-Cola from its tower.

'You want one?' she asks.

I say no, wincing at the loud snap as she pulls the ring. I swipe at my eyes, embarrassed by the lapse in my composure.

Perching on the edge of the table, she takes out her phone once more. Despite the confidence of her decisions, there is a nervous, caged-bird flutter about the way her hands move.

'I dropped my bag outside,' I tell her. 'It had all my stuff in it.'

Turning her phone towards me, she asks, 'You wanna contact someone?'

'I thought you said there was no reception.'

'There isn't. But you could line up a WhatsApp or a text. It would go through whenever this shithole picks up coverage.'

I think about Jeff, but what would I tell him? How could I explain myself?

'Thanks, but I'm okay.'

She goes back to her message, but my thoughts have strayed now to Jeff at home, watching rolling news reports of the attack, trying to call me again and again, only to get no answer. Will he call Kamila to check? Does he even know her number? I feel a drag of nausea in my stomach.

'I shouldn't even be here,' I say, and she looks up, mildly curious. 'I don't mean here, in this room – I mean in this part of London. I wasn't supposed to be here tonight.'

Her eyes take on a different sort of intensity. Do I imagine it, or do they flare a little with interest? Her hands grow still, and her fidgeting stops. *How strange this is*, I think. An hour or so ago I was sitting in a bar trading jokes at the expense of millennials, making disparaging remarks about snowflakes. And now here I am with one of them.

'What is it?' she asks, interest softening her voice.

'Nothing,' I say.

'You can tell me. I won't tell a soul.'

It feels strange. The way she's looking at me – the concern in her eyes, so unexpected. I'm a little drunk. All those Aperols are making my head feel heavy. And here is this stranger, offering me a space to confide in the most bizarre circumstances. But somehow it feels right. It feels necessary. Like refuge in a storm. Whatever happens, I need to unburden myself before I leave the room.

Everything in my life has been brought into sharp relief

with this terror attack. The swarming confusion of my feelings – the doubts, the regrets over decisions made – all brought into focus in the light of imminent danger, the threat prowling the street outside. Private thoughts that I haven't shared with anyone, stirred to life earlier this evening, now demand to be heard. And there is no one here except me and this girl with her dark eyes and plain face. There is something tranquil about her, as if she is unperturbed by the atrocities committed outside, but far from being wary of her unflappability, I find myself cleaving to it. Right now, she seems like the perfect person to share my secrets with, no thought given to the consequences.

I'm not sure how long we talk. Even afterwards, I cannot account for how much time we spend in that room. Whispered confidences in a strange place with a young woman I don't even know. Giving voice to things I had never openly admitted to, not even within the privacy of my own thoughts. The atmosphere in this cramped space crackles with the static of fear, of time running out. The two of us wait to be gathered up.

'I expect they're dead by now,' I say.

'The terrorists?'

'At Stoney Street, the police were there almost immediately. It was all over in less than twenty minutes.'

'I guess.'

She fingers the rim of her empty Coca-Cola can, stares down at it and says, 'I envy them.'

'Who? The terrorists?'

A slight tilt of her eyebrows, and she looks up. I notice how her chin juts forward just a tiny bit. It lends her an air of determination, or stubbornness.

'Not that they're dead, I mean. But I admire their conviction.'

'You do?' I cannot keep the incredulity from my voice.

Her gaze is calm, clear-eyed. In a quiet voice, she almost mumbles, 'I'd like to believe that much in something.'

There is something rueful and downbeat about her, but for the first time since entering this room, I feel wary of her. I think of all I have told her and feel the first shimmer of doubt.

When her phone skitters over the table, awakening like an angry wasp, we both jump.

She snatches it up, thumbs the screen, hesitates, then says, 'We can leave.'

'You're sure?'

'Yes. But go carefully.'

We've been sequestered in this room for what feels like hours, and now, leaving it, I feel some residue of the place has seeped into my bones. I go first, down into the darkness, and it feels like a game I once played as a child in my cousins' house: I was blindfolded, with all the lights turned out, everyone else hiding, as I stumbled from room to room, somehow afraid that I might never find anyone, that I would be trapped there alone, for ever.

I can feel her close behind me, and as I find the bottom step and move towards the door, fear clutching at my throat, instinctively my hand reaches out behind me until it finds hers. A hand that is cool and dry, papery skin over narrow bones. Our grip on each other tightens. Now is the moment. I reach for the latch, open the door, and slowly lead us out.

The street is cast in a greyish-orange light punctuated by

a flash of blue. On the ground there are bodies writhing; medics in yellow jackets lean over them, bent on their ministrations. Splatters of blood and shattered glass litter the tarmac. Uniformed police swarm the area, herding zombie-like survivors away from the carnage. Ambulances and police cars stand guard on both sides, a police-cordon tape flickering in the breeze along the perimeter. Someone starts shouting at us the moment we emerge. But what stands out above all else are the white sheets on the ground that cover the slain. The street is littered with them. My insides turn to liquid, bile comes up the back of my throat, and just then the girl squeezes my hand. I had forgotten she was there. Her nails dig into me, reaffirming our connection. It is only now as the police officer reaches us that I realize I do not know her name.

'Quickly,' the officer says, taking hold of my arm.

I don't look back, as I'm ushered away. But I do look down. And as we hurry away from that place, that glimpse of hell, my gaze is caught by a pair of feet emerging from beneath one of those sheets. Orange trainers. Lights that once danced in the soles, now extinguished.

2.

Amy

In the dim cave of the bedroom, I take a last toke before crushing the reefer into the scallop shell. I don't normally smoke weed, but under the circumstances I feel like I need it.

I've been online for almost three hours – nothing unusual in that. But tonight is different. It's not the usual grim slog through Facebook and Twitter and Snapchat. I haven't been wading through cyberspace, dipping into fan sites and online chatrooms, a swamp of useless information, the inane and virulent comments left by trolls, feeling the hot welt of anger growing inside me. There's a purpose to it now – something to look for.

Someone.

A quest of sorts. A treasure hunt. I'm looking for her face.

Pale skin, light freckles visible beneath her make-up, across her nose and cheeks. Shoulder-length auburn hair, parted to one side, salon-sleek with a hint of a curl. Eyes a marbled green that reflected her reserve, her intelligence, pupils retracting into pinpricks while the rest of her eye widened with fear.

Downstairs, the subwoofer gives out its blood-thunder bass beat. It's three o'clock in the morning but the party goes on. There'll be sore heads and scant attention in the lecture halls tomorrow but that's not my problem. I don't even know these people.

Brief stirrings in the bed behind me, as I click and click again, homing in on my quarry.

'Amy?' Sean says, his voice groggy with sleep and irritation. 'When are you going to turn that thing off?'

'In a minute,' I tell him, not even turning back to look.

Nothing showy or obvious in her beauty. A shy flower. Maddening how I cannot find her image, each search drawing a blank.

I'm dimly aware of my face reflected back at me from the window behind the desk, and beyond that the neat row of windows in the houses opposite, curtains drawn, everything locked up safe. All of it familiar to me. The street outside. Sean stirring in the bed. My night-trawls through cyberspace.

She reached for me in the darkness. Her hand held in mine.

Something has come over me. I look down at the keyboard beneath my fingertips, remember the pulse running through her blood communicating with mine, exposing my sudden need.

A change is coming.

The one I've been waiting for.

I can feel it.

3.

Cara

It is six hours since it happened. Six hours since I hid in that room. Beyond the windows of our apartment, a grainy light filters through the night sky. I can feel Jeff's hand in mine, the reassuring pressure of his thumb passing over the ridges of knuckles and bones.

A cup of tea sits cooling on the table in front of me. A cold skin has formed on the surface, the sight of which makes my stomach retract in tight revulsion. He has stopped urging me to drink it. I look down at his hand in mine, and note the whiteness of my skin, the unfamiliarity of it. For a disconcerting moment, I have the feeling that the hand is not mine, but a part of someone else. A foreign object. Everything in the room is impacting strangely upon me.

'What did the police say?' he asks gently. 'Will they want to speak with you again?'

'I don't know. I gave them my contact details.'

'But you did tell them what happened? You did tell them what you saw?'

'Yes. But there were so many people. So many accounts.'

All at once I am back there on the street, the strobe of blue lights cutting through the night air, white sheets on the ground concealing the lumpen shapes of bodies. A female officer's hand gripping my upper arm with a firmness that only served to remind me of the flimsiness of my own flesh, my mortality.

'You're alright,' she kept saying to me, her voice steady and reassuring, but I felt the urgency in her grip, the desire to get away from the site of all that killing.

I was ushered to an Italian café I knew well – a boisterous place, full of gentle mockery, each customer addressed in terms of intimacy. It was part of the strangeness of the night that this café now seemed to cower beneath a weight of hushed silence. Shaken survivors were herded inside to sit quietly at tables, some whispering into mobile phones, others holding their heads in their hands or staring blankly into the middle distance. The gregarious Italian waiters, sombre now, administered hot drinks while uniformed police hunkered down at tables, taking statements. It was only as I wordlessly accepted the hot coffee put in front of me that I realized she wasn't with me – the girl from the storeroom. I got to my feet and looked about, craning for a glimpse of that yellow-white hair, those trailing earbuds, but to no avail. She was gone, and I could not explain to myself the disappointment it made me feel.

'Cara?'

My thoughts snap back to the present. Jeff is staring at me, concern etched into his face. I look at him in the dawning light, still in his dressing gown, worry and lack of sleep making him look his age. It is only recently that his hair has thinned, whitish-grey hairs threading through a dark-brown thatch. The lines that run from the sides of his nose to the corners of his mouth have deepened into dark grooves. He is fifteen years older than me – a disparity that has never bothered me. When we got married five years ago, I believed that the difference in our ages was the only gap that could ever exist between us, and that it would blur in time. I believed that we were meant to be together.

'You still look shaken,' he remarks. 'I wish there was something I could do or say to help.' For just a moment, the way that he is holding my hand, the deep concern in his eyes, makes me think that this is the thing that will bring us close again. The knowledge that we could, so easily, have been violently torn apart. We love each other. We have made a life together. Surely that is all that matters?

'I think you should have a brandy,' he tells me, letting go of my hand and leaving his chair, heading towards the kitchen cabinet we call the drinks press. The thought of alcohol repulses me right now. I've already had a skinful, the dregs of it still spinning down the drain of my thoughts, making me feel heavy-limbed and overused, so I stop him and tell him no.

'You've had a shock,' he insists.

'Look outside,' I tell him, pointing towards our kitchen window. Beyond the glass panes, the sky shows signs of sunrise, dirty yellow clouds like nicotine stains.

'Mabel will be awake soon. I can't start the day with a drink, now, can I?'

He has his hand on the corner of the press, a frown puckering his forehead. His concern has morphed into something else. He no longer looks anxious. It's something closer to unhappiness.

'Have you called Kamila?' he asks, shaking me from my thoughts.

'Kamila?'

'Didn't you say you left her at the Tube station?'

A little trill of nerves pulses in my stomach.

'Yes.'

'Well, have you checked if she got home?'

'I –'

'Or let her know that you're okay? She must be worried.'

'I lost my phone, remember? How could I?' Despite my best intentions, these words come out sounding scratchy and irritable.

I have already explained to him how I dropped my bag on the street, offering it up as the reason why I didn't call him to let him know. Why his first inkling that something had happened was when I arrived through the front door, grey-faced and shaken, pushing past him to Mabel's room. I needed to feast my eyes on my sleeping child to reassure myself that even though my world had tilted in the night, the important things remained constant, true, safe.

'Besides, I saw her going down into the Tube station. She would have been well away by the time it happened.' I don't look at him as I say this.

'You should still call her,' he urges softly.

He is right, and I know it. My husband, who I have known and loved for six years now – the man I felt relieved and grateful to marry, knowing how safe and protected he made me feel, a harbour in a storm – is someone I trust and depend on, whatever the circumstances. But now, I feel a scream rising up inside me at his sound advice, his sensible approach. *Hold me!* I want to shout at him. *Can't you, just for once, forget about doing the right and sensible thing, and just hold me!*

'Do you want to borrow my phone?' he asks.

'That's okay,' I say calmly. 'I'll call her from the bedroom.'

And as I start up the stairs, I can hear him refilling the kettle, slotting bread into the toaster, flicking on the radio, and it occurs to me that an opportunity has been lost. That I might have sat him down and told him the truth – the real, deep truth about the night, about what happened. But I'm tired. Too tired for words. And part of me knows that the time for truths to be spoken has long since passed.

The weekend is a blur of tiredness, relief and obligation. I end up spending a good deal of time on the phone – not just to Kamila, but to other friends, who have heard the news and are calling to express support and horror. With each call, I find it gets a little easier. The repeated phrases act as a defence of sorts, keeping me at a distance from what I actually experienced.

By the time I call Victor, the presenter of the radio show I work on, the story has moulded itself into an identifiable pattern in my mind, its nuances hardening into historical facts. Victor Segal: shock-jock or voice of the people, depending on your opinion. He has been in the radio business for almost thirty years and for the last six, he's had me as his series producer. I know him better than either of his ex-wives and possibly better than his shrink. As I talk him through those moments of descending the staircase and stepping out into the street, my eyewitness account of the aftermath of carnage, it almost feels like a third-hand account of something that happened to someone else.

'Listen to me,' he intones gravely, 'who else have you spoken to about this?'

I start listing the various friends but he cuts me off.

'I mean at the station? Is there anyone you've spoken to about this, other than me?'

'No, not yet.'

'Do me a favour, will you, Cara? Just keep it to yourself for now, eh?'

'Okay. But why?'

I hear the cigar wheeze of his indrawn breath, and when he speaks again, his tone is softer, almost avuncular.

'You've had a bad night, love, but you were lucky. Put down the phone – better still, turn it off. The telly and radio too. It's a beautiful day. Why not get out there with your husband and child. Smell the roses, eh?'

Grousing, snappish Vic, my ageing *enfant terrible*. It's so strange to hear him speak to me like this. My guard falls momentarily, and for the first time since this whole thing ended, since leaving that room, I feel myself coming close to tears.

When I see Vic on Tuesday morning, it finally dawns on me why he urged me to keep my story to myself.

There's a sleepy feeling about the place, as if the city is reluctant to drag itself out of the long weekend. I'm crossing the office floor towards my desk, my mind roaming over impending tasks: a pre-recorded interview with a children's author will have to be bumped in order to make way for coverage of the terrorist attack and its aftermath; a decision will also have to be made about some of the other lighter segments we'd hoped to air; they might be deemed poor taste in light of Friday night's atrocity. These are the thoughts running pitter-patter through my mind when a sharp rap on the glass wall of the meeting room makes me look up. Victor and Derek, one of our producers, are inside, along with Katie, my assistant. Derek is beckoning me to join them.

It's still early – barely even dawn – and apart from Katie, I'm surprised the others are in already. There's a sheepish look on Victor's face, an eagerness on Derek's, and as I open the door it strikes me with force what it is they want from me.

I pause at the door and hold Vic's eye, then say, 'Forget it. I'm not doing it.'

'You have to, Cara. You were there! You saw it!'

I take my seat opposite him, the others looking on silently. Katie pushes a polystyrene cup of coffee towards me. It's my second one this morning but I feel like I need it.

'No way. It's crossing a boundary. I'm the series producer. I'm not meant to be heard on air.'

'What is it you always say when something big happens? *Get me an eyewitness who can speak coherently and let's put them on air.*' The exaggerated lilt of the bog Irish accent he affects sounds nothing like me. Apart from the soft 'r's and the occasional 'grand', all traces of my Irish accent were rubbed out long ago.

'It doesn't feel right –'

'Oh, come on!' he cries, exasperated, then gives me some guff about professional obligation and journalistic integrity.

'Vic's right,' Derek chimes in, capping and uncapping his pen – a tic of his that I've seen hundreds of times, but this morning it gets on my nerves. A hipster in his early thirties, with leather brogues and rolled-up chinos, Derek is looking at me with grave intensity above his pointy beard that makes me think, for some reason, of the last tsar of the doomed house of Romanov. 'When Vic rang me yesterday and told me what had happened to you, I was horrified. But I have to admit I had the same thought as Vic. This is exactly the kind of story our listeners are hungry for. It's too good to pass up.'

'Come on, love,' Vic wheedles. 'It'll be fifteen minutes, that's all.'

My eyes are scratchy with sleeplessness. I feel hung-over yet I haven't had a drop since that last Aperol spritz in the Water Poet on Friday night.

Beyond the glass walls of the meeting room, the office is filling up. I can see the cluster of desks I manage – the researchers and producers, the broadcasting coordinators, all in their places. By 10 a.m. this place will be humming with a melange of different people, from the young interns barely out of school to the seasoned old-timers coasting towards their pensions. A girl – one of the Marketing staff – passes the window. There are white iPhone buds in her ears, the slender cables disappearing into the collar of her shirt, and the sight of this touches something within me – a raw spot. That girl in the room. Jesus, all those things I told her. The memory of it brings a vertiginous swing. In my shoes, I feel my toes clench.

'Think of the ratings,' Derek says.

It starts to build again, that sense of unease, the moment I sit in front of the mike. There are three of us in the inner sanctum of the studio: Vic peering down at his notes through half-moon lenses, a pugnacious air about him as he smooths down his tie, Angela delivering the news and weather in a briskly elegiac tone, while I draw the hair back off my face, the heat of the room pressing down on me.

No small talk this morning – once Angela's done, Vic quickly dispatches her. Arms folded on the desk, he leans forward and launches into my intro. I've seen him do this hundreds of times, but always from the safety of distance. My heart thuds against the unfamiliarity of the situation. Everything seems slightly off-kilter, and as he announces my name to his listeners, I feel that drag of nausea again in my stomach and I shift a little in my seat.

'Tell us, Cara,' he says in a kindly tone, 'what did you feel when you looked up and saw a terrorist coming towards you wielding a knife and a gun?'

Unused to talking about myself so publicly, I begin clumsily, my voice sounding strange in my ears.

'It took me a moment to feel anything. It was all so unreal. There had been a buzz in the air, I was out enjoying myself, and then to see a man armed in that way . . . it seemed incongruous.'

Vic gives me a slight frown. *Keep it simple* is his motto.

'At what point did you realize the seriousness of the situation?'

My answer comes out clearer now, and I find myself relaxing into my account, Vic drawing me out with questions, leading me back up that staircase, placing me in the storeroom once more. I tell it like it's a story – something that might have happened to someone else. It is only the two of us in the studio now. There is intimacy here, a gathering hush that feels far from the busy industry of the office beyond, further still from the traffic and life percolating through the city below.

'And when you came out on to the street, what did you see?' Vic asks, the register of his voice dropping a little.

'I saw bodies. On the road, on the pavement. They had been covered with sheets. I don't know how many there were. It was awful. Shocking.'

He lets that sit for a couple of seconds, and then asks, 'And the two other people who had been in the room with you?'

He knows about Neil. When I gave my account to him on the phone on Sunday, I told him. The image comes again: the sheet covering whatever remains lay there, but those feet sticking out, immediately identifiable. A quiet impression branded on the mind. It advances and recedes, a pulse in my brain.

'I lost them,' I say. 'I don't know what happened to them.'

His eyes narrow. 'You don't?'

I talk quickly then about the time that followed, the confusion, the Italian café, giving my account to the police, and as my words fill the space between us I see Vic's eyes flicker to one side and know from this he is receiving a message through his headphones.

'Now, let's just leave things there for one moment, Cara, because we have a caller on the line,' he announces, his voice gaining authority, while at the same time indicating to me to put on the headphones in front of me. 'Someone you may recognize,' he adds, before booming into the mike, 'Hello? Is that Amy?'

I feel a soft-edged confusion as I slip on the headset and half-turn to glance back. Derek is in the producer's seat, his face unreadable.

There is a pause, and then I hear it: that same low throaty voice, the casual American inflection. I recognize it straight away. 'Hey, Vic. Hey, Cara,' she says.

I stutter through a response, something startled and awkward that conveys my unpreparedness. *How did they find her?* I wonder, my mind grasping for an answer.

'Amy, first of all, let me ask you if you are alright?' Vic asks, all concerned.

Her name doesn't suit her. It's too soft, too homespun for a young woman with her hard edges.

'Yeah, I'm okay. Glad to be alive, I guess. How're you doing, Cara?' she asks.

I try to keep my voice even, saying, 'Like you say, I'm glad to be alive.' My antennae are twitching all over the place.

'And we have you to thank for that, Amy,' Vic says, adding, 'So tell us what happened? How did you come to rescue Cara?'

It seems wrong, to put it that way, passing it off as some gallant act. In a way, it lessens the impact of what she did, by turning it into a soundbite. The gratitude I feel for her is immeasurable. Vic's schmaltzy tone somehow cheapens that. I think she feels it too.

There's a pause before she laughs a little – a mirthless breath that sounds closer to a cough – and then says, 'I don't know. It wasn't something thought out. I just saw her and pulled her back out of the street.'

Her shift had ended and she'd just shut up the shop with her co-worker, she explains, when they saw the terrorists coming.

'We backed into the doorway, towards the stairs. I just saw Cara standing there – this guy coming right towards her – and . . . I don't know . . . instinct kicked in, or something . . .' Her voice trails off, embarrassment radiating through the brief silence that follows.

Vic jumps in to fill it, asking, 'What happened when you were hiding in the storeroom together? What were your thoughts?'

'I don't know. We were all kind of panicked. Neil wanted to leave – to try to run – but I just thought we ought to stay there and wait it out.'

'So did one of you take charge?'

'Not really. Neil was kind of spooked, and after a few minutes, he ran back down into the street. Cara went to go after him, but I pulled her back.'

'Why?'

'I knew if she went down into the street, she'd die.'

'How did you know?'

'I just did. I can feel these things. It's like an instinct.' She coughs then, in a way that seems to ground the outlandishness of her statement. 'It was the same when my mom died. The morning when she left to go to work, I just knew something bad was going to happen to her. I knew I wouldn't see her again.'

Unlike so many of her contemporaries whose sentences rise at the end in an irritating up-tick, Amy speaks plainly, making definite statements. Her voice, though low and throaty, hums with quiet conviction.

'And when was this?'

'Sixteen years ago – I had just turned eight.'

'And, if you don't mind me asking, what happened to her?'

'My mom worked in the Twin Towers. She was killed in the 9/11 attacks.'

29

The declaration snaps like an electric current. Vic lets it lie there for a beat, allowing the significance to reverberate across the airwaves. My body has grown very still, but inside my thoughts skitter around madly. I feel the coffee churn in my stomach. But this girl's words affect me in a way I can't understand.

'So that's twice in your life you've been directly affected by a terrorist attack,' Vic states in a tone that lies somewhere between respectful and appalled.

'That's right.'

'Is this something you talked about when you were hiding in the room together?'

'No,' I answer firmly.

'I was listening more than talking,' she adds quickly. Do I imagine it, or is the manner in which she says this pointed?

'How so?' Vic asks.

'Cara was upset,' she explains. 'I felt like she needed to talk. There were things she needed to say.'

My thoughts slow. All the things I said in that room – the admissions and declarations, regrets, fears, unresolved passions – all of it seems to rise up now and fill the air around me with heat. A deep twang of nerves announces itself in the pit of my stomach.

'How long were you in that room together?' Vic asks.

'Two hours.'

'Two hours. I imagine in a situation like that, a situation charged with emotion, not knowing if you're going to come out alive, you must both have felt the need to reach out, to share confidences.'

30

'You make it sound like a Confessional,' she says in a wry tone, but her voice has gone quiet.

I don't trust myself to speak.

Vic glances at the clock.

'Well, Amy, I'm so glad you called into the show this morning, and that you two were able to make contact with each other after your shared ordeal,' Vic intones, and I feel the danger begin to recede. He is going to wrap things up now, deliver some pat line before offloading us both. I can almost feel the relief of escaping the studio, the heavy door closing behind me.

'Can I say something to Cara?' she asks then, and from her tone I know something is coming. Immediately the danger is back.

'Go ahead,' Vic urges, surprise in his voice.

Her breath echoes in my headset, as if she's steadying herself for something.

'He says I saved you . . . but really, you saved me. It feels like we were meant to meet that night. And what you said . . . what you told me when we were alone in the room . . . I just want you to know that I'll keep it close. I want you to know: you're safe.'

Vic's head is cocked with interest. Behind me I can feel the intensity of the others' gaze. All the unease I have been pushing away comes over me now in a wave, like sickness. My headset abandoned on the desk, I push through the door, out to the safety of the antechamber.

The broadcasting coordinator is there, her headset on, looking at me expectantly.

'She's still on the line,' she whispers, her hand held over

31

the mouthpiece. 'Do you want me to patch her through to your desk?'

I think of all I have told this girl – that crazed spewing out of secrets. A great sea wall of regret rears up in front of me.

With effort, I keep my voice steady and firm. 'No, that's not necessary,' I say, and I turn and walk away.

4.

Amy

My mom used to say to me, 'You gotta fly by the seat of your pants, honey. See where your shit lands.'

Every time she said it, my heart would sink a little, because it meant she was about to uproot us from whatever place we'd settled in. The signal that the school where I'd just started making friends, the bedroom I'd come to think of as mine, all of it was about to be tugged away from me as we'd gather up our stuff in a hurry and get back in her beat-up Subaru, no goodbyes, no onward mailing address, the two of us on the road again.

Fly by the seat of your pants.

Not much of a life philosophy, if you ask me.

I have the phone held to my ear but it's gone quiet. I don't know why, but I was half-expecting somebody to come back on the line – the girl who'd first spoken to me, checking my story, verifying the facts before patching me through. Someone, even just to say thanks for phoning in or we'll get Cara to give you a call once she's finished up – anything. But instead, there's silence on the line. My heart is still pounding though, a silly grin over my face. And when I put the phone down and stare out of the window at the morning sky, I feel something soaring within me – an unfamiliar feeling – and realize with surprise that what I feel is hope. It's happening. It's really happening. I can't remember when I last felt like this.

I dress quickly and straighten out the covers over the bed. Sean has already left for college. He said I could stay here while he was gone. I'd given him some scant details of what had happened, and I think he felt obliged to let me stay. In the hall, the radio is still playing, but I'm done with it now, so I switch it off on my way out. I hitch my bag over my shoulder and plug in my buds, and soon enough I'm on the bus with Kery James in my ears, rapping in a language I don't understand. Grey buildings flick past and merge into something homogeneous and familiar, and I think about Connie – about how she'll never get to see all this – and it's funny how she's back in my head again, after all this time. Her laughing voice worming through my thoughts, saying: *What* are *you up to, Amy Keener?*

I reach my stop and as soon as I round the corner on to my street, and see the police-cordon tape flickering, the wavering inside me starts. People are still going about their business and shops are open, but it feels different, like a sudden change in season. I stuff my hands in my pockets and keep my eyes fixed on the pavement in front of me, trying to hang on to the buoyant feeling, and when I walk inside the shop and Emerson greets me the same as he always does, with the V for victory sign, I feel better. Still, I don't go up the stairs to the staffroom, choosing instead to nip behind the counter and dump my stuff behind Lucy's desk. I wash my hands at the sink, pull on my apron and cap, and take my place alongside Haqim, who is already slapping egg mayonnaise on to granary bread.

'Didn't expect to see you,' he says without looking up.

'Ain't nothin' gonna keep me down, Haqim,' I say breezily, and for just a second I imagine that to be true.

Who am I kidding? Even as I pull bread rolls from their packaging, I can feel Neil's presence there by the sink, like it's Friday night again and the shutters are down, and we've turned the music up high, me mopping the floor while he scrubs the mats, whistling to the radio, the soles of his shoes squeaking on the wet lino. I've been trying hard not to think about him since it happened. For all I know, he could be lying naked in a drawer in a morgue right now, a tag on his toe. Or laid out in his best clothes in the front room of his parents' house.

I hold a bread roll in one hand and slice through it, and there's a shout across the kitchen.

'Amy! If I catch you doing that again, I'll cut your fucking hand off myself, d'you hear?'

I look up and see Monica, my kitchen supervisor – a small fat woman of Indian descent and indeterminate age – barrelling towards me and I can't help but be relieved, knowing that she's not going to tiptoe around me, subject me to pitying stares, or sympathetic murmurings. Dark eyes and crooked teeth that are crying out for a retainer, with her hair tucked up under her cap, she looks more like a twelve-year-old boy than the adult in charge of this kitchen.

'You alright?' she barks.

I can feel everyone else looking – Haqim sneaking a sideways glance, even Emerson taking a peek from the shop – and I say, 'Yeah, I'm fine.'

Nonetheless, she tells me to stop what I'm doing, gets Emerson to fix us two coffees, and soon we are perched on stools at a window table, Monica fixing me with a serious look, saying, 'You want to talk about it?'

I shrug and look down at my coffee, wonder if any of them heard me this morning on the radio – wonder if anyone I know heard it.

'Not much to talk about, really.'

Besides, I've told her all she needs to know already. I'd called her on Saturday morning to report what had happened – she's my boss, after all. And in a way, I saw it as a human resources issue, seeing as one of her humans was no longer resourceful, seeing as how he was dead.

'I couldn't fucking believe it,' she declares now. 'I still don't. D'you know, there was blood on the pavement outside when I came in this morning? I made Emerson go out there with a bucket of soapy water and a brush. This is still a civilized country, for fuck's sake.'

She shakes out a package of sugar, spills it on to the foam of her coffee. She's acting like the terrorist attack was a personal affront to her but I get the twitchy feeling that she's enjoying the drama of it. Blood on the pavement? Yeah, right.

She's like that, Monica – all fire and brimstone and righteous indignation. I like her, though. She's probably the closest friend I have right now, apart from Sean, and yet I can't talk to her about this, not really. She wants from me what everyone expects: horror, sadness, the special shiver that comes from looking death in the face. But what happened in the room – how to explain it? It wasn't like that. It was something else. Something coming to life inside me, like a match struck in the darkness. I'm afraid to even talk about it, in case it takes away the magic.

'You're to take things easy, you hear me, Amy? I know you think you're alright, but shock hits people in funny ways.'

'I'm not going to flip out in front of a customer,' I tell her, but she looks unconvinced.

'You don't know that. Your coolness isn't fooling me, you know.'

It's like something Connie would say to me when we were kids. She'd look down at me, her eyes crimping into a smile, nodding her head sagely like she was ten years older than she actually was, saying, 'You don't fool me, Keener. I see right through you.' And then we'd both laugh, and it was like whatever hurt or grievance I'd been nursing inside would just burst and fade like a firework disappearing into darkness. I miss Connie. At times like this, that missing feels almost physical.

'Listen, I've heard from head office – there's going to be a service for Neil sometime in the next few weeks. I'll be doing the rosters so I need to know: do you want to go?'

A hum starts in my head, right then when she says it. Barely three days have passed since I stood upstairs in that room and smelt the sharp tang of Neil's sweat too close to me, too dark to make out his eyes but knowing the fear that they held nonetheless.

Monica's talking again, saying how a bunch of them will go – Monica herself, of course, not wanting to miss the drama, Emerson and Pamela, both born-again Christians, always eager for a bit of religion – but how she wanted to give me first dibs, on account of my situation, my situation being I was the last one to see Neil alive. Like that gives me some kind of claim on him.

'So what do you think? You on for going? If it's not your thing, that's absolutely fine.'

She's talking, but it's like we're underwater or something, the words all bloated and indistinct, her face blurry and wavering. And swimming up through the water comes Cara's face, caught in the greenish light of the Emergency Exit sign. The way her eyes had fixed on mine – the need in them.

'Sure, I'll go,' I say.

But Monica's looking at me funny. She says, 'Fine,' in a tight voice.

It's only then that I realize I'm smiling – a big stupid grin charting its progress over my face.

It's Emerson's turn to pick the music, so we're subjected to Michael Bublé while we work, and this makes me think of Connie and that time she took me to the parking lot behind Toys R Us on a Sunday evening and gave me my first driving lesson. Bublé was on the radio singing 'Come Fly With Me'. Our moms were back at the house, all geared up and excited over some recipe Elaine had found for making toothpaste from scratch, or some other hare-brained scheme to 'get back to basics'. The two of them were so deep in their enthusiastic ministrations, turning the kitchen into a freaking laboratory, cooking up their potions while knocking back screwdrivers, that they probably didn't even notice Elaine's Pinto was gone. My feet just about reaching the pedals, the car lurching across the dusty lot under the orange floodlights towards a row of dumpsters, Connie squealing with laughter as the Pinto shuddered and shuffled like some old drunk relative, her hand over mine squeezing hard down through the gears.

I look down at my hand now, holding the scoop for the

tuna paste, and it's like I can feel the soft press of her fleshy palm against the back of it. For just a moment, the whole kitchen around me seeps away and there's nothing, only Connie's laughter and her hand over mine, and that feeling – like nothing else matters, only this.

I'm so absent, so lost within my own thoughts, that I don't see Haqim approach my bench. I don't register his presence behind me, or feel him reaching to slot the newly washed trays back where they belong on the shelf above my head. The trays are wet and slippery and Haqim is rough and imprecise, so that my jolt back to reality comes as they crash down on top of me. Eight or nine stacked aluminium trays skating off my head and over my shoulders, clattering on the ground about my feet. Even the customers by the windows can hear me screaming.

'You *fuck!* You *stupid fuck!*' I holler, and I can hardly hear myself above the angry hum in my head that has built to a crescendo as I round on Haqim and fling the metal scoop with force at his face.

It connects with his nose and instantly he bends double, holding his face and bellowing. When he straightens up, there's blood between his fingers and a fierce look in his eyes, but it's nothing to the anger that's inside me. The rage vibrates through me – I am shaking with it.

'You goddamned fucking terrorist!'

He takes a step towards me and I reach behind and find my knife. And when I hold it out in front of me, I am ready for him. I am full of intent. It's like something clean and beautiful – a pure thought: *I could kill you.*

'Amy!' Monica bellows from across the room. 'Put that knife down!'

I don't look but I can feel her propelled by indignation across the kitchen towards me. Still I hold the knife and Haqim's hate-filled stare. And just as I'm aware of Monica's approach, so I can feel the hushed stillness of all the others watching: Emerson and Lucy, Pamela by the coffee machine, the craned necks of customers gaping from the shop floor.

'What the hell are you playing at?' Monica shrieks, and she makes a grab for my wrist. I'm almost a head taller than her, but she's fearless and angry, and I let her take the knife. I don't look at her though, only at Haqim – the whites of his eyes yellowy-brown, like tobacco stains, his eyebrows curling above them – injured pride in his gaze.

'Both of you, upstairs. Now!'

My heart is beating fast, my stomach all twisted up. Everything is pressing down on me – the too-bright lights reflecting off every goddamned chrome surface in the place, the rows and rows of plastic containers neatly displaying the store's offerings like some kind of Stepford Wives' supermarket, how as soon as you leave the store's anodyne space and enter the Staff Only realm the whole place turns shitty, like they couldn't give a crap what kind of environment their sandwich-making goons would have to sit in on their breaks – and it makes me so mad, all the anger backing up inside me now, thinking of Neil spending the last few minutes of his life in this shitty place. And I'm especially mad at him because it was his fault we were still there – his fault for taking way too long over cleaning up. If he hadn't been so fucking dreamy we'd have shut up the shop ten, fifteen minutes earlier and then he'd still be alive.

I'm thinking of this and I'm so angry because I want to be back thinking about Connie and the times we had in that old Pinto. I want to be thinking about Friday night and Cara reaching out to grab my hand. I know I can't go up into that staffroom. The certainty of that thought hits me with force. I grab my things from the floor where I dumped them.

'Hey! Where do you think you're going?' Monica asks as I push past her.

I don't answer, not even to say that I fucking quit. I just take my baseball cap from my head and toss it like a frisbee out over the shop floor. My mom's voice is in my head again: *Fly by the seat of your pants, honey.* And, for once, it strikes a chord within me.

Emerson's eyes widen with astonishment, but that's all there is by way of goodbye. It's enough.

I sail out on to the street, pulling my jacket tight about me, no regrets. That episode of my life is over. Done with. I have a new purpose now. I push forward, no music in my ears, but happy nonetheless, knowing exactly where I'm going.

5.
Cara

A wind has picked up as I push open the doors, a welcome blast of it hitting me with a rejuvenating force. I should never have agreed to go on air. Foolish of me to allow myself to be pressured into an inherently uncomfortable situation. I'm mad at Victor for pushing me into it – mad at Derek for colluding with Vic. But mainly mad at myself for being vulnerable to them. So when the show is over and they suggest lunch in the Chinese nearby, I bluntly refuse. I need to go and buy a new phone anyway, to replace the one I've lost. Little chance of my bag turning up now. There's a Carphone Warehouse on Tottenham Court Road, and if I hurry, I'll have time to nip into Marks & Spencer's afterwards to grab a sandwich for lunch. These thoughts are chasing through my mind as I exit the building and turn the corner, when I feel a hand reach around my upper arm and roughly grab me. The breath catches in my chest as I swirl around and come face to face with Finn.

'Great. So you are alive then. Just checking,' he says, then dismissively releases my arm and continues on his way up the street.

For a couple of seconds, I stand there, watching him, the flare of his parka, caught in the wind, flapping around his long legs. I'm shocked by the ferocity in his demeanour.

Even the hunch of his square shoulders exudes anger. When I run and catch up with him rounding the corner on to New Cavendish Street, his face is set into a grimace of simmering anger, and he pointedly avoids eye contact with me.

'Wait,' I urge him. 'Let me explain.'

'What's to explain? You don't owe me anything.'

'Please, slow down. I can't talk to you like this.'

'Like what?'

'All injured and furious.'

'I think I have a right to be furious.'

'Oh, come on –'

He stops suddenly, turning on me. His eyes widen with incredulity.

'You walk away from me on Friday night right into a shit-storm. I have no idea if you are alive or dead. I spent all weekend calling you, messaging you, and nothing. Nada. Not so much as a text message to say you're okay. I was going out of my mind!'

He's looking at me intently, brown eyes ablaze. I have known him for so long now, his face almost as familiar to me as that of my husband. Reddish-brown hair greying at the temples. A mobile mouth that usually suggests humour – although, right now, there's no mistaking his anger.

'I couldn't call you –'

'Oh, please. Are you trying to tell me you couldn't find five minutes to hide in the loo and send me a text without your other half seeing you?'

'It's not that –'

'Instead, I have to resort to ringing around hospitals. Do you know, I even went over to your apartment block?'

'You didn't.'

'There I was on Sunday evening, steeling myself to call up to your flat, just to see if you were alive. I had a little speech all worked out in my head for when your husband answered the door. "Hello there, mate. Sorry to disturb. Just wondering if your wife made it home alive on Friday night? Oh yeah, and I'm the bloke she was sneaking off with. Cheers."'

I'm shocked by the notion. Finn has never been to my home. Up until now, those two parts of my life have remained separate from each other – inviolable.

'I wasn't sneaking off with you,' I say, my voice rising with sudden anger. 'Nothing happened between us.'

'You thought that was nothing?' He stares at me, then shakes his head in slow disgust, but I can see the hurt in his eyes.

The strain of the situation is showing in our voices. I can feel how dangerous Finn's mood is, and suddenly I don't want to be out on the street with him, having this conversation. People are streaming past on either side of us, hurrying on their lunch breaks. It seems altogether too public.

'Can we go someplace to talk?' I ask, searching his face for a hint of submission. 'Please?'

He doesn't look at me, fishing for his phone in his pocket, then checking it, as if there is some more important engagement he has overlooked. There's something petulant and childish about his behaviour, but strangely endearing too. I can feel the want in him battling against his own indignation.

'I owe you an explanation. Please? Let me buy you lunch.'

He is turning the thought over in his mind, and I feel him beginning to cave, his anger dissipating.

'Alright then,' he relents.

We go to a pub around the corner from Wogan House. I'm taking a risk going to a place like this, knowing there's a possibility that someone from work might be here, might see me with Finn, put two and two together. *We're just two old friends meeting for lunch*, I tell myself.

Whenever anyone asks me what a series producer does, I always answer, 'We manage egos.' Whether it's persuading a researcher, who has just spent three days on the phone with a subject, that their story has to be bumped for something more pressing, or if it's managing the whims and outlandish needs of some pampered celebrity, my job is to smooth out the wrinkles and persuade the various personalities to cleave to the greater needs of the listeners. It's something I'm good at, and God knows I've been well tested, particularly throughout the years of my relationship with Finn.

Live radio is the business I'm in, and I can't think of a better one. The feeling of satisfaction that comes at the end of a good show is something I crave. The spontaneous and responsive nature of it appeals to me, the risks involved in it. For underneath the sensible exterior, there lurks within me a particular kind of adrenalin junkie. It's not something everyone sees in me – but Finn does. Sometimes it feels as though most of the chances and gambles I have taken in my life have been intimately connected with Finn.

Take Friday evening, for instance. I had been leaving

work, fully intending to get the train home, when my phone buzzed and I looked at the screen and saw Finn's name flash up and experienced an immediate swoop of feeling in my stomach – fear or excitement, I couldn't be sure which. It was the first time in years I had heard from him. Instantly my mind went to the date, and knew it couldn't be a coincidence. When I answered the call, he told me outright that he had been thinking about me and wondering if I was okay. He was in Spitalfields, he said, killing time before meeting some friends later that evening. Did I want to jump on the Tube and whizz over there for a drink? I knew at once that I wanted to, even though there were many good and hard-learned reasons why I shouldn't. But it was years since I had seen him, years since I had spent time in his company, and I thought to myself: *One drink can't do any harm, surely?* So we sat together in the Water Poet on an oxblood-coloured chesterfield, elaborate Venetian masks peering down at us from their places high up on the walls above the bar. We sipped our drinks and talked and it was so easy – so comfortable – as if nothing bad had ever happened between us.

'I'm thinking of selling the house,' he told me, and despite the fact it was a part of my past, not my present, I still couldn't help feeling a pang, a sudden regret at the loss of that beautiful house.

'But why?' I asked, a plaintive note entering my tone.

He had shrugged and made a face. 'It's not right for me any more. It's never been right. Parsons Green – it's for families, not for single blokes like me.'

He had bought the house at a time when he and I were contemplating making our own family, but now that was firmly out of the question, it seemed pointless to linger there, he said. The words held no malice or accusation, more a statement of plain fact. And then the subject changed to less weighty matters, and I felt the alcohol loosening the muscles in my body, easing the clamps of wariness, and when he pointed to my glass and said, 'Same again?' I didn't have to think twice.

While Finn waited at the bar, I took out my phone and texted Jeff that I was meeting Kamila and would be home later, and then I stuffed my phone deep into my handbag, and tried not to think about my deception. The pub was beginning to fill up now that the offices were emptying, a Friday evening sense of release and possibility with the added excitement of the bank holiday. Finn was coming back to me, a drink in each hand, a broad smile on his face, his eyes locking on mine, and I felt that instant connection between us, still vital, despite the intervening years. It was an old, warm feeling of familiarity – of rightness. And all the time I sat there with him, I wouldn't allow myself to think about Jeff waiting for me at home. I refused to turn my thoughts to Mabel and the possibility of her disappointment at my absence. We had three rounds before leaving, my legs nicely wobbly as I walked Finn back towards Shoreditch where he had arranged to meet his friends, even though Liverpool Street Station and the train home lay in the opposite direction, just to savour those extra few minutes where I could pretend that we were still young and not embittered, shrugging off any scraps of sense or earned wisdom.

And now, as Finn slides on to the banquette opposite me in the Horse & Groom, shrugging out of his coat, I can feel again that dangerous tug, the desire to unlearn all I know, to turn back the clock. Underneath, he's wearing a worn grey shirt that I recognize with a pang as one I gifted to him shortly after we had first arrived in London, almost fifteen years ago. It was back in the early post-student days when a pay cheque seemed like a minor miracle, and lifelong love seemed like an inevitability. I almost comment upon the shirt, but he's still holding on to his injured air, perusing the menu in silence, so I say nothing. Still, I can sense a softening in him.

When the girl comes to take our orders, he snaps into his default charming mode, listening attentively as she goes through the specials. I notice how she addresses most of her attention to Finn, and it crosses my mind that maybe she recognizes him, or perhaps a vague suspicion has been aroused that he might be a minor celebrity. It's been almost ten years since he faded from the limelight of the television screen. As he puts it himself, 'I'm someone who was someone.'

The waitress smiles as he gives his order – waitresses always smile at Finn. He exudes a natural warmth and affability, when he's not radiating antipathy.

'Anything to drink?' she asks.

Finn gives a brief but emphatic shake of the head. 'Not for me, thanks.'

I'm tempted but refuse, wondering whether his denial was partly for my benefit, showing off his hard-won self-control. It was, after all, his lack of self-control in that department that had eventually killed us.

She caps her pen and moves away. Finn leans back in his seat and fixes me with a level gaze.

'Well?'

'I couldn't call you because I had lost my phone.'

He raises an eyebrow sceptically, then says, 'That sounds like "the dog ate my homework" for an excuse.'

'I know. But it's true. In fact, I was on my way to pick up a new phone when you accosted me.' And then I tell him about what happened after I left him on Friday night, how I had strayed into the path of murderers, briefly witnessed their bloody work, before being hauled to safety by a stranger. He listens to my account in silence, impassive. It's only when I get to the bit about Amy that he nods his head.

'I heard you on the radio,' he tells me gently, his elbows on the table, looking at me directly in a way that suggests his feelings are softening, anger giving way to concern.

'You were listening to the show?'

He shrugs, and says, 'Of course. I always listen to your show.'

I'm taken aback by this and strangely touched. For over six years we have been living apart, making lives separate from each other. It never occurred to me that he might be tracking the progress of my career from a distance.

'I was surprised to hear you,' he admits. 'Isn't that breaking one of your cardinal rules? Shouldn't the producer always remain firmly out of the spotlight?'

'I didn't want to go on air,' I tell him. 'It was a mistake. I kind of got coerced into it.'

He leans forward now. I can see from his expression that his interest is piqued, and it feels as if the restaurant has emptied out, grown quiet around us.

'The girl – Amy – did you know she was going to be part of the interview?'

49

'No. I had no idea.'

'How did they even find her?'

'She called in, apparently. Heard the show and recognized my voice. It all happened very quickly.'

'Just a coincidence then.'

'Yes. I suppose.'

His gaze feels a little heavy and I know where he's going with this. I drink from my glass of water, wishing it was wine.

'That stuff she said at the end – about how you're safe – what did she mean?'

'I don't know, Finn. She was just trying to be nice, I suppose.'

'Was she? Sounded like an oddball to me.'

I'm surprised to feel grazed by a sense of hostility at his remark.

'She's a little different, that's all,' I say in a tight voice.

'That stuff about her mother and 9/11 . . .'

'You didn't believe her?'

'Did you?' The look he gives me feels sharp and pointed.

'It's not completely implausible.'

'I suppose. A bit of a stretch, though. Did you notice anything strange in her behaviour when you were alone together?'

'No, I didn't. I was just bloody grateful to her for dragging me off that street and into safety.' My voice has risen, punched with indignation, and he notices it.

A small pause slips into the conversation.

'So what did you talk about when you were alone?' he asks after a moment. 'By her account, some pretty heavy stuff.'

I keep my gaze on the table, uncomfortable with the question.

'I don't know. I was upset. People had just been killed right in front of my eyes.'

'So why would she need to keep what you said safe? Why be all cloak-and-dagger about it?'

'Oh, for God's sake, I don't know! What does it matter what I said? Probably how I hoped to Christ I'd get out of there alive.' My voice has risen sharply and I realize how rattled I sound, how overwrought. I grab my glass and take a swallow of water. It hits a sensitive tooth and I wince, my fingers reaching to touch my jaw.

'Are you alright?' he asks, concerned.

'Fine. A tooth that's bothering me, that's all.'

He reaches out and puts his hand over mine. I feel the weight and warmth of it, and even though I know it's wrong, even though I've come through years of pain and regret to make myself strong against him, I feel the leaping answer of my own blood. I turn my hand over, and our fingers slip together, locking, like pieces of an old and familiar mechanism gently falling into place.

I met Finn in my second year of university. I knew who he was already – even then, back in Dublin, he was garnering fans, making himself a celebrity on campus with his active and often controversial participation in both the debating and drama societies. I was intimidated by him at first, far too cowed by his confidence, his little swarm of acolytes, to approach him for even the most innocuous conversation. Back then, I was fairly shy, awkward in crowds. I couldn't bear any kind of group attention. I had joined DramSoc in Freshers' Week, but it was not until the second semester that I plucked up the courage to participate in the society, and even then, it was in a backstage role. I was aware of my limitations. But I also knew my own strengths. Pragmatic and forward-thinking, I was a good organizer, qualities that were quickly recognized, and soon I was being relied on to stage-manage the bigger productions, a role I relished. It was a happy time in my life.

After my first-year exams, I went to Germany with three other student friends, to spend the summer working in a hotel in the Black Forest. It was there that I received a phone call from my father, telling me, 'She's gone, pet. Your mother's gone.'

The news spread quickly through university. I felt an edge to people's stares, the whisper of gossip wherever I went. I was 'suicide girl' – the one whose mother had killed herself during the summer. People don't know what to say to you when something like that happens. Yes, there is sympathy, but there is prurience too, a dark desire to know the gory details. Mostly it creates distance; people don't wish to get too close to someone marked by such a tragedy, afraid they'll be dragged down by it. That was why it was so surprising when, at a DramSoc party that autumn, I heard someone say my name, and turned to find Finn there extending his hand in introduction.

'I heard what happened to your mother,' he told me, his gaze clear and steady, holding my eye. 'That's really shit.'

I was at once taken aback at his candour, but grateful for it too. Unlike the others who pussyfooted around me, he took me aside, got us both drinks and then spent the night asking me about her – What had happened, how long had she suffered from depression, psychosis, did it come as a shock, how was I coping? – questions that, coming from someone else, might have felt invasive. But with Finn, they felt backed up by genuine concern, by warmth in those brown eyes, as if he had undergone something similar and was seeking a way to connect. He was easy to talk to, and I felt him drawing me out of myself, responding to his enquiry with an openness that was not usual to me.

There were raised eyebrows when we became a couple. Finn was seen as a star whereas I was a nobody, marked out in the worst way possible. We were yin and yang, my calm to his chaos, my quiet pragmatism to his firecracker charisma. But at night when it was just the two of us, our heads on the pillows, no one else saw the closeness there, the tenderness that existed. No one witnessed the passion he inspired in me, or the stillness and peace that came over him in our quiet moments together.

After everything that came later, it could be easy to forget the love that had existed between us, how intense and pure and uncompromised it had been in the beginning. A precious thing. A thing of beauty.

But on Friday night, turning to say goodbye to him on Redchurch Street, and here again in the post-prandial slump of this pub, feeling the steady beam of his attention on me, I can remember what passed between us once. I can believe in the rare beauty of it again.

'Do you know what I think?' he says quietly, after the girl has cleared the plates and brought the bill. 'I think your marriage to Jeff has been like an extra-marital affair. I'm the cuckold. All along, you have belonged to me.'

'Don't talk that way,' I say, breaking his gaze and looking down. My husband's name coming from Finn's mouth sounds wrong. My heartbeat has quickened at the mention of it. I cannot bear to have him malign my husband, and by extension our daughter. For all the little cracks that have appeared in our marriage, there is still love there, something deep and abiding. And when Finn utters Jeff's name like that, it is a reminder to me that by even sitting here with him I am betraying them.

'It's true,' he presses. 'You know it is. We were meant to be together. We just got a little lost along the way.'

'We both made our choices.'

'Did we?' he counteracts quickly. 'It seems to me that you were the one making all the decisions.'

'Well, someone had to.'

'I mainly remember trying to talk you out of those decisions.'

I shift uncomfortably in my seat, knowing where he is going with this.

'Like when I tried to talk you out of marrying him. Nearly succeeded too, didn't I?'

'Don't.'

'I was so sure that you were making a mistake. That you had convinced yourself that this poor bloke, grieving for his dead wife, and having to manage a heartbroken child to boot, would love you for life, when maybe he just needed some distraction – a crutch to get him through the difficult days.'

'That's enough,' I snap, my temper flaring.

'Sometimes I think you just married him to get back at me.'

'Well, you would, wouldn't you? Narcissist that you are.'

I slip my card into the leather folder and signal to the waitress. She brings the card machine, and all the while I'm punching in the numbers, waiting for my receipt, I can feel the blood in my cheeks, Finn's eyes on me. He is half-slouched in his seat, smiling across at me with fondness or knowingness – it's hard to tell which.

'That's what she was talking about, isn't it? That girl. Amy.'

I busy myself with putting my wallet back in my bag, shaking out my jacket.

'You told her about us. You told her how I'm the love of your life and that your marriage was the biggest mistake you've ever made – your one true regret. That's the secret she's going to keep safe. I'm right, aren't I?'

I slot my arms in the sleeves of my jacket, free my hair from the collar, and finally look up at him. His gaze is searching, and for all his warmth and openness, there is a reminder there within his question that I have my flaws, my weaknesses. I have made mistakes.

'Actually, you're wrong,' I tell him, getting to my feet.

'You're lying.'

'When have I ever lied to you?' I ask, a little heat coming into my voice.

The smile on his face has faded somewhat, his eyes narrowing in an assessing way.

'You haven't lied, Cara. But you have withheld the truth.'

The quiet way he says it, with all the layers of knowledge and experience it contains, causes a horrible little jolt of nerves in my stomach, and I think: *He knows.*

'When will I see you again?' he asks.

I shake my head. 'Let's not do this,' I say, and any last vestiges of anger have left me, replaced by a regretful sadness.

'Why not?'

'You know why not.'

'Oh, come on,' he pleads, flashing me a charming grin.

I steel myself against it, fix the strap of my bag on my shoulder. 'Bye, Finn,' I say.

Then I walk out of the restaurant, without waiting for him, and make my way back towards the office. My head is a blur of thoughts – about Finn, but also about that girl, Amy.

What you told me when we were alone in the room . . . I just want you to know that I'll keep it close. I want you to know: you're safe.

Stupid, stupid thing to have done. But I hadn't banked on the fact that I might hear from Amy again. I had thought it a fleeting contact – an opportunity to lay bare one's sins to a stranger, like kneeling in the darkness of the Confessional, and then walking away, feeling the lightness of absolution. My shoulders are high with tension and I attempt to shake them out as I stride away, as if I am shaking myself free of my own recent past.

I ring Jeff, just to hear his voice, to reassure myself of his presence, his love. As if by hearing it I can cancel out any thoughts or feelings stirred up by my meeting with Finn.

'I miss you,' I say, which makes him laugh.

'You saw me this morning! And you'll see me this afternoon.'

'I know. But I just wanted to tell you.'

'What's got you all sentimental?' he asks softly.

I can hear the tenderness in his voice, picture him sitting

there at his desk, half-turning away from his work, a smile on his face as he talks to me. Then he puts me on to Mabel, who sounds eagerly inquisitive, peppering me with questions I don't know the answers to until Jeff relieves her of the phone and in a voice of cheery optimism tells me he'll see me later, that he'll prepare something nice for dinner.

Back at the office, I am brisk and purposeful. Deeming it best to put today's disastrous show behind me, I run through the briefs for tomorrow's segments with Katie and Derek, make some calls to interviewees and have a quick meeting with my lead researchers to review progress on upcoming stories. It's fairly run-of-the-mill stuff, and when Katie hands me some afternoon mail, I've half a mind to leave it until tomorrow, my thoughts already launching themselves into the evening and the glass of warm Syrah that's waiting for me at the flat.

She is standing next to me, tapping in final prep notes on her iPad, and I'm explaining as I peruse the mail that we ought to do some kind of quiz for our listeners, some fun questions with maybe a science angle.

'Like what?' Katie asks, the end of her pen pressed to her lower lip.

'Like how much water do our bodies need?'

I smile, remembering Mabel's excitement when she put that very question to me over the phone, and take a plain-looking envelope with careful handwriting from the small stack of letters.

'Let's google it,' Katie suggests, and begins tapping away at her screen.

I'm slitting open the envelope now, taking out the single piece of paper.

'Sixty-four fluid ounces per day,' she says. 'That's eight glasses. Cara?'

'Uh-huh. Eight glasses,' I repeat, but my mind is not with Katie, and it's not with Mabel's question.

It's with the piece of paper in my hand, a simple message, unsigned, in small black handwriting:

I'm here for you, waiting.

6.

Amy

The security guard says I can use the bathroom. It's big and echoey, all marble walls and stainless-steel fixtures. I hang my bag off the back of the cubicle door while I pee, nervous excitement moving through me like it's a first date or an exam I'm about to sit. The bathroom smells like a hospital, which is not the worst smell, but still. I'd expected something more than plastic soap dispensers dribbling pink goo, green water stains daubing the enamel sinks.

I linger in front of the mirror, hypercritical as a teenager. My hair needs some attention but there's not much I can do about it now. Instead I take a tube of concealer from my bag and swipe two peach-pink smears over the carved lines beneath my eyes and then rub them in. A dab of lipgloss too, and I can hear Connie's voice right there in my ear, saying: *That's it. You slap that shit on, Keener. Have some pride. Make yourself presentable.*

Funny how she's come back to me again. After all these years. Her voice so clear these days, she could be standing right beside me.

Back out in the lobby, the security guard looks up briefly before returning to his *Daily Mail*. I take my place on the bank of leather seats that line the panelled lobby, and wait.

There's no one else here, apart from the occasional passing staff member, and as the time slips by, my mind flits over my current situation. As of Tuesday, I've no job – and so far, I've made zero effort to get a new one. I'm depending on Sean's continuing generosity to stave off homelessness. After my shopping trip to Lorraine Electronics this morning, I have £7.50 left in my wallet, and when I checked my balance at the ATM just now, I discovered I have £78 left in my account. I have my emergency fund – £900 in a separate account – but that's for when I need to return to the States, not that I can ever see myself doing that. Still, it's important to have an escape fund, and so far, I've been disciplined about not touching it. My Oyster card needs topping up, and I am clueless as to how the unemployment benefit works here, or whether I will even qualify for it. I could crawl to Pret and beg for my job back but something tells me I've burned my bridges there.

I suppose all this should make me nervous. More than nervous – downright fucking panicked. And it's true that I can feel panic at the edges, threatening to push through. But it's like I've been waiting all this time for something, not knowing what it was I've been waiting for. And now I have an inkling. A chink of light has been shed on it and it's like waking from a pharmacological dream, like I'm somehow coming back to my true self.

I'm so wrapped up in my own thoughts that I don't even see Cara coming out of the lifts, don't even notice her until she's right there in front of me, a security badge clipped to her jacket, her handbag tucked under one arm.

With a sharp little intake of surprised breath, I get to my feet, an embarrassed half-smile on my face.

'Hey,' I say, stuffing my hands in my jeans pockets, a little overwhelmed by her presence.

'Amy. This is a surprise.'

But she doesn't look surprised. She looks impatient, mildly pissed-off. It's taken me two days to pluck up the courage to come see her, but now that I'm here, I feel a nervous inward lurch knocking me off balance.

'So? What can I do for you?' she asks briskly, her eyes sharp with enquiry, and for just a second it's like I've gotten the wrong person – her fucking identical twin or something – that's how different she seems from the person I met last Friday.

'I just wanted to come and say sorry,' I explain. I lower my eyes, sweeping the floor with my gaze. 'What I said on the radio the other day . . . I shouldn't have. It was indiscreet.'

'That's alright,' she says stiffly. 'You didn't need to come out of your way to apologize to me. Honestly, there's nothing to be sorry for.'

'I felt bad. When we were talking during the show, I could feel how shocked you were, and sort of . . . disapproving.'

She takes this in, a tightness about her mouth. In fact, everything about her looks pinched and tightly wound. Even her hair, pulled back into a ponytail, looks severe, her skin pale and stretched. The phone in her hand buzzes.

'I was surprised, not shocked.'

'I put you in an awkward spot. I made you feel uncomfortable and I shouldn't have. I gave you my word, and I intend to keep it. I guess that's all I wanted to say.'

Someone walks past just at that moment, one of Cara's colleagues. 'Good show today,' he remarks to her in passing, and she smiles brightly, and thanks him, her prick-liness momentarily falling away. But then she glances down and reads her text, and her face darkens, the wall springing up again.

'I didn't mean to disrupt you or anything,' I say, the hopelessness leaking into my voice. 'You're probably in the middle of something.'

'Sorry,' she says, shaking her head, still looking at her phone. 'Childcare issues.'

She puts her phone away, looks in the direction of the lifts and then looks back at me, and I catch a glimpse of something there – a relenting. An opportunity.

'But I thought if you had a few minutes to spare,' I press, 'maybe we could grab a quick coffee?'

She smiles, for the first time in this exchange, and says, 'Alright. Just a quick one, though.'

I turn away from her then, busying myself with picking up my bag and fixing it over my shoulder so she cannot see the lip-twitching joy dancing across my face.

We head around the corner to a small Italian place with cheesy Europop oozing from hidden speakers. The coffee is good though, and we drink it at a table by the window – an Americano for her, a skinny latte for me.

'This is nice,' I say, looking around at the tourism posters of the Colosseum, the Leaning Tower of Pisa. 'I used to work in a place like this.'

'Oh? Where?'

'Back in Pennsylvania.'

'Is that where you're from?'

'Sort of. We travelled all over.'

'Your family?'

'Me and my mom. I don't have any siblings. My dad wasn't in the picture.' I say this like it's no big deal. Which it isn't. 'What part of Ireland are you from?'

'Donegal,' she tells me. 'In the north-west. But I've been living in London since I was twenty-one, so . . .'

'What brought you here?'

'A boy,' she says ruefully, but doesn't elaborate, sipping her coffee instead.

I know all about it, of course – the doomed relationship with some second-rate comic, played out in minor columns of the tabloids. I'd googled it already.

'So, how are things at work?' she asks, changing the subject. 'I imagine it's strange, after what happened.'

There's a formality to this conversation that I don't like. She's being nice and everything, but it's as if she's put a wall of politeness up around her, preventing any intimacy or warmth, so different from how it was when we were last together.

'Yeah, kind of. Actually, I'm not working there any more.'

'Oh?' Her face changes, surprise with a trace of concern entering her expression.

'It was just a temporary arrangement,' I explain quickly. 'Just while my family were away. I mean the family I work for.'

I give her a big spiel about how I'd been the live-in nanny for a family for the past year, and how the job in Pret was just for the summer while they were abroad. I can tell she's interested so I lay it on a bit thick about how close I was to the twins – four-year-olds, Kai and Lily – detailing all the excursions we used to do: kids' tours at the Tate, boating on the Serpentine. Deep in the tunnel of my ear, I can hear the ghostly echo of Connie's laughter.

'But during the summer, Peter – that's the father – he got a job in Stockholm, so they've moved. They've asked me to move out there too, so I can still mind Kai and Lily, but I don't know. There's the language barrier for a start. And the winters.' I give a little shiver, then smile shyly at her. 'I'm still deciding.'

'Did you go through an agency?' she asks.

'No. We had a mutual friend. It's better that way, I think, don't you? With agencies, well. You never know how well they vet people, do you?'

I smile at her again and sip my latte. I amaze myself, sometimes, with the bullshit I can come out with at barely a moment's notice. Ever since that text, that half-apologetic smile – 'Childcare issues,' she'd said – a winding thread has been set off in my head. There's an opportunity there and I intend to exploit it.

'So where are you living, if you're no longer with the family?' she asks.

'With Sean.'

'Sean?'

'He's kind of my boyfriend, I guess.'

'Really?'

The surprise in her voice is unmistakable and instantly, my defences rise.

'What?' I ask.

'Nothing, I just –'

'Did you think I was gay?'

She laughs then, embarrassed, and tries to bite down on it. 'I'm sorry, Amy. I don't know what I was thinking.'

64

It's there in her eyes, her nervous giggle. I'm not a dyke and I don't want anyone thinking that I am, especially not her. Dykes are people like Connie's mother, Elaine, butching around in a lumberjack shirt, tripping over herself to mention the gay community within ten seconds of meeting you.

'It's my hair,' I say gloomily, touching it half-heartedly. 'It was a mistake. I'm growing it out.'

'So where does Sean live?' she asks, changing the subject.

'He shares a house with other students over in Clerkenwell.'

'Do you like it there?'

'It's alright. I don't really fit in. I'm not a student, for one thing.'

I tell her about the house, music always pumping from some corner, the kitchen constantly a mess of spilt cereal and abandoned dishes. The living area where the guys sprawl on cinema seats, legs splayed and crotches on display as they drink beer and make jokes. Or girls playing the slot machines, draping themselves over the pool table, tossing their Kate Middleton hair. Shouty, opinionated girls with names like Cressida and Jemima. I know I'm not like those girls. I don't fit in.

'It sounds just like Olivia's digs,' she tells me, my attention snagging on the name.

'Your stepdaughter,' I say, to clarify. 'The one you told me about?'

'That's right. She's at Oxford.'

'Pretty handy, right? Seeing as how you don't get along.'

She laughs then in an embarrassed kind of a way.

'Did I say that?'

I shrug. 'Sort of. Not really. I was just reading between the lines.'

The skin on her neck has grown blotchy with nerves or regret, and I can almost see her thoughts tracing back over what she had told me about the first marriage, about Olivia and how difficult she makes things.

'I wouldn't really say we don't get on. We try our best, but it's not always easy.'

'How old is she?'

'Twenty-one. She was sixteen when Jeff and I married.'

'That must have been difficult.'

'You have no idea.' She gives a brief laugh but it dies quickly and so too does her smile. Beneath the facade there is a nub of disquiet. And I can tell, somehow, that there is trouble there.

'What happened to the first wife?'

'Ovarian cancer.'

'Wow. That sucks.'

'Yes. It was very difficult for them. Olivia especially.'

Then, as if anxious to change the subject, she continues. 'How long have you been going out with Sean?'

'A couple of months, I guess.'

'What's he like?'

I shrug. I could tell her that I like his smile – the warmth and shyness of it. I could tell her that when I first met him, I thought there was a clean, laundered look to him, like he had grown up in a home of hot dinners and clean sheets. But I don't tell her any of this. It's an effort to talk about him, now that she's made an assumption about me. About my orientation. It's hard to get past it.

'Well . . .' She glances down at her watch.

I realize that I've made her uncomfortable with my gloominess. 'I'm sorry,' I say quickly. 'I guess I've been a little off-centre, since, you know . . . since the attack.'

Her expression changes – that tightness re-entering it.

'I guess that's why I wanted to speak to you. There's no one else I can really talk to about it.'

'What about Sean?'

'He says I'm lucky to have gotten out of there alive. That I ought to be grateful. That I should put it behind me and look forward.'

'And what do you think?'

'I think it's easy for him to say that. He wasn't there –'

'By the way,' Cara interrupts. 'What happened to you that night? I was herded by the police into a coffee shop with all the others, but when I looked around you were gone.'

There's a sharpness about the look she's giving me, an edge to her question. Nerves announce themselves in my throat, and I take a swig of coffee.

'I don't know. I guess we just got separated.'

'Did they take you someplace else? The police?'

'Yeah, they did,' I say quickly. Then, changing the subject, 'So, what does your husband say?'

'Jeff?'

'Do you talk to him about that night?'

'Of course. And to friends. Most people are sympathetic. Horrified, of course. Some have suggested counselling.'

'Right,' I say, feeling the puff of indignation rise inside. 'Like that's gonna help.'

'You don't think it would?' she asks carefully.

'Spending a hundred bucks to talk to some stranger

who wasn't even there? Who cannot even begin to feel what it was like?'

'Jeff has been gently pushing me towards it,' she tells me. 'He's concerned I'm not sleeping. That I'm jumpy. That I'm overly worrying about things.'

'But that's natural, right? I mean it only just happened.'

'I suppose so.'

'Jesus, what does he expect, that you're going to see bodies lying on the street and then just carry on like normal?' Despite myself, the words come out more aggressive than I intended.

'Have you had therapy, Amy?'

'Yeah, I have. So I know what I'm talking about,' I continue, my voice still punchy. 'It's a crock of shit, let me tell you – some goon in a sweater-vest droning on about guilt and moral luck and being kind to yourself, but it's all just words. It doesn't come close to what's going on inside. Not even in the same ballpark.'

The anger flares inside me, rearing up so suddenly, heat in my chest, screaming in my ears. A woman at the next table looks over. My hands tighten around my coffee cup.

'Was this after your mother died?' she says gently, the question throwing me.

I'm still trying to get a handle on this anger, trying to push down on it. 'Huh? Yeah. Anyway, I guess I wouldn't recommend it, that's all.'

Her cellphone erupts suddenly on the table between us. We both look down – the name 'Jeff' is lighting up the screen.

'Excuse me a moment,' she says, and takes the phone while getting to her feet.

And then I'm left here alone, watching her through the window, wondering what it is she is talking to him about, what he's saying that's making her frown like that, press the heel of her hand to her forehead.

She's only gone a couple of minutes but it's enough time to do what I need to do. Her bag is on the chair where she left it and, discreetly, I take it on to my lap, reach inside my pocket for the plastic fob, slot it inside a tight fold of leather, making sure it's wedged there. By the time she's coming back in through the door, breathless and apologetic, the bag is back where she left it, and I'm draining my coffee.

'I'm so sorry,' she tells me, dropping her phone into the bag, checking for her security badge, 'but I really do have to go.'

'Listen,' I say quickly, 'there's gonna be a service for Neil. Sometime in the next few weeks. I'm not sure when yet, but I was wondering . . . I thought, maybe, you might be interested in going.'

She seems to recoil from the suggestion.

'Sorry, Amy. I kind of feel about funerals the way you feel about therapy.'

She's making a joke of it, but still I persist.

'Why don't you give me your number anyway? I can let you know the details, and then you can decide.'

I give her a sunny look, holding my phone ready to punch in the numbers, and feel her resistance battling with the dilemma of appearing rude. She caves gracefully enough, and I put the numbers in, then send her a text.

'Now,' I say, pushing down on my delight, 'you've got my number too.'

When I look up, there's a strange expression on her

face, like she's about to broach an awkward subject. I'm still seated, and she leans over the table, the fists of her hands pressed against the tabletop.

'Amy,' she says, keeping her voice light, but the way she holds my gaze tells me this is serious. 'What I told you the other night, when we were alone together – all those things I said about . . . Well, I was upset. I didn't mean it.'

'Okay.'

She keeps looking at me in that serious manner, not quite satisfied.

'I hope you can keep it to yourself. Or better still, forget about it. There are people close to me – my family – who would be hurt, and I just . . . Well, it seems unnecessary when there was no basis of truth to what I was saying. In fact, the truth is quite, quite different. Do you understand?'

'Sure,' I say, like it's no big deal.

She nods her head and gives a brief smile, but I can tell she is still uneasy.

'Don't worry. I'll keep your secrets.'

Still not satisfied, she opens her mouth to say something more, then changes her mind. She leans away from the table, checks to see she has her belongings and then holds out her hand for me to shake.

'It's been nice knowing you, Amy,' she says, giving me a stiff sort of smile. 'And thank you again for everything you did for me on Friday night. I'm very grateful.'

She takes her hand away, but keeps standing there, as if waiting for me to respond. But I can't think what to say. Her formality has thrown me.

'Well. Best of luck with everything,' she says, before turning away.

The bell above the door rings as she exits. I stay sitting in the window, watching her walk up the street. I keep my gaze focused on her, the straightness of her back, the way her reddish-blond hair catches the light, until she's lost from view. I sit back in my chair, the last remnants of feeling fizzling away to nothing. The long afternoon that stretches ahead, alone, empty, seems suddenly unbearable. And I think to myself of the finality of her handshake, her parting words, how cold and impersonal they had seemed. Is that really how it was to her? After all we had been through together, is this really how we part?

7.

Cara

The problems in my marriage began on the eve of the wedding day itself.

We were not having a traditional wedding, just a small gathering of our closest friends at Somerset House, preceded by a low-key registry office ceremony. No photographer, no big white gown, no flowers. I spent a small fortune on a Stella McCartney cocktail dress and Christian Louboutin heels, telling myself that I was only going to do this once in my lifetime so why not splash out a little. Because we had chosen to go down the less traditional route, it seemed a little silly for us to spend the night before apart. Olivia had gone to stay at Jeff's sister's house – she would meet us at the registry office with the others. I had left Jeff in the kitchen to iron his shirt, while I took possession of the bathroom to perform my final pre-wedding day grooming. I can still remember being perched on the side of the bath, in my bathrobe, dabbing red nail polish on to my toenails and wondering why I was bothering as my shoes had closed toes, when the door opened and Jeff stood there, grey-faced.

'Something's happened,' he said.

Such was the limit of my imagination, or rather the narrow sphere of my experience, that the first thing that came to mind was some vital disruption to our big day.

I was right, I suppose, but not in the way I'd thought. I expected him to say that there had been some mix-up with the restaurant – a double-booking, a misunderstanding over dates. So when he uttered the name of his teenage daughter in a voice so broken with emotion that it sounded scraped from the bottom of his lungs, I couldn't for the life of me understand what he was getting at.

'Olivia? What about her?'

And then I saw the shake in his hand as he ran it over his face, drawing down on his features, and I knew that it was bad.

'She's missing. That was Laura. Olivia never turned up at her house. And now she's sent a text message saying she's run away.' He was backing out of the bathroom as he said it.

I hurried after him, dropping the nail polish in my haste, saying, 'Wait. Where are you going?'

'To the police station.'

'Let me get dressed and I'll come with you.'

'No. You stay here, in case she tries to get in touch.'

'She's probably just holed up in a friend's house or –'

'I'm meeting Laura down at the station. I have to go.'

I watched him running around the apartment – locating keys, phone, wallet – feeling exposed in my bathrobe, inadequately dressed for this shock. When he kissed me on the lips and hurried out the door with a promise to call with news, I still didn't quite register what it meant. And then he was gone, and I was left alone in the apartment, my thought processes beginning to catch up now that the shock was fully absorbed. I went back into the bathroom, saw the spill of varnish in the bath, a scarlet daub hardened on to the enamel, and I got down on my hands and knees and with a nail scissors' blade I began to chisel away at it, gently at first, but then harder as I thought more about what had happened, forming my hypothesis, becoming angrier and angrier as I realized the true extent of what she'd done.

Olivia. Jeff's darling girl. Sixteen years old and already tipping over the cusp of adulthood. It's not that she didn't like me, she just didn't want *him* to like me – didn't want him to create room for any other woman in his life. It was understandable – up to a point. She was still hurting from the loss of her mother. I was careful not to intrude on her relationship with Jeff. I had tried my utmost to create a space where she and I could have our own friendship. But her feelings towards me were by turns scornful and indifferent. She made it very clear she considered me to be nothing more than a rebound, a temporary fling her father was having in reaction to his loss. She tolerated me with a patience that suggested I would pass – this relationship would pass – and it was just a bit tedious for her waiting for it all to blow over.

'Just give her time,' Jeff used to advise, 'and she'll come around.'

I should have guessed she'd pull something like this – she'd made no attempt to hide her contempt for our engagement – yet still, even I had not expected her to go quite so far.

It was after ten the next morning by the time they walked through the door. I had already been up for hours, and I was in our bedroom, make-up and hair done, getting into my dress when they came in.

'Oh, thank God,' I said, coming towards her with my arms outstretched, relief washing over me.

She moved straight past me to her room, slamming the door shut and locking it.

I turned to Jeff, my questions coming out in a rush: Where had she been? How did he find her? What did the police say? He looked shattered, drawn. I thought to myself that I should put an apron on over my dress, and fry an egg for him, make coffee and toast – the wifely duty already coming out in me, the need to provide him with some kind of sustenance to revive him, then get him into his suit and to the registry office.

He crossed the room and sank on to the couch and, for a moment, there was only silence. But when he looked up at me and said my name, I knew. The restaurant, our friends, my silk dress, all of it gone.

'We will do it,' he assured me. 'But not yet. Not until she's ready.'

There are certain things that are understood when you fall in love with a man who has children, and foremost among them is the concession that those children will always come first. Their previous claim on him, the nature of their bond, takes precedence. Best to understand that from the get-go, accept it, not try to fight against it – an argument you can never win. And so you prepare yourself for a life of interruptions, of delayed pleasure, of compromise, and I thought I was ready for that. But whatever I thought of Olivia and her machinations, I had not expected her to sabotage my wedding day.

That morning, as he sat looking hollowed out, bewildered by the night's events, I didn't say any of this. I held him in my arms and accepted his murmured apology, his promises that we would do it all later – the wedding, the lunch – just not right now. And then we each took up our phones and began the strained business of undoing our plans, negotiating with the restaurant, letting our friends know.

In the months that followed, Jeff made every attempt to make it up to me, and I made a concerted effort to improve relations with Olivia. It was in those months that I discovered I was pregnant. It was, in retrospect, a happy time, but the one thing that corrupted my happiness was the memory of what Olivia had done. The selfishness of her act, but more than that, the cold-hearted precision of it. For though I never said it to Jeff, I understood that what she had done had not been a cry for help, or a plea for attention – it was not even a protest over a marriage she did not wish to take place. It was an exercise of power. Her way of saying to me: *You see? I will always come first.*

We did get married, eventually. Four months after Mabel was born, the four of us went to the registry office in Westminster and in the presence of Jeff's sister, Laura, and her husband, we made our vows. Afterwards, Laura took Mabel for the afternoon and Olivia went out with her friends, while Jeff and I went for a celebratory lunch in the Savoy. It was quiet, intimate, romantic. I got to wear my Stella McCartney dress, my Louboutins, and I felt happy. But here's the thing – you lose something when you postpone the pleasure. That is what I learned. For all the noises of acceptance you make about the compromises, the delays, the interruptions caused by the children of the first marriage, in your heart you feel the toll they take. And you tell yourself that it won't always be this way, that those children will grow up, move on, have their own busy lives. But sometimes little niggles of doubt set in, so that while you are waiting for their lives to start so that yours can move on, a door silently opens within you, barely noticeable, ushering in uncertainty and dissatisfaction, doubt.

That evening, over dinner, I tell Jeff about the note.

'It just said: *I'm here for you, waiting,*' I say. 'There was no signature.'

His eyes are on the steak he's cutting, but I have his attention.

'It's odd, certainly,' he remarks, before looking up. 'What do you think?'

From the sitting room come clattering sounds as Mabel plays with her toys. The combination of Jeff's calmness and the noisy domesticity of my child playing takes some of the strangeness out of it. For even though the past couple of days have been busy, niggling thoughts of this anonymous note have lingered over everything. Now, saying it out loud, it sounds more silly than sinister.

'I don't know. It's probably just some loon who listens to the show. God knows, there are plenty of them out there.'

'Indeed.'

'Vic laughed when I showed it to him, said that I should see some of the poisonous missives he receives.'

'Ha! Yes, I can imagine.'

He smiles at me across the table, and I feel the warmth and steadiness of his presence. It acts as a reminder of why I first fell in love with him. His unflappability. His quiet reserve of strength. From the first time we met – at

77

a dinner party hosted by a mutual friend – I knew somehow that he was the sort of man who could be relied upon in a crisis, a decent man who would never deceive me, never let me down. He had a directness of manner coupled with an old-fashioned chivalry that I found greatly appealing. After the volatility of Finn's moods and caprices, my relationship with Jeff felt like sinking into a warm bath after battling through a storm.

'It must happen all the time,' he goes on. 'There are so many people walking around, disturbed, angry, looking for some outlet for their madness. People in the public eye can seem accessible. They are easy targets.'

'Finn used to get some weird letters and cards from fans, or from people who couldn't stand him.'

Jeff reaches for his glass, sips without saying anything.

'But I think he mainly enjoyed the attention,' I add.

Jeff snorts with amusement. 'He would,' he says with the slightest hint of malice. 'He probably sent them to himself.'

We both laugh, but it sparks a thought that unsettles me, for Jeff has inadvertently lit on a possibility. A lover of the practical joke, Finn has often gone to great lengths to construct elaborate webs to trap his unsuspecting victim. I remember how tenacious he could be and how this tenacity, which at the beginning was so attractive to me, could also be repellent, even dangerous. Could he be behind the note?

'So Ingrid got in touch again today,' Jeff says, interrupting my thoughts. 'About a project she's been working on.'

'Ingrid?' I ask, spearing some salad with my fork.

'Yes, remember? I did some work with her before

Christmas? Anyway, they've been looking for someone to manage the project for them and my name came up.'

'Really?'

'It's a fantastic opportunity, Cara.'

'That's terrific, sweetheart. Well done you.'

'The thing is, they'll need me to go to Berlin.'

I put down my fork.

'Just during the week,' he goes on. 'I can fly home at weekends.'

'How long for?'

'Six weeks, probably. I'll know more once I go over there.'

Consternation starts up in my chest. I try to keep my voice level.

'But what about Mabel?'

He laughs briefly, saying, 'Mabel will be fine! I'll call her every day – we can FaceTime. And I'll be home at the weekends.'

I get up from my chair, bring my plate over to the sink. I can feel him watching me.

'Come on, love. It would only be for a couple of months,' he protests.

'I thought you said six weeks,' I say quietly.

He sighs, puts down his knife and fork. I have my back to him, but I hear the scrape of his chair across the floor, and then he is standing next to me, putting his plate on top of mine.

'Cara –'

'Who's going to mind Mabel in the mornings when I leave for work?' I ask, turning to face him.

He's half a foot taller than me and he inclines his head

to meet my gaze. 'Couldn't you drop her off at nursery on your way in?'

'The nursery doesn't open until seven thirty. I leave here at six, or had you forgotten?'

'Perhaps you could juggle your working hours a bit? Start later?'

'Oh yeah. Sure. "Sorry, guys, we need to reschedule the show to a later hour, because my husband needs to go to Berlin. Just for a month or two. Then we'll return to the usual schedule. Everyone okay with that?"'

'There's no need for sarcasm. I just meant that maybe you could conduct some of your prep meetings the day before. I don't know.'

He turns back towards the table and starts clearing away the salad bowl, the glasses, the salt and pepper shakers. His excitement at his announcement has been choked off by the practicalities. But it bothers me that Jeff seems unable to grasp the fact that I am the main breadwinner and, as such, my working hours must be protected. It galls me that even though I earn more than him and my work is salaried and steady, I am still expected to drop everything when the childcare arrangements fall through.

'When are you going?'

'They want me to go over next week, to talk things through face-to-face.'

'Christ,' I say softly, wiping my hands on a tea towel.

This kitchen feels hot, like I can't breathe. All at once, I need to be outside in the cool air.

'I don't want to have a fight about it,' he intones softly in his reasonable voice. 'This is good news, Cara. Aren't you the one who's always going on at me to look for more challenging work? So that I don't slip into early senility?'

'I never said that. I merely pointed out that it would be good for you to do new things.'

'And now I am!' He catches himself, brings his voice back under control. 'There must be agencies that deal with this sort of thing. I'm sure we can get someone to live in – an au pair.'

'At this short notice? And for such a limited period? Besides, I'm not sure I like the idea of a stranger living with us.'

He puts the half-empty salad bowl into the fridge, then closes the door and looks about him to see if there's anything left to be put away. For a moment, the only noise in the kitchen is the buzz of the fridge. A thought flits across my mind – a possibility.

'I'll ask around at work,' I tell him. 'There might be someone who can help us out.'

We spend the next few minutes cleaning up the kitchen in silence.

On Friday, I spend my spare minutes in work on the phone to various agencies, as well as cornering other mums in the office to ask their advice. The responses are mostly negative. The short notice coupled with the uncertain time frame means my options are limited. By the time the lunch break arrives, I'm feeling despondent from all the fruitless enquiries, the apologetic tones from the agency contacts, the sympathetic glances from my co-workers. I'm also a little put out by the fact that it's me who's ringing around for a childminder, not Jeff.

Sometime in the afternoon, my phone pings with an incoming text, and when I check it, I see that it's from Amy.

'Lovely to catch up with you yesterday. Give me a call if ever you want to meet up.'

The possibility has been scratching away at the back of my mind, and prompted by her text, I call and put the proposition to her.

'It will just be for five or six weeks,' I tell her. 'A temporary thing.'

'That's perfect!' Excitement makes her voice sound light and breathy.

I'm not completely easy about the situation. But time is running out and I don't have many options. And at least I sort of know Amy. I take comfort in the memory of how sure and self-controlled she seemed on the night we were holed up together. In the face of all that fear and confusion she was calm and decisive.

'I'll need to get references, of course.'

She replies, 'Absolutely. No problem,' and promises to forward letters of recommendation from the family she has worked for, as well as from her manager at Pret. We make arrangements for her to come to the apartment at the weekend to meet with Jeff and Mabel, and then we say our goodbyes, but not before she gushes her thanks down the phone in a way that seems most unlike her.

I put the phone down and sit for a minute, thinking back to yesterday's conversation, in Gianni's around the corner. I remember the tension running between her square shoulders, defensiveness in the way she hunched over her coffee. She had seemed nervous and unsure; there was no sign of the almost casual complacency she displayed the night we hid in the storeroom. Sitting at the table opposite her, I noticed a tiny puncture in the side of her nose where a nose ring must once have been, and a tattoo in the crook of her arm – a black square. No text, no image. Just this oddly blank mark. It must be exhausting having to work so hard at looking tough. And yet there was something endearing about her nerves, her eagerness to please. There's some quality to her that I like.

The office around me hums with activity. There's a slew of emails I need to respond to, as well as a pile of post that Katie has left on my desk, wrapped in an elastic band which twangs as I remove it. I go through it hurriedly, most of it rubbish that I toss in the bin. I pause when I get to a white envelope, my name and work address written in black Sharpie ink. I open it quickly, draw out the plain white card and read the words:

25 August 2017. A night to remember.
Your Closest Friend
X

My heart gives out a little thud, confusion worming through my brain. *Is this Finn?* I wonder. *Or someone else?* For just a second, Amy's face flashes across my mind.

I look at the signature, the kiss, and I remember the moment on Friday night when I said goodbye to Finn on Redchurch Street. He had leaned in to kiss me and I had stopped him. Seeing the look of injury crossing his face, I'd tried to soften it, saying that we could just be friends. 'Friends,' he had repeated, then raising an eyebrow, his tone becoming teasing and lascivious, 'very close friends, I hope.'

There is still a chance that it's not him, but some crazy listener who's decided to concentrate their attention on me. I take the card and the envelope and roll my chair a few feet along to Katie's desk, and show it to her.

'Any ideas?' I ask.

She shakes her head blankly. 'It was just brought up with the rest of the post,' she says, turning it over. 'You could try asking down in the post room.'

'No point. It's external mail. They'll know as much about it as we do. It's probably just a practical joke.'

She hands it back to me. 'Kind of weird, though,' she says.

I've just exited Clapham Junction station on my way home when I hear my phone ping, and when I check, there's a text from Jeff, asking if I can pick up coffee on the way home – we're having friends for dinner, and he's realized we're running low. It's the first day of September and I note that the evenings are getting cooler already, even though it's barely six, as I reach the Lidl near our home and duck inside.

I'm in the aisle, hunting for coffee, when my phone pings again. When I look I see that it's a number I don't recognize, and the message reads: *You are everything to me. YCF x*

It makes me stop in my tracks. There amid the Nescafé and the Maxwell House, the Horlicks and the Cadbury's Bournville Cocoa, I try to process the tangle of thoughts turning over rapidly in my head. I text back quickly: *Who is this?* Then I wait. One person rises above all others in my suspicions. There have been missed calls and texts from Finn since our lunch on Tuesday, pleading with me to call him, and even though I've been studiously ignoring them, now I feel pinched with curiosity. Could this be his way of luring me into making contact? When there is no reply to my text, I call the number, a defensive feeling making my shoulders feel tight as I listen to it ringing. No one answers and eventually it rings out. There is no voicemail facility, and the deadness at the end of the line leaves me feeling frustrated. I scroll through my contacts for Finn's number and, despite my better judgement, I press the call button. He picks up straight away.

'At last. I was waiting for your call,' he says.

'Were you?'

'I've snagged tickets for Sigur Rós tonight. They're playing the Hammersmith Apollo. And I thought to myself, who do I know that loves Sigur Rós?'

'I can't, Finn.'

'Oh, come on! Make an excuse. Come out with me. You know you want to.' That pleading, cajoling voice I know so well.

'We have people coming for dinner.'

'Babe, that is just so middle-aged. Come on, say something's come up at work – some crisis or emergency. Tell them you're needed elsewhere. Because you are. I need you.'

For just a second, I imagine doing it. The memory of our recent evening together still shines inside me, and the prospect of another calls to me, like the old days beckoning.

'Have you been sending me messages?' I ask, remembering why I called him.

'Subliminal messages? Sexual messages?'

'Actual messages. Anonymous ones. I've been getting these cards sent to work, signed "Your Closest Friend".'

'A secret admirer. And you thought it was me?'

'Is it you?'

'I'm not telling. Where would be the fun in that? What do they say, anyway?'

'There was another one just now – a text message. It said: "You are everything to me." '

I wait for his response.

After a pause, he says softly and with sincerity, 'You *are* everything to me, Cara.'

I feel the blood rush to my face. Stupid, this silly schoolgirl reaction. This fast-beating heart, this flood of gladness.

'Finn,' I say gently, but firmly. 'This has to stop.'

I hang up before he can answer.

Our guests arrive shortly after eight, all of them landing in at the same time. I can hear laughter and raised voices through the intercom as I press the buzzer to let them in.

A little while later, six of us gather around the deal refectory table centred in our kitchen. All evidence of Jeff's culinary exertions have been tidied away, and there is candlelight and smooth jazz; the red petals of the geraniums growing in terracotta pots beneath the stairs are flares of bright colour against the soft grey walls.

I'm a little nervous at the prospect of one of our friends bringing up the terrorist attack. Kamila – my unwitting alibi for that evening – is among the guests, and I'm wary of any conversation that might reveal my deception. So,

86

from the outset, I make it clear that the evening mustn't become mired in gloomy doomsday conversation.

'I'm declaring a moratorium on all discussion relating to terrorism, Brexit and Donald Trump,' I say, before Jeff says, 'Hear, hear!' and then launches into a story involving a mix-up in the Airbnb booking for his Berlin trip.

He's on good form tonight. We both are. The difficulty that arose between us yesterday has dissipated, now there is a solution to the childcare problem, and he is once more buoyant with the news of his imminent work adventure. I watch him moving around the table, slopping wine generously into glasses, cracking jokes at his own expense. We always make an effort with friends, and are good at presenting a united front. Looking at us tonight, you would never know of the chinks in the walls of our marriage, the hairline cracks. There is a glow inside me, and even though I am present in conversation, in laughter, in joining in the fun, inside I am reeling with a wild dizziness. The thrill of it: *You are everything to me.* At the time, I had expressed disapproval, even annoyance. But now, in the warmth and safety of my home, I take pleasure from turning the thought over in my head. Finn's voice hums through me, sensuous and absorbing.

At some point in the night, Peter mentions how he spotted Phoebe Waller-Bridge from *Fleabag* in a restaurant during the week, and our conversation swerves in the direction of how promiscuity in women is depicted in modern culture.

'It's just getting so dreary,' Graham says, 'so full of self-loathing. I mean, aren't there any young women out there having fun?'

'Fun sex obviously doesn't market as well as complicated sex,' Kamila adds.

'But surely it's a step up from the old days when only men were allowed to sleep around in popular culture,' Jeff says, reaching behind him for another bottle from the counter.

'I don't see that it's much of a step forward,' Jenny offers. 'I mean it's still the same old story: promiscuity in men is seen as a rite of passage, but in women it must be punished.'

The men bray a bit at this, Peter saying, 'You can't win, can you? I mean, on the one hand you'd complain if all TV shows were depicting men getting their kicks, and yet you're not satisfied when these young women are getting laid on telly either –'

'I didn't say that,' Jenny interjects.

Beyond the entrance to the kitchen, on the little table where we drop our keys, I hear my phone ping with an incoming text.

'Jenny is right,' Kamila says. 'There's no fun in it for these young women. It's all so joyless and depressing.'

'Well, at least they're getting laid,' Jeff remarks with dramatic melancholy, and everyone laughs.

'Not fulfilling your wifely duties, eh, Cara?' Graham says.

I laugh and throw a look down the table at Jeff, and say, 'Poor neglected husband!'

But there's a barb twisting in the laughter and the jokey comments that only he and I are aware of. Since the night of the terror attack – the night Finn and I reconnected – Jeff and I have not made love. It's only been a week, but even before then, I could sense a staleness had entered our bedroom relations. And despite my attempt at deflecting his jokey remark, I am hurt that he would allude to it in this way.

I take the opportunity to leave my seat and go into the hall.

'Listen,' Graham pipes up. 'When I had the vasectomy, I was promised loads of sex. That's how the idea was sold to me. No, don't try to deny it, Jen.'

'I'm not saying anything!'

A blocked number. A simple statement: *Look outside. YCF x*

I stare at it. In the next room, the conversation has erupted into laughter once more, but here in the hallway, I am completely still, frozen. Is he outside? Would he dare risk coming so close to my home?

From where I am standing, I can see the night sky through the window of our sitting room. The curtains are still open, and in my mind, as I'm crossing the floor, I'm telling myself that this is perfectly normal, that if Jeff or one of our guests comes out into the hall and sees me, they will assume I am drawing the curtains.

It's a large window – one of those Victorian industrial jobs – that looks out on to the carefully tended grounds that front the building. There are mounds of dark shrubs down there, the spidery limbs of trees, hump-backed shadows of cars parked along the perimeter, but I am aware of these things as only vague familiar shapes in my consciousness. For what draws and holds my attention is the flickering of votive candles in the courtyard. Tiny lights in the darkness. There must be dozens of them burning away, all arranged into the shape of a love heart.

Once, when we were at university, Finn made me a Valentine's card. He was prone to spontaneous romantic gestures, but rarely went in for what he called Hallmark holidays. Only one time he made an exception. The card he gave me was a computer printout of a line drawing of a love heart, and above it was a mathematical equation. Mathematics was his principal subject, and although his passion for it was eclipsed in time by his love of comedy and celebrity, at that point it held a fascination for him. He spoke about equations in terms of beauty.

'You're giving me an equation?' I'd asked, half-joking.

And he'd pointed to the heart, explaining, 'The equation maps the line, you see? It's the equation of the heart.'

This comes back to me now, as I look out into the darkness at the flickering shape on the ground below, and the memory makes my heart pound. I lean my head against the window, feel the heat of my own skin against the glass. I wonder: *Is he down there in the darkness, watching?* My eyes scan the grounds, but there is no figure under the street lamps, no face staring up at me from the darkness. And yet, I feel that there is someone down there. I feel like I am being watched.

A smile passes over my face – I can't help it – and I raise my hand, a brief salute to my dark admirer.

An acknowledgement.

The response is almost immediate. The phone buzzes in my hand.

I look down, scroll to texts, and there it is – the blocked number. A simple message. No words, just an emoticon. Tiny though it is, it lights up the screen.

♥

8.

Amy

'I like your hair,' Cara tells me.

We're in my bedroom – or what is temporarily my bedroom, although it is Jeff's daughter's room really – and she's just shown me where I can put my clothes, my things. I'm still marvelling at the expanse of it, the softness of the carpet, the miracle of the en suite bathroom that I share with Mabel. She is skipping around the bed, picking up objects off the bureau and briefly inspecting them. I get the feeling that this room has been off-limits for her, and now she's making the most of the opportunity to absorb every little thing.

I put my hand to my hair, self-conscious suddenly. Two days ago, after Cara's phone call, I went into a place on the high street near Sean's house and, dipping into my emergency escape fund, spent over a hundred bucks dying it chestnut brown, and getting what the hairdresser laughingly described as 'a feathery cut', like I was some class of poultry looking to be groomed. It's more feminine, I guess, which is what I wanted.

'Thanks,' I say, and look down, feeling the sweep of my embarrassment.

'I hope it's not because of what I said?'

'Sort of,' I say, laughing to take the sting out of it. 'I mean, I was going to get it done anyway . . .'

'I'm sorry. It was a stupid assumption to make.' She's smiling at me, but it's a pained sort of smile, like she wishes she could take it back.

I don't want her to feel awkward. I don't want there to be any gaps or pauses between us, so I say, 'That's okay. Actually, my mom was a lesbian. Sort of.'

My eyes flicker over at Mabel, to see if she's listening to this. But the kid has picked up a fan and is busy spreading it, then collapsing it. She's a cute little thing, all dimples and curls. She looks like Cara, not a trace of her father in her, none that I can see anyway.

'I didn't know it for years,' I continue. 'Her friend that I told you about, Elaine? She lived with her daughter, Connie, in this house just outside Scranton in Pennsylvania, and when I was little my mom and I went there and lived with them for a while. I don't know how they knew each other – Mom and Elaine – how they'd met, but I just thought they were really good pals. I thought that for, like, ages. Until one day they were working on something in the kitchen – they were always doing these little projects together – and me and Connie were out on the porch and we could hear our moms in the kitchen hooting with laughter, and then Connie just looked at me with this kind of pained expression and said, "Fucking dykes." And that's how I found out.'

I lower my voice for this last bit, and lean in to whisper it conspiratorially to her. When she smiles, her mouth grows long and curved. I'm noticing small things about her: the slight discoloration of a lower tooth, a dimple in one cheek missing a twin. Each detail gathered up and stored away to be pored over later, treasured.

'How did that make you feel?' she wants to know. She's

sitting on the bed now, looking up at me, relaxing into this conversation. God, how strange it is to talk like this! I can't remember the last time I could be this honest with another person, this open.

'I was sort of shocked, I guess. A little disgusted too. I started spying on them, sneaking out of bed in the night, creeping down through the house to watch them together on the porch, sharing a beer, talking. Sometimes they'd reach out and hold hands. One time, I saw them necking.' I give a little shudder. 'They were pretty discreet, I guess. Like they had separate bedrooms and all that. But I remember feeling like she'd somehow betrayed me.'

'Your mother?'

'Yeah. Like she'd kept something about herself back from me – something that other people knew about but I didn't. It hurt that I had to learn about it from someone else. That knowledge came like a gut-punch. Like when you find out there's no Santa Claus.'

'Did you find that out from Connie too?'

I give a rueful smile that tells her she's guessed correctly.

'I'm making her sound like a real bitch,' I say. 'But she wasn't. She just wasn't good at keeping secrets to herself.'

'You were close to her?'

'Yeah. She was like my best friend. I could talk to her about anything. She could be really kind and sweet, and sort of practical, you know? Like you could always trust her to give you good advice.' And then, because I'm somehow moved to say it, warmed as I am by the release of this conversation, the welcome I've received here and the great opening out of possibilities that giddily present themselves, I say, 'You sort of remind me of her.'

93

Her smile broadens, her eyebrows tilt. 'Do I?'

But I'm embarrassed now. I've admitted too much.

'A little,' I say, and turn away to start unpacking my things.

The husband is not what I expected. Cara had told me how there's an age gap between them, but still. I can't get over how middle-aged he seems, grey spreading through his hair, the skin under his chin beginning to pucker and sag like an old frog. But it's like he hasn't noticed his age yet, or is choosing to ignore it. He wears jeans and green Asics, his hair a little too long on top as if going for that foppish, boyish look. He has that jaunty niceness – that English good cheer – that always seems like a wall to me, something impenetrable that could not possibly go all the way to the core. Everyone's got a dark side, I don't care how nice they are.

'Settling in alright?' he asks, and nods absently at my response. I was half-worried he'd start quizzing me about the night of the attack, and the first time Cara and I met. I'd had my answers all worked out, of course, but he never even asked. I get the feeling that his politeness is a veneer for his lack of interest. For all the conversation between us – the small talk – I don't think he listens to a word I say. Still, he's leaving in the morning, and I won't have to deal with him then.

The first night, I feign tiredness and slope off to bed early, deeming it best to show I can be sensitive to their need for privacy – let them have their romantic last evening away from prying eyes. Cara shot me a look of gratitude and I felt like I had done the right thing, a neat little

94

check-mark in the column of my private accounting. In my room, I slip off my shoes and socks, hang my jeans over the back of a chair, and then lie down on the bed, spreading my arms and legs wide and then pulling them in close like I'm making a snow angel on the covers, marvelling at the stippled softness of the waffle linen. Everything about the room holds a cloudy softness, from the thick-pile carpet to the chalky grey-blue walls. A port-hole window looks out on to a parapet tiled in Victorian slate, a sliver of sky beyond.

While I lie there taking it all in, amazed at the corner my life has turned, I hear Connie's voice in my head, say-ing, *Check you out, Keener. On the pig's back now, aren't ya?* And for once the voice doesn't sound like a mean kid, saying one thing but meaning another.

It's Mabel who tells me about the apartment. About how it belonged to the dead wife.

It's Tuesday afternoon, and I've just settled her at the table with her cup of hot chocolate after school, absently talking through what she learned that day while I get started on the dinner preparations. This week in school, the little kids are discussing houses. A kind of kiddie-class on rudimentary architecture, I guess. They've all been tasked with projects on their own homes – drawing pic-tures of their houses, answering questions like: Does your home have a fireplace? How many windows does it have? How many steps from the front door to the back door? Sounds like some busybody teacher having a good nose around the finances and properties of her young charges to me.

Mabel is drawing her picture. From this, you'd swear she lived in a red-brick Victorian mansion, but in truth, the building is split into apartments, some single dwellings, others, like this one, sprawling split-level affairs. The building itself is a bit of an aberration. It's called The Village, although I can't think why. A Victorian red-brick school conversion, more plush than forbidding after the job that was done on it, turning it into luxury apartments. It stands proud above the small narrow streets that surround it, lined with terraced houses that can't help looking mean and cramped in comparison. I'd done some snooping around property websites, and knew the purchase prices of these apartments easily top the million-pound mark. It's weird because the surrounding area is kind of run-down, streaked with poverty. Like someone airlifted a chunk of Belgravia and dropped it in Battersea.

Mabel puts down her pencil, looks up at me with some consternation, and asks, 'But how will they know which part I live in?'

'Why don't you draw arrows?' I suggest. 'Or you could circle your bedroom window?'

She does this – both the arrows and the circling – and then throws down her pencil in a hot little burst of temper.

'It looks silly!' she says, all mulish and unhappy.

'Come on, it's not that bad.'

'It's a silly house. I wish we didn't live here.'

'You're pretty lucky, you know, Mabel. Loads of people would kill to live in a place like this.'

'Mummy doesn't think so. She keeps telling Daddy we should live somewhere else.'

I put down my knife, turn away from the chopping board, my attention caught.

'She says that?'

'She says it's always going to be Claire's house.'

'Who's Claire?'

She rolls her eyes theatrically, then pushes herself away from the table and leaves the room. I think she's marched off in a strop, but she's back a few seconds later with a framed photograph she's taken from the hall table.

'Claire,' she says emphatically, thrusting the picture into my hands.

I look down at the image of a woman and a young girl, both smiling into the camera. It's one of those studio shots, and there's something stagey about their matching sweaters, the soft glow of their skin, their hair.

'This is your dad's first wife, right?'

'Mm-hmm.' She's back at the kitchen table, her burst of petulance easing, taking up her pencil once more.

'And this is her apartment?'

She doesn't answer, her little tongue visible at the side of her mouth as she concentrates.

'Mabel?'

'What?'

'How do you know all this stuff?'

'Because I hear them fighting,' she explains unhappily. 'I hate it when they fight.'

I press her on it, but she's clamming up and soon enough I go back to my prep in silence.

But as I stand there chopping onions and then leeks, I think about what it must be like – to live in a dead woman's house. This place is full of old furniture, antique

97

chests of drawers, slouchy sofas that look ancient, carved wooden chairs circling the table. I had it in my head that these were things that Cara and Jeff bought together, or maybe some family heirlooms. But now I'm rethinking it, wondering how much of this shit belonged to the dead wife. For a second, I imagine the ghostly sweep of her hand over every chair back, every door handle, on the bannister along the stairs.

When we were locked up in the storeroom together, Cara told me how unhappy she was living in this house. How she hated the sense of privilege that attached to the place, the fortress-like walls that surrounded it, the cruel-looking spiked fencing. Everything about it screamed a conservative entitlement that she felt she hadn't earned, and automatically rejected. That is what she told me. But she never mentioned the real reason. Not a word was spoken about jealousy, about the past. Not a word said about the dead wife.

By the end of the first week, we've settled into a routine of sorts. As soon as I hear the front door closing behind Cara in the mornings, I get out of bed. I like to have my shower finished, my room straightened up before going into Mabel to rouse her from sleep. She's a funny kid, a complicated mixture of childish innocence and worldly enquiry. Her questions often catch me by surprise: What would happen if the moon exploded? How did they make the first Tube? Why is bone-growing painful but hair-growing isn't? Such is the zone that I now patrol, the maze of questions forming the five-year-old mind.

After dropping Mabel at school, watching until she is

safely inside, I head back towards home and stop at Lidl or Asda to buy the ingredients for dinner. I have little experience of cooking, but I'm keen to learn, and have been trawling through the shelves of cookbooks in Cara's kitchen, picking out the ones I think I can manage. Any gaps in my knowledge are plugged by message boards and YouTube videos. I'm hoping to get more ambitious as the weeks go on.

Listen to me, already planning ahead. This is something new for me too, a reaction to the peace and joy I've been feeling since the offer was first made, the arrangements set in place. My happiness is occasionally corrupted by the worming thought that I should not get too comfortable here, but barely a week in and I'm way beyond that already.

I stop at Valentina's on Lavender Hill and buy diced beef, anchovies, bread, a bottle of Rioja. This last item is for the cooking, not for drinking, although I might have a little glass while I'm pulling it all together. At the cash register, I hand over two crisp twenties that Cara gave me for shopping, and as I wait for the change, my mind briefly darts to a time when I was a kid, shopping in the drugstore with Connie, the meaningful look she'd give me, picking up a lipstick or a mascara that she wanted me to lift. I had a blank, innocent face, easily forgotten, and I was good at it too, swift little fingers, done without fuss.

I'm making a beef stew – one of Nigella Lawson's recipes – something wholesome and nourishing. Last night, when she'd come in from work, Cara had looked pale and tired. As soon as Mabel came running at her, crying 'Mummy!' her face became animated, all smiles.

But I'd caught the expression just before that — in the moment that she stepped into the hall, leaned back against the door and stared up at the skylight. Like she'd just stepped in from a storm. She hates the walk from the station to home, especially at night or in the early mornings when it's still dark — the spooky rush through the railway underpass, the scrubby grass alongside the supermarkets strewn with litter, the shadows lurking in the disused playground of Lavender Gardens as she scurries past in the darkness. She'd hid it well for Mabel, for me too, I guess. Making happy noises about the smell of the lasagne cooking in the oven. But I could tell it was an act. Underneath she was troubled.

'You know what you need?' I'd said. 'A glass of wine.'

She shook her head, saying, 'I really shouldn't. It's a school night.'

Crazy, the rules these people make for themselves.

'I won't tell,' I said, feeling her relent.

'Alright, but only if you'll join me.'

So we sat at the table, the three of us, eating the food that I'd made, a bottle of smoky Rioja open between us. After I'd finished cleaning up and Cara had put Mabel to bed, I tipped a little more wine into my glass and settled on the couch in a warm, happy fug, watching the TV with the sound down, listening to the hum of Cara's voice through the ceiling. She was on the phone in her bedroom, to Jeff, presumably. I couldn't tell from her muffled tone whether she was happy or sad, but when she came back downstairs a little while later, she had that strained look again, like her mind was loaded down with worry.

'Everything okay?' I asked and she said yes, fine, then

said something about a tooth that was giving her some trouble, her hand held against her jaw. But I caught the small, hard glance she gave the wine glass in my hand, noting the top-up with unspoken disapproval, her eyes flicking from there to my feet propped up on the edge of the ottoman, my flip-flops abandoned to the side of the rug. I could tell I'd overstepped the mark, caught the quicksilver thought crossing her mind that I was like a teenager slouching on her sofa, and so I sat up a little, withdrawing my feet and making a mental note to wait, in future, for her cue before replenishing my glass.

'Listen,' she said, 'I know we agreed you'd stay for a month, but there's been a slight change in plan.'

Here it comes, I thought, *my dismissal*.

But instead, she went on, 'Jeff needs to stay in Germany a little longer than expected. I don't suppose you'd mind staying on with us? Maybe even until Christmas?'

Of course I agreed. Embarrassed myself with eagerness as I jumped to accept.

'Thank you, Amy,' she added, putting her hand to her head, fingertips touching her temple as if there was pain there. 'I'd be lost without you.'

Not long after that, she retired for the night, claiming exhaustion, while I sat there on the couch, polishing off my glass while watching *The Deuce*, a big warm feeling spreading through my insides.

It's Wednesday morning of my second week here, and I've dropped Mabel at school before coming home to the big, roomy apartment. Cara is at work and Jeff's in Berlin, so it's just me here alone in this vast space. There's something delicious about the echoing silence as I pad from room to room, plumping pillows, straightening out towels on the rails in the bathroom, fantasizing that this place is my own. It gives me pleasure, this busy domesticity, like I'm watching myself in a play, performing the role of lady of the house, watering the pot plants. I touch these things as if they are mine, running my fingers along the mantelpiece of the redundant fireplace, cupping my hands around the carved wooden head of some African sculpture with drooping earlobes, a collar of beads winding around its neck. I'm tempted to pour myself a drink – a glass of ice-cold Chardonnay from the fridge, a finger of vodka with ice – but it's not even midday and I've responsibilities now, so I make myself a coffee and drift through the rooms, clutching the mug to my chest.

In all the days I've been alone here, I haven't yet gone upstairs to Cara and Jeff's bedroom. It seems off-limits. Private. Even though this has never been made explicit. I stand at the foot of the stairs that lead from the kitchen up to their private space. The quietness seems forbidding, but my curiosity is stronger. I put my coffee cup down on the table and then tiptoe up until I find myself in a lofty room decorated in the same tasteful tones as the rest of the apartment, the only jags of colour in the abstract art above the bed, and in the armchair and footstool in the corner. There's an electric guitar propped against one wall – an old Gibson, that must be worth a mint – and I almost laugh, picturing Jeff balancing it on his knee, plucking at the strings with a plectrum, his public schoolboy fringe of hair flopping forward.

I open Cara's wardrobe and start trying on shoes. By

happy coincidence, we are the same size, and I slip on a pair of Christian Louboutins and strut over to the bathroom then back again, amusing myself with a wiggle of the hips. Perching on the edge of the bed, I pull open the drawer on his side of the bed. There's nothing of interest — some magazines of the financial variety and an inhaler, a foil-backed sheet of paracetamol, two of the blisters empty. Kicking off the shoes, and rolling over on to Cara's side, I lie with my cheek on her pillow, breathing in the now-familiar smell of her shampoo, perusing the messier contents of her drawer — tubes of lipstick, moisturizer, a box of tissues, a pack of birth-control pills, a faded photograph of a smiling woman I guess is her mother. I stare at the photograph for a moment, struck by the thought that Cara never mentions her mother. Even when I opened up to her about my mom and all I'd been through, still she said nothing about her own.

I put the photograph back and close the drawer. The bed is comfortable — not too hard and not too soft. I'm like frigging Goldilocks here, testing the mattress. I wonder if this is where Jeff slept with his first wife? Was this their marital bed? I think of the woman in the photograph, her arch smile, her perfect grooming. Who knew what pain she might have gone through in this room, as the disease ate away at her? And how must it have felt for him, taking Cara to bed here after all of that? Did they feel, in some way, watched?

An image creeps into my mind of the two of them having sex, Jeff's thin-lipped smile lowering to Cara's breast, sucking in the hard nub of her nipple. A rogue thought that lingers and excites. I spend a breathless few minutes, rubbing at myself, holding that image in my mind, my face pressed into the pillow.

Afterwards, I straighten out the bed and return the shoes to the wardrobe. I back out of the room slowly, my eyes scalding the surfaces for any stray evidence of my visit.

When Cara comes through the door that night, the beef stew is ready, Mabel pink from her bath, and I'm folding laundry at the kitchen table, my face a perfect mask of innocence.

The same thing happens on Thursday, and when Friday morning comes, after the drop-off I don't bother about the shopping. The lure of that bedroom is too strong. I get back to the flat, throw my stuff in the kitchen, and then I'm back upstairs, flinging open the wardrobe, trying on clothes, taking another turn on the bed. I've left my phone downstairs on the kitchen table and I'm vaguely aware of it ringing, but I've the iPod on, plugged into the speakers by the bed, and Nick Cave is crooning menacingly above a cheesy organ. It's probably just Sean again, and I don't feel the need to speak to him, not now that things have changed. So I let the phone ring out and reach into the wardrobe for another dress.

Something happens to me when I'm alone in this room. It's like I'm mooring myself to a world that's unfamiliar and exciting, a world I want to greedily swallow. In these hours alone in this space, it's hard to believe that barely three weeks ago I was bored and groundless. The clothes are spread around the room in disarray but I don't care, consumed by this tremulous need to explore, like I'm nine years old once more, Connie and I dressing up in my mother's clothes, Connie sipping beer she'd stolen from the fridge.

I've chosen a kimono-style dress made of silk, a sleek image of a stork screen-printed along the side – it's a piece of clothing I can't imagine Cara ever wearing. She seems to live in a uniform of jeans and suit jackets, Gap T-shirts underneath. Half the clothes in her wardrobe sit on hangers wrapped in cellophane. There's something forlorn about them, like orphaned children, so it feels like I'm doing this dress a favour when I push the plastic away and take the material in my hands. I've shed my clothes, my bra too, and the silk slipping over my naked flesh is like rippling water, cool and fresh and cleansing. I muss up my hair a little, and then, taking one of the lipstick tubes from Cara's drawer, I coat my lips with scarlet, and step my feet into heeled ankle boots, little zippers at the back, fastening them tight. I take a couple of steps back to observe the full length of myself in the mirror. The dress is a little big on me, my body requiring some augmentation in the chest area in order to fill the fabric, and I pull at the neckline so that it scoops and plunges, the white skin between my breasts clearly visible. I'm imagining myself at a cocktail party downstairs in the living room, guests milling around, the occasional eye glancing over at the young woman in silk, murmured questions circling: Who is she? I pose and pout in front of the mirror, miming drinking from a champagne flute. And then a mischievous thought enters my head and I pretend that I'm leaning down to pluck a canapé from a tray on the ottoman: my dress sags open and some old crusty work colleague of Jeff's snags an eyeful of my breast; and I'm actually doing this now, watching myself in the mirror, when the music snaps off, silence tearing through the room, and I swing around and see a person I have never met before standing there at the door.

Her hair is long and dark, a sharp geometrical fringe cut high above thin eyebrows. She's about my age, maybe a little younger, and she's fixing me with a look of horrified fascination, like I'm some weird exhibit, a grotesque. My heart is fighting like crazy beneath the silk, and I can feel the nerves blotching my throat.

The girl stands still for a moment. And then she removes the bag from her shoulder – a baby-blue leather tote – and drops it on the ground by her feet, not once taking her eyes off me.

In a voice that comes out in a rasp of slow, disbelieving enquiry, she says, 'Who the fuck are you?'

9.

Cara

We're in the meeting room talking through the briefs in the minutes before the show starts — it's Friday, so we're keeping it light: a comedian who's flogging a book, and a model/actress with a new play opening in the West End. Katie has acted upon my suggestion and put together a small quiz, and she's going through it now, fending off the grim march of negatives from Vic's corner, when I notice a new hashtag in my Twitter account. Throughout the meeting my phone has been sporadically lighting up with news feeds, but this one catches my eye:

#ParsonsGreenAttack

Just as I'm picking it up to scroll down and investigate, I notice a flurry of activity on the office floor. It's heading towards nine o'clock and the place has filled up considerably since I arrived a couple of hours ago, but now I can see a huddle forming underneath the flat-screen TV that's broadcasting the news channel. Murmurs are filtering through into the meeting room.

'Are you seeing this?' Derek asks, his eyes pinned to his phone, and then he reads aloud. '"Reports are coming in of an incident on a Tube train in west London. There are unconfirmed accounts of an explosion on the District Line at Parsons Green station. Eyewitnesses have spoken of a device detonating as the train left the station. As yet, there is no information regarding casualties. The station is being evacuated and emergency response units are at the scene.""'

'Fucking hell,' Vic declares. 'Not another one.'

Derek is already moving far ahead of us, announcing we'll have to change our plans, rethink our approach. 'We'll need to talk to senior management, get a steer from them as to how much airtime to devote to this terrorist attack –'

Vic interjects, 'The bloody show is becoming *Let's Talk Terrorism*. For fuck's sake, it's supposed to be light entertainment! People want a break from this stuff – let's give it to them. It's Friday, after all!'

They're debating it now, the two of them, going back and forth, and I can see Katie looking at me. She's expecting me to intervene, I can tell. Or perhaps she's thinking what I'm thinking: that as the series producer, I'm the one who should be suggesting a rethink, I'm the one who should consult senior management. Derek is overstepping the mark and he knows it, but the truth is my breathing has quickened, my mouth dry. The skin of my face feels stretched taut over bones.

'Are you alright?' Katie mouths, so that the men aren't aware.

I nod my head briskly and, with an effort, take control of the situation. Somehow, I manage to get my head together enough to issue terse instructions to all of them, assigning tasks before we all disperse – Derek and Katie heading for the control room to meet the sound operator, Vic ducking out for a quick smoke before the show begins. I make a great effort to maintain a normal walking pace as I move through the office, and head towards the toilets.

Once inside, I splash my face with cold water, then blot my skin dry with a paper towel. I sit in the cubicle for a full five minutes, waiting for my heart to stop thumping, for the sweat to stop oozing from my pores. Finn lives in Parsons Green.

Eventually, I get it together enough to return to my desk, where I pick up the phone and, breaking my own rule, I call him.

When there's no answer, I send a WhatsApp.

Heard about Parsons Green attack. R u ok?

The show is about to begin, but Derek is in the seat this morning, so I stay at my desk and open up the web browser, fishing through the various news websites for information. On Facebook, I look for Finn's profile in my Friends group, hopeful of a green spot next to his name, but there's nothing. I try his number a few more times, leaving voicemails now. There're no blue ticks to indicate he's read my WhatsApp message, and so I send a text and an email too, trying to keep a tone of neutral enquiry, trying not to veer into hysteria.

I make an effort to focus on my work, contacting my senior in head office, and getting the steer from him, before joining the others in the control room to say the word is we'll go with our original plan, but to warn the guests lined up that they may be bumped at the last minute should any further serious developments occur. I think of the words I've just uttered. Serious developments. A thread of fear passes coldly through me. *Let him be alright*, a voice whispers in my head.

Somehow, we get through the morning show without incident, and I'm just walking back to my desk, when the phone starts ringing. I break into a run.

'Hello?' I say, breathless with anticipation, and when I hear Jeff's voice at the other end, I cannot hide from the stark feeling of disappointment that shoots right through me.

'I'm fine,' I tell him. 'We're all fine,' thinking he's calling because of the attack.

'Good,' he says. 'Thank God . . .'

And then there's a pause, and into this brief silence comes the understanding that he's not ringing because of Parsons Green. He's ringing over something else.

'I was wondering,' he begins, 'is everything okay at home?'

I'm briefly baffled by the question. Then I answer, 'Yes. Why?'

'Well, I just had this odd call from Olivia. She's been round to the apartment, and bumped into Amy, and . . . I don't know, she sounded a bit worked up about it.'

As soon as he utters Olivia's name, I feel myself hardening against the conversation. I make little effort to keep the chill from my voice as I say, 'Really? What's bothering her?'

'She says she found Amy in our bedroom. She says Amy was trying on your clothes.'

'*What?*'

He gives a nervous laugh, and says, 'Apparently. According to Olivia.'

'Look, this is just a misunderstanding,' I say, feeling an unwarranted rise in my temper. How easily his daughter gets under my skin.

'Okay,' Jeff says, reasonably, but I can hear him waiting for the explanation.

'I asked Amy would she mind doing a little laundry

for me. She was probably just putting my clothes away, that's all.'

'Why did you ask her to do laundry?'

I am tempted to snap at him, *Why should you care who does the laundry? It's not like you do it!* But I don't Working hard to keep my voice level, I say, 'I'm swamped in work this week. Everything was piling up. She offered and I accepted, that's it.'

'Alright,' he says on an exhalation.

'Why is Olivia home, anyway? I thought she had some internship lined up at the university before term starts?'

'I don't know. Some mess with a boyfriend.' There is a note of mild exasperation parcelled in his tone. It touches upon the soft bewilderment so frequently inspired by his beloved but wilful daughter, the flurry of dramas that tend to kick up around her.

'Is she staying?'

'Just until Monday, I think. We'll need to think what to do about the rooms –'

'Don't worry about that,' I say quickly, and then ask him when he'll be home.

'Tomorrow afternoon,' he says brightly. 'Tell Mabel I'll be home in time for tea.'

'I miss you,' I tell him.

He answers straight away, 'I miss you too. This week – it's been good at work and everything. But the evenings, the nights in the hotel, they really drag.'

'You should get out – see the city while you can,' I tell him.

'Yes, but . . . it's not the same, being here without you.' And in the instant that he says this, and for several moments after we say our goodbyes, I forget the fault lines running criss-cross through our marriage.

Lunchtime comes, and Finn still hasn't called. I try to limit the number of times I check my phone. News reports speak of an improvised bomb exploding on the Tube. There is footage of ambulances leaving the scene, police swarming the area, the shocked faces of passers-by. I scan the newsreels for his name, his face, trying to quell the rising panic by rationalizing: his lifestyle meant he was rarely out of bed by nine o'clock, let alone dressed and on a Tube heading into the city. His work is patchy and freelance, he keeps his own hours. Still, I can't help feeling the deepening nudge of anxiety – intuition telling me that something is wrong. I am longing for some kind of sign from him. Even a message from YCF would be welcome – any indication that he is alright.

I have no appetite, but I force myself to leave the building and run to the nearest coffee shop for a sandwich. Is it just my imagination, or is there an edge of nerves in every face, the sway of fear taking over? Everywhere I look, there are TV screens showing the news, people craning their necks, looking for updates. Halfway through my sandwich, I scan the contacts on my phone for Gerry Higgins – one of Finn's closest friends. I haven't spoken to him in almost a decade, and when he hears my voice on the line, his surprise is evident.

'I was just wondering if you'd heard from Finn?' I ask, nerves jumping in my voice.

'Um, no, not today,' he answers, questions pinging in his tone. 'The last time I spoke to him was a month ago. Is everything alright, Cara?'

'Yes!' I say, a little too eagerly. 'It's an old college reunion thing I've been told about. I'm just trying to get in touch with him, and there's been no answer, so . . .'

'Well, you know Finn. He hates that kind of thing.'

'Right!'

There is an excruciating moment of chit-chat, and I know Gerry is reading through the thin layer of my small talk to the real context of my call. The TV screen in the corner is showing footage of ambulances parked beneath the underpass outside Parsons Green station, shocked onlookers standing on the street. I hang up quickly.

Back at Wogan House, I scan through the security barriers and jab the button to call the lift, and when it comes and the doors open, and I look into the gaping maw of the blank, innocuous space, a coldness comes over me like a douse of icy water.

The doors to the empty lift stand open.

I have been working so hard to push down the thoughts of that night in Shoreditch, to keep the memory of it at bay, but now, suddenly, I am staring not at the lift but at that cramped, windowless room. The smell of disinfectant invades my nostrils, I can see the dull sheen of plastic encasing the bottles of mineral water, the glare of the overhead light.

The eyes of the security guard are on my back now, and there's a prickling of sweat between my shoulder blades. The lift waits in front of me like a trap.

Get in, you idiot.

I take the stairs instead.

It's past four o'clock, and I'm usually out of the office by now, but I take the time to make one last call.

'Hi, Cara,' Amy says as soon as she picks up, and I read some nerves in her voice, some prescience about why I might be calling.

'Is everything alright at home?'

'Yeah. We're just in the door.'

Then I ask, 'Is Olivia there?'

A hesitation, before she says, 'No. She went out.' I can tell from the way she's holding her breath, so different to her usual gushy optimism, that Jeff was right: something happened between them. But right now, I've got my own worries to deal with, my own problems to sort out.

'Look, I don't know what happened between you, but we'll talk about it when I get home, okay?'

She says, 'Okay,' in a very small voice, and then I tell her that I'm going to be late. That something's come up at work. Her voice lifts a fraction as she tells me she'll save some dinner for me, but there's a deep note of unhappiness there.

I carry something of that note with me as I head out into the afternoon. The streets seem unusually busy for this hour, as if the commuters have all decided to leave early, perhaps anticipating the disruption caused by the shut-down of part of the Underground network. There's little chance of getting where I need to go by public transport, and to walk would take an hour and a half, so the first chance I get, I flag a taxi and climb in the back seat.

The cabbie, when I give him the address, squints at me through the rear-view mirror.

'Not sure about that,' he says. 'It's murder down there. Traffic-wise even.'

'Just see how close you can get,' I tell him. 'I can walk the last part.'

He turns off Regent Street on to Conduit Street, telling me how large parts of Parsons Green have been cordoned off.

'A complete no-go zone,' he says.

Blocks have been set up at all the airports and major transport hubs, trying to apprehend the terrorist.

'Waterloo is a fucking nightmare, apparently.'

Rosary beads dangle from the rear-view mirror. The traffic chokes the city streets and we make agonizingly slow progress; I feel the frustration building up inside me as I keep thumbing the screen of my phone for updates, desperate for a sign.

By the time the taxi has reached the Kings Road, every way seems clogged with cars and trucks. I can't sit still any longer, so I get out and walk.

It's been years since I walked through this part of London, once so familiar to me. I pass the Chelsea Theatre Company where Finn and I once spent an afternoon watching an experimental theatre production featuring sock puppets. Fairly sozzled at the time, the two of us had snorted and giggled our way through the performance, expecting at any moment to be asked to leave. Finn had started doing the quiz show by then, and was already experiencing the first flush of fame. When we walked into a venue, you'd see people doing a double-take, nudging their friends, eyes turning in our direction.

It seemed like a boon when he landed the gig – a panellist on a popular quiz show on Channel 4, every Friday night. One of the scouts had spotted him at the Edinburgh Fringe, then later in the Comedy Club. The money was colossal – far more than either of us had ever dreamed of. By sheer fluke, I had landed a production job with GLR, and was pulling in my own wages, but these were eclipsed by the deal Finn signed. By the time he renegotiated his contract for the fourth season, he was able to buy the house on Elphiron Road – a four-bedroomed Victorian in the middle of the row. Our neighbours were bankers and lawyers and diplomats; a successful actress lived with her boyfriend and their child several doors down. The money seemed to be pouring in, and we went a little mad redecorating, installing a bar and a games room, a hot tub in the garden. It was Finn's house, paid for with his money, but it felt like ours.

It was not until after he bought the house that the cracks in our relationship properly developed. He was drinking heavily then. A few pints after the show would turn into a three-day bender followed by swift and debilitating remorse. He would just about have picked himself up when Friday night would swing round again and it would start all over. There were always people hanging around the house. One time I came home from my shift at GLR to find half the cast of *EastEnders* partying in our kitchen. The only time we seemed to be alone was when we went out – quiet Sunday pints in the White Horse, or cocktails at the Eelbrook, next to the Common.

The show, which had once seemed such a godsend, eventually proved his undoing. Yes, it brought him fame and wealth, but he couldn't seem to get over his disdain for the way he achieved it. Once, in a rare moment of truthful self-assessment, he told me it would have been different if he had achieved these things through some higher art – writing or painting perhaps – instead of grubbing it out making cheap cracks about celebrities for a booze-riddled Friday night audience. He could be contemptuous of his fans and even though onscreen he came across as wry and boyish, in private he became increasingly demanding, occasionally cruel. Money was an obsession, even though he was raking in more than either of us had ever dreamed of. Still, it wasn't enough. He would bitch about how others earned more than he did, eventually quitting the show in a childish fit of scorn when he discovered one of the other panellists was commanding a higher fee. Rumour had it that he quit before he could be fired. The drinking was well out of hand at that point.

I had left by then. It was a quiet enough parting in the end. No histrionics, no hurled accusations, no tearful pleading. I simply told him that there wasn't a place for me in his life. Squeezed out by the booze, the crowds, the demands of the show, he hardly even noticed I was there any more. Some shadowy background figure emptying the ashtrays and taking out the bottles. I pitied him, I suppose – the self-loathing, the dips towards melancholy. But it was not enough to keep me there.

I did love him, though. There was never any doubting that. Even after I left him, those feelings remained. And as I cross the Common, turning the corner on to Crondace Road, I remember the pain in my heart the day I left. All those feelings of anger and grief in a complicated knot alongside the deep burn of first love. And now, as I trace the route back towards that house I once called home, feelings with the same mix of complexity announce themselves: fear, anxiety, frustration, concern and the ever-present hum of love.

The door has been repainted a glossy aubergine, but otherwise, the place is utterly familiar. I ring the doorbell, my heart pounding, and wait. I ring again and stand back, looking up at the bedroom windows for signs of life. The curtains to the living room are drawn shut against the dusky evening light. When there is still no answer, I reach up to the ledge above the electricity meter box, fingers feeling around for the key we used to keep hidden. I'm up on tiptoe, frantically rummaging there, when the door opens and Finn stares at me.

'What are you doing here?' he asks.

There's a bewildered look about him, standing there in his bathrobe, his hair dripping. The bloodshot eyes, the downward cast of remorse in them, it all sweeps through me, so fucking obvious and yet I've been blindsided by it. Falling off the wagon, taking to the bottle, any communication with the outside world blocked out, knowing the guilt trip it will inevitably bring. I'm so angry and relieved at the same time that when I open my mouth to speak what tips out is not words but a gasp. Tears shudder through me, and I'm standing there, my whole body shaking with spasms, when I feel him grab me by the arm, pulling me inside. The hall door slams shut, the sound of it reverberating hard in my head as I press back against the wall, the muscles in my chest still jagged with emotion, and feel him leaning into me, the familiarity of his smell, of his mouth when it meets mine, his arms around my waist. And I realize, with a sense of inevitability or honesty, that I knew all along that one day I would be back here, being led up the stairs by this man in this house where nothing much has changed except for the silence.

The rooms around us are empty now, the party long over, as he brings me into the bedroom, mercifully dark, the shutters pulled fast against the gloaming. Until now, my behaviour has been somewhat defensible – harmless flirting, a couple of meetings, no bodily contact, save the holding of hands. But now, I feel myself unfolding to his touch. When he peels my top off, unclasps my bra with well-practised ease, I do nothing to resist. I don't hesitate or pause for even a second to marvel at or recoil from what we are doing. I feel, for the first time in so long, utterly present. Completely real. Desire pulses through my flesh and bones, it prickles along my nerve endings, traces routes over my scalp. When he enters me, a sound is emitted from my throat. Not the sharp intake of shock or excitement; this, rather, is the exhaled burst of surprised relief, the shuddering joy of finally – after so many years of waiting and longing, even though I didn't know it – finally, coming home.

10.

Amy

I put down the phone, my heartbeat cranked up to ninety, a blizzard of thoughts storming through my head. Had she been cool with me? She seemed cool with me. Something stiff about her words: 'Look, I don't know what happened between you, but we'll talk about it when I get home, okay?' What did she mean by that? Talk to me about it, like showing me the door? A little kick of panic at that, which makes me think of the Gibson upstairs. Should I just take it now? I'd done a little googling, reckoned I could get a couple of grand for it. I'd made a list of vintage guitar stores where I could try my luck, once the time comes when I have to leave.

Fuck that stupid bitch, Olivia, I think, a stab of venom piercing my heart as I go back into the kitchen and try to arrange my thoughts. *Supercilious cow, staring down her long nose at me. Why the fuck did she have to walk in?*

I take out vegetables from a net bag, slamming carrots down on the counter – bam! Followed by onions and peppers – bam! bam! I have no earthly idea what she said to Cara, but it can't be good. The kitchen is so hot, sweat rolling off me. I open the window and then pull off my sweater, and as it comes over my head, I have a sudden flash of me in that gaping dress, giddy as a schoolgirl drunk on rum, nipples flashing, and that bitch silently gawking in the doorway. Bile comes up the back of my throat, and I steady myself at the chopping board, the handle of the knife anchoring me to the present.

'I want something to eat,' Mabel announces.

I haven't noticed her drifting into the kitchen, and now I look down at her by my side, hair in lopsided bunches, a cross expression on her face.

'Dinner will be ready soon,' I say, taking an onion and slicing off the hairy nub of the end.

'I need something now.'

'You can wait,' I tell her, keeping my voice low as I peel the bulb and chop it up small.

If Cara tells me to leave, what should I do? Beg her to let me stay? Tell her that I'm sorry – cry, even?

I put the gas on under the pan, slide a knob of butter in to melt.

Or should I haul her secret out for her to see, take the pin out of that grenade and wave that baby in her face? *Don't make me do it*, I'll tell her.

'But I'm hungry now!' Mabel whines.

'I said to *wait*.'

Part of me thrills at the prospect of pushing Cara that far. It's been sitting there between us from the get-go, this little parcel stuffed under the table that nobody mentions, but we can all hear it ticking away. How fucking good it will feel to release it. Cathartic. Cleansing.

'But I've a pain in my tummy from waiting.'

'Then go to the toilet. Jesus.'

With two hands, I scoop up the chopped onion and dump it in the pan. The butter sizzles and spits, the air filling with the smell of it.

But if she calls my bluff, what then? I'll have to leave, and there won't ever be a chance for us. Where would I even go? Back to Sean's? The prospect fills me with sudden revulsion. All those stupid guys and those dumb-ass girls, uppity as hell, looking at me like I'm some kind of freak.

The thought of it sends my attention back to the hob, stabbing at the frying onions with a spatula, shaking the pan so it rattles over the iron grid.

But the hollow realization pooling out like cold water over the floor of my gut is that there is nowhere else. Nowhere in this whole city for me to go.

'Amy, please –'

'Goddammit!'

With lightning speed, I whirl around and fling the spatula across the room in a spray of fat and onions.

I bend down to her now, and say the words loud and slow into her face. 'What the fuck? Didn't I just tell you to wait?'

The fury is zipping through me, fed by that phone call. That stupid bitch, Olivia!

Mabel's hands aren't pulling at me any more. They're drawn away to her sides and she's tucked her chin in a bit, but beyond the shock at my outburst, I can see mutiny forming.

'Daddy always makes me a snack when he's cooking!' she shouts.

I grip her tightly by the arm and haul her towards her bedroom so fast I'm almost lifting her off the ground, snarling, 'I couldn't give a fuck what your daddy does.'

Her chin is tucked even further in and her chest is puffed up, her face reddening, like she's holding in her breath, and when I let go of her arm and shove her towards her bed, it bursts out of her in a hot explosion of snot and tears.

'I'm telling my mummy on you!' she yells.

'Knock yourself out,' I tell her, slamming the door behind me.

Back in the kitchen, the onions have burnt, the acrid smell surfing the air. The pan hisses angrily when I plunge it into the sink. I'm shaking from the encounter, that sudden burst of rage. She's just a little kid but she shouldn't have pushed me. I go to the drinks press, take down the vodka. I tumble ice into a glass and slop the vodka in, the ice knocking against my front teeth as I tip it back.

She had a play date after nursery with this spoiled brat she's friends with – Leslie – who lives in this goddamned mansion over in Kensington. Mabel's always dissatisfied after going there, in the way little kids get even when they're too young to really understand what envy is.

After the second hit of vodka, I'm calmer. I'll give her a minute, then I'll go in, say I'm sorry, hug and make up. Buy back her affection with ice cream. At this point, I still think I can fix this.

The spatula's on the floor by the dishwasher where it landed, and as I bend to pick it up, thinking how I'll have to cook something different now the onions are ruined, the truth hits me like a sudden rush of blood to the head. I have fucked up. Badly. The way I'd gripped her arm, there could be marks. Bruising. A plunge of nerves goes through me. *I'm telling my mummy on you.* I put the spatula on the table, then put my hand to my mouth.

Bad, bad girl, Connie says. *Now look what you've gone and done.*

I go to the sink, squirt detergent on the pan and start scrubbing.

Who's in trouble now? she sings sweetly, and her ripe laughter spins out behind her words, soaring with hysteria.

'Fuck!' I say, dropping the pan back in the sink and turning away.

The kitchen table is a goddamned mess. I need to think. I need to work this out, but Connie's laughter is so loud and mocking, it drowns out all thought.

Mabel's schoolbag is on the table and I pick it up, the flap swinging open, and it's as I'm dropping it on the chair that the toys fall out. A couple of rabbits in dresses. A plastic picnic table with a pink umbrella. A collection of minuscule imitation goblets scattering over the kitchen floor, one of them lodging in the crack between the floorboards. Sylvanian Families toys – or as Mabel calls them, Sylv-aliens. She has been coveting these things for ages. Leslie has a whole rake of the things, a goddamned Sylvanian compound – and it's been driving Mabel wild with jealousy.

I know that she has stolen them. And once I know that, the next bit is easy.

'Leslie's mum called,' I tell her, when I go into the room.

She's curled up under the duvet – it's pulled right over her head.

'Some of Leslie's toys have been stolen.'

She doesn't move, but I can tell I have her attention.

'They've called the police,' I say.

She sits up.

I cross the room, crouch down next to her.

'This is serious,' I tell her. 'The police are involved, now a crime's been discovered.'

'What?' Her eyes, red and squinty from crying, seem to open a little wider, searching my face.

'Do you know what the police do with people who steal?' I ask, and she shakes her head but her lip is trembling. 'They put them in jail.'

'Even children?' she asks, her voice very small.

'Of course. They have special prisons for bad little girls and bad little boys.'

A flash of terror crosses her face and then she presses her face down into her knees, her body shuddering with sobs, and despite myself, I'm moved by the pathetic performance. I shift so that I'm sitting alongside her, my arm going around and drawing the little body to me. 'Shhh,' I whisper. 'It's okay. Do you know what we are going to do?'

She leans away from me, a look of desperation on her face.

'I'm going to take those toys and put them somewhere very safe – somewhere secret. Somewhere the police can't find them.'

She nods gently, but the fear is still there in her eyes.

'We're not going to tell anyone about this, okay? It's going to be our secret.'

'Mummy and Daddy say I'm not allowed to have secrets.'

'Yes. But Mummy and Daddy wouldn't want to find out you are a thief, would they?'

She shakes her head slowly, the tears threatening to return.

'They wouldn't want to see their little girl taken away to jail.'

'I don't want to go to jail!' she wails.

'And you won't,' I whisper. 'I promise. I'll protect you. I'll keep your secret. But Mabel, you have to promise me something too.'

'What?'

'That you won't speak about this to Mummy and Daddy – about anything that happened today. Do you understand?'

She nods her head and looks down.

'Even if they keep asking you about it. Even if they tell you that nothing bad will happen to you. Because they don't understand what's at risk, do they? They don't know about the stealing, about the police.'

I put my hand to her face, run my finger over the wet chub of her cheek. And then I smile at her. I positively beam. The anger is all gone now. Connie's voice is quiet in my head. Replaced by a happy note of contentment. Funny how you can do that – turn the current from rage into something peaceable, something pure.

It's almost eight by the time Cara comes in. I've been half-dreading it, the vodka buzz having worn off, replaced now by a dull emptiness. Mabel is asleep at least – a small mercy. Worn out from her tantrums, her fear, she hardly ate the dinner I made – macaroni and cheese. I wound up eating hers and mine, the pleasing tackiness of it, pasta moulding itself to the roof of my mouth.

I'm in the kitchen cleaning up when Cara walks in, puts her bag on the table and shrugs out of her coat. As I turn to say hello, she greets me briskly, then disappears into Mabel's bedroom just like she always does. My heart is hammering away, powered by remorse as much as anxiety over being found out. But when she emerges, closing the door softly behind her, she gives me a brief smile, saying, 'Fast asleep,' and gratitude washes through me for I can see that whatever it is she's going to say to me, all is not lost. There is still friendliness there.

'I saved you some dinner,' I tell her, a puppyish eagerness in my voice that even I can hear, but I'm just so freaking grateful, I can't help myself. 'It's just mac and cheese, but I could heat it up –'

'God no, I can't eat,' she tells me, and half-laughs before going to the fridge. 'I need a drink,' she says, drawing a long-necked bottle of Riesling from the wine shelf, and holding it up for me to see. 'Want a glass?'

I'm half-toasted on vodka already, but I say, 'Sure. Why not?' all the school rules thrown out the window tonight.

There's something different about her, like she's charged with a new kind of energy. Not nervy exactly, but there's something zippy there – an excitement. She unscrews the bottle, turns away to take down two glasses from the press. And as she closes the cupboard, I catch her, just briefly, pausing. Two hands placed to her cheeks, staring at nothing. A stillness has come over her, like she has just remembered something, or is suddenly taken aback. Her face is reflected in the glazed panel of the door, and I see the widened eyes, the ghosting smile, and the look is one of marvel. Wonder.

She breaks her reverie to pour the wine, handing me my glass, saying, 'So, you met Olivia then,' watching for my reaction as she takes her first sip.

'I'm so sorry,' I say. 'Whatever she told you . . . This is all a big misunderstanding.'

'Were you trying on my clothes?'

The skin on the bridge of her nose wrinkles, not with

distaste, but with amusement, and I'm confused by it. I thought I was in trouble, but she's taking it like it's a joke.

'I was putting away laundry for you,' I begin cautiously. 'Trying to be helpful. I thought I'd put the clothes away rather than just dumping them on your bed or whatever.'

'And?'

'And . . . I saw this dress hanging in your closet, this silk dress.' I hesitate now, trying to gauge her reaction, but I'm getting the feeling that an admission is called for, so I continue in a rush, 'It was just so beautiful, I couldn't help myself. I'm sorry, Cara, you've every right to be mad at me. I shouldn't have taken that liberty. I don't know what I was thinking. I wasn't thinking. I just tried it on to see what it felt like, and that's when she walked in.'

She tips a little more wine down her throat, gives me a smile that's kind of mischievous.

'Did you know it was my wedding dress you were trying on?'

I put one hand up to cover my mouth. For an awful second, I feel sure I'm going to laugh. But I push down on it and say, 'Oh God! I'm sorry! That makes it so much worse. I'll get it dry-cleaned for you, I swear.'

'Don't worry about that,' she says breezily, moving past me out into the hall with the bottle.

I can hear her in the living room, moving around, drawing the curtains. When I follow her in there, she's crouched in front of the fireplace, cranking the lever. It's mid-September but there's a slight chill in the air, and I'm guessing it's been months since this fire has been lit. The mechanism gives a whizz-bang, and then a skirt of flames appears among the fake coals, and she straightens up.

'If you want me to leave, I will,' I tell her. 'I'll pack my bags right now.'

'Oh, for God's sake!' she laughs, kicking off her shoes and throwing herself into one of the club chairs. 'I'm not going to fire you over something so silly. Although I'd rather you didn't repeat the offence.'

'I won't. I promise.' I'm grinning like an idiot, can't stop the goofy smile from breaking out over my face. When I sit down on the couch, it's like a great weight has been lifted from me. I try my wine. There's a dried apple flavour to it that I don't like, but I still sip away greedily.

'Did Olivia say where she was going?' Cara asks.

I shake my head. 'We didn't talk much, to be honest. She seemed kind of angry or . . . disgusted.'

She lets out another laugh, an involuntary yip. 'Yes! That sounds about right. She's good at disgust, is Olivia.'

'I see now why you don't like her,' I say.

Her expression changes instantly, giddiness draining away to something more serious. 'Of course I like her,' she corrects me in a quieter voice. 'It's just . . .'

She sighs, sits forward, splashes a bit more Riesling into her glass.

'Things are a little difficult between Olivia and me. The stepmother thing – it never really took off. Not in the way I'd hoped it would.'

'You don't seem old enough to be her mum.'

'No. I suppose that's part of the problem. I just thought that it would be easier. That she would realize that I understood what she'd been through. That I could relate. I had it in my head that we'd be close because I'd had the same experience.'

'Your mom died?' I ask.

'Yes. I was a little older than Olivia was when it happened. But only barely nineteen. Still just a child.'

'What happened to her?' I ask.

She looks briefly into the contents of her glass, as if to find the answer there. Then says, flatly, 'Suicide.'

Something moves inside me, a disconcerting lurch.

'How?' I ask, barely keeping the shock from my voice.

'Pills,' she says matter-of-factly before a sharp smile glances off her face. 'Nothing too gruesome, thank God.'

'No, I mean how could she do that?'

I can't explain it – how stricken I am at this information. How could I know her this well – be so close to her – and not have known this vital thing about her? That she went through this pain, this awful betrayal. It's like I'm feeling it myself. Like it's my own mom we're talking about. And then I remember the lie I've told and a wash of shame comes over me, so sharp and sudden I have to sit forward quickly just to slough it off.

'Amy, are you alright?'

'I just can't understand it.'

She's looking at me now, concern in her face.

'She was depressed,' she explains softly. 'It was very sad, but I had my dad and . . . well.'

'Don't you miss her?'

'Of course I do. But life goes on. I've learned to accept it.'

I look down at my hands holding my wine, aware of the crack of emotion that's come into my voice, aware of the watchful look she's giving me. My nails are shredded and rough. Fingerprints smudge the glass.

In a quiet voice, I ask, 'What was she like?'

'Like?' She thinks about it for a moment, before alighting on the right word. 'Bookish. When I look back, that's how I remember her – always reading. I used to think she preferred books to people.'

'Yeah?'

'She was a solitary person. Shy. I think the world frightened her a bit. By the end, she had almost completely withdrawn. I wasn't allowed to have friends over. She wouldn't have anyone in the house. She suffered, the poor woman.'

'You make it sound like it's a distant relative you're talking about,' I comment, not unkindly.

'Do I? It's years ago, now. I suppose that's why.'

The softness of her tone – the kindness in it – all of it is suddenly too much. I put my wine glass down, and press the heels of my hands against my closed eyes, holding them there for a moment, my shoulders high with tension.

'Amy?' she prods lightly. 'Are you okay?'

'I shouldn't have . . .' I begin, but the sentence breaks, the back of my wrist gently knocking against my tightly shut lips as I lower my hands.

'I'm sorry,' she says hesitantly. 'I didn't mean to upset you. I should have thought.'

And it's all there in her face – the wariness, the caution.

I shake my head quickly in a gesture of irritation with myself. I've been trying so hard to get close to her, all this time. The thought that this one stupid lie might threaten that closeness infuriates me.

'No . . . It's just . . . Shit!' I fix her with a fierce gaze. 'I lied to you. I shouldn't have, but now, after what you've told me about your mom, I just can't . . . Shit!'

'What is it?' she asks gently. 'Tell me.'

I realize now that I have to tell her the truth. It's a gamble, but I'm banking on her unexpected good humour, her openness tonight, that a corresponding openness in me might just cement our bond, rather than breaking it. The opportunity is there and I seize it.

'My mom didn't die,' I say quietly. 'She wasn't killed in 9/11. The truth is she walked out and left me. I was thirteen years old. We were living with her girlfriend, Elaine, and . . . I don't know . . . things weren't going well, and so she just left one day. I kept thinking she'd come back, you know? Send for me once she got herself settled. But she never did.'

I shake my head, angry at myself for getting so upset or for revealing the truth or for lying about it in the first place.

She's trying not to react but I can see the spike of interest in her eyes, the shock.

'And the 9/11 thing?'

'That's just something I made up. The kids at school used to give me a hard time about it – about my mother abandoning me. You know what kids are like,' I say, shrugging. 'They can be cruel. And there was this kid in my class whose father really did die in 9/11, and they never bothered him about it. Like his loss was something noble or worthy or, I don't know . . . patriotic. Whereas mine was just pathetic. So later on, after I left that school, I began pretending that my mom had been killed by the terrorists.' My voice drops a little. Saying it out loud, I can't help but feel ashamed. 'I made up this whole elaborate tale about her working in the Twin Towers, about her coming in to say goodbye to me that morning. Some-times, it felt like that's what should have happened, you know? Telling people . . . after a while, it didn't even feel like a lie. But then you tell me about what happened to your mom and it just makes me feel –'

I stop, shocked to find there are tears spilling down my cheeks.

'I suppose I can understand why you said that,' Cara offers gently.

And I feel so goddamned grateful to her right then, and so fucking relieved, I can hardly speak.

'And after your mother left?' she asks. 'Who took care of you then?'

'The Millers – Elaine and her daughter, Connie, the one I told you about? I guess we were like sisters. We had kind of been living with them already, so . . .'

All this time we've been talking, there's been this loosening inside me, this opening up, and I'm starting to feel like I can finally say my truth, that I've finally found someone I can be safe with. But then I hear it, that whis-pery voice, running like an undercurrent in my brain: *Tell her about me, Amy. Tell her what you did.*

And then the laughter, horrible and mocking.

'Did you ever hear from your mother?' she asks softly.

I shake my head quickly and pick up my glass. 'If Olivia needs her bedroom, I don't mind,' I say, getting to my feet.

Consternation briefly sweeps across her face, but then she also stands and says, 'No. Stay where you are. I can make up a bed for her in Mabel's room if she comes back.'

I know she's confused by the sudden shuttering of my

admissions, but I'm teetering on the edge of an uneasy threshold.

Just before I turn in for the night, she holds me with a long look and says, 'I'm really glad we had this talk, Amy. I feel like we understand each other better.'

And there is such warmth and feeling in those words that it is all I can do not to fall into her arms, sobbing with gratitude.

Cara goes to bed not long after I do. And in the darkness, I listen to her moving around up there, going through her nightly routine. I lie in my bed, watchful and restless. My phone pings and I read the incoming text. It's from Sean.

Everything okay? Haven't heard from you in so long.

I barely glance at the message before deleting it. The memory of his voice is a distant echo. A whine reaching out from the past. But I don't need him any more. I've moved on.

Something happened between me and Cara tonight – another twist in our tale, bringing us closer together. And I think of how she listened to what I said, how she gave me the space to say it, invited me to open up in a way that no one else ever has. This is not like Connie – this is something else. Something deeper. Something pure. I feel the roots of it spreading through me, anchoring me to her in a way that makes me feel whole.

All is now quiet upstairs. She must be asleep.

You are closer to me than anyone, I think, my phone still in my hand.

Then, somewhere beyond the ceiling, in the sleeping room, I catch the fleeting buzz of a phone, thrilling to the knowledge of how close she is. I turn over, burrow down into my pillow, happy in the belief that soon I will be free to say these words directly to her, no distance between us. We will be together, lying in each other's arms, and no one will be able to separate us, ever again.

PART TWO

II.

Cara

Thursday comes and I leave the office as soon as the show is over. I take the Tube to Parsons Green and walk for five minutes until I reach the surgery on the New Kings Road that Kamila has recommended. My journey takes me close to Finn's house and I try to push down on the excitement I feel. It has been raining all morning, the pavement slick from the latest downpour, the trees on the green dripping. I'm nervous, as I always am whenever I have to see a dentist, but this time, the anxiety is leavened by hopefulness. My childhood phobia had been a millstone around my neck until Kamila handed me the card of one of her university friends – a dentist who specializes in conscious sedation – and instructed me to call her.

I like Dr Nichol from the moment I meet her. She is small and very beautiful, her pregnant belly swelling beneath her clinician's tunic. Warmth emanates from her ready smile, her light touch, her liberal use of endearments as she probes me for information to determine the seriousness of my phobia.

'One time I chipped a molar while chewing a sweet,' I tell her. 'It took me over a month to pluck up the courage to get it seen to. I just kept popping paracetamol and eating on the other side of my mouth.'

She laughs and nods, and then asks if she can examine my teeth.

My heart is beating hard and fast as the chair reclines and while her examination is gentle at first, I feel my hands gripping the armrests as she begins to scratch away plaque, and prods the enamel of my teeth. As she works silently, I count in my head – an old childhood habit to ward off fear. Her belly brushes against my arm as she leans in close and I think about the baby curled inside her. My own experience of pregnancy was of mood swings and amazement – the hormonal soup in my veins held sway but, every now and then, I would catch myself with wonder, and think: *Is this actually happening? Is this real?*

Perhaps that's the closest I can come to describing how I have been feeling in the days since it happened – it's like the hormonal daze of pregnancy. Life has carried on, outwardly normal, but there have been times when I have been sitting at my desk perusing emails, or at home up to my elbows in the kitchen sink, when it will suddenly come at me, what we have done, and I feel breathless with amazement. Amazed at my own audacity. Amazed at the circumstances that led up to it. I think of him pulling me into the house and slamming me against the wall. I think of myself being led submissively – excitedly – up the stairs to bed. Not a day has passed since it happened when I haven't thought about him, about the pressure of his body against mine. It can take a few moments for me to compose myself after these recollections.

It has only happened once. Does that constitute an affair? The very thought of it – even now, pinned to this chair as Dr Nichol conducts her examination – sends a trill of hilarity through me. An affair – me! Casual sex – illicit sex – has always seemed the domain of others. It's for younger, more modern people. In this new Tinder age, casual sex seems to have become de rigueur once more, but for me sex has always been about some level of commitment, or at the very least some spark of hope that it will go somewhere. Perhaps some shreds of my Catholic upbringing stubbornly remain. But what happened last week seems to spin and turn in my head with little thought of where its orbit is taking me, let alone the consequences of what might happen.

Outside, the rain hisses against the window pane, but here in this quiet room, classical music playing softly on the radio, I allow myself these gentle musings. It's only happened once, and can, arguably, still be contained. I know I should be overwhelmed by remorse for my infidelity – my betrayal – but if I'm honest with myself, those feelings of guilt have been occasional and not as searing as I imagine they ought to be. Perhaps this is helped by the fact that Jeff didn't come home last weekend after all; an unscheduled visit from a client kept him in Berlin. The distance helps. In a way, the distance feels normal. I feel brushed by guilt, but not impaled by it. I don't like to think what that says about me.

In the last week, Your Closest Friend has fallen silent. It's like he's been calmed, satiated, made peaceable. Or, perhaps, the device has served its purpose. I've had two phone calls from Finn at work, and a couple of WhatsApps. But when I leave here today, I will see him. The clinic is within easy walking distance of Elphiron Road. We have arranged to meet for coffee, to sort things out between us, set the matter straight. Yet, if that's what we're doing, then why do

I feel this burst of happiness in my heart, this frisson of nervy excitement? My reward, perhaps? A naughty little treat for overcoming my phobia. One fear trumped by an even greater risk.

I have been so caught up in the delirium of my thoughts that it is not until Dr Nichol runs a tiny hook-like instrument between my teeth and gums that my terror rears up from the shadows. I raise my hand for her to stop, and sit up suddenly in the seat.

'I'm sorry,' I tell her.

'That's alright, dear,' she says peaceably. 'Take your time,' and she offers me a paper cup filled with water.

After I've sipped, I try to explain. 'It's just I had a bad experience as a child – a toothache that was allowed go untreated for too long.'

'I understand,' she tells me, drawing off her latex gloves.

'You must think I'm a little mad,' I laugh, and a thought of my mother stirs briefly in my head, drawing me down the dark avenue of childhood memories. Her agoraphobia trapping her in our house for weeks on end, until the pain in my mouth became so unbearable I was sobbing for help. In the end, a teacher at my school intervened, but at that stage the damage had been done.

'You would be amazed how many patients of mine have shared your experience,' she reassures me. 'Now, you have a couple of molars that need attention, and there's a scratch on your front tooth we ought to take care of. I think the best thing is for you to make an appointment with our hygienist and then once your teeth have been cleaned, come back to me and we'll set about fixing those teeth.' She must see the anxiety on my face, for she lowers her voice and touches a hand to my upper arm. 'Don't worry, dear. I'm going to give you a prescription.'

She turns away, rolling on her little wheeled stool over to the countertop that runs the length of the room. Clicking her pen, she begins scribbling on a pad, explaining as she writes: 'It's a script for temazepam. A mild sedative. You take it an hour before your appointment. You'll find that it will take the edge off things and ease your anxiety.'

She runs through a list of questions to assess whether there's anything in my health or history that might preclude me from taking the drug. Then, satisfied with my answers, she pulls the script from the pad and hands it to me.

'This will cover your visit to the hygienist, as well as the subsequent visits with me.'

I ask about the possible side effects, remembering my anxiety outside the lift at work. The last thing I need is to crank up my paranoia. But she tells me the most likely effect is drowsiness, and warns me not to drive after taking them.

When I step outside on to the street, I feel a sense of relief that's akin to escape. I begin to breathe normally, as if I've been holding my breath the whole time I was in there.

It has stopped raining. Finn and I have arranged to meet across the road in the Eelbrook. At a break in the traffic, I run across, tucking my rolled-up umbrella into my bag. I'm standing under a canopy, checking my phone for the time, and a droplet falls and bounces off the back of my hand. Its coldness draws attention to how hot I had become sitting in that chair. It's early, and I'm considering whether I've time to take a stroll around the Common to compose my thoughts, when a dog barks and I look up and there he is.

Finn. Crossing the green at a leisurely pace, watching me with a broad smile on his face.

Both of us raise our hands in greeting, and I see him laugh at our simultaneousness, then put his hands in the pockets of his old familiar parka. And as he steps across the pavement towards me, I know with deadening certainty what will happen. There will be no coffee, no long chat, no wistful what-might-have-beens. I know that as soon as he reaches me, he will put his arms around me and I will let him kiss me, even though it is the middle of the day on an open street, cars and vans whizzing past on the New Kings Road. And I realize how much I have been wanting this.

'Hello, you,' he says, taking one hand from his pocket so he can reach around the back of my head, grasp the hair at the nape of my neck and draw me towards him.

I can feel the smile lingering in his kiss.

Afterwards, we lie together in the bedroom we once shared. Neither one of us speaks. Some of the passion we've just spent still clings to the air. The windows are shuttered against the afternoon sunlight, which came on suddenly, burning away the memory of rain. Distant sounds of traffic filter into the room, and somewhere down the street, there are children playing in a garden, their voices rising and falling.

I'm lying on my side, facing the shuttered window. Finn's arm lies beneath the crook of my neck, his body pressed close against mine. The skin along my back, my thighs, my heels, tingles with the contact. His breathing comes slow and even but I can tell he's not asleep. In this murky half-light, familiar shadows announce themselves: the tall mahogany dresser by the window that we bought together at an auction on the Fulham Road. Some framed Ralph Steadman prints that we never got around to hanging still propped against the skirting board. The half-open door to the bathroom, the penny tiling on the floor reflecting light thrown by the frosted-glass window.

Soon, I must leave here, and that makes me feel sad. We have yet to speak of when we will see each other again, although I know we will. I can feel the weave and pull of greater complexities around us, now this has gone deeper. My handbag looks prim, almost stern, sitting on the chair alongside the bed, as if it has observed us having sex in silent disapproval. My phone lies within it, on silent. Once I look at it, there will be messages and emails that will demand my attention, but for just a few minutes more, I want to hold on to this peace.

After a while, I feel Finn's free arm stirring. His fingers come to rest on my shoulders, then trace gently along my arm to my wrist.

'What are you thinking about?' he asks.

I'm thinking about the risk I am taking by being here and how I only ever take risks when Finn is involved. All my adult life, I have been unable to decide whether Finn is good for me or bad for me. When I'm with him I feel brave, ready for the challenge, willing to leave my comfort zone. When we're together, I can feel myself coming alive. But there is always the niggling doubt that it's a path to self-destruction. At the back of it all lie the memories of how he has hurt me. My life without him seems safe and secure, but also tame, timid. Unlived? The question I'm turning over in my mind, unable to answer, is which version of myself is the more authentic? Which version is true?

I don't tell Finn any of this. Instead, I say, 'I'm thinking of a party we went to once. It was in Canary Wharf, I think. A media party of some sort – I don't remember. Everyone was wasted. You especially.'

'No surprise there,' he says lightly.

'Some of us went up to the top floor of the building and out on to the roof. It had a sort of terrace, surrounded by railings, but you weren't really supposed to go out there. One of the guys who worked in the building took us up to show us the view. Do you remember?'

I turn to look at him and he takes the opportunity to free his arm from under my head and then half-props himself up with it, so that he is looking down on me.

'No. I don't remember.'

I can feel some trace of the exhilaration I felt that night, being up so high, the nauseous excitement of looking down at the glimmering lights below.

'You'd done a little coke,' I go on, 'and you went over to the railings – which weren't very high at all, actually – and slung one leg over. You really don't remember?'

He smiles and shakes his head, traces a fingertip down the line of my breastbone.

'Your foot was on the outer ledge, straddling that rail. All you had to do was shift your weight on to that outer foot and you'd have slipped, fallen – what, thirty, forty storeys? Everyone was shouting at you to get down, to stop messing. I went over to you to tell you to stop it. And you just looked at me. I put out my hands. And for a few seconds, watching you balanced there precariously, it was like I could see the fall happening, like I could feel the drop myself.'

'So what happened?'

'You said . . .'

He waits. His finger has grown still.

'Well? What did I say?'

I've strayed too far into this memory. It's too intricately laced in events unmentioned. An old anger waits on the margin, ready to be summoned.

'Never mind,' I say.

'What?'

'You took my hand and climbed back to where it was safe.'

I turn away from him and sit up, leaning forward to reach my clothes on the floor. Behind me, I can feel him watching, unsatisfied. I pull on my bra, step into my knickers. I'm standing by the bed, zipping my jeans, when he says, 'I asked you to push me. Didn't I?'

He's lying back against the pillow now, but his eyes are still fixed on mine. There's no levity in his voice, no impishness.

'You said you didn't remember.'

'I don't.' He breaks his gaze away, stares at the ceiling. 'But it's the kind of thing I'd do.'

Dressed, I pick up my shoes and grab my bag, in two minds over whether to kiss him goodbye. The euphoria of our reunion has died away now, replaced by something quiet, almost sad. It feels uncomfortably like regret. He grabs me by the waist and pulls me to him, his grip around me tight and assertive. From the slight frown on his face, I think he's about to ask when he'll see me again.

But instead, he asks, 'Were you tempted?'

'What?'

'To push me.'

'Don't be ridiculous,' I say.

I smile then, bat him lightly on the chest, but inside my heart is a fluttering moth beating at daylight beyond a pane of glass. His grip on me briefly tightens. Then, released, I sit back, reflexively smoothing a hand over the sheets.

He keeps on looking.

'Of course you were,' he says, and his voice is cold.

12.

Amy

The church is on a busy road, across from a McDonald's; there's a Primark on the corner. Hard to imagine achieving any kind of solemnity here amidst the grubby high-street commerce, the grey rush of traffic on the street beyond, the impatient beeping of horns. Rain hits the flight of steps up to the entrance, making them treacherous, and the mourners don't linger. It's the end of September, and it feels like the seasons have shifted. I duck my head down and hurry up the slippery steps and into the blank modern church.

The congregation are loosely scattered among the pews. It makes the space feel emptier somehow, even more depressing. I can see the crew from Pret huddled together. Monica's squat form bunched between Emerson and Pamela.

I take a seat in a pew on my own. My eyes glance over the heads of those gathered here. The white-haired relatives, the youthful friends. It's been a month since the death, long weeks rolling past waiting on a post-mortem, the release of the body, some mix-up involving burial requests.

Neil's coffin stands close to the altar, propped up on some kind of metal trolley. There's a framed picture of him on top, the kind taken by a high-street studio photographer – grey backdrop and cheesy grin. I can imagine Neil cringing in his coffin at the thought of it. And then my mind is in the coffin with him, and I'm wondering what clothes they've put him in, whoever dressed him. Probably not the ripped jeans and T-shirts with corny logos that he used to favour. Almost definitely not those godawful trainers. I'd bet anything his mother or someone picked out some sensible chinos and a nice sweater for him to wear for all eternity, and the thought makes me feel depressed and angry. I have to pinch the skin on my inner arm, twisting it a little, just to keep myself present, stop myself from slipping off.

A man comes in and takes the space next to me. He's older than I am, with the greyish appearance of an uncle or a distant relative of the deceased. A puff of air comes out of his lungs as he dumps his weight down, the wooden bench rocking a little. There's like fifty empty pews in the freaking church, but this guy has to pick mine.

'Terrible, isn't it?' he says to me, like we're already acquainted. 'A young man, shot down in the prime of his life. Shocking.'

I say nothing, but take out my phone.

'A friend of yours, was he?'

I hate this kind of busybody. All my life, I can't fucking stand them.

I keep my eyes on my phone, refusing to look at him, and say, 'I don't know you.'

I can feel the wave of surprised resentment coming off him.

'Charming,' he mutters, and makes a big deal out of getting up and clambering back out into the aisle to find someone else to torment.

'Asshole,' I say under my breath, my eyes straying after him.

I catch Monica looking. She's spotted me hunched in

my jacket off to one side. Her face is flat and expression-less, her eyes combing over me. She turns to Emerson and whispers something to him, then he too turns to look.

I glance down at my phone, at the message I've typed. *Here at St Saviour's. About to start. U coming?*

My thumb hovers above 'send', indecision nipping at my edges. I've already texted a reminder earlier this morning. I don't want to piss her off.

I'd told Cara about the funeral a few days ago, reminding her about it yesterday. Both times, she'd been non-committal. I know she's got to work, but still. She was in the room with him too. At the end of his life, she'd been there. Me and her together. That's got to count for something.

From some unseen place up above, an organ groans out a hymn, and we shuffle to our feet to pay our last respects. I've always kind of liked churches. Liked the feeling of stepping out of your life for a short interval, any real interaction suspended while some stiff in a dress drones on in a way that allows your mind to drift.

So now, while the priest intones about the mysteries of life and death, I try to zone out of this space, put my mind somewhere far from this church, these people, that corpse in a box. What I think of is Connie, one evening back when I was sixteen and she was twenty-three, the two of us in this bar in the town near where we lived. I was too young to be served, but Connie bought me a soda. And when the bartender's back was turned, she tipped some rum into it from a small bottle she kept in her purse, a bottle like one of those miniatures you see in hotel-room fridges. Connie'd already had two or three Buds – she'd been in here drinking since her shift at the dry-cleaner's ended. Booze made her skittish, restless eyes roaming the bar for trouble.

There were two guys in suits sitting up at the counter, ties loosened, relaxed. Youngish guys, I don't recall wedding rings on their fingers. I knew, even before Connie clapped eyes on them and said to me, 'Hey, let's have some fun with those guys,' how it was going to play out. At least I thought I did. She didn't get her kicks from flirting, or attracting a guy's attention – she could do that easily enough. She liked to shock.

At first she waited until one of them noticed us, held his stare for just a second too long, then threw her head back and laughed, displaying her whole long, lovely neck, as if I'd just cracked the funniest joke in the world. I knew how to play along, how to act like we were enjoying each other's company immensely and didn't require any third parties interrupting, thank you very much. Not so hard to act, really. Once she was sure of their attention she focused in on me, petting my hair, resting her hand on my knee, leaning in close to whisper nonsense in my ear, the two of us giggling and making eyes at each other, all the while pretending we weren't performing to an audience.

We'd done it before. Stupid stuff to titillate dumb guys. It was fun to see how easy it was to turn them into slavering dogs. It never went any further than that. But this evening, there was a side to Connie that I hadn't seen before, like she was lit up from inside with a different-coloured light.

'We should kiss,' she said, and I laughed and hiccupped. It was dark outside and I knew I should get back – Elaine would be getting worried.

'You heard me,' she said again, and I felt it even sharper now, the edge in her voice pushing me, the way her green eyes seemed to draw me in.

She was holding herself very still, that little smile lingering on her face, like she was waiting, and I understood it was up to me to cross the divide. The invitation sitting there plumply between us. My heart thrumming hard in my chest, I swallowed my hesitation, and leaned forward, set my lips on hers, felt the soft give in them, an opening. I had kissed a few boys. Hell, my virginity was gone a full year at that point. But this was something different. All those other kisses had felt transactional – a pushing and pulling, an exchange, an exploration – this felt like something I was offering with no return. I drew away, confused, and the look she gave me stoked up all sorts of feelings inside.

We left the bar not long after that, neither of us speaking as she drove us home. But what I remember clearly was the next morning, me and Connie sitting over breakfast while Elaine whistled out on the porch where she was swapping out rotten wood for new planks. I was sipping coffee while Connie polished her nails, those two odours fighting each other, heat gathering in the morning air around us.

'Hey, that was some crazy shit, wasn't it?' I said to her. I wanted to tell her how I'd lain awake half the night thinking about it, reliving it, trying to make some sense of it.

'Uh-huh,' she'd answered, dabbing at her nails with the little brush, like she wasn't really listening.

'Those guys. I'll bet we were in their dreams,' I went on, pushing her towards it.

'Just a pair of dumb guys. So what?'

She screwed the lid back on the polish, wafted her nails around in the drying air.

'The looks on their faces. After we kissed.'

Her eyes flicked sharply towards me, shards of ice flecking those green irises.

'What in hell are you talking about, Keener?' Her voice light as innocence.

It was a question that held a warning in it. A disavowal. And I saw straight away my mistake. I had broken the rule. Brought the secret out into the light, hardened it with words. In my mind I scrambled backwards, desperate to claw it back, to make it unsaid.

We never mentioned it again. But it was there between us, all the time. A wound that wouldn't close up.

I don't know why I'm thinking of this now, my thoughts knotting and twisting around this memory. Gnarled as it is, I can never tell, each time I relive it, how it will make me feel.

The air in the church fills with a foreign smell, incense rising from the brass censer swung on chains around the coffin. From where I'm standing, I can hear the thrup of holy water flicked on to the wooden casket. These ancient rituals drawing it all to a close – a whole life ending in smoke and water. If I had charged out into the night, instead of Neil, it would be me in that coffin. I feel cold, the damp ends of my jeans chilling my ankles. And then the coffin goes past me and some people make a hasty sign of the cross and lower their gaze, but I don't. I follow the casket's progress down the aisle with my eyes. I catch sight of Monica looking across at me. Her eyes are large and flat, a kind of baffled interest in her stare. Is she wondering what happened between us in those last moments before Neil ran out into the night? Or is she thinking of my sudden departure, the craziness of my actions? Her hand raises in a tiny wave – a little chink of an opening. And I think of how easily I could drift over to her afterwards, chat to her and Emerson and Pamela, trot out some tired and facile remarks about Neil's character, our loss. Then afterwards, we'd all go somewhere for a drink, sit in some crepuscular pub with the rain dampening the windows and the floor, making everything smell musty and off. I think of how they'd chat about Pret, and the dull stream of my old life appears fleetingly before me, and I know that I can't do it. I'm well past it now, that life stale and finished. I break Monica's gaze and file out of my pew.

Outside, the crowd of mourners huddle in groups under a canopy of umbrellas, but I'm done with all that grief. I hurry away, across the paving stones oily with rain, past the Coral towards the high street, moving with purpose. I'm a different person now. I'm not the drifter that I was. There is a goal now, a meaning. Before I met her, I felt like an absence. But since she burst into my life, I have become a presence. The fact that she didn't come today doesn't change that. She's with me always. I carry her in my heart.

I check my phone for updates and see that she has an appointment with the dental hygienist this afternoon. A few days ago, when she was in the shower, her laptop open on the kitchen table, I quickly installed the programme I'd discovered. Among other advantages, it gives me access to her Google history, and from this I find the details of the surgery she is attending. It's not far from the vintage guitar shop I'd planned on sussing out, and I've a good few hours left before I have to collect Mabel from nursery. If I hurry, I can catch Cara just as she's coming out. My plan is to surprise her and then suggest a coffee, tell her about the funeral, reminisce about the night that we met and maybe use that to gain access to her thoughts and feelings, seek out an opening to push this thing to a higher level.

I take the train to Charing Cross then change to the District Line and even though the connections are quick enough, I arrive late, and have to run from my station to the surgery. I'm not familiar with this part of London, and have to keep stopping to check Google Maps to prevent myself from getting lost. I'm standing on a road with shops on one side, a wide expanse of grass on the other, when I hear it. Laughter, so familiar to me now, that it makes me look up. A couple are walking along the footpath bisecting the green, hand in hand, and at first, I think: *It can't be.* Jeff is in Berlin. I don't know this man with his reddish-brown hair, his loping walk, so it can't be her. But even as my mind works furiously through this, the reality surfaces like oil separating from water.

Oh, of course, I think as I watch them move away together, their step easily falling in with one another. I watch her say something to him and see his face turning to hers, leaning in easily to kiss her. That kiss is a needle in my heart. All the work I have done, all the careful building, the labour and time and effort and sheer fucking longing, and despite all of that, she's here, proffering her mouth to this guy, this interloper. I can't believe it.

Jealousy is churning inside me as I start to follow them,

across the green on to a residential street. It burns like acid sloshing around inside, but it has nowhere to go. I don't notice anything about the houses I pass, the cars lining the streets, the trees and shrubbery. I'm careful to keep my distance, and yet part of me wants her to turn and see me. I want to witness the look on her face when she realizes her dirty secret has been discovered. I fantasize about a scene where she's begging me, here on the sidewalk, to forgive her, to not tell. *I'll do anything*, she pants, *anything*.

They round the corner, and a few seconds later I round it too, and I stop, stricken with momentary panic. The street is empty. My eyes scan quickly, and then I see. Two of them outside a doorway. The house registers with me vaguely in terms of its grandness. Huddled there together, they seem dwarfed by the size of the door he is unlocking, the arch of the portico a good deal higher than their heads.

He opens the door and before stepping inside, he turns to her, slides a hand around her waist. My stomach lurches as I watch her melting into him, their faces mashing together in a nauseating blur. I watch for longer than seems decent but I cannot draw my eyes away. And when the door closes behind them and I am left alone, stranded out here on this street, I feel bereft, a wave of grief surging in my chest. I stand there looking at that closed door, imagining what is happening beyond it. The explorations, the shudders of ecstasy, the low moans and cries.

It is a long time before I turn away.

I am silent for the rest of the day. When I collect Mabel from nursery, I avoid eye contact with the other minders, the moms. Her hand in mine feels hot and soft as she trots along beside me in a stream of banal chatter. I stare ahead stony-faced, the strap of her schoolbag cutting a line across my arm.

Cara is having an affair. I can't believe it, and yet there's something so pedestrian and obvious about it that I can't help but be disappointed. I know I should be thinking of how I can leverage this new knowledge, calculate how best to deploy it as a tactic, but I'm too heartsore, and paralysed by this impotent rage charging around inside.

When I open the door to our building, and Mabel complains about the stairs, 'I'm too tired!' she whines, I pinch her hard high up on her arm. She lets out a piercing yelp, but then falls silent, snivelling quietly as she follows me. I know she won't tell. I've made sure of that.

Partly to appease her, and partly because I just can't deal with her demands right now, I let her watch a DVD even though it's a weekday and that's breaking one of the rules. But I've had it with sticking to the rules. Why should I bother after what Cara's done? Her betrayal sits inside me like a dull pain, heavy and relentless.

I sleepwalk through the afternoon, going through the motions – getting Mabel's snack, emptying the dishwasher, tidying and putting things away. There's a stack of laundry, and I fill a basket, tucking it under my arm and leaving Mabel alone, descending to where they keep the washers and dryers. It's cold and dank in the basement, but the laundry room holds a warm fug, a couple of machines humming through their loads. There's an ache in my back as I bend down and start to feed the clothes into the drum. Everything this afternoon has been a blur, my attention skating off the surface of things, unable to settle. But now, as my fingers touch upon something cool and satiny, and from the tumble of clothes I draw out Cara's nightdress, something coalesces inside me. The shimmery, airy weightlessness of the nightdress, the sensory ripple it elicits, galvanizes the anger inside me, stirring it up into a rage.

I realize my hands are shaking. Knuckles whitening, my grip on the fabric tightens as I hold it against my chest, all the sorrow and rage building in my body until I can't bear it. The fabric is light and rips easily, and I hear the echo of my furious sobs bouncing off the walls and machines, as I tear it with my hands, picking up scraps off the floor only to tear them again. And when that is done, I shove the shredded gown into the hole of the machine and slam the door. It bounces straight back and I slam it again. Over and over, I keep slamming and slamming, grunts of rage channelling through me.

13.

Cara

When I ask him the question, he answers no.

'Oh, come on!' I say, one finger teasing out a curling chest hair.

We are lying in his bed in the lingering hours of Thursday afternoon. The sharpness that marred the ending of our previous encounter has been forgotten. The draw of him throughout the intervening days apart has softened my feelings, desire eclipsing memory, so that now as we lie together there is no hint of animosity or regret. There is peace in this bedroom, and also, strangely, forgiveness – for all that has gone before, all the hurts and betrayals, the deceptions.

How easily we have fallen into a routine. I leave work early and get on the Tube, meet him in some quiet out-of-the-way coffee shop, and inevitably, we wind up back here, in this bed that I once thought of as our marital bed, spinning out the afternoon in acts of passionate rediscovery followed by a lazy hour of gentle musings before I rise and dress and return to my ordinary life. I try not to think about what this rekindling of feeling between us means, or where it might lead me to. In the same way, while I am in this room, I try to keep all thoughts of Mabel and Jeff at a distance. Some trick of the mind allows me to view these encounters with Finn as within a capsule. He and I, alone together, are separate and apart, distinct from my ordinary life, removed from it. And it is this trick of the mind that allows the affair to persist, keeps me going as I tread the rocky path through my marriage. For I know, in my heart, that it is a fleeting thing – something that must end, and soon. But just for now, I am here because of some need within me, an unresolved question, unfinished business.

'Surely there must have been someone,' I persist, softly, but I want to know.

'I'm not saying I've been a monk,' Finn replies. His eyes are closed, and there's a blurred quality to his words, like he's just coming out of sleep. 'After you left . . . well, there were a lot of girls. I was lonely and angry.'

'At me?'

'Partly. Mostly at myself. Fucking was like revenge. There was no joy in it.'

It's strange, reliving that part of our history. When either of us touches upon it, inevitably an air of sadness or regret stirs in our thoughts, silvering our conversation.

'And when you became sober?'

'Then I was too boring for anyone to fuck.' He says this in a morose tone, and I pinch the skin on his chest.

'You could never be boring.'

'Couldn't I? You threw that word at me once. Don't you remember? In the heat of one of our rows towards the end. You turned on me and said I'd become just another boring pisshead. Spat the words at me. I didn't mind the pisshead part, but boring hurt.'

'I'm surprised you remember.'

His eyes are open now, and he's turning to me, awakened, his hand finding my breast, cupping it hard. 'You'd be amazed the things I hold on to,' he says, leaning in to kiss my neck, starting things up again.

'Don't,' I tell him gently, but make little effort to stop the progress of his kisses as they chart down my body, raising goosebumps over my flesh. It seems such a long time since I've felt this way – desired, sexual. That side of my marriage has tended to feel more loving than passionate, gratitude and comfort taking the place of desire. But now the thought of Jeff has wormed its way into my head, I cannot escape from it. Finn's kisses reach my stomach and I pull away firmly.

'I have to go,' I say, forcefully, but still tinged with regret.

'Stay,' he whispers.

'No.'

His body is holding me there, one hand clasping my wrist to the pillow.

'Stay and we can make love. Then afterwards we can shower and sit around in bathrobes. I'll order in some food, and we can watch a movie – something romantic. Your choice. *Casablanca. Brief Encounter.* Whatever you want.'

I laugh at the idea. He hates those films.

'You know I can't,' I say gently. 'I have to get home.'

'But he's not even there.'

'He's coming back tomorrow.'

Neither of us, I have noticed, use Jeff's name when we speak of him. At least not when we're in the bedroom. It is, perhaps, a conscious choice, an effort to keep at bay the powerful feelings of guilt that wash over me if I'm not careful. Since this thing started, I seem to lurch between euphoria and guilt, joyful abandon and debilitating remorse.

I am alternately amazed and horrified by what I am doing. I suppose it makes things a little easier, Jeff being away. It's not like I have to face a nightly confrontation with my treachery. Still, that doesn't prevent these feelings of guilt from sneaking into the bedroom, lying plumply between us like some bitter third party in the bed.

Today, things are made easier by the temazepam I have taken. My first appointment with the dental hygienist preceded this meeting, and I followed Dr Nichol's instructions and took the sedative in advance. I had been curious to learn the effects of it, envisaging myself riding the Tube to the surgery, half-dazed, my mouth slack and drooling. But in truth, I felt fully conscious, in control of myself. And yet there was a definite ease inside me, like a gentle lull in my thoughts, a warm feeling of untouchability. Like nothing could harm me.

I suppose I carried some remnants of that into the bedroom with Finn. Those trailing feelings of calm. Happiness, even. But now, when he presses me to stay, and I hear the whine coming into his voice, a wariness starts inside me, the effects of the drug wearing off.

'So? That leaves us tonight,' he presses.

'I can't. Mabel needs me.'

'Well, bring her over here! She can stay too. We'll set her up in one of the spare rooms where my nephews sleep when they visit.'

The notion strikes fear into my heart and I tug my wrist free of his grasp and sit up. I can feel my heartbeat quicken as I reach for my clothes. By raising the notion of introducing himself to Mabel, Finn has defiled something. I can't explain it. Although I trick myself out of thinking about

Jeff, the mention of her name touches upon a nerve that is too raw. I cannot contemplate bringing her here. It frightens me to think of it, because I know that any such meeting between my little girl and my lover would mean the breaking apart of my marriage. It would mean wrenching my little girl away from her father, and that is something I cannot countenance.

'I have to go home.'

'This is your home.'

'No, it's not.'

I pull my T-shirt on, reach for my jeans.

'It's more your home than the place you live in,' he continues, a dangerous edge coming into his voice. 'The dead wife's place. You said it yourself.'

He's making no effort to get out of bed, but he's moved over to my side of the mattress, leaning in as I bend down to look for my shoes.

'What kind of a man does that? Insists on living in his dead wife's apartment? How could he do that to you? Doesn't he know how weird and uncomfortable that makes you feel?'

'I've already told you,' I say quietly, keeping my voice level, even though something is rising in me now. 'It's because of Olivia. It's been her home since she was born —'

'But it's not her home now, is it? She's been at university for two years. Christ, even before that she was packed off to boarding school! That place ceased to be home for her since you moved in.'

'Just leave it, Finn. Christ.'

There's anger in my voice that I don't try to hide. Why is he doing this, saying these things? I thought it was understood between us that while we are here together, neither one of us can talk about the realities of our separate lives. What we share in this bedroom is an escape from the everyday. Why is he inviting it in, knowing how dangerous such a conversation might be?

I'm fully dressed, ready to leave, but he pulls me down so that I'm sitting on the edge of the bed, his arm holding me there.

'Face it, sweetheart. He's stuck in the past.'

I look down at him, read the need in his face. 'Maybe he's not the only one.'

'I love you,' he tells me, the words and the naked hope in his expression making him vulnerable.

It's been years since that expression has been used between us. My anger, having flared briefly, dies away. I lean down, cup his face with my hands, kiss him softly on the lips.

'I'm sorry,' I say.

A recalibration happens after I leave him. As I walk away from Elphiron Road towards Parsons Green, I spend those last minutes replaying our time together in my mind, shoring it up for when I must let it go, put it behind me, resume my normal life. This happens somewhere after West Brompton. By the time I've changed to the Overground, I'm feeling more like myself, returned to my usual persona. I am no longer a lover, an adulteress, a cheat. I am mother, wife, stepmother, successful radio producer. I am all of these things. I take out my phone and turn off flight mode, wait a few seconds before the barrage of emails and texts comes at me. I check my phone messages first – among them is a missed call from Jeff. He hasn't left a voicemail. The knowledge of this leaves me curiously unmoved. No needling of guilt. Nothing. Perhaps it's some vestige of the temazepam still coursing through my system. Or maybe it's an indicator of how far I've drifted from him.

I go through my emails next, taking out a notepad I always keep in my bag, and jotting down a To Do list: people I need to contact, messages I need to respond to, fires that will have to be put out and others that need igniting. The text messages I leave until last. There're not many – one from my dad, another from the dentist reminding me of the date and time of my appointment. Finally, there's one from my closest friend. Despite myself, I feel a little jolt of nerves, a pleasurable fritz of electricity going through me right to my groin. It's been so long since I've received one of these messages, and I picture Finn still in bed, thinking about our afternoon together, reaching for his secret phone. I open up the text, savouring the transgressive moment of it a little before I re-enter normal life. My eyes pass over the words.

Bad girl.

That's it. No signature. No kiss. Just those two words.

I stare at them for a second then close the message. The sexual excitement drains away into disappointment, and something else. A feeling of unease. The message could be read as teasing, but there's something bad-tempered about it. Sulky. When we were together in the years before, there were times when I glimpsed a nasty streak running through Finn, particularly when the show became an all-consuming part of his life and his fame began to grow. That success seemed to breed within him a needy child, selfish and petulant and occasionally cruel. If those around him did not respond to his demands with sufficient urgency, he would turn on them with lacerating scorn. Sometimes, he would hold back his anger and plot a more elaborate revenge. A lover of the practical joke, this also manifested itself in darker moments as nasty stunts, set-ups designed to humiliate, precursors to cutting that person off. I think of his neediness, his evident unhappiness at my refusal to stay and the dangerous edge when he spoke of Claire: 'the dead wife', as he called her. *Bad girl.* Was it an admonishment for my behaviour, and if so, then how dare he, knowing the risks I was taking just to be with him?

Angry thoughts stir in my head like wasps as I leave the station and walk home. Evening has come on quickly, the sky already dark, orange street lamps illuminating a gentle mist that leaves my hair and skin feeling damp as I enter the building. I've deleted the text, buried my phone in my bag, and as I climb the stairs to my home, I resolve not to look at the damn thing until tomorrow morning.

The apartment feels different, as soon as I walk in, busier, an air of quiet industry about it. I can hear the TV on in the sitting room, although the room looks empty. As I place my keys on the hall table, Mabel comes hurtling out of the kitchen towards me, flinging herself into my open arms, shouting, 'Mummy!'

Her joy tears at my heart, and I swing her around, and clasp her to my hip even though she's five years old and almost too big for this kind of lifting.

'Daddy's home!' she cries.

Nerves in my chest kick out with fright. I've barely time to take this in, when Jeff appears from the kitchen behind her, and comes forward to kiss me.

'You're home,' I say when he draws back, the blood rushing to my face.

'I'm home,' he echoes.

'We weren't expecting you until tomorrow.'

I busy myself with putting Mabel down and walking with her into the kitchen, grateful for the distraction so I can compose myself. The thought crosses my mind that I need to shower. I'm terrified my body will give away the secrets of my afternoon.

Olivia is sitting at the kitchen table, dabbing purple polish on her fingernails. The whole room reeks of the chemical odour. She looks up briefly, but doesn't reply when I greet her.

'I had nothing major on, so I thought I'd come back early,' Jeff says, giving me a quick assessing gaze. 'You look shocked.'

'Do I?' I laugh, and put a hand to my cheek. My face is burning, my heart thumping all over the place. 'What time did you get in?'

'This morning, just after eleven. And I don't have to be back in Berlin until Tuesday.' He picks up a knife and resumes chopping an onion. 'I called at the office, thinking I'd surprise you, but they told me you'd gone for the day.'

'I had an appointment with the dental hygienist.'

'I saw that on the calendar. But that can't have taken all afternoon, surely?'

'Depends on how dirty her mouth was,' Olivia says softly, not looking up.

The bitchiness of her comment barely grazes me, I'm so consumed with desperation, clutching around the recesses of my brain for a plausible alibi. I'm aware of

168

sweat beading on my upper lip, nerves trembling in my stomach. But I'm also aware that Jeff has made no attempt, beyond a weary intake of breath, to admonish his daughter for her remark. Finished with the onion now, he pauses, knife in hand, awaiting my answer.

'She was with me.'

I turn around and see Amy in the hall. A paperback is in her hand, and there's something reluctant about her, like she can't decide where to go to read her book. Jeff looks past me towards her.

'There was a service for Neil,' she continues in her quiet voice. 'The guy we were in the room with – the guy who got killed. His funeral mass was in Lewisham this afternoon. We both went.'

'I see,' Jeff says. His eyes glance back at me, caution in them. 'Are you alright?'

'Yes,' I say brightly. 'I'm fine.'

I turn towards the stairs that lead to our bedroom, relieved at my reprieve. At the return, I pause to look back down. Jeff has started chopping peppers, Olivia is chatting about some play that's on at the New Vic that she's thinking of seeing. But my attention is drawn to Amy. She stands a little way off by the sink, wrapped in her own little bubble. She runs water into a glass, then turns to drink it, and I think perhaps she will glance up and see me, and I can flash her a quick smile of gratitude. But she doesn't look, just keeps on standing there, taking sips from the glass, her face blank and unreadable.

The following day, when I come home from work, Jeff is there with Mabel. He has made arrangements for us to go to dinner. There is no sign of Amy.

'I told her she could have the day off,' Jeff tells me. 'No point in her hanging around if I'm here.'

'But what about dinner? Won't we need a babysitter?'

He has it all arranged. Olivia is going to stay and do the honours. He tells me she's quite content to spend a night in for once.

I don't question him about Olivia's continued presence or when she might return to Oxford and her internship, trying to keep my uneasiness about the situation hidden. It's not that difficult to do. There are so many things I'm hiding from him now – so many thoughts and feelings – that when we go out to dinner and spend a perfectly pleasant evening together, it feels like the front I present him with is only a representation of me, a cardboard cut-out, a reanimation of the person I used to be.

Later, when we come home and I'm alone in the bathroom wiping off my make-up, I stare at myself in the mirror, pink-cheeked and tired-looking now the mask has dropped, and think to myself: *Fraud*.

What the hell am I doing?

On Saturday, Jeff and I take Mabel to Kensington Zoo. As we move from one enclosure to another, I note the russet tinge already starting to eat through the green of the ancient oaks and sycamores that punctuate the sky-line. I am ready for autumn, longing for it, in fact, nourishing the naive belief that putting the heat-heavy summer behind me can make my future clearer, ease this trouble that's been kicked alive inside.

That afternoon, I take a long hot bath while listening to Radio 4 and afterwards, Olivia and Jeff make curry while Mabel and I cuddle up on the couch and watch *Moana* together, the occasional drift of conversation and laughter from the kitchen reaching me as I curl around my little girl. A mild, relaxing day, the only dent in it the latest text from my closest friend playing on my mind. At first, it had seemed a device to get my attention, a romantic ploy to win my affections. But now that we are deep into our affair, it seems to have changed its purpose. The tenor of Thursday's message was a marked shift from the earlier notes of love and desire. This one, though brief, seemed mulish and pouty, the voice of a spoilt child brooding over not getting his way.

Amy is gone for the whole weekend. There has been no opportunity to speak to her alone since her muted performance in the kitchen on Thursday evening, lying to Jeff, unprompted. My thoughts keep returning to that moment: *Why did she lie for me? And how did she know I needed an alibi?*

As it happens, the first chance I get to speak to Amy about it is on Monday morning.

I'm at work, in the editing suite, making a final cut of an interview we'd pre-recorded last week, when my phone rings.

'I need to talk to you,' she says when I answer.

There's an intensity to her voice, an urgency. *She knows,* I think.

I tell her that I'll come home early. I'm thinking that we can take Mabel to the playground, and have a quiet word, just the two of us, while Mabel's on the climbing-frame.

But Amy cuts me off. 'I'm downstairs,' she says, interrupting my thoughts. 'Can I come up?'

I meet her at the lift, having overcome my recent fear of it, and walk her across the office, pointing out the various parts that might interest her – my desk space, the studio, the green room where the guests wait. I pass Heather in conversation with another producer and we say hello. I whisper to Amy afterwards, 'Heather Foley. My boss.'

In the editing suite, I ask Richard to give us a few minutes, and Amy sits down, looking around her with interested eyes at the consoles and decks, the computer monitors showing waving lines in staccato beats.

'I'm afraid to touch anything,' she says, laughing in a shy manner as I take a seat opposite. 'How do you even know what any of this is for?'

'I don't – well, not all of it. This is the sound engineer's domain.'

'Oh.' She looks down at her hands, an air of disappointment about her.

'I wanted to talk to you over the weekend, Amy, but there wasn't an opportunity.'

'No.'

'I wanted to ask you . . . Why did you tell Jeff I went to the funeral with you?'

She blinks, shrugs. She can't seem to bring herself to look me in the eye.

'I dunno. I just thought . . .'

'Thought what?'

'Thought I was helping you out.'

'I don't need you to lie for me, Amy –'

'Don't you?' She looks up now, defiance in her voice that catches me off-guard.

'Are you angry with me?'

She shakes her head, looks down again.

'Then what? You're behaving like I've done something to offend you. If there's something bothering you, something you're not telling me –'

'It's Mabel,' she blurts out.

The name catches at my heart.

'What about her?' I ask.

'I'm worried about her. She's been acting strangely –'

'In what way?'

'I dunno. Quiet. Kind of . . . closed off, you know? Like there's something troubling her but she won't say what.'

The editing suite is in the heart of the building – a windowless room that tends to be stifling and hot despite the air conditioning. The coldness that comes over me is unexpected.

'At first, I thought she was just tired,' Amy goes on. 'Or maybe she was coming down with something. But she's not sick. And then I realized. She's frightened.'

The word turns over inside me.

'Frightened of what?'

'I've tried to coax it out of her gently but she just clams up. When I pushed her on it, she got upset, said she couldn't tell me. That it's a secret.'

All my fears come alive. Traces of every parent's paranoia – that someone will secretly harm their child. A stranger. A family friend. The horror of molestation. All of it teems through me, as I splutter out questions: How long has this been going on? Was there anything specific that triggered her suspicions? Who might it be?

Her answers are vague and non-committal, yet I get the sense that she is holding something back. That she is fearful of saying too much.

'Please, Amy, just tell me what you think. I won't tell anyone that it came from you. Just please . . .'

She holds my gaze, and I read a wavering inside her.

'When I got her dressed for school this morning,' she begins, still reluctant, 'I noticed there were bruises on her back. They were hidden beneath her vest. When I saw, she tried to hide them from me. When I asked her about them, she said she didn't know how she got them.' She hesitates, before adding quietly, 'They looked like pinch marks. Bad ones.'

I suck in my breath, try to quell the nausea inside. 'Is it some kid in nursery, do you think? Another child that's picking on her?' In my mind, I'm thinking that some little brat picking on Mabel, whilst not a happy thought, would be far better than the horrors summoned by my initial fears.

'I don't think so,' she says firmly. 'I don't think a child did this. When I helped her change out of her uniform on Friday, there were no marks on her back. I'd have seen them. She didn't see any of the kids from nursery over the weekend, and yet the marks were there this morning.'

I'm baffled by this, my mind running over the past few days, recalling how Mabel has been with me. A little quiet, yes. Perhaps subdued. But I hadn't observed anything in her behaviour to arouse suspicion. She had seemed relaxed and happy.

'Did you see anything?' Amy asks me now. 'When you gave her a bath at the weekend?'

'I didn't give her her bath,' I say slowly. Something is coming over me.

'Then who did?'

A beat of anxiety.

Olivia.

I walk Amy back down to Reception, my arms folded tightly over my chest as if I'm cold, which I am. The chill I felt in the editing suite hasn't left me.

'Thank you for talking to me about this,' I tell Amy, as we stand by the glass doors.

'I don't want to get anyone into trouble,' she says. 'But I'm just worried about Mabel.'

'I know. And I appreciate that.'

'What will you do?' she asks.

I run a hand over my face. I know that what I must do will change things. By solving one problem I'm creating another. But nothing comes before Mabel and her safety. Nothing. And just as I acknowledge that thought, it is chased by another: I failed to notice there was a problem with my own daughter. It had to be pointed out to me by her minder. And the knowledge of this raises questions about my own fitness as a parent. Have I been looking the other way? So caught up in my own affair that I have neglected to notice real distress in my beloved child? The thought crushes me, and at the same time galvanizes something inside me.

I need to sort my life out. Simplify things. Set things straight.

Perhaps she reads the flurry of thoughts in my head, the charging emotions at play, for she leans into me suddenly, her arms going around me, and I allow her to pull me into a hug. She holds me there for a moment, and I feel the press of her against me, the urgency of her hug.

'I'm here for you,' she whispers. 'Let me help you.'

The words, while well intentioned, feel clumsy, and I'm awkward in her embrace. When I draw back from her, I have to battle the distaste I feel at the sudden physical display. But more than that, a resolve is forming inside me. My unforgivable preoccupation with Finn has blinded me to my little girl's trauma. I feel ashamed of my actions, and determined to change. For I believe there is still time to turn things around. To fix this.

'Don't worry,' I tell her, my voice firm. 'I'll sort it out.'

14.

Amy

How much do they realize I can actually hear?

That's what I'm wondering as I sit in my bedroom by the door, my ear pressed against it. If I was to open it just a crack I'd hear it all, but I dare not do that. Things are tricky enough as it is.

It's almost two hours into the fight. A lot of it is done. Olivia has left, in a storm of bitter accusation and tears. I guess it was pretty ugly, what went down between them, despite Cara's cagey diplomacy. No matter how carefully she put it, you couldn't get away from the starkness of the accusation. Jeff was incredulous, Olivia incensed, spluttering in her denials. She insisted that Mabel be hauled out to give testimony, something Cara railed against. She was overruled in the end, Jeff caving in to Olivia's wishes. I was pretty nervous then, straining to hear what the little kid was saying, whether she'd spill her guts and drop me in the shit. Moments before they brought her out, I took her to one side and warned her.

'Remember what you stole. Don't make me tell the police.'

It seemed to do the trick. She didn't give them anything.

Now she's back in her bedroom, and I've given her my laptop and headphones and plugged her into a Disney movie as my way of saying sorry. It's hard to know how

177

much of this she understands. She's only five, after all. But then, just as I was retreating back through our shared bathroom to my own bedroom, I'd caught her reflection in the mirror. She didn't think I could see her, but there it was – a quick flash of her little tongue sticking out at me. Pretty stupid, but it unsettled me.

I put it out of my mind and concentrate my attention on what's going on in the kitchen.

'What's the point?' Cara says. 'You're never even here these days, so why should you care?'

'I'm away working!' he shouts in reply. 'You make it sound like I'm on holiday!'

'You didn't have to take that job.'

'Oh, for crying out loud – you were the one who guilted me into it!'

'Guilted you –'

'Yes! Jesus Christ, if I'd had to listen to you making the point one more time of how we relied on your salary –'

'That's not fair –'

'You've no idea, have you? The way you play the martyr. The overworked, unappreciated wife. How I'm supposed to fall on bended knee out of sheer gratitude at the way you juggle work and motherhood. Saint Cara of the kitchen sink! No wonder I snapped up the opportunity once Ingrid suggested it. Work of my own – money that was mine, that I didn't have to feel guilty about.'

'Don't you dare throw this back at me! I never stopped you looking for a job. It suited you well enough, having me go out the door every morning so you could lock yourself in your little man-cave and play at writing your books.'

'That's fucking low, Cara, even by your standards,' he

remarks, then, on a rising note of frustration, he shouts, 'Jesus, your phone? Seriously?'

'Sorry,' she says.

But he snaps back, 'You're always checking it these days. Who the hell are you expecting to hear from?'

'No one,' she mutters, then adds in a catty tone, 'Here, it's off. Happy now?'

There is a pause then, and I flatten my ear closer to the door, wonder what they are doing. All the bustling about the kitchen has stopped. Are they standing facing each other, finally exhausted? Is she crying, hugging herself by the kitchen sink, while he sits fuming, watching her?

When Jeff speaks again, his tone is calmer, conciliatory even. 'I didn't mean what I said. I know you have never tried to make me feel bad about not being the breadwinner. But I have felt, sometimes, that you're not particularly proud of me. You love me and you need me. But to a certain degree, everything I do is domestic. I know I accused you of wanting gratitude, but I suppose I envied you a little – that you could excel at a demanding job and still come home in the evenings and have Mabel fawn all over you. It's silly to say it, but I felt that even though I was the parent who was present for her most of the time, it was you she really wanted. You she preferred.'

'That's not true.'

'I know but –'

'Every little kid does that. They always rush at the parent who comes in the door. Mabel loves you.'

'Yes.'

The pitch of the row has fallen away completely. What's left is something quiet and wistful and almost tender. It makes me edgy. All the anger and retribution that stormed through here has fallen away. It's worn them out. They're spent.

'I thought, for a moment,' he admits, sounding almost bashful, 'that you were going to add that you love me too.'

There's a soft clink, a glass being put down on the table, perhaps.

'I do love you, Jeff,' she says quietly, and I feel my cheeks grow hot, anxiety billowing out inside me. It lasts only a second or two, until she adds, 'But something is broken between us. It's been broken for a very long while. Surely, you must feel it too?'

He doesn't answer at first, and I strain to listen.

'How do we fix it?' he asks, and there's hopelessness in his tone. He knows it, as surely as I do.

'Let's go sit down,' she says, in a tired voice full of resignation.

And I listen as they leave the kitchen, cross the hall, and retreat to the living room. They're too far away, their voices too low, for me to hear. But in the quiet of my bedroom, I know. The sombre turn their voices had taken, the warm glow inside me. I know, without having to listen, that they're sitting down quietly, like reasonable grown-ups, admitting to each other, quietly, sadly but unmistakably – and a little thrill goes through me at the thought – that it's over between them. What is broken cannot be fixed.

Jeff goes back to Berlin the next day. Nothing is said, but everything is different. I can tell by the change in Cara – a quietness that has come over her like sorrow, an unwillingness to talk. When she comes in the door now in the evenings, her face is drawn and I see her having to dig deep for the energy when Mabel launches her little body at her mother, mustering a smile, a sense of cheer, even though she's not feeling it.

I keep wanting her to confide in me, but she responds by closing herself off, making herself remote. Connie was the same. Whenever she'd have a row with Ray, her boy-friend, coming home red-eyed and thin-lipped, she'd never open up about it, no matter how much I begged. Kept it all locked down deep inside, guarding her griev-ances tight like treasure. But I don't want to think about Connie, and certainly not about the rows she had with Ray. Not while her voice is silent in my head.

Instead, I think of my mom the morning that she left. How she came into my room and sat on my bed in the darkness, not really saying anything, just stroking my hair and saying, 'Hush, baby, it's okay,' which confused me because she was the one that was crying, not me. I couldn't make out her eyes in the darkness but she had that sinusy note in her voice that she got whenever she was upset. It wasn't even dawn, and I figured she'd had a late one, and that when she got up off my bed it was to go back to her room. The whole thing was like an episode in a dream, and I think I must have drifted back to sleep then, so I didn't hear the car pulling away down the dust track to the road. The first real inkling I had was when the light drifted through the curtains and found my face. I woke up and heard Elaine downstairs, crying at the kitchen table, hav-ing found the note.

Cara doesn't cry. Or if she does, then I don't hear it. She

keeps the sorrow at bay by keeping busy. In the evenings, after Mabel's asleep, she spends time going through her things – clothes, old papers, boxes of memories. 'So much junk,' she says under her breath. A spring clean, even though it's October. A declutter. I guess it's therapeutic. I wouldn't know – I've never been one to hoard, preferring to travel light. Jeff spends the weekend in Berlin, and neither of us remark on it.

It's a Thursday evening and I'm prepping the dinner, a hunk of bloodied beef that I'm slicing into thin strips for a stroganoff, when she stops at the doorway to speak to me. There's a bag stuffed with clothes resting against the side of her leg, the plastic handles cutting lines in her hands. Stuff she's throwing out, or donating to Oxfam. She's hauling it outside to take down to the lobby.

'Listen, Amy, you should probably know – I've an estate agent coming to view the apartment tomorrow, to get an estimate. It would be better if you and Mabel could make yourselves scarce before she comes.'

'You're selling the apartment?' I ask, shock in my voice. For some reason, I had assumed that even after Jeff eventually packs up and leaves for good, Cara and Mabel and I would remain here. That this would still be our home.

'Yes. It's been on the cards for years, and now, under the circumstances, we feel it's the best thing to do. But Mabel doesn't know yet, so could you please keep it to yourself? I imagine it will take some time to arrange, and I don't want her getting upset about it.'

Under the circumstances. The phrase sticks in my head. The meaningful way she'd said it. Excitement bubbles up inside me.

'You're getting a divorce.' It's a statement, not a question.

Cara's eyebrows shoot up in surprise. 'A divorce? Whatever gave you that idea?'

The brightness of her laughter leaves me cold.

Confused, I stammer, 'But why else would you sell? When you said "under the circumstances", I thought –'

'I meant what happened recently. With Olivia.' She lowers her voice as she says the name.

She sees the stricken look on my face and puts down the bag of clothes. I turn from her, fix my attention on the meat, slicing carefully.

'I know there's been a bit of upheaval lately – Jeff being away so much has required an adjustment – but everything is fine between us. And selling this place is something we have talked about on and off over the years. This apartment has always felt more like Claire's home than mine. We think it would be good for us to get someplace bigger – a house, maybe, with our own garden. Bedrooms for Mabel and Olivia –'

'For Olivia?' I cannot keep the disgust from my tone.

She picks up on it. Do I imagine that she flinches?

'Of course, for Olivia,' she says in a patient tone, like I'm a child she's explaining it to. 'She's not my favourite person right now, but she's still Jeff's daughter.' Then, as if in an aside, she adds quietly, 'Besides, I'd prefer she had her own room, rather than having her share with Mabel.'

I almost laugh out loud at the craziness of her optimism. How could she be so blind?

'There'll be a room for you too, of course,' she adds, coyly, like she's dangling a treat in front of me. Despite my disappointment over the non-divorce, I feel a giddy kick of gladness that's doused out almost immediately, when she adds, 'Or for any future minder or nanny we might have.'

My temper flares inside me. She deserves her unhappy marriage, her piss-weak husband, the crummy leftovers of a dead woman. Thinking all that is needed is a new house, thinking that will change everything, make Olivia forgive her, turn her marriage all new and shiny, with no cracks in it, erase her own betrayals.

At the door, she picks up her bag of clothes, and lingers for a few seconds, as if thinking about saying something more. I don't say anything and neither does she, and then I'm alone again with the metallic smell of the meat hitting my nostrils, filling it with a cloying odour of something faintly rotten.

Getting through the next couple of weeks is a struggle. It feels like there's a stone in my heart, like it's not pumping the blood around properly. I'm sluggish and drained, so that even the smallest task is an effort. I walk like a cow, heavy-jointed and slow.

The estate agent comes and I take Mabel to the cinema to see some totally forgettable kids' movie. There's a trailer for *Paddington 2* and I'm vaguely aware of the deep chuckle of her laughter at the bear's antics, but I don't laugh. The ice-cream-coloured version of London shown onscreen is so phoney it makes me depressed. All that schmaltz, that fake goodwill, makes me nauseous.

Afterwards, Mabel's tired and difficult, and a surge of fury comes through me out of nowhere and I nearly yank her arm from its socket, dragging her to the station. On the Tube, I'm sweating and remorseful, Mabel pale-faced and silent. I have to be careful now that Olivia's not around. No telltale marks, no bruising.

The apartment goes up for sale, signalling an end for me. I can feel it. So I'm not even all that shocked when I'm going through Cara's emails and I come across one she's sent to the nursery school, looking for a recommendation for a new live-in nanny. She requests their discretion in the matter, and this is the part that makes my blood boil. The secrecy of it. After all the secrets I've kept for her! This is how she repays me? It dawns on me then, the deal they've made – Cara and Jeff. He has agreed to sell the apartment in exchange for her letting me go. The obviousness of it takes my breath away. I've noticed a change in the way he talks to me lately. Before, he'd been polite and cheerful, although brief, but now that brevity is marked by a new curtness, like he can't stand to be in the same room as me. I worry that he suspects I might be behind Olivia's fall from grace, and that maybe Cara has used me as a pawn in their trade-off so she can finally be free of the dead wife's home.

Once I've made the connection, I sink even lower, wallowing in thoughts of my own misery, my own self-loathing. It's my fault this has happened, just by being me. It's not hard to trace back the pattern of rejection, all the way to my mother hightailing it in the early hours, abandoning me to Elaine's goodwill.

I lie awake at night, and listen to Connie. She's back with me again, perched by my bedside, mean and mocking.

What the hell did you think would happen, Keener? That you'd stay with them for ever? That they'd fucking adopt you?

I turn over in my bed, and as I do so, I hear the change in her voice as the penny drops, the mocking laughter that follows.

Oh no. You didn't! That's *what you wanted? How was that ever going to happen – you and her?*

The gale of her gusty laughter pollutes my dreams.

A few days later, I drop Mabel at nursery, then linger for a while in a coffee shop, making my latte stretch until the waitress comes over and starts scrubbing the table next to me in a hostile kind of way and I know I've outstayed my welcome. Part of me knows I should be doing something, looking for a job – who knows, maybe go back to the States? That thought lasts hardly a minute before I remember that I can't go back. Certainly not to the state of Pennsylvania anyway.

I am on my way back home, a light drizzle dusting my hair and the sleeves of my jacket, when I turn the corner on to the road outside the apartment block and see a man standing under a tree. Straight away, I notice something odd about him. He's standing there with his hands in the pockets of his parka, his eyes fixed on the building. I guess he could be waiting for someone, but surely he'd wait by the doors, or on the little paved square where there are wooden benches surrounded by plant pots? The drizzle is thickening, coming down harder, and still he stands there, making no effort to seek shelter. There's something furtive about him, a tension running through his shoulders, the way his weight shifts from one foot to the other. I stare at him as I walk past, wanting to see his face. I'm thinking maybe he's a prospective buyer, checking the place out, but then I see who he is and know this is something else.

'Can I help you?' I ask, turning back to address him.

He gapes at me. It takes him a second to speak.

'Uh, no thanks.'

'Are you waiting on someone?'

'Sort of.' He gives a brief wheeze of a laugh but it's not meant for me. His eyes are back on the building and there's a bleary look to them, like he's been awake all night. Even from this distance I can catch the stale whiff of booze on his breath.

'You're wasting your time,' I tell him. 'She isn't home.'

His eyes whip in my direction.

'Who?'

'Cara.' I state her name plainly, watch him blink in confusion.

'Do I know you?' he asks, hostility in his voice now that he's been caught out, his little spying mission aborted.

'No, but I recognize you. And I'm a friend of hers, so . . .'

He tucks in his chin, hunches a little further in his jacket, swept by sudden shame.

'Do you want to come in?'

'No,' he answers quickly, shaking his head vigorously. There's something vulnerable about him, like he's teetering on the brink of collapse.

'Hey, are you okay?' I ask gently, reaching out to touch his sleeve.

He sniffs and looks up and there are tears streaming down his cheeks. *Goddamn*, I think, the idea slowly turning over and forming in my head.

'Why don't we go somewhere?' I suggest. 'Get a coffee and talk. I'm Amy, by the way.'

And even though I'm a complete stranger, he allows me to draw him away. I take him up the hill to the Café Parisienne and he talks for well over an hour, fuelling himself with a string of espressos. It's his dollar so I keep ordering cappuccinos until I'm hopping with the caffeine, my stomach churning.

I already know about the affair, so it's no shock. The juicy details make me queasy but I nod and smile my sympathy, drawing him in. I try to imagine him sober. Even in this sodden, dishevelled state there's a kind of roguish quality to him that could be charming, if that's what you're into. I've seen the house he lives in – a goddamned palace – but right now he looks like a tramp. Greasy, stringy hair, three days' worth of stubble, clothes that look like they've been lived in and slept in for the best part of a week. That's what rejection does to some people. Sends them over the cliff. I should know – I've been there.

I'm starting to lose interest in him, the confessional bilge that's coming out of his mouth, and I'm about to interrupt with an excuse for leaving, when he says, 'I've been playing this game with her.'

There's an air of apology about the way he says this, but also something furtive about the way his eyes won't quite meet mine.

'What sort of game?'

'This sort of secret admirer joke. At least it was meant to be a joke, but also a coded way of reminding her how close we've always been.'

'What kind of joke?' I ask.

And that's when he tells me about the messages, the texts.

'Your Closest Friend?' I repeat, and I can barely keep the disgust from my voice.

'I know,' he says, half-laughing in an embarrassed way. 'Pathetic, right?'

He's misread the look on my face for pity, when what I'm feeling is sudden and intense anger. This strung-out mess of a man thinks that *he* is closest to Cara? The audacity of his assumption – the sheer wrongness of it – makes me twitchy and tense and I have to pinch the skin on the back of my hand under the table while I listen as he explains it all to me: the separate phone, the untraceable number, the array of text messages, as well as the occasional postcard sent to her workplace.

'Does she know that it's you?' I ask.

He nods. 'She guessed.'

'So why continue?'

He shrugs, and mumbles something about romantic gestures and excitement, but it's all just bullshit. I see clearly what he's like – the type who needs to control, even when he's not with her, pushing and cajoling her with his little game. Have her dancing on strings like a goddamned puppet. He's a fucking stalker and I understand immediately how dangerous he is to her.

'You've got to stop,' I tell him.

He winces. 'I know, I know. It's just – what else can I do? She won't talk to me. She won't answer my calls.'

He exhales, a sharp burst of breath, and for a second it looks like he might start crying again.

'Let me see if I can help you,' I offer.

The look that comes over his face is so nakedly hopeful, it almost makes me feel ashamed.

'Give me your number,' I tell him.

He obliges without question. I punch in the digits, then stow my phone away in my back pocket as I get to my feet.

'You're going?' he asks, desperation leaking into his voice.

He's clinging to the bottom rung here but I've had quite enough. All this time I've been sitting here, listening to his sob story, a hard stone weighing down my heart, thinking: *This is what she loves? This is what she chooses?* I push the thoughts away from me, storing all those bad feelings up for later.

'I'll talk to her,' I tell him in a kindly voice. 'Then I'll call you.'

I can feel his eyes on my back as I walk away – I can almost imagine the light of hope in them. But when I get to the door and glance back, he's sitting with one elbow on the table, supporting his head, eyes fixed dully on the next table. He's not looking at me at all.

I don't call him. Instead, I wait until Saturday and then go around to his house.

'Amy,' he says with surprise.

He's standing in the doorway, dressed in jogging pants and a T-shirt, flip-flops on his feet. His hair is still wet from the shower.

'I hope you don't mind,' I say. 'I was going to call but I was in the neighbourhood, so . . .'

I smile, lifting my arms a little and then letting them fall back to my sides. He's still looking confused, questions milling around behind his eyes, but then he shakes them away and opens the door wide.

I try not to gawp at the surroundings. The cathedral height of the hall ceiling. The kitchen island – a fucking continent, more like. An empty cereal bowl and spoon are marooned in the middle of it, a smattering of cornflakes litter the surface.

'Listen, I'm sorry about the other morning,' he begins, scratching at the side of his face. 'I was in a state. You were very good to entertain my . . . well, my grievances.'

'It's alright,' I shrug, standing awkwardly by the island. I don't know whether or not to sit, suddenly unsure of myself. I'd wanted to get inside the house, but now what?

'I feel terrible, having involved you,' he goes on. 'It's a private matter, between me and Cara. I should talk directly to her, rather than dragging you into it.'

'I don't mind being dragged.'

He nods but looks uncomfortable. A frown of confusion forms and he asks, 'How did you know where I live?'

'I looked up her Rolodex.'

'Did you speak to her? About meeting me?'

'Yeah, kind of.'

He puts his hands to his hips, exhales briefly. He's sober and clear-headed, but he looks unprepared for this.

'Could we sit down and talk?' I ask.

He nods, directing me to a round table in the curve of a bay window. The garden outside looks overgrown and neglected, drifts of yellowed weeds waving in the breeze.

'Let's have coffee,' he says, fiddling with the Gaggia, but then he stops and says, 'Fuck. I've run out.'

'Oh.'

'I've no milk either. Maybe we should go out?' He's pointing to the door, like he wants me to go with him.

Sensing my opportunity, I say, 'Can I use your bathroom first?'

A brief hesitation appears on his face, and then he says, 'Tell you what. I'll head to the shops while you're in the loo. I'll be back in five minutes.'

He directs me to the cloakroom in the hall, and I wait inside till I hear the front door slam, then I'm out and flying up the stairs, two at a time, not even bothering with the living room or any of the spaces on the ground floor. He said five minutes, but I'm guessing it will be more like ten and I don't intend to waste any of them. I go straight to the bedroom. People always hide their private shit in bedrooms, even in massive houses like this one. The bed is a giant raft in the middle of the room, still unmade, heat coming from the open door of the en suite where he recently showered.

The phone is on the window ledge, plugged into the charger. A clunky-looking thing. I check to make sure it's not password protected, then slip it into my pocket quickly, the charger too. I have a quick rummage in his chest of drawers before snooping in the wardrobe. At the back, behind the rows of shoes, is an old cigar box. I kneel on the floor and draw it down on to my lap, open it and peer inside.

'Goddamn,' I say to myself. I cannot believe my luck.

I'm back in the kitchen, staring out into the garden, when he comes in. As well as coffee and milk, he's bought fresh pastries, and we sit at the kitchen table and chat, tearing pieces off the croissants and pains aux raisins, stuffing them into our mouths as we talk.

'She does love you,' I tell him, 'she's just really messed up at the moment. It's like she doesn't know what she wants.'

He's staring at me intently, hunched over his coffee, quietly considering everything I say. So different to the last time, when I had to endure a loose stream of verbal diarrhoea from the guy.

'Take this house sale she's orchestrated. Where the hell did that idea come from? I can't help but feel she's running away from something.'

'From what?'

I shrug and take a slug of coffee. 'Isn't it obvious?'

When he doesn't answer, I explain. 'The attack. That's when all this started. When things started getting out of control for her.'

'But she seemed okay after it.'

'Yeah, on the surface. But I gotta tell you, I'm worried. I think she might be suffering some kind of stress.'

'What? Like PTSD?' He sounds incredulous.

'Why not? It was pretty fucking traumatic. That guy was coming right for her when I whipped her off the street. When we came out, there were bodies everywhere, blood on the pavement. It could so easily have been her. Don't you think she'd have been spooked?'

'I suppose. She's just always been so level-headed. So . . . steady. Even in the face of deep personal tragedy. She just has this way of keeping herself together. Unlike me,' he admits, in a self-deprecating way. 'I suppose it's one of the things that drew me to her.'

'She's a Capricorn,' I say, as if that explains it.

He shoots me a sceptical glance. 'Right. If you believe in that kind of thing.'

'Why? What are you?'

'Pisces.'

'Ah!' I laugh and nod, as if that explains his scepticism. He laughs too.

And then I say it, lightly so as not to seem too obvious, 'Like Mabel. Cara's daughter. She's a Pisces too.'

'Is that so,' he says, but he's not really interested.

'Although she should have been born in May. Does that matter? Is she really more of a Taurus?'

'May?' he asks.

'Right. She was, like, two months premature. She nearly died. Didn't you know that?' I ask, innocently, noting the confusion tracking over his face.

'No. I didn't.'

'That's strange. That Cara never mentioned it to you. I wonder why she didn't? Anyway, thanks for the coffee. And the pastries.'

I suppose I could say more, press the button a little harder. But I can tell from the concentration on his face, the calculations going on in his brain – dates, places, all of it taking shape – that, really, I need say no more.

'It was nice, having this chat with you,' I tell him at the door, giving him a sunny smile.

He hardly speaks in reply, a greyish look on his face. And when I round the gate and wave, he's still standing there, unseeing, beached upon his own doorstep, the waves of realization crashing over him.

15.

Cara

On the last day of October, I drive to the airport with Mabel in the back seat. A gloriously surprising sun beams across the city. It's Hallowe'en, and as we head down the M25 towards Gatwick, I tell Mabel about the costumes I used to wear as a child, how a group of us would troop around the housing estates, bonfires burning on the green, calling from one door to another, threatening vengeance should the treats not be forthcoming.

She listens with interest, my child. I see her face in the rear-view mirror, eyes round with concentration, sucked into the circus of her own vivid imagination. It's a relief to see how she has recovered since the incident with Olivia. Even though she has never openly acknowledged the harm done to her by her half-sister, I sense an ease in her behaviour in the weeks since Olivia stormed out. I've been making a special effort since to come home early from work, to be more available to her in the afternoons and evenings. It's as much a balm to me as it is to her, filling the void left after ending my affair by throwing myself into family life. A new determination has taken hold of me, renewing my belief that I can make this marriage work.

'When will we be there?' she asks, with excitement more than fatigue.

'Not long now, sweet pea. Looking forward to seeing Daddy?'

'I can't wait!' she replies enthusiastically.

Her buoyancy matches my own. It's been ages since I've driven the car, and now, behind the wheel, speeding towards the airport, I feel calmly optimistic. Happy, even. For the first time in months, things seem clear to me and I am hopeful for the future. Jeff and I have come to a new understanding of each other. Despite the difficulties of these past few weeks while he's been away, I can see how energized he is by the work, how bored he had been at home. When this project ends, he will look for another, and I will be supportive of his endeavour. We are moving into a new phase of our lives together and I'm excited at the prospect. Earlier today when I'd spoken to our estate agent, she informed me that there was a second potential buyer now, and while their offer still did not reach our asking price, it was edging closer and she remained confident we would achieve it.

Spurred on by this news, I'd called Jeff. He was at the airport in Berlin, awaiting his flight. Recently, we'd started speculatively trawling some property websites, and there was a house that had caught our interest; it had an open viewing this afternoon.

'What do you think?' I'd asked him, fully expecting him to say no, advising against counting chickens before they'd hatched, et cetera. But to my surprise he'd responded with enthusiasm.

And when we meet him at the Arrivals gate he swings Mabel around, then turns to me, planting a warm kiss on my lips, before he draws back and grins, saying, 'Come on, then. Take me to see our house.'

The house is beautiful. Loftier and more generous than the photographs depicted, each room feels elegantly proportioned, solid, with a patina of age suggesting generations of living within these sturdy walls. The viewing is well attended, and we have to squeeze through doorways to assess each room, as other prospective buyers mill about, making their observations.

'What are all these people doing in my kitchen?' Jeff growls in my ear.

I smile back at him, relieved and delighted that he feels it too. The sense of belonging – like this house was meant for us. I'd felt it the minute we'd walked through the front door.

Jeff corners the estate agent, peppering him with questions about heating systems, plumbing, who the vendor is, their reasons for selling, while I take Mabel outside. The back garden is long and narrow, scarcely tended to. A concrete path bisects a strip of patchy lawn, leading down to a clutch of fruit trees, their windfall harvest rotting on the ground. Mabel skips about me, happy to be outdoors and away from the bovine crowd being herded from room to room.

I look back at the house, and imagine us living here – the three of us. Already I am envisaging a brick patio outside the kitchen, summer mornings spent breakfasting there, reading the paper, Mabel playing on the lawn. I feel calm and relaxed, sure in the knowledge of how right this feels. After the chaos and difficulties of the past few months, the way seems clear.

It is nearly a month now since I told Finn it was over. I was calm and reasonable when I broke it to him, explaining that it had been a mistake, taking full responsibility for it – apologizing, even – for reawakening something between us that was best left sleeping. Some pasts aren't worth returning to. Some loves should be allowed to wither and fade.

I'd been rigorous about not caving in to his pleas to meet, to reconsider, disciplining myself not to respond to his texts and voicemails, which had grown more whiney and desperate as the weeks progressed. During that time, there were messages from YCF, pleading in tone. *I'm waiting for you.* And *Tell me you'll change your mind?* I read them, then deleted them. Put them to the back of my mind. Part of me was tempted to confront him about these messages. *What is the point of all this?* I wanted to ask. But I knew him of old. There was no point, not really. They were just a part of his twisted logic. A ploy that had been set in motion and now could not be abandoned.

Standing here in the garden, I breathe in the autumn air. A breeze trills through the garden, silvering the leaves on the trees next door.

'Will Amy be living here too?' Mabel asks, interrupting my thoughts.

I look down at my little girl, remembering my conversation with Amy and briefly regretting having left her with the impression that there would be a place for her in our new home. I will have to set her straight about it soon.

Mabel waits, and I answer, 'No, sweet pea. It will just be me, you and Daddy.'

I watch her think about this for a moment, and then her face breaks into a grin, and she runs back up the path to where Jeff is emerging from the kitchen. I go to follow her, wondering why she hadn't reacted negatively to the news that Amy will be leaving us, my hand pressed to my bag, when I feel the buzz of my phone.

I take it out, thumb the screen, my heart turning over.

'Ready to go?' Jeff asks, scooping Mabel up in his arms as he comes towards me.

I stash my phone back in my bag, look up and force a smile.

'Ready,' I say, the one-word message burnt on my retinas.

Bitch.

After that, the messages start up in earnest. Your Closest Friend is angry with me, the messages dripping with fury.

Liar.

Cheat.

Whore.

They zip through, lighting my phone up with their toxic rage, pinging at all hours of the day and night. I know they will die out eventually, once his fury is spent, but they're bothersome nonetheless, and untypical of Finn. I've learned in the past how nasty he can be once he feels abandoned or scorned, but the brevity and sharpness of these messages, little fragments of digitized shrapnel, seem inconsistent with the more complex and thought-out nature of his previous attacks.

I'm sitting at the kitchen table the following Saturday afternoon, making the most of a quiet half-hour to catch up on some work administration. Jeff has taken Mabel to buy new shoes, and Amy is down in the basement doing her laundry, when my phone lights up with a message. That now-familiar sinking feeling comes over me as I read it.

Traitor.

I put the phone down and think. How am I going to get this to stop?

The door opens and Amy comes in from the hall, her basket of clean laundry tucked under one arm.

'Hey,' she says in a hollow tone as she passes, her flip-flops scudding over the floor.

There's something downcast about her lately, like she's lumbering under the weight of her own little cloud. It's been mildly irritating, but now it makes me pause.

'Amy,' I say, stopping her as she reaches her bedroom door. 'Did you just text me?'

'What?'

She takes a few steps towards where I'm sitting at the table. I hold up my phone.

'I just got a message and I was wondering if it was from you?'

'No. Look.' She points to the worktop and I see her iPhone plugged into the charger.

'Have you tried calling the number?' she asks.

I explain that I have, but any time I do, the number rings out or gets cut off and there's no voicemail facility.

'How many messages have you got?' she presses, and I feel her rising curiosity.

'Not many. A few.'

'YCF,' she reads over my shoulder, and hastily I flip my phone over. 'What does that mean?'

'Nothing,' I say quickly, regretting this line of

conversation. I get to my feet and turn to face her. 'Actually, Amy, there's something I wanted to talk to you about, while we're alone.'

'Oh?' She hitches the basket a little higher on her hip, and waits.

'It's about Christmas. One of Jeff's colleagues in Berlin has offered us the use of his holiday house in the Black Forest, and we've decided to take him up on the offer. It will be fun for Mabel – mountains, snow. Also, we've accepted an offer on this place and it looks like the sale will go through towards the end of December –'

'But where will we live?' she cuts in.

The word 'we' snags in my head. 'That's what I want to talk to you about. You see, we've found a house that we love –'

'Where?'

I hesitate, surprised by my own reluctance to tell her. 'Near Dulwich. We've put in an offer and we're hopeful of getting it, and if we don't, then we'll have to rent while we keep looking . . . Anyway,' I stop myself from divulging too many details, 'it seems like a good time for you to start thinking about what's next for you.'

'For me?' There's a stunned look about her, like she hasn't seen this coming.

'Yes. Soon it will be a new year, a new start for all of us.'

'You don't want me any more?'

'Amy,' I laugh gently. I can't help it – the baldness of her statement, the hint of desperation in it. I'm embarrassed for her. 'It's not that we're not happy with your work, or that we're not grateful for all you've done. I don't know where I'd have been without you these past couple of months! But we think, once we move, that we might make some changes. Mabel can stay in after-school club until I finish work, and we want to arrange for someone to come in for the mornings when Jeff's not there – someone who lives near the new house, we hope, who can help us out with the school run.' I say all of this carefully, aware of the brittleness of her mood. I can sense how close she is to tears. 'This was always supposed to be a temporary arrangement. Come on. Surely you wouldn't want to live with us for ever!'

She flashes me a look that I can't quite fathom, and just as quickly averts her eyes.

'No,' she says softly.

'You are welcome to stay here over the Christmas holidays if you've nothing else arranged,' I tell her. 'But once we get back . . .'

I leave the sentence hanging. She's looking straight at me now, no sign of those tears. It's a hard, flat stare.

'I understand,' she says in a monotone, then hugging her laundry to her hip, she turns and disappears into her bedroom.

I think I hear her inside, talking, and presume she's on the phone to a friend, bitching about me, probably. But I don't give it much thought. I turn my attention back to my laptop, go through a few more work emails. It's only after I've finished, and closed the laptop, that I realize Amy's phone is still plugged into the kitchen wall. When I pass her door a minute later, there is nothing, only silence.

The next few days pass in a blur of activity and obligations. I'm stuck in the office until Thursday, when I meet with a group of students from UCL. It's for a follow-on piece from one we ran last month on political activism within third-level institutions, and we've arranged to meet on campus in Bloomsbury. The group are passionate and engaging, and we talk for the guts of an hour. I'm just wrapping up when I get a call from Katie, and when I answer she sounds breathy and anxious, speaking low into the phone.

'You need to get back to the office,' she tells me.

'Why? What's going on?'

'Look, I can't talk about it over the phone, Cara. I'm sorry to be so cloak-and-dagger, just . . . Just get here as quickly as you can, and come straight to the meeting room. We'll be waiting for you.'

I hang up, nonplussed, distractedly saying my good-byes to the students, and then I jump in a cab and head back to Wogan House. In the back seat, I glance over my emails, my Twitter feed, then look up the news headlines, but nothing alarming jumps out.

As soon as I go through the swing doors on to the office floor, I feel it. Groups are huddled around computers in individual cubicles, chatting conspiratorially. Instinctively, my eyes flick to the TV screen in the corner showing the news, but there's nothing of note, the only information scrolling the ticker-tape is the Dow Jones Index and the NASDAQ 500. Besides, there isn't the same charge in the air as there was the morning of Parsons Green. There is an edge of amusement to this – like some shared joke being passed around. Down at the end of the room, I can see some of the lads in Marketing standing around laughing. I catch sight of Heather, my boss, her arms folded while she talks to another producer. Finished with their conversation, she nods dismissively and turns to head back to the lifts. Seeing me, she seems to refocus, saying my name as we pass, but holding my gaze just a fraction too long, her expression inscrutable.

They are gathered in the meeting room, waiting for me – Victor, Derek, Katie, and Mark from IT. His presence throws me. They are standing close together, looking grave, and when I enter the room, the huddle breaks up and the expressions they present to me range from nerves to something mournful.

'What is it? What's happened?' I ask from my place at the door, waiting for an answer.

Katie is rubbing at her lip, Vic is staring at his shoes. It's Mark who breaks the silence.

'An email was sent from your account,' he says, taking his hands from his pockets and leaning towards the laptop open on the table. 'Brace yourself.'

He clicks on it and an image pops up. My legs weaken.

It's a large-scale photograph of me. Not a recent one. And in the photograph, I am naked.

'You should sit down,' Katie says, and I allow myself to be ushered into a chair.

All the blood has drained from my face. I'd always thought it was an exaggeration, that expression of growing faint, your legs failing, in the face of great shock. Even when I learned my own mother had died, I remained upright, all my limbs functioning. But this is a different kind of shock entirely, and it hits me physically.

'I take it you didn't send this?' Mark asks.

I can only shake my head mutely. I'm furiously trying to process this, my eyes fixed on the picture. I'm aware of some level of humiliation, but the full extent hasn't sunk in. I'm too busy calculating where this has come from.

It's an old picture, obviously, taken at a time in my life before children, before marriage, before any real responsibility or maturity kicked in. Just a silly photograph, the two of us messing around, experimenting. Seen under a different light, it could be playful and innocent, part of a burgeoning sexuality, an exploration of self. But now, writ large across the screen, the word 'SLUT' screaming above it, it has become something else. Something lurid and obscene. Something shameful.

'Close it down, for God's sake,' Vic mutters, and Mark snaps the laptop shut.

Vic's hand falls heavily on my shoulder, gives it a squeeze.

'You alright, love?'

'No,' I say, my voice a whisper.

He squeezes again.

'You've been hacked,' Derek announces, and I can't help feeling he sounds just a little pleased about it.

'Well, that's stating the bleeding obvious, isn't it?' Vic seems more pissed off about this than I am. But I'm still at the shock phase. Anger has yet to reach me.

'When's the last time you changed your password?' Mark asks.

I shake my head. 'I don't know.'

'Well, that's the first thing you do. Change it immediately. Then get on to the police.'

The word shakes me from the dreamlike trance I've fallen into.

'Wait – what? Police? Is that necessary?'

'This is clearly malicious,' Mark states, his hands back in his pockets. 'It's a criminal offence. You'll want to find out who did this –'

'But I know who did it.'

They are all staring at me now. A brief pause falls over them, and I realize they're waiting for me to say who it is. Who I suspect. I put my hands up to cover my face.

'Who was this sent to?' I ask from behind cupped hands.

Katie replies gingerly, 'It seems like most people on this floor, and a few from upstairs.'

I think of the look Heather gave me, then shutter my mind to it.

'Anyone else?'

Another silence.

Then Katie pipes up once more, 'I looked at the list. I'm sorry, Cara. They sent it to Jeff.'

I arranged to meet him outside Topshop on Regent Street. I was terse in my instructions.

'Now,' I told him. 'Come right now.'

He will have picked up on the livid fury seeping through my coldness.

I have picked a street corner because I don't want to sit down in a coffee shop or restaurant with him where we will be forced to keep things civil. This is not a cosy chat or a civilized conversation. Blood roils inside me at his betrayal – his malice. Whatever hurt I may have done him is far outweighed by this wanton act of extreme vengeance.

I am there first, nerves dancing, and as I wait I try to imagine the conversation we're going to have, a defence mechanism perhaps, so I can circumnavigate whatever he throws at me. Fury channels through me. I am certain of the moral high ground here and for all his spite, his self-regard, he will know it too. He'll have had time to think about what he's done, time for regret to start nudging its way in, and when he rounds the corner and comes into view, I fully expect him to look guilty and a little cowed, braced for recrimination, shrunk in his jacket now that the bravado has worn off. That is why I am so surprised to see him come towards me with an expression on his face that mirrors my own righteous indignation back at me.

'You've got some bloody nerve,' I tell him as soon as he's upon me.

My arms are crossed tightly over my chest – an obvious display of disapproval perhaps, but I won't risk any opening for physical contact. I don't want him to touch me.

'Me?'

'Yes, you! You and your little games. Jesus, do you think I'm stupid, Finn? Did you think I wouldn't know it was you?'

I am reminded all over again of why things didn't work out between us – the way he could be petty and mean, vindictive when he didn't get his own way. I'm reminded of the jokes that turned nasty, the air of chippy entitlement and lack of scruples, the smart-arsed throwaway remarks that cut too deep. I'm reminded of all of this, and with it comes a blinding sense of my own stupidity.

'I've been trying to meet with you for weeks. You wouldn't talk to me. You wouldn't answer my calls. I needed to speak to you –'

'So this is how you choose to get my attention? By humiliating me?'

He blinks, the ghost of confusion momentarily breaking up his anger.

'What?'

'Oh, please!' I say, hard, mirthless laughter bursting from me. 'Don't even try to pull that one. I should call the police. In fact, I think I will.'

'Hang on – police?'

'Your Closest Friend? Don't tell me you're going to deny it was you?'

'Listen,' he says, recovering his anger, 'if you want to make a complaint about a few stupid texts, then be my guest.'

'My closest friend. Jesus, what a joke.'

'It's what you want, isn't it? Friendship.'

The word comes out of his mouth like something distasteful, unclean. His flippancy causes my anger to flare and suddenly, there on the busy street outside Topshop, pedestrians passing us, I launch myself at him, my bare fists pounding against the drum of his chest.

Startled by this sudden violence, he raises his hands defensively before grabbing hold of my wrists. We struggle against each other for a moment, and up close I can see the broken capillaries in his face, the exertion turning his skin blotchy and almost purple, his eyes rheumy and bloodshot. He's nothing but a drunk – a washed-up, vain, self-centred has-been.

'How did I ever love you?' I ask when we eventually break apart. 'How did I ever think what we had was something precious, something lasting? If you could do this to me?' And I'm crying now as I say it. 'If you could take something private – something intimate between us – and send it to my colleagues, my boss, my husband? Those photographs – yes, it was stupid of me to let you take them – but it was part of our relationship. Something cherished – a gift to you. How could you twist it like that? Do you really hate me that much?'

My voice comes out tremulous and weak. The anger has dissipated, replaced by a terrible sadness like a gaping wound. The full impact of his betrayal is crashing over me, and I feel weakness in my body, a nervy undoing as he fixes me with a look of astonishment.

'What are you talking about?' he asks, shaking his head, and even through the lens of my own hurt, I can see that his confusion is genuine. 'I never sent any photographs.'

'But you must have.'

I'm bewildered at his expression, his repeated denial, as he asserts his innocence.

'Look, I admit that I sent a few texts. But I haven't sent any in ages. Even if I'd wanted to, I've lost the bloody phone. And I certainly never sent any pictures.'

'But the photographs were in your possession –'

'I haven't looked at them in years! I'm sorry, but I haven't.'

'They must be on your computer –'

'They were Polaroids.'

'Well then, you must have scanned them, uploaded them. Someone must have hacked your computer.'

My voice is rising. I'm aware I'm sounding a little manic, and he's giving me a patient look, like he's waiting for me to rein myself in. But my thoughts are so scattered and confused. I can't make sense of them.

'I didn't do this, Cara,' he says, gently but firmly. 'And I don't know who did. Frankly, right now, I don't care.

That's not why I came here today. That's not why I wanted to talk to you.'

'Oh, Finn, it's over,' I tell him. 'Can't you just let it be? Can't you just accept it?'

He shakes his head, and a wash of exhaustion comes over me. But it quickly goes cold, at what he says next.

'I don't want you back, Cara. Not now, with all I know. I'm not sure I even want to know you after what you've done. I came here today to find out the truth, from your own mouth,' he says quietly.

'What truth?'

We're standing close to each other, close enough for me to see the pulse jump in his neck.

'About Mabel,' he says, and my heart lurches uncertainly in my chest. 'About my daughter.'

16.

Amy

For some people, it happens slowly. A winding down of the marriage. No screaming matches. No discoveries of betrayal. Just a quiet falling off of closeness, a smooth-growing distance. And then one day, they sit down at their kitchen table and have a solemn, respectful conversation during which arrangements are made about the children and who gets to stay in the family home, some tears are shed but nothing heated or dramatic, no insults flung, no last-minute pleas to stay. A civilized ending to a civilized relationship. That's how it happens with some marriages.

Others need a push.

I linger near the bottom step, listening for as long as I can. Mabel has long since gone to bed, and in the living room, I've left the TV on loud so Cara will think I'm in there watching, not standing here straining to hear what's going on upstairs.

It's easy to tell myself that this is meant to happen. There's a fateful air to everything that's happened so far. The way she ran into my path that night, how I chose to snatch her from the darkness and save her. Everything from our teenage years spent under the shadow of absent mothers, to the shared meaning of our names. *Beloved.* And she is beloved to me. Maybe more so in these last days when she seems to drift from day to night, exhaustion and stress making her zombie-like, her mind elsewhere. And I'm there, always, in the background, caring for her, looking out for her. Waiting.

I know she's on the phone to Jeff. I've come to recognize the strain in her voice when things are difficult, and I imagine things are difficult now. That picture. A stroke of genius. It was a toss-up, whether or not I would send it to him too. But then I thought, *What the hell? Two birds, one stone, job done.* I wonder how she's explaining it to him, what possible reason she can come up with to lessen the harshness of it. I guess it's not evidence of a betrayal – not when the photo was taken so long ago, before the marriage – but no one wants to be reminded of their partner's sexual past. Especially when it serves to highlight how flagrantly different and more colourful that past was when compared to your own staid, boring present.

Feeling brave, I tiptoe up a few steps to listen. The words are muffled but when I hear her mention the police it sends me scuttling back down to my room.

I close the door and sit on my bed, still listening for a voice overhead. But it's too distant to make out. The word *police* has scooped out a cold cavity inside me, and for the first time since coming here, a feeling of deep unease comes over me. What if she does call the police? What if she has already? For a long time, I sit there in the cloudy room I've come to call my own. With my knees drawn up to my chin, alert to every sound, I wait for her to come and find me, to tell me to stand up – that she knows it all now, every single thing I've done.

*

And then, finally, it happens.

I wake in the middle of the night. A creaking floor-board overhead alerts me to her wakefulness. Checking my phone, I see it's almost 3 a.m., and I wonder if she has slept at all. I follow her footfall across the room and down the staircase. I'm out of bed when I hear the faucet turn in the kitchen, water running.

'Hey,' I say.

She looks back with a guilty air. I can't be sure, but it seems like she's just popped a pill into her mouth. She doesn't respond to my greeting, just takes a swig of water from the glass she's holding, then leaves it on the counter.

'Sorry if I woke you,' she says, and turns to face me.

Except she's not looking at me. Her arms are folded protectively over her chest, even though it's not cold in here, and there's something funny about her mouth, the downturn at the corners, a sort of wavering about it.

'That's okay. Are you alright?'

And then her mouth does that wavering thing again, and I realize how upset she is. The cries burst out of her and she claps both hands over her mouth, a furious look entering her eyes, as she pushes past me, towards the sitting room. Instinctively, I follow her, my awareness heightened by the drama of her emotional display – moved by it, in fact. That she can feel free enough in my company to break down.

'Cara? What is it?' I ask gently. 'What's happened?'

'Everything's a mess. And I . . . Oh, Jesus,' she says, shaking her head furiously, holding a balled-up tissue to her nose.

There's a manic energy to her as she paces between fireplace and window, unable to settle.

'Calm down,' I tell her.

But she snaps at me that she can't. How can she?

'Not with all this going on!'

'All what?'

She gives a small cry of frustration, and continues with her manic pacing. Looking at her, you'd think she was angry. But I know it's not anger that's powering this display. It's fear. And for a second, I feel guilty about the picture, about what I've done.

I walk to the drinks cabinet, and pour her a large vodka – neat. Then I order her to sit down, and I put the glass into her hand, cupping it with my own as I instruct her to drink. It's amazing how easily she consents, like she just wilts. And I can tell she's been longing for this – aching for someone to take charge, to guide her, to ease her burden.

'Now,' I say firmly, once she's taken a couple of big sips. 'Tell me what is wrong.'

And she does tell me – most of it, anyway. About the text messages, about the picture sent to every staff member, her humiliation. Falteringly, pausing every now and then to gulp at the vodka for courage, occasionally shaking her head or rolling her eyes in an effort to acknowledge the outlandishness of what she's describing. But underneath it all, I can see how deeply this has affected her. The slow corrosion of those messages. The insidious nature of the email threat.

'God, I could kick myself for being so stupid. For allowing myself to be photographed like that in the first place!'

'Lots of people do stuff like that. It's not something to be ashamed of.'

'Oh, Amy – yes, it is! If you'd seen the way people were looking at me. My boss . . .'

She drops her face into her hand, shaking her head as if trying to dislodge the memory.

'It's just so fucking vindictive of him! Not that he's owned up to it,' she adds, with a snort of derision.

'Have you spoken to the police?' I ask. I'm taking a gamble here, but it's worth it.

She shakes her head. 'What's the point? I'd prefer to sort it out myself, anyway. Keep it private.' And then, remembering the public nature of her humiliation, she laughs – a short burst like a hiccup. 'If that's even possible.'

'Have you spoken to him? To Finn?'

'Yes.'

'What did he say?'

'He says he didn't do it. That he didn't send the photograph. But if he didn't do it, then who did?'

She looks at me then, and I'd swear there is something behind that stare, something searching and interrogative. Nerves tremble in my stomach. I turn away and walk to the drinks cabinet and help myself to a vodka. Her eyes are on me the whole time, and then she says it.

'He knows about Mabel.'

My heart tightens and I sip my drink, steel myself and then turn to meet her gaze.

'How does he know?'

She shakes her head slowly. 'I don't know. I've never told another living soul. Except you.'

Her voice is low and steady, a test in it. I hold my nerve,

keeping my voice level, and say, 'Well, he didn't hear it from me. How could he? I've never even met the guy.'

Confusion or irritation crosses her brow and she gives her head another angry shake before lifting her drink to her mouth, the glass almost empty.

'Of course,' she relents. 'Sorry. I don't know what I was thinking.' Then, with vehemence, she adds, 'I wish to Christ I'd never met him.'

'I thought he was the love of your life?' I say, softly probing.

A burst of harsh laughter from her, then she asks, 'Is that what I told you?'

'Yes. When we were alone in the storeroom. You said you'd married the wrong man. That you'd mistaken comfort and safety for love. That you should have been brave enough to make a different choice. You said —'

She looks up sharply. 'Go on.'

'You said your child was his, and he didn't even know it. That your husband didn't know. A mess of lies, you called it, that needed to be sorted out, unravelled, no matter what the consequences. And if you got out of there alive, you would put things right.'

Just saying it aloud brings it all back to me — how I felt the night she'd told me. The thrill of the illicit. Sharing a secret like that, it binds you to a person, weaves them into your life in such an intimate way.

She shakes her head, stares into her empty glass with contempt. 'I must have been drunk. Either that or I am a fool.'

I take her glass from her hand and she doesn't protest as I refill it.

Watching me, she says, 'One time, we were at a

party – Finn and I. Some friend of his from TV. While we were there, the house was raided by the police, and I panicked because I knew Finn was carrying. I'd seen him myself before we'd left our house, slipping a few grams into his pocket for later. The police didn't search all of us, but they searched him . . .'

She pauses, wordlessly accepting the refreshed glass I put into her hand, before resuming her story. In a tired but somewhat hardened voice, she goes on.

'They didn't find anything. I assumed he'd flushed it down the toilet or thrown it out of a window, and when we got out of the house with a few of the others, he was euphoric. I wanted to go home, but he wouldn't have it, insisting we move on with the others to another party that was happening in Canary Wharf.'

'Did you go?'

'Yes, I went,' she answers, with the ghost of a regretful smile. 'And when we got there, Finn turned to me and said, "Give me your bag," and when I did, he reached inside it and found the little bag of cocaine he'd hidden there. I couldn't believe it. He'd planted his drugs on me to save his own skin.'

'What did you do?'

She draws in a breath, as if to steady herself. 'I confronted him about it. Obviously, I was furious. But he just laughed it off, said I was overreacting. Said that he knew the police wouldn't search someone like me.' She shakes her head slowly, then repeats: '*Someone like me.* There was real contempt in the way he said it. And then I watched while he snorted a couple of lines, shared it with a couple of the others, and we all went up on the roof –'

She stops, but I can sense there's something she's not telling me.

'And?' I prompt, but already, I can see her shutting down.

'And nothing,' she answers despondently. She drinks deeply from her glass, her eyelids lowered.

'Can I ask you something?' I say tentatively. 'Why would you go back to him? After he's behaved like such a prick . . .'

She smiles down at her glass, and there's something wistful and yet bitter about it.

'I've asked myself that,' she replies, 'a million times. It's like some kind of addiction, I suppose. Because even though he has hurt and betrayed me, behaved selfishly beyond imagining, when it is good between us there is such intensity of feeling it's like nothing I've ever known before. The greatest rush. Can you understand what that is like?'

I can understand. Of course I can. I've been there myself. With Connie. And now, with Cara. There are so many parallels between us: the way she latched on to Finn after her mother died mirrored my own attachment to Connie in the wake of my mother's abandonment of me. That same rush she talked about – I knew it. I had felt it. It had driven me to the darkest of places.

She opens her mouth to say something, and then closes it. Something changes in her face, anger draining away into a pained expression that betrays a deeper worry – one she won't speak of.

Except to say, 'I'm frightened, Amy. I'm frightened of what he might do.'

Her voice is barely above a whisper.

And then the anger gathers again inside her, and she says, stormily, 'God, I could just kill him!'

'Don't say that,' I tell her, surprised by the sudden thud of conscience in my heart.

She smiles at me, her eyes glassy and unfocused.

'Why not?'

'Because you don't know what it feels like.'

Her eyes are on me now. I'm flirting with an uneasy threshold. Alighting on the raw graze of a hidden insecurity.

'You don't know what it's like to really hurt someone.'

'And you do?' she asks.

The air has grown still around us. There's no car alarm now. No noises from without or within. I feel the weight of her attention and find myself thrilling to it.

'My friend, Connie – the one I told you about?'

She waits.

'She . . . there was an accident.'

The word crackles in the air between us.

'It was my fault.'

Cara's still sitting on the sofa, her hands wrapped around her glass, but she's looking at me oddly. Despite the vodka and whatever pill she swallowed, she's still together enough to register the weirdness of my admission.

'What do you mean?' she asks, her voice hoarse and wary.

It's like I'm back there once more, the cold night air hitting me in the face. I'm winded all over again, realizing what I've done. I'm sitting at the very edge of the couch, the tumbler held in my two hands, and I can feel my throat closing over with unexpected emotion so that I have to drink quickly to try to calm myself. The vodka worms its way down to my stomach, warming me and opening me out a little. Still, it's hard.

'I need another,' I say, getting to my feet. 'This is difficult . . .'

She doesn't say anything, just watches while I fetch the bottle, and pour us both another measure. I leave the bottle on the floor by my feet and resume my position, only this time her body is turned towards me, one elbow resting on the seat of the couch.

'What happened, Amy?'

I take another sip of my drink and begin.

'It happened when I was nineteen. I had this job in our town waiting tables and I was coming home one night, in early Fall. I guess I was pretty tired. It was late and dark, and I was driving along the road that led to our house. We lived about four miles outside of the town – a kind of remote place, nothing much around except trees. It was just me and Elaine by then. Connie had a boyfriend – Ray. This Polish guy she'd met at a barbecue. They were renting a studio apartment on the other side of town and she was talking about getting married.'

I take a sip from the glass. It's been so long since I've told this story, I'd half-forgotten the power it has over me. But something is happening to me now. The smell of diesel in my nostrils, the headlights sweeping over the road lighting up the sugar pines that grew on the margins, some tinny pop song playing on the local radio station – Shit FM, we used to call it – the only station that piece of junk could pick up.

'I'm driving along and suddenly I feel this impact,' I tell her. 'At first I thought it was a dog or something. I hadn't seen anything, just felt the bump of it. I stopped the car and got out. There was blood all over the road.'

I have to stop for a moment. How vivid it had been, even in the darkness.

'And there's this person lying there, crumpled, by the ditch.'

I can't look at her as I tell her this, but I can feel Cara's eyes on me, her attention like a held breath.

'I knew it was Connie before I even got to her. She had this purple suede jacket she used to wear everywhere, and so I knew at once it was her.'

I suck in my breath to beat the nausea that has come on me all of a sudden. Pink matter glistening on the asphalt. Her mutilated face.

'Later, we found out she'd had a fight with Ray. She'd walked all that way and was nearly home when I —'

My throat tightens. I put the glass to my lips and find my hand is trembling. When I go to speak, the words won't come, and instead I gulp in air like a fish pulled from the water. Cara's hand is on my wrist, her fingers encircling it in a firm grip. She doesn't say anything, but I can feel her willing me to go on.

'I called 911, and then I waited with her, whispering all the time that she was okay, that I was going to stay with her, that help was coming.'

Her grip on my wrist tightens. I look down and see the clasp of it whitening my skin.

The tears come now. I can't stop them. All this time I've been pushing them down, but they spurt up now in a rush, spilling out ugly and crude, my whole body shuddering with the force of them, the back of my hand against my face to hold back the messy tide of it.

And then she's reaching up for me and I slide down on

to the floor beside her. She draws me towards her, pulling me so that my head lies in the crook of her neck, my hand still over my face. I can feel the pulse of her right there by my ear, the heat from her body, her hair brushing my forehead. Every nerve ending is popping, so I can barely make out the words she is whispering, something about how it wasn't my fault, how it was a terrible accident, and because of the murmuring softness of it, the sweet warmth of her, I almost believe it.

My breathing slows. The tide of emotion subsides, overtaken by something quite different. I feel her drawing back from me, and dare myself to bring my eyes up to meet hers. I'm holding myself so still, knowing we are on the cusp of something. Her eyes are locked on mine, and there's this pause. The air between us shrinks with anticipation.

Which one of us will reach across it? Who will be brave enough?

My courage is summoning itself, my fever stirred, when she shakes her head, and says, 'So what happened to Connie?'

And like a punctured balloon, all the anticipation shrivels.

I turn my face away, look at the fake flames in the phoney fireplace, and feel a sharp nudge of disappointment.

'She had a concussion. Some broken ribs.'

'But she was okay? She recovered?'

I press the heels of my hands into my eye sockets, try to calm myself. Then, taking my hands away, I give a brief shake of my head, stretch out my neck a little.

'Yeah. I guess. I didn't stay.'

'You left?'

Shrugging, I say: 'I kind of had to. It was an accident, and all, but . . . I dunno. I didn't like the way Elaine looked at me after that. So I took off.'

'Where did you go?'

'Philadelphia, for a while. Then New York. But, there were always reminders. I couldn't stop feeling guilty about it, you know?'

'Is that why you had therapy?' she asks, tripping over the words.

Despite myself, I roll my eyes. Just remembering those sessions with Dr Krauss droning on about agent-regret and not blaming myself for my bad luck makes me itchy with irritation and impatience.

'He used to tell me that I was feeling responsible for an act of which I was not culpable. That I was taking the blame for a situation that had been created through no will of my own. That I was suffering from self-imposed pain, and that was the thing that really annoyed me, you know? Like I was wallowing in it, or something. And I kept wanting to scream at him, "But *I* hit her! Not anyone else. *I* did it! Why don't you understand this?"'

I feel myself getting worked up, and she draws back from me a little, rests her elbow on the couch again, puts her fingers to the side of her head. Her eyes keep half-closing, like she's having difficulty staying awake.

'I need to sleep,' she murmurs, the vodka dipping to one side as the glass begins to slip from her hand.

I take it from her grasp and put it on the floor, and when I straighten up she is already lying back against the cushions, her eyes closing.

A lock of her hair rests against her cheek and I reach

out and push it back. She hums with pleasure, her face turning into my hand.

'You're so good to me,' she says, her voice thickened by alcohol or sleep.

Slowly I draw my thumb over the smooth planes of her cheek.

It's like a hunger inside me. A hunger I've long felt but have never been able to satisfy. Her skin beneath my touch makes me dizzy. She's so close now. Could I?

Fear holds me back, but desire is stronger. I am helpless to it. And when I lean in and kiss her, feel the heat of her mouth against mine, the desire is stoked, like an animal nudged awake. She makes that noise again, that happy moan, and our lips open to each other, and it's like I've been travelling for so long across arid, lonely plains, and now it's all behind me, the hard journey.

I'm home.

17.

Cara

I don't know where I am.

Cheek stuck to the sheet, I breathe through my mouth and try to focus. I'm vaguely aware of the pain but I'm more alive to the guilt – a thick wash of regret that always heralds a hangover. My vision clears slowly. A dim light brushing against a chalky-grey wall. A rug on the floor stitched and woven in shades of beige, tufts of lamb's wool, that I have only the vaguest memory of buying. A sour taste fills my mouth, a backwash of bile, and it's an effort to swallow, my tongue and teeth tacky and dry. I have the feeling that somewhere in the back of my head there is a bank of thoughts and images and revelations waiting to burst forth, but I'm holding them back, not ready – not able – to deal with them yet. It's all I can do to peel my face off the mattress, stare blearily at a clock face I don't recognize. Someone shifts in the bed next to me.

I struggle to get up, all of it coming at me now. This is Amy's room, Amy's bed, her head flattened into the pillow next to me. I have the sensation that I am propelled from the bed – like an ejector seat suddenly released – and I find myself standing by the wall on shaky legs, assaulted by confusion and the awful panic that comes from over-sleeping. A cacophony of thoughts come crashing in: I have spent the night in her bed with no recollection of how I came to be here. What happened between us? Spidery thoughts crawl around my head. Was there some kind of intimacy? A sexual act? One small mercy: I have my clothes on, and, as far as I can see, so does she.

I step out of the room without disturbing her, and rush up the stairs to my bedroom. The bed is unmade, as I left it. I am disastrously late for work. On the nightstand, my phone sits, almost throbbing with malice. I pick it up and swipe to the fourteen missed calls from Victor, Katie, Derek. There are texts with varying levels of urgency and annoyance. I haven't the stomach to listen to the voice-mails. It's almost 9 a.m. – the show will be on air in fifteen minutes and today it's supposed to be my turn in the producer's chair. Swimming up from the deep comes the memory of Finn's assertion yesterday. 'My daughter,' he had snarled at me. And it is this that frightens me the most.

Downstairs, Amy is sleeping. I know that I need to find out what happened between us, but there's no time for that now. I focus on the most pressing emergency – work. In all my professional life, I've never once allowed a lapse like this. I call Katie.

'Where are you?' she hisses into the phone.

'I overslept.'

'Are you alright?'

In the background, I can hear the patter of voices, the industrious din of the office floor so familiar to me now.

'I'm fine. A bit of a bug, maybe. I'm on my way in now.'

I press her to fill me in on what's happening, trying my best to scramble some air of authority and to conduct proceedings from this end of the phone, but there's a queasiness gathering inside me and my head throbs with pain.

'Can you put me on to Vic?' I ask, and she says sure, and I can hear her voice distantly, telling him I'm on the line. I cannot hear his response.

A minute later, she's back with me.

'I'm sorry, Cara. He's with Derek in the studio. They've asked not to be disturbed.'

She delivers this in an awkward manner and I sense her discomfort, but it's overpowered by my own feelings of sudden anger, a jolt of hot anxiety.

'Look, are you sure you want to come in?' Katie asks, her voice softening with concern. 'Especially after yesterday. Maybe you should just stay in bed and get well.'

I close my eyes briefly, shutting them against the memory of that photograph, humiliation crawling over me like a virulent rash. The thought of running the gauntlet of all those stolen looks, those judging glances and whispered asides, is almost unbearable. I could stay at home, pull the covers over my head, cry off sick for once.

But I don't like the thought of Vic and Derek pushing me out. Riled by fear of exclusion, I tell her that I'll be there in forty minutes. Underneath the noisy anger and queasy anxiety, a small voice whispers: *You just don't want to be alone with her.* I push it away.

There's no time for a shower or breakfast. So, I dress quickly, scrub my face clean and brush my teeth. I knock back a couple of painkillers and grab a cereal bar, and soon enough I'm on the train hastily applying make-up and trying to calm the squalls in my brain and stomach. I need to get on top of things at work. What happened yesterday will be gossip for a day or two but then it will be forgotten. The important thing is to rise above it, stick my chin out and act like I don't care. Derek has been openly flouting my authority lately, no longer bothering to hide his attempts to usurp me. This morning's error only tipped the balance more in his favour, and I struggle to remain clear-headed; I must not be pushed into any corners by him.

It's not until I emerge from the Tube station that my thoughts turn to Jeff. I am astonished to find that I have hardly thought of him since waking to this nightmare. Have things fallen this far between us? I take out my phone and call him, propelled by guilt, and when he doesn't pick up, I can't tell if I feel disappointed or relieved. I listen to his voicemail recording, and then leave a message.

'Hey there. Listen, I'm so sorry again about yesterday. I understand how painful it must have been for you to see that photo. It was a stupid, reckless thing I did many years ago before I met you, and I'm sorry it's come back now to cause you hurt. I hope you'll forgive me. Call me if you get a chance.'

And then I hang up. Briefly, I imagine telling him what had happened last night, but know that it could only compound the difficulties of yesterday. And how would I attempt to explain it? That at some stage last night I passed out? That I awoke this morning in bed with our nanny? A plunge of horror goes right down through me, and it unearths something – a hard little kernel of memory: a hand on my breast, eager, probing.

Oh Jesus. It comes at me so suddenly, I have to stop in the street. Did that happen? Or am I just imagining it? The buildings around me tilt. Everything is blurry and indistinct. Memories are opaque and unreliable. They swerve through me and I push back against them, battling to regain my equilibrium, hurrying now towards the office, pulling my jacket tight around me.

I need to work, to keep busy. Work will save me. Work will stave off all these feelings of insecurity and doubt. The show is on air when I arrive, and I can hear Vic's voice piped through the speakers in the lobby as soon as I push through the doors. I take the stairs two at a time, don't even bother stopping to dump my jacket and bag at my desk, instead heading straight for the control room, ignoring the heads that bob up above the partitions as I pass, the knowing smiles, the trace of laughter that skims my progress across the office floor. *Rise above it*, I tell myself. And it's not like I haven't been the subject of whispered gossip before. I can still recall with icy clarity the trail of whispers that followed me through university in the wake of my mother's death. Back then I had Finn as my support, my protector. How crushing it is now to realize that this time he is the perpetrator of my pain.

In the control room Derek and Katie huddle alongside the sound engineer and the broadcasting coordinator, peering through the Plexiglas at Vic, who is wrapping up the segment and nodding to Anna, who is poised to read the news.

Derek gives me a sidelong look as I come in and says, 'There you are. Pick up the *Evening Standard* on your way in, did you?'

'Ha fucking ha,' I say, but I catch the glint of malice in his eye. 'Well, I'm here now. So I can jump in the chair, let you go.'

He swings around, his expression incredulous. 'I don't fucking think so.'

'Why not?'

'Because you reek of booze. Heavy night, was it? Not that anyone would blame you, after what happened yesterday.'

A rogue thought slips into my head. Her hand cupped around mine, her mouth close to my ear. 'Drink,' she kept saying, pushing the vodka to my lips.

How much did I have? The vodka, on top of the temazepam, made me bleary and confused. But to what extent? What had I allowed to happen?

A sudden lurch of bile comes up my throat, and I dip my head and swallow it down.

'You know the rules,' Derek tells me. 'No hangovers in the control room.'

I have no choice but to concede.

'Fine. I'll see you in the meeting room with the others at eleven thirty for the post-mortem. Okay?'

Not waiting for his reply, I grab my bag and push through the door. I need the loo, so I walk briskly down towards the Ladies, ignoring the glances, the glare of the fluorescent lights overhead. Once inside I check my reflection in the mirror, then run the cold tap and take a spare toothbrush out of my bag – an old habit – and give my teeth a quick going-over. I don't look too bad, considering, and after reapplying lipstick and a quick dab of concealer in the hollows beneath my eyes, I look almost human.

My nerves begin to calm. I can do this. There's a message on my phone from Jeff.

I know things are difficult. We'll talk it over at the weekend. See you tonight.

I send a reply.

Can't wait. X

Then I comb my hair and spray on some deodorant.

I am coming back to myself. The headache is abating, reason returning. There's a simple explanation for what happened. The temazepam mixed with the vodka must have hit me harder than expected. I probably crashed out in the living room, and Amy must have tried to help me up and get me to my room. No doubt she manoeuvred me as far as the kitchen, then realized she'd never get me up the stairs. It must have been at that point, weighing up the options, that she decided it was best to just dump me on to her bed to sleep it off. That would explain why we were both still fully clothed. Of course. It's the only explanation. The logic appeases me. If I hadn't been so panicked when I'd awoken because of the lateness of the hour, then I would simply have asked her and she'd have explained, thus saving myself all this unnecessary anxiety.

How ridiculous! I almost laugh aloud. I imagine myself this evening, telling Amy of the fright I had gotten waking up in her bed, imagine the two of us laughing at all the crazy notions leaping around in my imagination.

When I was a student, in the months before Finn, before my mother killed herself, I got entirely wasted one night on a bottle of Southern Comfort and lost a chunk of time. It was my nineteenth birthday and we were celebrating. The last thing that I remembered was knocking back shots with my friends in our dorm room, and after that: nothing. I woke the following morning in someone else's digs, off-campus, cream cheese was smeared over my T-shirt and there were grass stains on my white jeans. The hair on one half of my head was sopping wet. I had no idea what had happened to me. At first, I was too hung-over to be alarmed. It was only afterwards that a sense of unease came over me, at how vulnerable I had been. Later, I managed to piece the night together based on accounts from other people. How we had decided to move the party to one of the lads' flats, which involved walking across campus, and because I was so plastered I kept falling over in the grass. Back at his place, I declared myself famished, and attempted to eat toast with cream cheese, making a mess of myself. One of the girls thought it would be hilarious to pretend my parents were downstairs and wanted to see me, causing me to run to the bathroom and shove my head under the cold tap in an attempt to sober up. And so my movements were all accounted for. But I never managed to retrieve the memories myself.

All of us, back then, had our black-out stories. It was like a rite of passage. Alarming, really, when you think about it, the boastful way we would state, 'I can't even look at Southern Comfort – I got completely out of it one night on the stuff.' Or, 'Just thinking about tequila makes my stomach flip. I lost a whole night because of it.' I have friends who've woken up in strange places with strange people. One recalled coming to in a dentist's chair. These are stories from my youth that we used to laugh about and cringe at. But they were part of my youth, firmly put behind me. Or so I had thought.

And now, here I am, a grown woman, hung-over at work, trying to piece together the facts of the night before as she straightens herself out in front of the mirror. Pathetic.

I turn from my own reflection, lock myself into a cubicle and hang my bag on the back of the door.

It's clear what I need to do. I need to stop drinking and get some early nights. I need to have a frank discussion with Jeff about the problems between us, possibly raise the notion of some kind of couples' counselling. I need to set things right with Finn. And I need to tell Amy it's time for her to move on.

I lift the lid of the toilet, pull down my jeans, and it's only when I'm sitting down that I see it.

On the inside of my upper thigh. A bruise. Reddish-brown in colour, darkly veined towards the centre. I stare at it in disbelief.

Moments ago, I was thinking of my student days of carelessness, and this too is a reminder of those days, when I would wear a scarf to lectures on warm spring days to conceal the love bites of some overly amorous boy I'd copped off with the night before.

The ideas that I have been pushing away begin slowly surging forward. A love bite on my inner thigh. Not just one. As I lean in to examine myself, I find another peeking out behind it, further up. I stare at these bruises with horror and all the ideas explode in my head. Her mouth on my thigh, kissing, sucking. My insides churn and I have to put a hand out to the cubicle wall to steady myself. The tiles of the floor – grey with some kind of grit engrained – zoom and jag in my vision. Light gleams too brightly off the chrome handles of the door, the toilet-roll holder. My head is a mass of lewd horrors, and I get to my feet quickly, needing to pull my jeans up over that part of my body, as if by concealing it I can somehow erase what has happened.

I don't know how I get through the next few hours. The post-mortem is excruciating and I'm relieved when it's over. Victor pulls me aside afterwards, and having slagged me mercilessly in the meeting over my hangover and my lapse in professionalism, he lowers his voice to a rare note of softness, enquiring, 'You alright, love? You look shocking.' It's all I can do not to fall, sobbing, into his arms.

Back at my desk, I take a few drops of Rescue Remedy, then call Jeff.

'What's up?' he asks, hearing the weakness in my voice.

'Nothing. I'm just coming down with a cold or flu or something.'

'Oh dear. Have you taken anything for it?'

'Some paracetamol. Look, I know I said I'd pick you up from the airport, but I don't think I'm up to it.'

'Oh.' A note of disappointment echoes down the line.

'I'm sorry, sweetheart. I'm just wiped.'

'No, of course. Go home, have a hot bath and get to bed early, eh?'

'Yes,' I say, feeling the ache of not telling him.

I get off the phone as quickly as I can, and after answering any pressing emails, Katie and I briefly run through the next day's schedule, before I grab my things and head for the door. The effort of trying to appear normal is exhausting.

On the Tube, I take a seat, instinctively crossing my legs, and straight away I feel the pinch of discomfort along my thigh. I uncross them, and sit forward, hunched, pushing down on the anxiety that has been gathering inside me all day. I do not look at my own reflection in the window opposite. I wonder what she is doing? How will she react to my questions, my accusations? Will she leave quietly without a fuss? Will I get her out of there without Mabel noticing, before Jeff gets home? I feel sick at the thought of the confrontation, and when the train pulls into my stop, the temptation to stay sitting here and not get off is overwhelming.

As soon as I open the apartment door I am hit by the smell of cooking. Spices undercut by the sickly-sweet decaying scent of stewing meat assault my senses. I realize I haven't eaten all day. But rather than feeling ravenous, instead the prospect of food makes me nauseous.

She's in the kitchen, hunched over the hob, with her back to me. She hasn't heard me come in. Her phone is plugged into speakers and French rap fills the air. For a moment, I stand there watching her – the steady syncopated nodding of her head in time to the music as she prods at the flesh cooking in the pan. There are various clattering noises coming from Mabel's room, the soaring voice of some Disney princess lifted in song alerts me to the laptop entertaining her in there.

The pan spits, and Amy steps back, swearing under her breath. When she turns around, the heel of one hand is pressed against her eye. She catches sight of me and takes it away.

'Hey,' she says, her cheeks flushed. I can't tell if that's from the cooking or a sudden wave of awkwardness upon seeing me. She's biting down on a smile that insists on surfacing, and it makes her look younger than she is, guileless.

I almost feel embarrassed for her, so obvious is her crush. How have I been blind to it?

She turns the heat down under the meat, and begins hurriedly clearing the mess strewn over the kitchen table.

'I didn't know you'd be home this early,' she explains, gathering plastic bags of vegetables, packages of nuts and dried fruits. 'I thought I'd do something special – as a surprise. You mentioned you like Asian food and I found this great recipe for tempura, so I thought I'd give it a go.'

'Please stop that, Amy,' I say, and her voice peters out. 'You and I need to talk.'

'Okay.'

'About what happened last night.'

She looks down, blood rushing up her neck, mottling the skin. From where I'm standing, I can see that she has carefully parted and combed her hair. Underneath her apron, she's wearing a button-down top, a smart, newish-looking pair of jeans. Her usual look is unkempt, almost slovenly, but there is something neat and put-together about her now, like she has taken care with her appearance. And that is when I realize that she has dressed with care for me. She looks up and her eyes meet mine and I see they are opened with a sort of wonder. *Christ*, I think. *She's in love.* The nausea, the light-headedness, the sickening feeling of abuse – it all flees now, chased away by this revelation. She has no idea of what she's done.

'I don't remember what happened between us, Amy. Last night is a blank. All I remember is waking up in your bed this morning.'

'You left so fast. I was still asleep.'

But I remembered her turning over, and had the sense that she was only pretending to sleep.

'I need you to fill in the blanks for me. I need you to explain what happened.' I'm gripping the back of the chair for support. Part of me is crying out to sit down, but the greater part demands that I hold my ground.

'You don't remember?'

'No.'

She smiles, and reaches to touch the ends of her hair. This new girlishness – this coquettishness – seems alien and strange. It's like all her hard edges have been blurred and smudged.

'You were upset,' she says in her new soft voice. 'You needed someone to listen. To comfort you.'

'I took some medication last night – something to help me sleep. And then, with the vodka . . . Yes, I was upset. But I think you might have misconstrued . . .'

'I helped you. You needed me and I helped you.'

There it comes again – this new beatific smile of hers. An ache runs up the backs of my legs and I tighten my grip on the chair.

'Did we sleep together?' I ask, and she dips her head, made shy by the bluntness of the question. It angers me, pushes me to add, 'Did we fuck?'

The word visibly knocks her. The smile falls from her face.

'Don't call it that.'

'Did we?'

She frowns, plucks at the apron around her waist, looking down at it with an air of regret. Mulishly, she says, 'It wasn't like that.'

'Tell me then, because I have no clue what happened. Tell me what it was like.'

'Why are you testing me like this?'

'Christ, there are bruises between my legs. I have a bite-mark on my thigh! What the hell happened?'

'Don't say it like that, don't twist it —'

'Twist it?'

'You're making it sound like something smutty or dirty, when it wasn't like that at all. It was beautiful.'

She throws out the word but it's mismatched with the dark, sullen expression that has come down over her face.

'Beautiful? Oh my God.'

I'm suddenly overwhelmed. Hurrying to Mabel's bedroom door, I gently pull it closed, fearful lest my little girl walk out of her room and into this hissed confrontation. When I round back on the kitchen and come to the table, she has taken off her apron and is regarding me carefully.

'I was out of it last night, Amy. You must have seen that.'

'You were upset. You reached out to me —'

'Not in that way! What? Did you think I fancied you? That I wanted to seduce you?'

'I just —'

'You took advantage of me!'

She flashes me a look of teenage defiance, then shakes her head and looks down, mumbling something incoherent.

'What did you say?'

I wait for her response. Her eyes sweep the table furiously. She can't seem to meet my gaze. I can barely make out the words when she repeats them.

'It wasn't just me. Don't make it out to be all one-sided.'

I wait for a beat.

Finally she brings her eyes up and says, 'I know you care for me. Why are you pretending that you don't? After last night, there's no point.'

'Amy, you sexually assaulted me.'

'I . . . no. That's not how . . . not even remotely . . . no.'

Her chest is moving with the effort of all the emotion rising up inside her, tears spill over her cheeks.

'*You* reached out to *me*,' she says. 'You let me kiss you, you let me touch you. I could tell you wanted it, that you wanted me –'

'Stop it!' The images are coming at me too fast, making me nauseous.

But something has been released inside her, and she can't seem to stop.

'From that first night, I knew there was something between us. You reached out for my hand. You needed me. All I wanted was to help you. That's all I've been doing. Don't you see? We were supposed to meet that night. It was supposed to happen. You weren't happy – you needed something to fill the hole inside –'

'I was upset that night! That's all. The rest is in your head! There was no gaping void inside me waiting to be filled. I have everything I want –'

'Your marriage is a sham – anyone can see that.'

'How dare you?'

'You don't love him. You love me.'

I want to get her out. Nothing matters more than that.

'You'd better go, Amy. Pack your things and leave. Now.'

'But –'

'I said, now!'

My voice cracks on the heated note. I can't remember

the last time I felt this enraged. It's like my blood is bubbling and surging in my veins. It takes a moment for her to take it in. She just stands there in front of me, a liquid mess of tears and misery like some sulky adolescent throwing a tantrum. But she's not a teenager. She's a grown woman who has strayed way too far into my life. How have I let it come to this? I'm appalled at my own negligence. My recklessness.

She takes a deep breath, tries to gather herself. With an aura of martyrdom, she walks past me to her room. I hear the door close, and I wait. I'm aware of the tension in my shoulders, the iron grip of pressure at my temples. I pour myself a brandy and knock it back at the sink to steady myself, then fill the glass with water and knock that back too.

When she emerges from her room a few minutes later, she has her coat on and a duffel bag in one hand, a shopping bag stuffed with possessions in the other. Her face has a raw look about it from the crying, but her mouth is a grim line across her face. She takes her iPhone from the speakers, then pauses by the entrance to the kitchen and gives me a last look, as if waiting for a late reprieve, a last-minute pardon.

'Leave your keys on the hall table,' I tell her, my voice deliberately hard. No good luck, no take care. No goodbye at all.

Sadness briefly flickers across her face, but it's chased by something cold and hard.

In a small voice, she tells me, 'I'm going to make you see. I'll show you how much I love you.'

And then she flips her keys and they land on the hard

surface of the table with a small clatter that makes me flinch. I wait until I hear the firm click of the front door closing behind her, before releasing the breath that I wasn't aware I was holding. In the silence that follows, I try to compose myself. The muscles in my body begin to unclench. And even though my mind still teems with the horrors of what happened between us in the night, I feel a sweeping sense of relief, like I am reclaiming my space, taking control of my life once more. I pluck her keys from the table, feel the hard angles of them pressing against the flesh of my clenched fist.

18.

Amy

In the hallway, I hesitate, guts wrenched into a ball, like all my inner organs are clamouring up towards my mouth. I'm so fucking angry I can't think straight. A big part of me wants to turn back and hammer on that door until she opens up and then explain it to her until she sees that we love each other, that what we have goes deeper and far beyond anything either of us could ever feel for anyone else. I'm so convinced of it that I do turn back. I put my forehead to the door. Inside I can hear Mabel squealing, and Cara laughing. How could she do that? Be so cruel and disdainful with me, and then switch on her joy for her kid? Through the door, I can smell the tempura I'd been cooking, oily and heavy like thick globules of fat hanging in the air. My stomach does a kind of flip, and I back away, nauseous, pick up my bags and call the lift. But my expression reflected back at me in the elevator doors is pained and frightened and I don't want to look at myself. So I take the stairs instead.

Darkness has come on and there's a damp cold lingering beyond the brick walls of the apartment complex. Sounds of traffic zoom in the distance, and I can hear someone laughing from an open window, a can being kicked and bounced across the street. I'm walking away from the place I've called home but I've no idea of where I'm going. And it comes to me that I will always be like this. The person who's in the wrong, the person who's forced to step out into the evening with her belongings, the person who's forced to leave. My limbs are shaking like I'm cold or something, and the bleakness of my indecision seems too much to handle.

A wooden bench sits on a platform of concrete pavers, around which are various plantings of trees and bushes, prissy little round orbs of box hedging. All the weeks I've lived here, never once have I seen a person sitting here. *These people*, I think with a push of anger as I throw my weight on to the bench now, slinging my bags alongside me.

Lights are coming on in the apartments as people come home from work, set about their cosy evenings – dinner, a glass of wine, some TV before bedtime. How easily I came to accept it, to rely upon it. I badly want a drink. Never much of a smoker, I find myself itching for a cigarette now. Any kind of hit to jolt me out of this quivering uncertainty. My eyes scan the building.

A voice in my head whispers: *Where is she? Where is she?*

Two floors up, on the right side, I can make out the tall blank rectangle of the living-room window, darkness beyond. A little to the side, the neat rectangles of the kitchen window panes, illuminated from within, but there's no passing shadow, no silhouette, and my anger turns to something more muted. Sadness. Despair.

Aw, poor baby, the voice in my head says. *Sitting all alone, all broken-hearted, missing your little lady-friend.*

'Shut up,' I murmur.

But I do miss her. I miss the smell of her, the familiar

sound of her voice. I miss the certainty of her return every evening, that moment when she turned her green eyes to me. I miss the touch of her hand against mine, the sweetness of her mouth.

You miss twiddling her rosy nipples, Connie says in my head, and I hiss at her, 'Shut your fucking face, Connie.'

For weeks, her voice had disappeared from my head. I've had no need of it. But now she's back with me again, needling. The ribbon of her laughter shimmers on the night air.

And then the light in the living room snaps on and I see Jeff walk to the shelves by the fireplace to switch on the lamp. How did he slip past without my noticing? He's pausing at the window to look out and I keep myself very still, wondering if he can see me here in the shadows. Something calls his attention away and he turns back to the room. And then I see him bending down and when he straightens up, he has Mabel in his arms, swinging her around. A third figure joins them, standing a little distance away, hands on her hips. I strain in the darkness towards her, desperate to know what she's saying. I almost want to stand up and shout, wave my arms at her, so desperate am I to offer her this one last chance. A warm look, a kind word could turn this whole thing around. And then Jeff puts the child down and goes to his wife, his arms reaching for her.

I'm sitting in the darkness on this chilly bench, willing them to stop, willing him to let her go. And when he does, she comes to the window and looks down. I raise my hand.

I'm here, I want to say.

She tugs the curtains shut. And I think about them in

there, the memory of their embrace imprinted on my mind, and my thoughts unspool, imagining them sitting down to eat the meal that I prepared, then, after the kid is in bed, settling on the sofa with an open bottle of wine – the sofa where only last night she had opened herself to me, asked me to take a plunge deep into her depths – her turning to him and explaining my absence. *I had to let her go, Jeff. Her behaviour had become a bit odd – clingy. You'll never guess what she said to me.* Maybe she'll act all upset, like I'd scared her with my feelings, and he'll be suitably horrified. Or maybe they'll laugh about it, make a joke of it, turn it into a story they'll trot out for their friends over a nice dinner.

The skin on my wrist is bleeding now where I've pinched and twisted it.

Fucking callous bitch, Connie says softly.

I head into the city. I've only half a mind on where I'm going. It's getting dark and I know I should be thinking about checking into a hostel for the night but I'm still reeling from what happened. My brain churns from the effort of scrabbling around to find an excuse for her, for what she did. Street lamps have come on, orange lozenges fizz through the purple gloom, a teaming mass of tail lights on the Tottenham Court Road all blurring into a blinking red stream as I pound the pavement, barely noticing anything. How do I make her see what I see? Her vision has been clouded by duty and responsibility and shame. But we don't have to be ashamed. What we have is something pure and clean. It deserves to be celebrated, not hidden in the shadows.

For the love of God, I hear Connie say, her mocking laughter scratching inside my skull. *You sad sap.* I push down on her voice, crush it as I head underground.

I get the Tube to King's Cross, the strap of my duffel bag cutting into my shoulder as I trudge up to Attneave Street. Friday night, and the house is loud, music blaring from deep inside. I have to lean on the buzzer for a full minute before anyone comes.

'Look who's back,' Jez says when the door opens. He leans against the door jamb, legs crossed at the ankles, and stares at me unsmiling. 'Thought we'd seen the last of you.'

'Is Sean here?'

'No.'

'I need to see him. I need . . . I've got to . . . Is he –?'

'He's down the boozer.' A tilt of his chin towards the corner of the street.

'Right.'

I'm so tired, for a moment I'm not sure if I can make it as far as the pub. I'm half-thinking of asking Jez if I can sit down here in the doorway for a minute, just until I get myself together. And then I catch the way he's looking at me, his head to one side, a slight wrinkling of his nose.

'Are you alright? Has something happened?'

'No.'

'So why are you crying?'

From behind him, in the pit of the house, comes a small crash, chased by the squawk of a girl's laughter, but Jez doesn't turn to look. He's watching me bringing my hands to my face, my skin tingling to the touch, my fingers coming away wet. Like some freaky dream where the shape of it keeps changing, I can't get a handle on my emotions.

I go to turn away, and trip on the shopping bag I'd left down on the ground. The contents crash and spill out – jumpers and books, a box of junk I've no idea why I'm hanging on to, some coins spinning gleefully away from me down the slope of the pavement until they dip and plummet down the drain.

'Hey, maybe you should come in for a while,' Jez says. His eyes are steady but the alarm's there in his voice.

A door opens behind him, a billow of music and voices blows out, and I'm already backing away down the street.

'Hey!' Jez shouts after me. 'Your stuff! Amy!'

But I don't go back. I don't need that shit. Clutter keeping me slow and tethered. What does it matter, anyhow? I can still hear him shouting as I reach the end of the street and turn the corner, disappearing for good like those spinning coins.

Sean is way down the back of the pub, squeezed into a corner behind the slot machines, his arm around some girl I don't know. She has long, lank hair in a nondescript colour, the same flannel-clean skin as he has. The only mark of colour about her is the single earring dangling from her left ear – a beaded thing with a lurid blue feather at the end.

The two of them are wearing polo necks and drinking his 'n' hers beers, laughing about something that probably isn't even funny. It's all so goddamned pure and happy, it makes me want to puke. And maybe I should just walk away but I can feel the anger building inside me, so I order a Captain Morgan's and Coke at the bar and take a quick swig, the ice clanging against my teeth.

'Hey there,' I say, and I realize how breathless I sound. The girl's smile fades as they both look up at me.

'I was just passing, and Jez told me you were in here, so . . .' I smile and then swoop forward, my hand extended to her, saying, 'I'm Amy. Who are you?'

Gingerly, she takes my hand, darting Sean a little look. He says, 'What's this about, Amy? What do you want?'

'Nothing. Just wanted to know your girlfriend's name. So, what is it?'

'It's Margot.'

'Margot?' I say, beginning to giggle. It's like I can't stop laughing at her stupid name, even as the girl draws her arms back off the table, lowering her chin to her chest.

Sean gets up from his seat. 'What the fuck's got into you?' he snarls, grasping me by the elbow so hard it hurts, and drawing me away from the table where his chick is sending out sulky little glares.

'What's got into me? What about you? Cosying up to that weedy drip. Fucking love's young dream.'

'So? It's got absolutely nothing to do with you, who I see.'

'Oh, well jeez, I thought we were friends –'

'We're not friends. I haven't seen or heard from you for weeks – months, even.'

'I know. I'm sorry. There's been stuff going on. That's why I'm here. That's why I needed to see you.'

He makes a halt gesture with his hands, momentarily closing his eyes while he shakes his head. 'No. I'm done with this, Amy. I can't be the person you use whenever you feel lonely or get into trouble.'

'But –'

'I can't do it any more.'

'I wouldn't ask you unless I had nowhere else to turn.'

He chews his lip, his eyes flicking over my face.

'Please, Sean,' I say, hating myself for the wheedling tone. We're standing some way off from Margot, but I can feel her gaze pinned to us, tracking every gesture, reading something into every lean and glance. I put my hand out to gently touch his waist.

He flinches like he's been burned. 'No!' The word flies out of him. 'I'm sick of being used by you, Amy. I can't help you with your problems any more. Find someone else.'

And then he turns from me and goes back to her, and it's crazy how much this cuts me. All the time we were together, we never once sat in a pub or across from each other at a restaurant. The sum total of all our contacts took place in the confines of his house, and even then, now that I think back on it, he was always anxious to scuttle me off to his room, not wanting to hang out with me in front of the others. It comes to me now that he was ashamed of me. Like his attraction to me was something dark and shadowy, something he would disavow in the daylight. And I think again of Connie, how she was the morning after we kissed, her lips curling into a sneer of disgust, the husk in her voice, saying, 'What in hell are you talking about, Amy?' like I was crazy. Like I'd just made the whole thing up.

And I'm standing here now watching Sean squeezing back behind the little table and sitting down, her scooching in close beside him, and I feel the great screaming unfairness of it. So I go up to them one last time, ignoring the heave of angry impatience in his breath, instead focusing on her, eagerly putting my hand out again for her to shake, saying, 'Well, goodbye, Margot. It was nice meeting you.' I'm aware of how manic I sound, how wound-up and erratic my behaviour must seem.

She keeps her hands in her lap, shooting me a bitter, pitying look. People at the next table have stopped talking and are looking over.

Sean says, 'Just fuck off, would you?' his voice a rising note.

And then I reach forward, so quickly she hasn't time to react. My hand finds that single earring and I yank it down, feeling it tear through the lobe. The scream she gives is more a yelp of surprise, and then she's leaning forward, both hands going to the wound, blood streaked between her fingers.

He's still yelling at me as I whirl out the door into the night, high-pitched anger or terror in his good-boy voice. 'You're fucking crazy, d'you know that, Amy? Crazy!'

But I'm laughing now, the earring still in my hand, and Connie's laughing along inside me.

I sit in a Wetherspoon's drinking beer until midnight when they throw me out. At a Burger King near Leicester Square, I buy a coffee and make it last, scrolling through arguments on various online forums, feeding the angry hollow inside me. After an hour, I call Monica – that's how desperate I am. The phone rings three times and then cuts out, and I imagine her seeing my name flash up on the screen, the startled puff of anger it elicits before she decisively rejects the call. I don't like the way the security guard by the door is staring at me and the thought of being cut off like that makes my spirits plummet, and all of a sudden, I'm crying again – great heaving, wracking sobs that bring the woman out from behind the counter, a heavy-set, Slavic-looking woman with purple hair and a nose ring, who asks, 'You alright, miss?' But she sounds more pissed-off than concerned, so I blow my nose on a serviette, and leave.

A light rain is falling now. There's a crowd outside the Underground station, but I don't feel like going down there. I don't have the money for a cab but I need to get back to Battersea, even if it means sleeping on a park bench. I've nowhere else to go. The first car that stops is a silver Renault – one of those people carriers moms use to cart their broods to soccer matches and swimming lessons. It's not a mom, but an older man with a paunch and wire-rimmed glasses who sits up very straight behind the steering wheel.

'Used to live near Battersea myself,' he says after I've told him where I want to go. 'Had a girlfriend lived just off the Burns Road. Nice boozer near there – the Duke? The Earl? Something like that. Do you know it?'

'No.'

'Maybe it's called something else now. This would have been, what? Twenty years ago. You'd only have been a baby. American, are you?'

'Look, can we not talk? Please.'

He shoots me a swift assessing glance. There's a nip of aggression in it.

'Suit yourself.'

I should be nervous. Getting into a car with a strange

man in the middle of the night. What's he even doing, driving around alone at this hour? He's not a cabbie – I don't know what the fuck he does for a living. But I'm too tired to care, buoyed and lulled at the same time by the heat of the car, and I close my eyes and half-doze.

In the lidded darkness, the strobe of street lights echoing the shadows in my mind, I hear her voice in my head. *Amy, Amy*, I hear her call to me from the tunnel of memory, luring me back down there after her, to a night tucked deep in my past, unearthing it now like a treasure, long buried in the garden.

When I was little, sometimes I'd wake in the night to hear my mom and Elaine fighting. A voice raised in anger, a smashed plate. Their feelings made raw by one too many screwdrivers and the proximity of everyday living. When I was little, it frightened me when they fought. Sometimes I'd cry, and Connie would sit up in her bed, and say, 'Hey, wanna come over for a visit?' and I'd scoot across the room and curl in alongside her, smelling the warm fug of her breath. Later, when I was older and other things were biting in on me – a teacher who'd made fun of me in front of the class, some burning humiliation inflicted by a friend or stranger – I'd still find my solace there beside her, the steadiness of her breathing lulling me to sleep. And when I'd wake in the morning, a tangle of limbs and bedclothes, I'd feel like everything had been made new in the night.

And then Connie met Ray and moved out.

'The whole place to yourself now,' Elaine had commented, looking at the space where Connie's clothes, shoes and army of cosmetics had once been strewn, now a barren plain. All of her belongings filling another room on the other side of town, her bed shared with a Polish builder who played the saxophone and smoked rollies and promised to marry her and take her back to Krakow to meet his mother. Love's young dream. Until he threw his cellphone at her face one night and chipped a front tooth, and she walked the whole five clicks to Elaine's, crying all the way.

And there she was, back in her bed, like the year and a half had been nothing – an aberration, a blip – everything made right. I lay awake, listening to her crying, and this time I was the one who sat up and said, 'Want to come over for a visit?'

She let me hold her until she fell asleep, turning in my arms so that the back of her was spooned into me, the chamomile scent of her shampoo filling my nostrils. It seemed strange to have her there like that, and yet it felt like the clicking together of two lost pieces eventually joined. It made me breathless and peaceful at the same time. In her sleep, I felt the fullness of her breast beneath her T-shirt, filling my hand as I gently found it. The thrill of the hard little raspberry nipple grazing my palm. Excitement bore me along, until she shifted next to me, half-raised on her elbow, the rising tide of curious revulsion in her voice as she said, 'Amy? What are you doing?' I drew my hand away. She was on her feet, staring down at me, words hissed into the darkness: *sick, pervert, dyke*. I'd pushed my face into the pillow to suppress the sounds of my pleasure, and now I kept it there to bury the shame.

I felt the nausea rising as she switched on the light and dressed in a hurried huff of incredulous fury. The door banged shut behind her, and seconds later I heard the scuff of her heeled boots on the asphalt, carrying her away from the house, away from me, everything we had ever shared broken, making what we had seem smutty and cheap when I knew it was something special. Something beautiful. She would forgive Ray the chipped tooth and then she would tell him what I had done. She would tell everyone, and all the kids I'd gone to school with would know, the guys in the grocery store would know, people in bars, people at church. It was a small town. Eventually, Elaine would find out, and I just couldn't bear it.

'This alright for you?' a voice says, and my eyes snap open.

The car has stopped. Outside, a grey street, a shopfront.

The man is looking at me, waiting for something. He's turned on the little roof light, and his face looms beneath the ghostly glow of it.

'What?' I say, fear coming on me suddenly. 'What is it you want?'

His brows curl with confusion.

'Battersea. That's where you said, right?'

I fumble for the handle and almost fall on to the kerb.

'You alright?' he calls after me.

But I slam the door and his voice is cut off, and I stagger away from it into the night.

19.

Cara

We talk over the weekend, about the picture. Jeff's feelings of shock and revulsion are tempered with reason and objective thought. He understands this is not something I intended to happen, but even though he doesn't articulate the thought, even though it happened years ago, I can tell he thinks that letting myself be photographed like that shows a serious lapse in judgement.

'What I don't understand is why he would send it now?' Jeff asks, and I feel myself swallow, my mouth dry. 'What possessed him to resurrect that photograph in such a malicious way?'

I mumble something about Finn's unpredictability, feeling the rising pressure in my chest. Finn knows about Mabel. The knowledge of this hovers in the background like a device primed to explode. Perhaps now is the time to tell Jeff. A shot of fear goes through me at the thought.

'After all these years,' Jeff says. 'You'd think his vindictive gaze might have fallen on someone else by now.'

'You would think,' I agree.

On Saturday, there are two missed calls on my phone, both of them from Amy. She doesn't leave a message and I don't call her back. I am actively trying not to think about her, about what passed between us. Every time I'm brushed by a rogue memory of that night, a shudder of revulsion goes through me. The bruising on my thighs is fading, and I resist looking as much as I can, or even thinking about it. I have always been good at compartmentalizing the various aspects and episodes of my life. That night is a small dark attic room, the door to it firmly locked. Besides, I have bigger things to worry about, chief among them what I should do about Finn.

On Saturday night, Jeff and I go for dinner at Graham and Jenny's house. The food is good, and the other guests are all people we know well. The conversation around me is lively. But even though I am among friends, I cannot seem to relax and get into it. As we pass from one course to another, I replay the angry exchange with Finn over and over in my head. The words he spat at me, his eyes lit up with righteous indignation.

'You were very quiet tonight,' Jeff remarks in the taxi on the way home. 'Is anything wrong?'

How to explain to him the events that have been set in train? The creeping feeling of foreboding that has come over me?

'Just tired,' I say, offering an apologetic smile.

On Sunday the rain comes down all day. I duck out of the apartment for a couple of hours to buy a present for Jeff. It will be his birthday in a few days' time. I'm in a bookshop near the Tate Modern, searching for a book on Vanessa Bell. Jeff had mentioned an exhibition of her work in the Dulwich Picture Gallery that he'd enjoyed. I'm looking for an illustrated biography, when I get a prickling sensation, like all the nerve endings along the back of my neck are suddenly brushed awake. I turn around and feel a swish of air, the movement of a person who's just disappeared behind a bookcase. I cannot account for the sudden apprehension I feel, nor the urge I have to follow them – an urge I act upon, rounding the corner and hurrying towards the closing door.

Outside on the street, I look one way and then another. Pedestrians move in different directions – women, men, a courier on a bicycle, a mother pushing a child in a stroller – but no one I recognize. There is a figure hurrying away at the far end of the street, wearing a grey parka with the hood pulled up, but they're too distant for me to identify them, too far ahead for me to catch up.

I don't go back into the bookshop, and all the way home I mull over that grey parka – does Finn wear something like that? – and I feel apprehension inside me like the low hum of a detuned radio, barely audible but troubling nonetheless.

It stays with me. The murmur of fear. And when I come into work on Monday morning and there's a letter waiting for me in a crisp white envelope bearing the embossed insignia of the legal firm Waters and Slater, it roars to the surface. I scan the contents, baffled by the onslaught of all that the letter promises: paternity tests, litigation, custody battles, court. A tide of fear rises within me. I look at the letter in my hands and see it tremble and think to myself: *I cannot do this. I cannot cope.*

All weekend, I have been trying to convince myself that Finn's anger was just a passing reaction. That if I remain calm and wait it out, he'll get over it and move on. At the sight of this legal letter, I realize how foolish I've been, trying to kid myself. I know him better than that. I know he's not one to let things go.

I pick up the phone. After two rings, he answers.

'Can you meet with me?' I ask. 'I need to talk.'

I wait while Vic reads the letter, the tufts of his eyebrows lowered as he concentrates.

We're in his club not far from work. It's a wood-panelled affair, all leather chairs and plush carpets, with a lingering odour of cigars. I sip my coffee and look at the sheaf of papers in his hand, thinking: *Someone composed all that just for me, constructed those threats couched in legalese and then aimed them directly at me.* I'm trying to picture Finn sitting in a solicitor's office, discussing this – discussing me, my daughter – trussing up his anger and spite into a list of grievances, giving them my name, my place of work.

Vic puts down the letter, removes his glasses and breathes out heavily through his nose.

'Christ,' he says. 'He's some piece of work.' He looks up at me with his inquisitor's gaze. 'I have to ask, is it true?'

I put my cup down, answer in a small voice.

'It might be.'

'Well then, you really are in the shit,' he remarks, not unkindly. 'Does Jeff know?'

I shake my head.

'He's going to find out, you know. Now that the bloodhounds are on the case.'

Having gone through two divorces, Vic is no fan of the legal profession.

'I have to say I'm surprised,' he admits. 'I hadn't thought you'd be the type to get yourself into a scrape like this.'

'It's complicated –'

'It's always complicated.'

'Finn and I . . . it's hard to explain.'

'Try,' he urges, but his voice is kind.

'I've always been vulnerable to him,' I say. 'When my mother died, he was there. It helped take the pain away. He's always been able to do that – make me feel better.'

'Apart from when he was making you feel like shit,' he reminds me.

'We had this agreement,' I begin, tentatively, because this is something I don't tell people, 'that every year, on the anniversary of my mother's death, we would do something together. Something fun, celebratory. Life-affirming.'

'Even after you broke up?'

'No. Just this one time after we broke up. I was with Jeff by then and things were getting serious between us. There were a few problems in the relationship though – Jeff's daughter, Olivia, was making things difficult and I wasn't happy with the support I was getting from him. So when Finn rang me up and suggested we meet for the anniversary, I thought: *Fuck it. Why not?*'

'Let me guess,' Vic says. 'You met up, had too much wine, got carried away reminiscing about the good times, starlight and violins, and hey presto, you're in bed together.'

He sits back, takes a slurp of his coffee. There's no judgement in his tone, but the summation stings a little.

'You wake up the next morning,' he goes on, 'wallow in remorse for a while before putting it behind you. Then you discover you're pregnant, do the maths but persuade yourself that, in all likelihood, it's the product of your marriage bed, not this extra-marital coitus. You have the baby, don't say a word, put it from your mind. Am I right?'

I nod.

'So, then what? How did this all erupt?'

I lean on the elbow of my chair, my voice lowered.

'The night of the Shoreditch attack,' I begin, 'back in August, I was with Finn. It was my mother's anniversary, you see, and we'd met for a drink. During the course of the evening, he made various overtures. He wanted to start things up again between us. I was unhappy, Vic, at the time. I can see that now. I might have encouraged him. It was just so easy – so comfortable – being in his company again. Nothing happened. I walked away – stumbled into that terrifying night – but later . . .'

'You began an affair,' he finishes the sentence for me.

'Yes.'

I explain how when I ended it, Finn took it badly.

'I take it he's the one behind your photo shoot?' Vic enquires, and when I nod my head, he murmurs, 'Little prick,' and there's real feeling in his tone.

'What I can't figure out,' I tell him, 'is why he has become suspicious about Mabel.'

'He's only doing the maths now?'

'Mabel was born two months prematurely. Finn doesn't know that. To him, the calculations would add up differently.'

'He must have found out –'

'Yes, but how? No one else knows besides you and one other person. And she's never even met Finn.'

I drop my head in my hands. I feel suddenly tired. Exhausted. The thought of getting up and walking back to the office feels like a Herculean feat. Talking to Vic has, on the one hand, served to calm me, but on the other hand, it's made me feel even more isolated. This is my problem, and no one can help me with it.

'What am I going to do?' I ask him, staring at the swirling pattern of the carpet.

I feel his hand reach out and land on my knee.

'From where I'm sitting, you can play it one of two ways. You can lawyer up and fight back, inform the police about that little stunt he played on you last week, take your chances in court. But there are real risks involved there. It might further inflame his anger and malice. This could, after all, be an act of desperation on his part – just a way of getting your attention. So, instead, you could try reaching out to him on a personal level. Leave the lawyers out of it. Talk to him – reason with him. Save yourself the legal fees.'

I remember the scene on the street – the way he stood there jabbing his finger in the air near my face. 'You lied to me,' he hissed. 'All these years, you've been deceiving me. Depriving me of my own child.'

No matter how much I denied it, feigning indignation and astonishment, still he kept coming at me with an insistence that intimidated.

'I'm frightened,' I tell Vic, and somehow admitting it out loud seems to reinforce my fear, make it real and large. 'I don't want to lose my family.'

'You won't,' he assures me.

But deep down I know that they're just words – empty and hollow. With a growing sense of anger and helplessness, I realize that this is out of my control. I'm at Finn's mercy.

*

Back in the office, Katie meets us as we go through the swing doors.

'Cara, you're needed upstairs. Heather wants a word.'

I look at Vic.

'Maybe she's promoting you,' he suggests, then slaps me enthusiastically on the back. 'Glass half-full, eh?'

Heather is the head of the radio station, and my boss. Her involvement in the show is distant and occasional, the way I like it. She is a cool, level-headed woman, a little frosty and severe. Rarely does she seek a meeting, and never at such short notice.

I have to wait outside her office for what seems an age until she is finished on a call, and during that interval I press my thumbnail to my teeth, a nervous habit, pondering my conversation with Vic and whether I ought to brief a solicitor, how on earth I am going to break the news to Jeff.

The door opens and Heather is standing there, an expectant look on her face.

'Cara. Sorry for keeping you waiting, do come in. This won't take long,' she tells me, sitting in an armchair at a glass coffee table where a laptop lies open, and indicating to me to take a seat on the couch alongside.

Heather is a tall, slightly gangly person, made even taller by the two-inch heels she wears, the smart tailored suit.

'How are you getting on?' she asks, fixing me with her unsettling gaze.

Her face has an avian quality to it, and in the black-and-white suit she's wearing today, she looks like a magpie. For a moment, I babble on about today's show, as well as making some positive noises about what we have lined up for the week ahead. I'm conscious that I'm doing a sales pitch here, but I'm also thinking about the latest quarterly ratings figures from RAJAR, wondering if she's going to bring it up. We've suffered a slight dip, but hardly enough for my head to roll, surely? Unless there's some sort of reshuffle planned, I can't tell what this could be about.

She smiles and nods in a swift, slightly dismissive way that makes me sense she's impatient for me to finish.

And then she says, 'How have you been, yourself, Cara?'

And that's when I know this has nothing to do with the ratings or the show. This is entirely about me.

'I'm fine. Why?'

'I heard about what happened last week.'

'Oh God,' I murmur, dipping my head, before mustering my courage and looking her in the eye. 'Look, I'm sorry about that. Obviously, I'm very embarrassed that it happened, but you must understand that I had no hand in it. Someone I used to have a relationship with is lashing out at me, and has chosen public humiliation as his way of doing it.'

'I understand,' she says reasonably, but I can tell she's not finished with the subject. 'Revenge porn is happening more and more these days, unfortunately.'

The word clings to the air between us, pulsing with disapproval.

'So long as this person – your ex – doesn't make a habit of it.'

'Don't worry,' I say coolly. 'I've taken steps to address the matter. It won't happen again.'

But even as I say the words, I feel disingenuous. What

steps have I really taken, beyond confronting Finn in the street? The only thing that achieved was a legal threat in the post. And how do I know he won't pull another similar stunt? Unpredictable at the best of times, there's a dangerous edge to him when he's angry, like a cornered rat ready to spring.

Heather is giving me a look that suggests she can read my doubts. 'Are you sure about that?' she asks softly.

She rubs her palms slowly against each other, then touches the mousepad with a manicured finger and brings the laptop to life. 'I received this.'

She presses a key, and turns the screen towards me, fiddling with the volume so I can clearly hear the audio-clip. A crackling silence, and then I hear Finn's voice, saying:

What are you thinking about?

His voice sounds distant, slightly muffled, as if heard from behind a door. And then I hear my own voice, saying:

I'm thinking of a party we went to once.

'What is this?' I ask Heather.

But she is staring at the screen, concentrating.

It was in Canary Wharf, I think. A media party of some sort – I don't remember. Everyone was wasted. You especially.

I remember this conversation. In his bedroom. Even though the recording is muffled and indistinct, there is the occasional creak of the bed, the rustle of sheets.

Some of us went up to the top floor of the building and out on to the roof. It had a sort of terrace, surrounded by railings, but you weren't really supposed to go out there. One of the guys who worked in the building took us up to show us the view. Do you remember?

My brain is struggling to catch up. I'm so shocked by

the knowledge that he recorded this – a private, intimate conversation between us. And if he recorded that, then he must also have recorded our lovemaking. Dear God, has Heather heard that too? Is she playing me the full clip or just an edited version to spare my blushes?

'Please,' I say to Heather now. 'Don't play any more.'

But she doesn't turn it off. She's looking at me carefully, watching for signs on my face – of what, exactly? Recognition? Shock? Humiliation?

I know where this is going. And it's building inside me now, a sense of growing horror at what has happened, at what he's done. Still I have to sit and listen to it play, a fury ramping up inside me. I hear the tone of Finn's voice, remember the lingering desire between us as he watched me dressing, his body still sprawled naked across the sheets – and it all seems utterly foreign.

'I can't listen to any more of this,' I tell Heather, my voice harsh and clipped with emotion.

She frowns but leans forward and stops it.

'Where did you get this?' I ask. My fists are so tightly clenched in my lap that I can feel my fingernails cutting into the flesh of my palms.

'It was on a USB stick that was posted to me.'

'I don't know why he would do this,' I say, trying to sound calm. 'I don't know why he would hurt me like this.'

'Don't you?'

Anger surges upwards in my throat.

'To be quite frank, Heather, I think it's inappropriate that you're even confronting me about what was a private conversation that has nothing to do with –'

'You work here, Cara. I'm your employer. This was sent

to me, surely you don't expect me to ignore it?' Her voice has hardened, sharpness entering her tone.

'No, but –'

'Listen to me now. I know you well enough, and I know that you're a capable woman who likes to remain in control. But sometimes situations can get on top of us.' She takes a breath, considers her next statement, then says, 'There has been some talk about your behaviour recently.'

'What talk?' I demand, and I can feel my face flushing. My mind jumps instantly to Derek, that snake in the grass.

'It seems you've been behaving erratically. That you've been late for work, that you've turned up smelling of booze –'

'Oh, come on! Seriously? That only happened once.'

'Are you sure about that? Your work hours are your own affair, Cara – no one has to clock in and clock out. But you've been absent from the office a lot, lately. And yes, I know a lot of your meetings take place off-site, but still. There is a general sense that your mind has not been on the job.'

I am staring at her fiercely but I don't open my mouth. Anything I say in my defence will sound weak and pleading and false. We both know there's some truth in what she's saying.

'I heard what happened to you in August. I heard how you got caught up in that awful attack,' she says.

'I don't see how that's relevant.'

'You've been through a traumatic event. Perhaps you need to stop and take some time to consider that.'

I frown in disbelief.

'Are you suspending me?'

266

'I'm suggesting that you take some time off. A couple of weeks, perhaps. Rest, get your head together. Talk to a professional.'

She's winding up the conversation, and I'm helpless to change things.

'What about the show?' I ask, a last feeble attempt to stave off this unwanted hiatus.

'Let Derek manage it. He's hungry and arrogant. And he's been snapping at your heels for long enough. Let him have a go – see what kind of job he makes of it. My guess is he'll have a greater sense of respect for you after he's had to carry the can on his own for a while.'

Her response is sympathetic but firm, and she gets to her feet, signalling the meeting is over.

Before I leave, I ask if I can have the USB stick. I don't like the thought of it staying here, my words being replayed for whoever she might deem fit to listen. Even though she's probably made a copy already.

'No, I'm going to hang on to it, Cara,' she says crisply. Raising a hand to ward off my objection, she continues, 'It was sent to me, after all.'

'And there was really nothing with it? No note?'

She frowns and returns to her desk, picks up a small brown padded envelope, peers at it.

'Just these letters written on the flap,' she tells me. 'YCF.'

It comes over me like a second skin tightening around my own. Cold rage.

Your Closest Friend.

The words dart around my brain, lacerating every corner,

propelling me out the door. I barely hear Katie's voice calling after me as I grab my coat and bag and flee the office. I'm so caught up in this shaking fury that the next thing I remember, I'm on the Tube, holding on to the pole, resting my forehead against it, inhaling the metallic smell of it, the vibrations from the tracks travelling up into my skull.

I must have got off at Victoria and changed to the District Line, but I have no recollection of it. Later I will be shown CCTV footage of myself walking along the tiled passageway of that station – footage taken at different angles from security cameras perched high up on the walls. It is so strange, looking at that woman, her bag slung over one shoulder, walking not too slowly, not too fast, her eyes set on somewhere in the distance. From the set of her features, there's no telling what she's thinking about: what to have for dinner that night, whether to book those theatre tickets, how to handle that problem in work. I certainly don't look like I'm being propelled by rage. I don't look driven by any kind of emotion.

Records show that I tapped out my Oyster card in Parsons Green station at 16.43. Daylight would have been fading then – it was mid-November, sunset taking place shortly after four. Then I walked through the underpass and crossed the road. I remember this bit.

I am stepping out without looking both ways, and a cyclist whizzes past me in a blur of bright orange, shouting at me, 'Watch where you're going, bitch!' He is wearing sporty sunglasses that give the impression of an angry wasp glaring back at me. My heart is thumping, and it almost rouses me from my sense of purpose, shakes me awake. But instead, fatefully, I plough on.

I go past the coffee shop and the estate agents, and round the corner on to Ackmar Road. My phone starts ringing, but I don't answer it, don't even look to see who is calling. Everything is impacting on me – the hurts of the day and the weeks that have gone before this – all of it building inside me. I think of Finn and how I had loved him, and how it had all come to nothing. But then I have loved before and felt the pointlessness of it – right back to my own mother. Perhaps all love is a waste of time and energy and feelings. It feels like all my life I have loved where I shouldn't. Like I am finally beginning to see how misplaced my affections have been over the years, putting my faith in the wrong people, acting on false impulses. Perhaps the only real pure love I have is with Mabel. I cannot allow it to be threatened – I will do anything to protect it, regardless of my own personal cost.

I stand under the high arch of the portico and ring the doorbell. There's a brass knocker in the shape of a fox, and when he doesn't answer I hammer with that, so hard the door rattles in the frame. I know he's in there. I can sense it. The anger inside me is nearing a crescendo, and when he fails to answer, I find the key where I know it's hidden, and let myself in.

There's a radio playing in the kitchen. Apart from that, there are no sounds. I walk through the hallway purposefully. I don't even call out his name. Later, I will wonder why I was so silent. It's almost as if I knew what was coming.

The living room is empty, as is the kitchen, two empty mugs on the counter, coffee rings staining the marble surface, an empty bottle of whiskey. The rooms at the back of the house are dimly lit, but the front of the house is already darkened.

I don't feel afraid. I'm too full of rage to allow any other emotions in. The stairs creak underfoot, and I have a moment of unexpected calm, the sudden feeling that I can still get a handle on things. This crisis can be resolved. It won't be easy, but it will still be possible. This strange pragmatism comes to me, even as I push open the bedroom door and see him there, the metallic odour of blood rushing at me.

A small cry comes from my throat. It echoes in this empty, cavernous space.

And it is empty. For even though he's lying there in the bed in front of me, I know that he isn't really there at all. Not any more.

His body lies on the bed, naked, one leg slung over the side, his head disappearing under the pillows. Some trick of the mind makes me think I can see the rise and fall of his breathing, like he's just asleep.

I know he is not sleeping. The livid wounds across his ankles, his wrists, testify to that, the veins emptied into the mattress.

Gingerly, I remove the pillow from his head, and see his face, his eyes closed fast, a grey cast to his skin. Nausea surges, as if all my internal organs have suddenly come alive and are rushing up towards my mouth. The pillow falls to the floor. And then I do what I can't possibly explain. I turn from him, flee the room, my footfall thumping down the stairs. And then I'm outside the house, gulping in great lungfuls of air, clutching my bag to my side as I run down the little path to the street, the gate clanging behind me, and I don't stop running until I'm back on the platform, my heart hammering away in my chest, watching the oncoming train with widened eyes, as if staring into those rushing headlights will erase what I have seen.

20.

Amy

'What are you doing here?'

There is frost in the night air, and the grunt and chortle of a DHL van shifting gears and turning the corner of the street.

'I needed someone to talk to,' I begin, and watch the confusion gathering in his face. 'About Cara.'

He lets go of the door only to shove his hands into his pockets, not to let me in. Suspicion is etched into his features, emanating from the stiff pose, drawing him up to his full height, which is a good deal taller than me, seeing as how he's standing on the step. From the way he's looking at me, I can tell how dishevelled I must appear. For the past two nights, I've been sleeping on a park bench in Lavender Gardens, waking every hour or so to wander down the road and stare up at her building, hopeful of a sign.

Behind him, from somewhere in the recesses of the house, music plays – some syncopated jazz, the blare and wheedle of a trumpet.

'What about her?' he asks.

'We had a fight.'

I keep my voice flat, raise a hand to my face so he can see me wipe away the tear.

'I'm sorry to hear that,' he replies, his hands jiggling in his pockets with impatience or irritation.

'It was about you.'

'Me?' The word snaps out into the darkness. I see his breath misting on the cold air, then swiftly disappearing.

Behind me, there's a sudden interruption of laughter, two guys hurrying past sharing a joke. The echo of their voices lingers like a third party to this conversation.

'I'm sorry. I shouldn't have come here, bothering you with this. I just couldn't think where else to go.' And now the tears are really falling, effortlessly pouring out of me without my even trying.

'You'd better come in,' he says reluctantly, standing back to let me pass, but there's a look of distaste on his face and I can tell he's not happy, his evening interrupted by all this emotion.

Inside the doorway, I stand there, shoulders hunched forward, snivelling like an orphan.

He says, 'Come through,' and leads me down into the kitchen.

It's so bright in here, all the lights lit, filament bulbs burning over the island, hidden fluorescent strips back-lighting glassware in wall cupboards.

'I'll fix us both a coffee,' he says over his shoulder, fiddling with the Gaggia, which I suspect is as much of a distraction from my state as anything else. 'I'm sorry, I've nothing stronger in the house.'

I perch on one of the stools at the island, bring my bag to rest on the veined-marble top.

'Don't worry about it,' I say, opening my bag. 'I came prepared.'

When he turns around, a coffee in each hand, and sees the whiskey, something comes over him. A drawing down of his features.

'No. Not for me,' he says quietly, coming forward and putting my coffee in front of me, sipping from his while his eyes remain on the bottle.

'It's Irish,' I tell him, attempting a watery smile. 'We could have Irish coffees.'

'You go ahead.'

I unscrew the lid and pour a shot into my cup, then hold the bottle out, pointing to the label.

'Look. Writers' Tears,' I say, with a sad little hiccup of a laugh. 'Cara told me you were a writer, so I just thought . . .'

'She did?'

God, the neediness in his voice, like he can't even hide it.

'Come on,' I whisper, leaning in to give him a secret conspiratorial smile. 'Keep me company. I promise I won't tell.'

And that's all it takes. That's how easily he caves. I keep my disdain tucked away behind my smile as I tip the bottle into his cup, a generous measure.

'She let me read one of your stories.'

'Which one?'

'The one about the guy travelling home on the bus. It was lovely. Funny, but kind of moving too, you know.'

He ducks his head and shakes it, a show of false modesty. 'It feels like a million years has passed since I wrote that.' Then he says, 'I can't believe she kept those stories.'

'Well, it's not like they're on display on her coffee table,' I say frankly, and he laughs and I can feel him warming to me, loosening up. *This is working*, I think. 'But she did tell me that she always thought it a shame – that you didn't pursue your writing. That's where your real talent lay, she thought.'

He's hanging on my every word, drinking it up, and it's pathetic how easily he's buying this. Not that I'd be much better. Slavering for the smallest crumb of a compliment from her. In a way, we are the same, me and him. Survivors, shipwrecked and washed up on the shore, gasping for air, desperate for a sign of rescue. But of the two of us, only I know that we are not comrades but rivals. Only I know that my presence here tonight is not a comfort – it is a duel.

I slop some more whiskey in our cups and this time he doesn't demur.

'So, what were you fighting about?' he asks.

I make a show of sighing and seeming downcast, then I lay it on thick about how she'd confessed her true feelings to me – that she didn't love her husband; that her heart belonged to someone else.

'She didn't mention your name, but I guessed it was you,' I tell him.

'How?'

'She said it was someone from her past, someone she used to live with. "Even when we were breaking up, we still vowed to always love each other," she said.'

He stares hard into his mug, then, leaning on one elbow, he puts his hand to his head.

'Why would she say that to you and then act like . . .' He lets the words drift, and into the silence I read his exasperation, the turmoil of his thoughts and emotions. 'You know, I'd take her back, that's the crazy thing!' he laughs, suddenly animated. 'I'd take her back in a heartbeat. Even though she lied to me about my own child.'

His eyes flick in my direction, narrowing. 'But you knew that, didn't you? Lobbing your little grenade.'

My heart tightens, a jump of fear at the weight of his suspicious gaze. It's not too late for me to back out, to walk away.

In a small voice, I say, 'I thought you had a right to know.'

Still skewering me with that cool look, he says, 'I suppose you thought you were helping,' and I can't tell if he's being caustic or sincere.

Slowly, reluctantly – because it's a gamble – I reach across, put my hand over his.

'I just saw two people who should be together,' I say softly, seriously.

I wait for him to respond. Woozy from the whiskey and intimidated by my own dark purpose, my hand rests over his in clammy hesitation.

'Okay,' he says, turning his own hand so we are palm to palm. His fingers give a quick squeeze of reassurance and a thrilled shiver passes through me.

The coffee dries out, but we keep drinking. I have to be careful not to let myself get too crazy, although part of me needs it. Despite everything, I'm still frightened at the prospect of the night ahead, the rattle of nerves rubbing up against the hardness of pure resolve. It helps numb the boredom too, because he's one of those drunks that talks and talks. About himself, his past mistakes, the wrong turns taken, how things could have been different. Coulda, woulda, shoulda. Boo-fucking-hoo. I tip my whiskey back and pour more into his cup. The night's getting on and he's showing no signs of slowing. I'm waiting for the slurred voice, the lull in conversation, the sinking down into sleep. But I need it to be a deep sleep, so when he's staggering over to the stereo, squinting at Spotify until he finds that perfect jazz track that's running through his head, driving him crazy – 'What was the name of that fucking song?' he mutters – I take the opportunity to spill my powdered gift into his cup. Nothing deadly – I'm not pouring hemlock down his throat. A couple of sleeping pills to ensure I'll get the job done.

Next thing Ella Fitzgerald is in the room with us, her caramel-smooth voice warm, and he's swaying to himself by the stereo under the bright lights, smoking a cigarette, locked in some private moment of his past.

So I go over to him, and take his hand, saying, 'Come on. We gotta dance.'

And he lets me pull in close to him, fixing his arm around me, the cigarette clamped between his dry lips, and we dance with our eyes holding each other's gaze and I'm humming the song and imagining this is not his body I feel pressed against mine, nor his eyes looking at me in a new and speculative way. He takes the cigarette from his mouth and puts it to mine, and I push down on the revulsion I feel at the wetness of his spittle on the filter adhering to my lips. I barely have time to release the plume of smoke when his mouth is upon mine, desperation or greed in that kiss, sucking my tongue into his mouth.

My heart is pounding when we go upstairs. There's an urgency about him, like he wants to do this quickly before he changes his mind. Or maybe it's me who's thinking that, my own resolve wavering and stumbling. When I feel his hand like a cold claw on my breast, it takes every-thing I have not to spring back from him and flee.

But then I remind myself of my purpose – steeled by the memory of my promise. *I'll show you how much I love you.* What I'm doing here is an act of liberation. I have to remember that. I have to remember the danger he poses to us. And so I try to put my mind elsewhere while the act takes place. My body is a doll on the bed, a hollow thing that he is pawing and probing and pushing into, and as he does, it crosses my mind that this was her bed once, a place where she found pleasure and abandon. In the photograph I had stolen from his wardrobe, it was this bedhead that she reclined against, smiling, one finger pressed coyly to the corner of her mouth, both knees drawn up a little and pressed to one side; but there was nothing coy about the spread of her breasts or the light in her eyes. And as he pumps and groans above me, I know that it is not me he's fucking – it's her. The eagerness of his exertions, his rising excitement – none of it is for me. I'm just a proxy – a tem-porary stand-in. And that's when I start laughing.

'What?' he asks, still pushing into me, but he's starting to laugh too, like he's in on the joke.

I keep laughing, pausing just long enough to tell him, 'I'm going to kill you.'

And he giggles like it's a figure of speech I'm using, not a statement of intent, and besides, he's hurtling fast down the avenue of his own pleasure, no words are going to throw him off-course.

It's over quickly enough. I feel something cold and wet against my thigh as he slips out of me.

And then we're both lying on our backs, staring at the

ceiling. I can hear him panting, see the rise and fall of his chest, while I remain perfectly still and wait.

A calmness has come over the bed. It is almost time.

I lie in the semi-dark of the room and listen. I hear the creaking of floorboards expanding and contracting, the late-night twitter of a bird high up in the rafters. Downstairs, the jazz is still playing, and far outside, the low rumble of traffic. Somewhere in this city, she is waiting for me. I can feel it. And it is the knowledge of this that keeps me steady, causes me to rise carefully, not that I'm afraid of waking him, he's that far gone. Like a child, worn out from the playground, falling instantly down deep into sleep.

I don't dress yet. Instead, I tiptoe naked back downstairs to where I've dumped my bag. The blades are in a small plastic envelope, and I have taken the added precaution of packing surgical gloves which I snap on now. Creeping back up the stairs, I can't help laughing at the picture of my own self.

He is splayed naked across the bed, one arm thrown over his head. His nose whistles as he sleeps. I perch on the side of the bed and say his name. Then I reach up and take his wrist, drawing his arm down so it lies by his side. I pinch the skin on his chest hard. But he's down so deep, he doesn't stir.

Now is the moment. But I'm not afraid. I'm not charged with any emotion. This is a mercy killing. A form of euthanasia. Putting the poor bastard out of his misery. But most of all, this is my gift to her. With this act, I am saving her.

The blade is sharp and surgical. It draws easily through the skin. Blood spurts violently but he hardly stirs. Only when I cut through the arteries in his leg does he turn his head, a groan released from the floor of his chest.

It is hard to believe how calm I am, how self-possessed. I put the blade into his right hand, taking care to curl his fingers around it, like a treasure I am pressing on him, urging him to keep safe. After the initial spurts, the blood gurgles and gulps, draining steadily out of him. I pick my way carefully over the floor to the bathroom, keeping my surgical gloves on while I shower, wash my hair, sluicing the blood down the drain. By the time I am dressed he is dead. At least, that's how it appears. I don't draw close enough to check. It's more a feeling I have – the way the room holds the air: an emptiness there.

It's well past midnight when I leave the house. I am taking a chance, no matter what time of the day or night I choose. My hood pulled up, I stand in the hallway, gathering my nerve, waiting for the right moment before venturing out into the night.

The road is quiet, the only living thing I encounter as I walk away is the russet swish of a fox, disappearing over a wall in a shiver of waxen leaves.

PART THREE

21.

Cara

'Well?' he asks.

I can already feel him leaning in, the air between us shrinking.

'Don't,' I say, when I mean the opposite.

On this warm night, on the side of this street, the sounds and smells of city life impacting upon us, it feels like a negotiation is happening. A base animal instinct – reading each other's signals. I see the dilation of his pupils, the smile pulling at the corners of his mouth, read his intent in the way he won't break my gaze, pushing for a response. And in my own body, I feel my increased heartbeat, a chemical arousal happening in my bloodstream, the magnetic pull silencing the voice screaming from the rational side of my brain. Emotion holds sway. Ignoring my warning, he leans in and kisses me. A closed-mouth kiss of short enough duration, but there's nothing chaste about it. A kiss loaded with intent.

We smile at each other as he draws back from me, and then I turn from him and walk away. This is not a dismissal, and I know that he knows this. Nor is it an invitation to follow. It's part of the game.

I resist the urge to look back, walking steadily, confidently, my bag over my shoulder, one hand slipped into my jeans pocket. The zing of cocktails in my bloodstream mingles with my hormones to make a cocktail of their own. A magical elixir – it's like the years have fallen away and I'm nineteen again, willingly enslaved by an all-consuming crush.

I turn the corner on to Redchurch Street, out of his view now, but still I feel his watchful gaze, bask in it. I wonder how long I must wait until he contacts me. Will there be a text from him as I sit on the Tube, feeling the sway of the carriage taking me home? Passing The Owl and Pussycat where the punters have spilled out on to the street, perching on bar stools as they down pints, I realize I am smiling to myself, the cacophony of their happy inebriation striking a familiar chord inside me. I get my facial expression under control, and look up, and that's when I see him.

Eyes, blank and glassily malevolent. The gun in his hand.

Fight or flight. Hyperarousal. Acute stress response. Call it what you will, it amounts to the same thing. The triggering of glands in the brain, a cascade of hormones that activates responses in the autonomic nervous system. This same control mechanism, ironically, also fires into action during sexual arousal. Perhaps it was because this system had already been called into play moments earlier when I stood in the street with Finn and felt the tug of my desire, the same glands poked alive, the stream of hormones already released, that when I see the terrorist coming towards me, I neither flee nor fight. I freeze.

Screaming splits the night. There's a sound like a firecracker as the gun goes off. I watch bodies fold over on themselves, then slump to the ground. It feels as if the whole street is already in motion by the time my nervous system wakes up and I start to run. I run and I keep running, right up until the moment I feel her hand reach out and clasp my arm, hauling me back into the darkness.

Later, I learn that not everybody ran. Some people stood their ground – a few have-a-go heroes, their fight instincts outweighing all others. Those lads drinking outside the pub, their pint glasses sailing through the air in a barrage of shots. They'd picked up their bar stools and flung them at the attackers, then rushed back inside the pub to retrieve chairs, tables, more artillery.

You don't know how you'll react until you're in the situation, and I suppose I learned something about myself that night. When danger rears up, my instinct is not to stay and fight, but to run. It's evolution. The way I am wired. I'm as helpless to resist it as I am to change the way I digest food or how my pupils dilate and contract. But when I heard about those people outside the pub and how they'd fought back in the face of danger, I'd felt the tiniest nudge of shame. For all the science to explain it, my response felt cowardly. Perhaps, in the end, that is what I am. A coward.

Now, I get off the Tube at Earl's Court. My legs are shaking. I have no idea why I am here, why I have chosen this stop. Propelled by an instinct I cannot fathom, I emerge from the Underground, blinking in the street lights. I pull my coat tight around myself, and walk, head down, along the high street. I don't know this place, and yet anyone would think I'm moving purposefully, as if I am going somewhere, when really what I am doing is escaping. Fleeing. Running, even though I'm walking. My mouth is dry. It feels like there's some kind of constriction in my throat, making it impossible to swallow. In my mind, I am counting – an old habit to ward off anxiety. I count the number of steps I take. Like a child, I stare at the pavement, avoiding the cracks. I take care not to brush against strangers. These tics and habits all guard against an invasion of thoughts, of images – his body on the bed, those blood-drenched sheets.

I walk until the dryness in my mouth becomes unbearable. There's a Boots on the corner, and I go inside, pluck a bottle of still water from a refrigerated shelf, then stand in line for the cash register. I hold the water to my chest, rock back and forth a little, toe to heel, toe to heel.

'Is that everything?' the shop assistant asks me.

The bottle beeps its price, and she hits a button on the till.

'Miss?'

Her voice comes at me from a distance, like I'm not really there at all. I'm back in that bedroom, the tang of blood in my nostrils, the air cloying with death.

'Oh God,' I say, leaning forward involuntarily, my arm knocking against the display, cereal bars and packaged biscuits tumbling to the floor.

'Miss!' I hear her calling after me as I stumble out on to the street. 'Your water!'

It takes over half an hour for me to get back there. The wait for a train, the dash back along Ackmar Road. I keep thinking that I should call the police, ring for an ambulance, alert them, but another part of me thinks I should go back there first, as if needing to double-check – to make sure I didn't dream it up.

286

When I turn on to Elphiron Road, I see the fluorescent vehicles, the blue lights spinning although the sirens are turned off, and realize that I am too late. A small cluster of bystanders has formed on the pavement outside. A middle-aged man holding plastic shopping bags bulging with food, a mother jiggling a fretful toddler on her hip, an older woman in a dressing gown, one hand pressed to her mouth, are all staring at the house. I see these people but I don't approach, thoughts clattering and careening through my head: *How will I explain myself? My reasons for coming to the house, and then my erratic behaviour: fleeing the scene, failing to call the police?* Even in my shocked state, I can still see that the optics aren't good.

A uniformed officer is putting up police tape. He raises his hands and, in response to their queries, asks the bystanders to be patient and keep their distance. An unmarked car draws up – a maroon-coloured estate – and two men get out, dressed in smart suits: one grey, one biscuit-coloured. They duck under the tape and proceed to the crime scene.

Crime scene. Those words echo in my head, provoke something inside me, push me forward.

'Excuse me,' I say to the uniform.

He gives me a patient look that seems practised, well-worn, but before he can launch into his patter I cut him off.

'I need to speak to someone,' I tell him, and my voice, to my ears, sounds remarkably calm, given the tumult inside. 'I have information,' I continue, 'about the person who lives here.' And then I catch myself and add, 'The person who *lived* here.'

The patient look leaks away, curiosity or suspicion creeping in.

And then I stand and wait for what comes next, knowing I can't stop it now.

When I left the house earlier that evening, fleeing the scene of the crime, my flight instinct in full force, I left the front door wide open. In my haste to get away, I had not considered closing it carefully behind me, restoring the key to its hiding place. In fact, the key is still in my pocket when I arrive at the police station. I take it out and place it on the table in the interview room, staring at it with as much surprise as the detectives sitting opposite me.

The open door caught the attention of a neighbour across the street, I am told. She saw it from her bedroom window, and then alerted her husband who was outside in the garden. He had crossed the road to the house, rang the doorbell a few times, and when there was no response, he'd ventured inside to investigate. The police and the ambulance had arrived on the scene only moments before I returned.

All this I learn in the police station. The biscuit-coloured detective provides the information after he's brought a cup of tea into the interview room for me – plus a biscuit for the shock. It's a slightly stale custard cream. It adheres to my molars when I chew it. His name is Detective Constable Andrew Lewis. He introduces me to the female detective who's sitting to his right but her name flies past me. I'm surprised he needs to be flanked by this colleague. In my head, it should just be the two of us sitting down to talk – not exactly for an informal chat, but not this level of seriousness either. It is partly the reason why I decline a solicitor – I don't feel I need one. I am still, I suppose, at that point where I think all of this can somehow be contained. That I can come forward with my information, tell them what I know, and leave.

'Let's go through it again,' DC Lewis says, leaning his forearms on the table. 'What you told me back at the house.'

'Alright,' I say. 'I called to see Finn earlier – I think it must have been about half past four. I rang the doorbell and there was no answer. When I tried the brass knocker and there was still no response, I let myself in.'

'You had a key?' Lewis asks.

'No. But I knew where there was one hidden.'

That's when I remember the key is still in my pocket. I lean back to insert fingers into the tight jeans pocket and draw it out.

'Why did you take it with you?' Lewis asks.

'I don't know. I was shocked –'

'So you let yourself in, and then what?' the female officer prompts. Her hair is drawn off her face and held by a lozenge-shaped clip at the nape of her neck. She is young but there's a drabness to her appearance, and a sharpness in her eye that speaks of ambition. She offers me a thin smile.

I say, 'I checked the rooms downstairs. When there was no sign of him, I went up.'

'You went upstairs to the bedroom,' she clarifies.

'Yes. I saw him lying there on the bed. From where I was standing, I could see he was dead.' Then, steeling myself, I go on in a more forthright tone. 'I moved towards him – the pillow was covering his head, but I could already see his wounds, the blood on the sheets. I took the pillow away and saw his face was lifeless, and that's when I ran. I was shocked and panicked,' I say by way of explanation.

But DC Lewis isn't interested in that right now. 'Did Mr Doherty know you were calling to see him?'

'No. It was a spur-of-the-moment thing.'

'Did you often turn up at his house unannounced?'

'No. Not often.'

'How would you describe the nature of your relationship with the deceased?' This from the thin-smiling female detective.

'We were friends.'

'Good friends, I assume – if you know where he keeps his key hidden.'

'Look, it's no secret that we were once in a relationship. I knew where the key was because I lived with him there a few years ago.'

'And you remained on good terms after your relationship ended?'

'Yes. Good enough.' But the words have a hollow ring to them, and all I can think of is the rage I felt upon leaving Heather's office – was that really earlier today? – the wound of the solicitor's letter still fresh.

'So why were you calling to see him this afternoon?'

'I wanted to talk to him.'

'About what?'

She's still smiling, but it's so thin her lips have almost disappeared into a narrow line. DC Lewis has his hands clasped in front of him, patiently waiting, while I scrabble around my thoughts for an answer. I know that I should just tell them the truth about the paternity test, about our recent affair, but I'm also thinking that if I tell them the real reason, they might suspect some involvement on my part and begin poking around in things that don't matter any more, not now Finn is dead. It seems pointless to send them down this cul-de-sac and waste their time, when it's so obviously a suicide.

'He had been troubled lately. He'd been sending me odd text messages and things.'

Thin Lips visibly straightens up. DC Lewis remains still.

'What kind of text messages?' she asks.

And so, I start explaining it – how a couple of months ago, these anonymous texts began appearing in my inbox, signed YCF.

'Your Closest Friend,' I say in answer to the eyebrows raised in enquiry.

'There were other things too,' I go on, 'notes sent to work – all innocuous at first. But then they started getting nasty.'

Liar. Cheat. Bitch.

They listen without interruption.

When I tell them about the photo sent to my work colleagues, remembering the vicious manner in which he used my image, not to mention the violation of my trust, my voice begins to wobble.

'Take your time,' Lewis tells me.

I steady myself enough to relate the incident that took place this morning in Heather's office, the recording he had sent. Thin Lips takes down the details, asking for Heather's name and how she can be contacted. They will need to hear the recording and to see the picture. I take a sip of my tea. A cloudy film has formed on the surface – it breaks apart and smears the sides of the cup when my lips come into contact.

Just as it dawns on me only now how deeply they intend to delve into my personal life, so it occurs to me that I have not cried over Finn's death and that perhaps I should. Outwardly, I am calm and composed – apart from that one wobble, and that was prompted by the memory of my own violation, not a reaction to his suicide.

Suicide. The word looms in my imagination. It pulses with its own dark energy.

'These messages,' Lewis asks, 'when did you realize they were from Mr Doherty?'

I think carefully before answering:

'I must have guessed it early enough. It's the type of thing he would do. He loves practical jokes, winding people up. He often orchestrates fairly elaborate hoaxes.'

I'm still talking about Finn in the present tense. That part of my brain hasn't quite caught up with the cold reality.

'Do you have any proof that he was sending these messages?'

'Well, not exactly. But he admitted it to me –'

'When?'

'I don't know. On the street, the other day. We met . . .' I am momentarily flummoxed, trying to rein in these words as they unspool from me. 'Thursday. It was Thursday, I think.'

'Why were you meeting?'

'Because of the messages. He had just sent that picture of me to my colleagues –'

'You wanted to warn him?' Thin Lips interjects.

'I wanted it to stop.'

'Were you angry?'

'I was upset, obviously. I was hurt.'

'How did he react? Did he apologize?'

'No. He . . .'

They wait for me to go on. This room is small, window-less. The plastic seat of my chair feels hot beneath me, making the backs of my legs sweat. What had he said? I remember the confusion on his face, the snap of indignation in his denial, and it occurs to me with a watery feeling in my bowels, that that was the last time I saw him alive.

'He denied sending it. He admitted to the texts, but denied sending the photograph.'

'Could we see these texts?' Thin Lips asks.

'I deleted them.'

She frowns, jots something down on the notebook in front of her. The scratch of her pen on the page unsettles me.

'So, when you went over there this afternoon, you were going to confront Mr Doherty,' Lewis surmises.

'I wanted to sort it out between us,' I try, 'amicably.'

'You must have been pretty angry though. Under the circumstances.'

'Look,' I say, reasonably, trying to break up the tension and introduce some perspective. 'However I felt about his behaviour, I wouldn't want him to kill himself. I'm telling you all this because it points towards his deteriorating mental health. I see that now. I couldn't at the time because I was too close to it all. But now, don't you see? It all points one way. It explains his suicide.'

They stare impassively back.

'If it is suicide,' DC Lewis says.

For the first time since entering this room, I feel my chest constrict with fear.

'What do you mean?'

He shoots a look at his colleague, then shuffles his paperwork on the table.

'We'll have to wait for the pathology report and the inquest before we can deem it a suicide.'

'How long do you think this is going to take?' I ask. 'My husband will be worried. I should have been home by now.'

While not exactly exchanging glances, they seem to shift their bodies in a synchronized readjustment that suggests boredom or irritation.

'I'd like to call my husband, please,' I say, my voice tight now, genuinely worried that they won't allow it. The absurd fear creeps over me that they're going to hold me indefinitely – even though I have come of my own free will – and no one will know I'm here.

It comes to me now, as DC Thin Lips caps her pen, that I'm one of those people mentioned in the papers and in the news – a person of interest. Someone who's helping the police with their enquiries. How has this happened? How have I allowed my life to stray so far into the grey?

'Call your husband,' Lewis says, picking up his own phone as he gets to his feet. 'Tell him you'll be here for a while.'

My solicitor's name is Helen Molloy. She comes from 'a huge Irish family in Liverpool', she tells me when we meet, which makes me feel some affinity with her. Her accent is fairly neutral with only a faint flavour of that city in it. A friend of Jeff's colleague, Ingrid, she is a brisk, no-nonsense sort of person, in her belted suit and with her sharp, interrogative gaze – I feel better having her by my side, more secure in myself.

It is almost nine o'clock now, and I've had nothing to eat save the BLT that Helen thought to bring me. I'm tired and a little hollowed out by the grim monotone surroundings of the police station. Mostly I just want this all to be over so that I can go home and have a hot bath, scour away all traces of this dreadful day from my body, then swallow my one remaining temazepam – to hell with my dental work, I'll brave it unsedated – and fall way down into the deepest of sleeps. And it is to this end that I sit down to face DC Lewis and DC Kirkby (I have found out her name), prepared to answer their questions.

'Take us through what happened after you discovered the body,' DC Kirkby says.

She has her notebook in front of her, pen uncapped and in hand like an eager schoolgirl.

'I was shocked,' I begin. 'I just panicked. I realize that I should have stayed where I was, that I should have called the emergency services, but I was scared and I just wanted to erase what I had seen, so I ran out of there.'

'Where did you go?' Lewis asks.

'I went to the nearest Tube station: Parsons Green. I took the District Line as far as Earl's Court.'

'Why Earl's Court?'

'I don't know. I wasn't thinking straight. I wasn't thinking at all. It's like my brain was just closing down and I was all instinct.'

He walks me through what I did next – the high street, Boots, my reversal and subsequent journey back to Parsons Green, but there's something distracted about the way he's listening – like this isn't the part that interests him.

'Why did you panic?' he asks when I've finished.

'I told you. I was in shock. What I saw in that bedroom – it was so violent.'

'Leonard Parkes was in shock too but he didn't run.'

'Who?'

'Mr Parkes. The elderly gentleman who discovered the body,' DC Kirkby says, adding pointedly, 'after you did, of course.'

I feel pinned by her unspoken accusations – her judgement.

'We all have our own reactions,' I say, a little flint entering my voice to match hers. 'That's hardly a crime.'

'In many jurisdictions, it's against the law to leave the scene of a crime. In France, it's a criminal offence not to come to the aid of someone in mortal danger –'

'This isn't France, Detective,' Helen interjects. 'Nor, might I add, was Mr Doherty in mortal danger. He was dead when my client came upon him.'

'We only have her word for that,' Kirkby retorts snidely.

'Ignore that,' Helen instructs.

We lose the first battle. They keep me there overnight. The seriousness of the incident, coupled with the blanks in my statement, the searing error of failing to report my discovery of the body, all add up to them holding me until morning when the questioning begins again.

I've slept badly. Intimidated by my surroundings, my

thoughts crowded with the overwhelming events of the day, the struggle to find a comfortable position, imagining all the others who have slept here before me, the bodies that have tried to find comfort on this thin mattress, the eyes that have scoured these walls. How many of them were guilty? I wonder. And how many had felt the angry thump of indignation in their hearts at the injustice of their treatment – their incarceration? And at the back of all of this is the whisper: *Finn is dead.* I feel the words hissing in the ancient pipes, echoing around the old walls. And in the hours before dawn, my thoughts fixate on the slide my life has taken since the night of the Shoreditch attack. Amy flickers briefly in my mind, and I wonder where she is right now, whether she's still in London – or has she left the city for good?

They've taken away my phone, so I can't contact Jeff. I have no idea how he has reacted to this news, and part of me shrinks from imagining.

'He's fine,' Helen tells me in her brisk tone when I ask the next morning. 'Worried, naturally, but looking forward to seeing you later today.'

'Do you think they'll release me soon?' I ask.

'I expect so,' she answers, with a brief, sharp smile.

Something of my hope fades a little. I would have preferred something less speculative, more definitive. I miss my little girl – ache to feel her warm little body in my arms again. I have no idea how Jeff has explained my absence to her, and I cannot bear to think of spending another night away from her.

DC Kirkby has let her hair down today. It hangs loosely to her shoulders, and despite the hard line of the parting, it makes her look softer. Her colleague is wearing a dark-blue suit, and he carries the tangy odour of some citrusy bodywash into the room with him. Both of them look fresh, well rested, which only serves as a reminder of how worn and wrung-out with sleeplessness I am.

'I want to play something back for you,' DC Lewis tells me after the interview has formally resumed.

He fiddles with his phone for a moment – a large, clunky-looking BlackBerry – and then puts it down on the centre of the table. I think it's going to be part of yesterday's interview. Both Helen and I lean in to listen.

What are you thinking about?

It's disconcerting, hearing Finn's voice, now that he is dead. It makes me sit back suddenly, as if struck. Even when the sound of my own voice follows – *I'm thinking of a party we went to once* – still I don't lean forward to listen. Unease starts up inside me, knowing what is coming.

DC Lewis plays it in its entirety and when it gets to the part where Finn says: *I asked you to push me. Didn't I?* I close my eyes, feeling myself tipping into danger.

DC Kirkby is staring at me when I open my eyes, her face solemn and unrevealing. But there's no escaping the voices on tape, Finn asking if I was tempted to push him, my weak denial. A beat of excitement in the air, or trepidation. In the seat beside me, I can feel Helen tense.

Of course you were, he says, and it feels like judgement. He's damning me from beyond the grave.

DC Lewis swipes the audio off, then puts the phone back on the table, returning his hands to their default clasped position. I stare at the nest of his fingers.

'Why do you think he recorded this exchange?' he asks.

'I don't know.'

'And why would he send it to your boss –?'

Helen interjects, 'She can hardly be expected to account for the deceased's actions or intentions.'

'Well, she can speculate, can't she?' he says, then looks back at me.

'He was doing it to try and hurt me.'

'That's one explanation,' he acknowledges, then adds, 'or perhaps it was an insurance policy.'

'Against what?' I snap the words at him.

'When did this encounter take place?' he asks, unfazed, and instantly all hope I have of an imminent release seems to vaporize.

'A few weeks ago,' I admit, quietly, my eyes not meeting his. I slump in my chair, arms folded like a recalcitrant teenager – the polar opposite to DC Kirby's school prefect efficiency.

'When you were asked in an earlier interview to describe your relationship with Mr Doherty,' she tells me, 'you said that you were friends.'

She waits for me to answer, but I'm tired and defenceless, swamped by the futility of it all.

'It is clear from this recording that your relationship was in fact of a sexual nature,' she tells me sharply.

'It wasn't like that. Not really.'

'Then tell us – what was it like?' she asks brightly, sitting forward, all ears and eyes and antennae.

'What I said was true – we had been friends. But then, he began agitating for something more. A couple of times, I slipped.'

'You slipped.' Her tone drips with disdain.

'We saw each other – in that way – a few times over the course of a month, and then I ended it.'

'*You* ended it,' she says, to clarify.

'Yes, I ended it.'

'How did Mr Doherty take it when you ended the relationship?' DC Lewis asks in a speculative tone.

'He didn't take it well. That's when the messages became nasty.'

'The text messages.'

'That's right.'

'And the photo to your work colleagues –'

'Yes –'

'And the audio recording of the two of you in an intimate post-coital conversation sent to your boss.'

I feel a rising panic inside. The narrative he is constructing – it's like he's putting together a motive for me to have killed Finn. All along I have been so sure that I am the victim in this thing between me and Finn, but now – and this is what really frightens me – past events are being twisted to fit into a case against me.

'This man was clearly harassing you.'

'Yes,' I acknowledge quietly.

'So why didn't you report it? Why didn't you come to us?'

'I didn't want the police involved. I didn't want anyone involved. I was hoping that we could sort it out ourselves without involving any third parties.'

'So you arranged to meet him on the . . . the ninth,' he says, checking his own notes for the date. 'You met him outside Topshop on Regent Street. You asked him to cease this harassment.'

'That's right.'

'And did he?'

'No.' I stare at him. He already knows the answer to this.

'Then he sends the audio tape to your boss. You're angry, humiliated. You decide to call around to his house to confront him and then when you get there . . .'

'He was already dead,' I say, obligingly finishing the sentence.

'Convenient, wasn't it?'

'Not really, no.'

'Well, it puts an end to the harassment,' Lewis counters.

'I suppose –'

'And you don't have to worry about a paternity suit now. Not now he's dead.'

He doesn't blink. Doesn't alter his expression in any way but I can feel him alert to any changes in mine. He looks long enough to capture the fleeting astonishment that crosses my face. Then he picks up his phone again, swipes it until he finds the scanned image of a document and holds it out for me to see. It's a copy of the legal letter I was sent by Finn's solicitors. DC Lewis continues to hold the phone out patiently while Helen takes down details, and I have to suppress the urge to snatch the bloody thing from his hand and fling it at the wall.

'Not the first time you slipped, was it?' DC Kirkby asks, almost sweetly.

The pitying look she's giving me, like I'm some recidivist who can't be saved.

'I didn't kill him,' I say quietly but firmly. It's the first time I've stated it out loud – the first time those words have been uttered since I entered this room.

'Then who did?' Kirkby asks.

'Don't answer that,' Helen instructs.

I shake my head, tired of the games now.

'There must be any number of people Finn's pissed off over the years –'

'And yet you're the only one he instructed a solicitor against,' Lewis cuts me off coldly. 'So far as we can see, you're the only person he had an active and serious grievance with. You say you didn't kill him. That he was already dead when you arrived on the scene. But tell me this, Cara,' and he leans forward, eyeing me with undisguised distrust that sends a cold shiver through me, 'seeing as how you have real and pressing motive, seeing as how you have lied to us already, why on earth would we believe you?'

22

Cara

The pathologist saves me. From the police, at least.

Once the report comes back establishing the time of death as between midnight and 4 a.m., they have to let me go. I was at home during those hours. My movements for the rest of the day have been corroborated by various sources. I think of Victor and my other colleagues and how they must have reacted when questioned by the police about my whereabouts. I think of Heather handing over that USB stick. And I wonder how I will ever face them again.

A small scrum of reporters and photographers are gathered on the steps as we leave the police station, and I am appalled to find that already I am tabloid fodder. They turn en masse as we push through the double doors and hurry past, one hand up to shield my face from the intrusive glare of the lens, as Helen and I hurry to the car where Jeff is waiting behind the wheel. We tumble inside and the car roars away, out into the morning traffic.

In the back seat, Helen turns to me and instructs me as to what will happen next.

'The police have yet to come out definitively with a cause of death,' she says. 'But you are still a material witness, and until death by suicide is firmly established, the police will likely seek further information from you.'

I glance at the back of Jeff's head, try to catch his eye in the rear-view mirror, but he is focused on the traffic he is carefully negotiating. It's the first time I've seen him since this kicked off, and so far, he has not said one word beyond confirming to Helen that he will drop her back to her office. I suspect that he can feel me looking and is studiously ignoring my gaze.

Helen advises me not to leave the country without informing the police first, and to contact her immediately if and when I'm hauled in for more questioning.

'Is there anything you want to ask me? Anything you're unsure about?'

'Can they change their minds? I mean, if it turns out not to be suicide. Decide I'm a viable suspect after all?'

She makes a face. 'Highly unlikely. The time of death is pretty definitive. The report from Forensics should put you in the clear too.'

Her words should reassure me, but I can't stop thinking that perhaps it wasn't suicide. All that time I spent in police custody, I'd been so focused on defending myself and getting my story straight that it's only now the thought catches up with me that this might really be murder. Someone out there might have inflicted that violence upon Finn. But who?

'Listen,' she says kindly, as Jeff pulls the car up outside her offices, 'you've had a rough night. Go home, have a nice hot bath and a cup of tea, then get yourself into bed. Hmm?'

She squeezes my arm and I manage a smile.

I watch Helen in her high heels and pencil skirt clattering up the granite steps to the glossy black door, and I think of the question that I have not put to her:

Should I be afraid?

I haven't asked her because I know she will feel that the question has already been answered. The pathologist's report, my corroborated alibi for the time of death – as far as my solicitor is concerned I am safe from any charge. But that is not what I mean.

I know I didn't kill Finn. I know that I was not the one to wield that knife and draw it across his wrists. And even though I have no idea who did it, or why, I can't help thinking that just by happening upon that scene, I have somehow endangered myself too. It's not the fear of prosecution or prison that I was referring to – although those things scare me too – it's the fear of the knife, of the unknown assailant. The creeping feeling that the same violence might find its way to me.

We don't speak for the rest of the journey. I can sense that Jeff doesn't want to. And so I sit in the back of the car like it's a taxi, sightlessly staring out the window at the passing streets of south London until we reach our flat. Home is quiet, with a stillness that feels foreign, and when Jeff closes the door behind us, I turn to him and speak.

'I know we need to talk. You deserve an explanation but –'

'That's okay,' he cuts me off. 'You should do what Helen suggested. Have a bath, sleep . . .'

He speaks quietly and I can hear all the anxiety and fatigue in his tone as he stands by the front door, his hands in his pockets, making no attempt to take his coat off. His eyes are trained on the hall rug. Since this happened, he hasn't once looked at me. I feel the pain of that, a peculiar punishment.

'Besides,' he continues, moving to the door now, 'I have to go out. There are things I need to do.'

I don't ask him what those things are. I don't ask him anything. But just before he closes the door behind him, I say his name, and this time, he raises his eyes to me.

'I'm sorry,' I say softly.

He opens his mouth to say something, but then he drops his head, silently backing away, the door clicking shut.

We do talk, but not until much later.

In the immediate aftermath, I run a hot bath and empty half a bottle of bath oil into it, then spend a good half-hour wallowing. I cry a little, hot sobs of self-pity but also tears for Finn. Despite having seen his corpse, I still can't fully fathom the fact that he is dead, and that I will never see him again. Even in the years we were apart, he has been a constant in my life, in some shape or form. I try to imagine his last moments, the terror he must have felt, the pain, and find myself flinching at the memory of his body. All that blood. The pastiness of his skin. When I feel the guilty nudge of relief – relief that he can no longer bother me, relief that he is dead and I am not – I slide down in the bath so that my head is fully immersed under water, as if that can somehow cleanse me of these shameful thoughts.

In my bathrobe, my head wrapped in a towel, I boil the kettle to make tea. As I wait for it to come to the boil, my mind turns to that Hallowe'en day when Jeff and I took Mabel with us to view the house in Dulwich. I think of those moments in the garden with Mabel happily singing to herself as she skipped along the broken path, Jeff back inside the house making enquiries, a joyful hope blossoming in my chest at the thought that it might become our new home, a place where we could be happy. I think of those moments in the garden just before the text from Your Closest Friend, and it seems to me that was the last time I felt truly happy. If only there was some way I could burrow back in time, try to find that feeling once more.

My stomach is empty and growling, but I can't face more than a slice of buttered toast. I go through the motions of eating, and tidying the crockery away, but in my head thoughts twist and tangle, unseating any calm achieved by bathing. The slashes across his limbs, the drenched sheets. Whoever did this must have had their reasons, must have crept in during the night. Some shadowy, watchful figure. And if they were watching Finn, then do they know about his affair? Do they know me?

Another stray thought: where was Jeff when that text was sent to my phone? I know he wasn't in the garden with me and Mabel. I turn the memory over in my head: do I imagine it, or can I recall him coming out into the garden, tucking his phone into his pocket?

I'm careful not to turn the radio on, or the TV. Before I go upstairs to bed, I check the front door twice to make sure it is locked.

I sleep for hours. Pulled way down deep into a dreamless depth. When I finally emerge from it, the sky has darkened, the bedroom is full of shadows. I have that fug of confusion that comes from waking after a deep sleep during daytime hours. It's compounded by the fact that I've left my phone – which I rely on for the time as well as communication – downstairs, so I roll over to Jeff's side and check the little clock he keeps on his nightstand. I'm surprised to find it's almost nine o'clock. The entire day has passed without my noticing.

The flat feels quiet as I pull my dressing gown on over my pyjamas and pad downstairs, the quality of the air suggesting emptiness. I go to the tap and run water into a pint glass, then drink deeply. I am parched. That dry-mouthed feeling I've had since finding Finn's body has eased off but not gone away. I refill my glass, and hold it to my chest as I cross the floor to Mabel's bedroom and look inside. Her neatly made bed is empty, the lights turned off. A spill of Lego on the floor by her toy box is the only evidence of recent activity. I look at her empty bed again and feel a pang of loneliness. Jeff must have taken her away, perhaps to his sister's, and I've no doubt that he's done it with the best of intentions. But I need my daughter right now. After all I've endured over the past forty-eight hours, I have a strong and urgent desire to hold her in my arms, to smell her skin, her hair, feel the density of her flesh and the warm trickle of her laughter.

I back out of her room, closing the door, and turning to look for my bag in the hall, thinking I'll retrieve my phone and call Jeff, I stop suddenly, momentarily shocked. Jeff is sitting in one of the leather club chairs by the fireplace. A glass is balanced on one arm of the chair; it contains an amber-coloured liquid which I'm guessing is whiskey – it's a large enough measure. He seems calm and still but I can tell from the grim-faced look he is giving me that he is very angry. For a moment, I just stand there holding his gaze. The lamp on the shelf behind him is lit, but apart from that the room is in shadow. The greyish light in here makes him look old, a gauntness about his cheeks that I haven't noticed before, a watery cast to his eyes. I'm tempted to pour myself a drink to match his, but I need my wits about me, and so I take my glass of water and come forward, sitting in the chair opposite his.

'Where is Mabel?' I ask him gently, after a moment.

'She's at Laura's. I thought it best.'

'What did you tell Laura?' I can't help asking.

He says wearily, 'I told her the truth, Cara. She reads the papers, like everybody else.'

I picture his sister's horrified reaction. The scandal.

'And Mabel —?'

'She doesn't know anything,' he says curtly. 'She thinks you're away with work.'

'Good. Thank you.'

I say this sincerely but he gives a little huff of impatience, then snatches his drink from the arm of the chair and takes a swig of it.

Jeff isn't the sort to get angry. He simmers and sulks, conveys his fury through silence and stillness – an immeasurable calm. That is why it's so strange to see him physically agitated. The whiskey, the shifting in his chair: there's something caged about him, like at any moment he might spring forward.

'I didn't mean for any of this to happen,' I tell him.

'What were you doing there?' he asks, ignoring my statement, his voice rising. 'At five o'clock on a Monday afternoon, you just call around to your ex's house? Why?'

'I wanted to talk to him.'

'About what?'

All this time, I've been trying to find the right moment to tell him – waiting for an opening to appear. But now that it's upon me, I feel reluctant and unready.

'Were you having an affair with him?'

His words cut through the air between us. There is a challenge in his stare, and despite his outward composure, I can tell his temper is ready to flare.

'Not any more,' I answer quietly.

A little burst of air escapes his lips. 'I knew it,' he intones.

'It only lasted a few weeks. It meant nothing –'

'Spare me the platitudes, will you?'

'Sorry, I just – it was a stupid thing that I did. An inexcusable thing. I kept wanting to tell you about it –'

'So why didn't you?'

'Because I was afraid.'

'Of what I'd say? Of what I'd think?'

'Afraid you'd leave me.'

'And now?'

'I'm still afraid you might.'

Something occurs to me during this exchange: his lack of shock. He hardly seems surprised at all. Perhaps it's because he's had time to process the information – no doubt since my phone call from the police station yesterday evening, he's been turning different possibilities over in his mind. Still, a suspicion has been aroused within me.

'How long have you known?' I ask.

He peers down at his glass, considers this for a moment, then says, 'I've had my suspicions for a while,' before sipping from his drink.

I wait for him to go on, and when he meets my gaze, there's a challenge in his eyes.

'It was Amy, if you must know,' he states.

I feel a lurch inside – a push of betrayal.

'Amy?'

'Yes, albeit unwittingly. I was in my study one afternoon and she knocked on the door. She'd been down in the basement, doing some laundry, and a slip of paper had fallen out from the clothes. It had a phone number on it. She didn't want to throw it out, in case it was of importance to either you or me. I took it from her and called it.'

I get a sinking feeling inside.

'You can imagine my surprise when he answered.'

'What did you say to him?'

'Nothing,' he says, and there's something quiet – almost sheepish – about the way he admits it. 'I recognized his voice straight away, and the suspicion just reared up, so I put the phone down.'

I'm trying to take all this in while at the same time processing the information about the phone number. Did I write down his number? Did I slip it into a pocket? For the life of me, I cannot remember.

'I had noticed an oddness in your behaviour – a kind of withdrawal – ever since the night of the attack. But I was putting it down to some kind of shock, an unresolved trauma of some sort. But when I heard his voice, I began to wonder.'

I sit still and listen as he continues:

'All the time I was in Berlin, my mind kept coming back to that phone number. I kept telling myself that it was some sort of misunderstanding. I was driving myself crazy thinking about it, so I booked myself an early flight home one Thursday morning. I called to your office, hopeful of surprising you, but you weren't there. Some young guy you work with – David?'

'Derek.'

'He told me you regularly disappeared on a Thursday at lunchtime.'

I feel a push of anger at this – the thought of Derek deliberately stirring things up – but I don't say anything.

'No one there knew where you went,' Jeff continues. 'I knew you didn't come home – Amy told me as much. It wasn't hard to guess the rest.'

'Did you follow me?' I ask. 'Did you go to his house?'

I'm looking him in the face as I say this and I swear I see a flash of something cross his eyes.

'No, of course not,' he answers. 'I was humiliated enough without adding that to it.'

He looks away.

All the years I have known him, I have always relied upon his honesty. I have trusted him implicitly, taken him at his word without question. Now, for the first time, doubt creeps in. That look in his eyes, his denial. I realize I don't believe him.

'You say it was over between you,' he says.

'Yes.'

'So why were you at his house yesterday?'

'I needed to speak to him.'

'In person? Couldn't you ring him?'

'It was delicate.'

His eyes narrow, and a new tension comes into his shoulders. 'I'm almost afraid to ask,' he says, and there's weariness in his voice, and the faintest hint of malice.

But all of this changes when I tell him, 'It was about Mabel.'

His anger momentarily falls away, replaced by a look of surprise and naked fear. And it is this obvious fear, so quickly aroused by the mention of his little girl, that causes the first real surge of regret to go through me. Regret that I have brought this upon us, all this unhappiness. What kind of person am I that I would risk it all – my marriage, my home, our happiness – in this game of chance? All along, I have been telling myself that it's because I was unhappy, because I had made a mistake in marrying Jeff, like I was trying to convince myself that the real infidelity was giving up on Finn in the first place. I know that what I am about to tell him will break his heart, and I know too that it will break us apart. Tear our marriage asunder. Whatever happened over the past few weeks, it is nothing to the betrayal caused by that lapse in judgement on a night in August six years ago. There will be no going back, no forgiveness for what I have done. I just can't quite believe that I have been so stupid, so reckless, so blind as not to foresee the consequences.

After I have told him about the solicitor's letter, about Finn's assertion that she is his daughter, he asks in a voice barely above a whisper, 'Is she?'

'No,' I reply. But my voice is not strong, made even weaker by my next statement, 'I don't believe so.'

'You don't believe so.' He shakes his head, genuinely baffled. 'Does that mean there's a possibility she could be?'

He knows the answer already, but I nod wearily. There's no point in fighting it. No point struggling. I'm tired of all the lies, the deceit, and so I tell him in a quiet voice about my infidelity.

He is sitting on the edge of his chair, his head in his hands, taking all this in wordlessly. His glass, not quite empty, sits abandoned on the floor by his feet. From where I am sitting, I see the slump in his body, the hair thinning on the top of his head, the quietness of his hurt, and for the first time in months, I feel a wave of tender love for him, so surprising, it causes a lump to rise in my throat and I have to stop for a moment.

Jeff rises from his chair and walks past me out into the hall. He can't take any more. I understand that. I've been keeping all this unwanted information succinct and to the point, but I know that his mind must be filling in the details, all sorts of unwelcome images conjured by his imagination. I hear him clattering about in the kitchen, opening cupboards, taking things down, his anger manifesting itself in the sharpness of contact between glass and wood.

When he returns, he has the bottle of whiskey in one hand and a spare glass for me. I watch as he fills it, moved by this small gesture of compassion. It gives me hope.

He splashes whiskey into his own glass, but doesn't sit down. Instead, he walks to the window, peers out at the night sky, at the lights coming on in the apartments opposite.

'I suppose I should have a paternity test done,' he says quietly, but before I can protest, he adds, 'but I'm not going to. Mabel is mine, and I won't allow that to be corrupted by the ravings of some creep who is now, thankfully, deceased.'

His words, while softly spoken, are shot through with venom. He has every right to be resentful. Still, it sends a chill through me, the way he says it. Makes me look at him anew. How long has he been harbouring these dark feelings? Since yesterday when I phoned to tell him Finn was dead? Or did it go further back, to when he first suspected my affair?

Turning away from the window, he stands four-square on the carpet, one hand holding his drink, the other tucked into his pocket.

'Is there anything else?' he asks. 'Anything else you haven't told me?'

His shoulders are rounded and tense – I know he can't take much more of this. He is weary and heartsore and he – like me – just wants it all to be over. But when I tell him about the texts, about the solicitor's letter and audio, a change comes over him. He paces from one side of the room to the other, starts switching on lamps and drawing the curtains, a pantomime of busy domesticity that serves to highlight his pent-up vexation and rage.

'Jeff . . .' I say.

How rare it is that I address him by his Christian name. It's a match to tinder, and he swings around, gives a gesture of frustration.

'Why didn't you tell me about all this? I don't understand it! You're being harassed by this prick and you don't think to tell me?'

His voice breaks a little, and I realize that his anger is powered by hurt. He slumps down on the sofa, shakes his head from side to side, finally defeated.

'I don't feel that I know you any more,' he confesses.

'You're like a stranger to me. Your behaviour, the things you've done ... it's like you've had some kind of a breakdown.'

The word hits me with force, and I feel ashamed all of a sudden.

'Ever since that night of the terror attack, you've been acting differently. You've become secretive and closed off. And now I find out this has been going on, that you've been put in this situation — that you've been intimidated and frightened. I mean, am I so terrible that you felt you couldn't tell me? Are things really that bad between us?'

I bring my eyes up to meet his, feel my heart constrict at the open hurt on his face.

'I don't know what's happened to me,' I answer, and it feels like the truth. Ever since that night, my life has changed. That night was the start of it: when I took that tentative first step towards an affair with Finn. The same night I first met Amy. 'I can't explain it.'

He leans forward, his arms resting on his knees, and his voice when he speaks is softer, more forgiving.

'What happened that night was distressing. Is this some kind of post-traumatic stress?' He shakes his head, bewildered.

We both feel the flimsiness of his thesis. Neither of us speaks for a while.

Outside, I can hear the rumble of an aeroplane passing low overhead. I look past Jeff to the window and see lights blinking in the darkness, and judge the plane to be heading west. For a moment, I have the purest longing to be up there on that plane, to fly far from here and the troubles that have come over me of late, like a sickness.

'We were alright before that night,' he says quietly. 'We could have told each other anything then.'

Does he really think that? The words jar with me, for I know that the sarcoma that has formed over our marriage has deeper roots than that, ones pre-dating the night of the attack. But I'm too tired to raise the matter, shying away from the inevitable argument it will bring. And from the sense of deflation emanating from him as he sits on the couch staring into the middle-distance, I know he's not capable of it either.

Instead, I ask, because I need to know, 'Are you going to leave me?'

His eyes flick in my direction, alert now.

'It would be understandable if you did,' I say.

Quickly, he sits forward, his anger renewed, his voice shaking with indignation and hostility as he says, 'Sometimes I think you want me to. That you are *pushing* me to leave you. Christ!'

I am shocked by the words, even more shocked when he gets to his feet and flings his glass across the room where it clips off the marble fireplace and shatters in the hearth. For a moment, he stares at it with widened eyes, as if he can't believe he's just done that. It lasts but a moment, and then he recovers himself sufficiently to cast a look of such hostility in my direction, it makes me draw back.

'I could almost imagine,' he says in a voice so low and deadly it is nearly a snarl, 'that you'd orchestrated this whole bloody nightmare just to force me into it.'

He leaves the room, and a few seconds later the front door slams, the air still quivering with the remnants of his rage. With a shaking hand, I raise my untouched glass to my lips, but the smell of the whiskey curdles my stomach. Instead, I put it down, and then slowly cross to the fireplace where I crouch down and carefully begin picking up the pieces of shattered glass.

Helen rings two days later with an update. The police have come up with another lead – a couple of witnesses have reported seeing someone calling at Finn's house the evening before his death, and they have yet to identify the person. This should make me feel better but it doesn't. I can't help thinking that whoever hated Finn so viciously that they would kill him, might somehow be aware of my entanglement with him. She tells me that there will be a short segment about the incident on the local news next Monday. My heart constricts when she says this, fearing that they'll do a reconstruction and I'll have to sit back helplessly and watch an actress made up to look like me re-enacting my shameful actions in front of the whole nation.

It's a relief when she clarifies that it's just an appeal for information – a police officer will give the particulars, describe the event, but that's all.

For the rest of the week, I'm like a prisoner in my own home. I cannot go to work, and apart from my trips to the nursery with Mabel, I daren't leave the apartment. Jeff has taken to going out in the evenings alone, to concerts, to meet with friends, sometimes to sit in the pub alone with the paper and a pint. It's clear to both of us that he's avoiding me but I don't confront him about it. We barely speak beyond the necessary communications of everyday family life. He's tired and drawn, the pressures of the situation taking their toll, and it pains me to see it, his unspoken dismay. If only there were some way I could reach out to him, make him understand how badly I regret my actions and how much I want to find a way back to him. But part of me understands that he needs time to think this thing through for himself, resolve his own feelings before opening up to the possibility of forgiving me.

I don't tell him about the television appeal, and as it happens he is out the night it airs.

Once Mabel's asleep, I put on my pyjamas, slosh some Riesling into a large glass and park myself on the sofa with the TV on.

The presenter announces the segment, and then there is DC Lewis with his hair neatly combed, an eager but serious look on his face. He's wearing his biscuit-coloured suit and he looks handsome for a cop, the camera likes him. I'll bet his mother is beaming with pride, on the phone to all the relations. I drink from my glass and watch through narrowed eyes as he runs through the details I know already.

My phone buzzes. It's on the floor by my feet; glancing down, I see the screen light up with an incoming text.

DC Lewis has finished his appeal, and the presenter is announcing the number to call with information. The details appear in white text at the bottom of the screen. I picture a bank of telephonists in police uniform, headsets on, feverishly fielding calls while DC Kirkby struts up and down with a severe look on her face like some second-rate fascist commander in a B-movie.

My wine glass is empty. I get to my feet, retrieving my phone as I do, and I'm heading across to the fridge for a refill when I check my messages and stop.

I stare at the screen. My hand starts to shake.

No. It can't be.

My mind whirls with confusion.

I look at it again, but this is no trick of the mind. No mistake.

Happy now? YCF x

23.

Cara

The waiting room is cold. There's a sour smell, dampness in the air, and I shiver while I wait. Perhaps it's the memory of the last time I was in this police station, or maybe it's exhaustion. I haven't slept. All night, I lay awake, thinking of that text message, turning it over in my head, lining up possible suspects. A colleague I've alienated. A friend I've pissed off. Briefly, I think of Amy, her parting words to me: *I'm going to make you see. I'll show you how much I love you.* My mind flits over my work colleagues and lands on Derek. Heather's comment: *He's been snapping at your heels for long enough.* The sly look of satisfaction on his face when I was floored by that picture. There is always the possibility that it's some random nutter completely unconnected to me. But then, for some reason, the thought flits through my head that when it comes to murder, the initial suspect is always the spouse. The person closest to you.

My name is called and I look up and see DC Kirkby. She nods to me as I get up and fix the strap of my bag over my shoulder, nerves announcing themselves as she holds the door open for me. As she leads me at a clip down the corridor to the interview room, fear stirs inside me. I've come here to seek her help, but I can't escape the thought that somehow I'm walking into a trap.

It's just the two of us this time, no sign of DC Lewis. She seems put out this morning, grim-faced as I explain what happened, hand her my phone and watch as she reads the text. I wonder if she's pissed off he got the TV gig – another example of male favouritism in the workplace?

'Okay,' she says slowly, putting down the phone. 'So, why are you showing me this?'

'Why? Because I'd told you before about the texts and you didn't believe me.'

'There was no evidence of them because you'd deleted them –'

'Exactly! But now this new one has come through so you can see – I wasn't lying.'

She looks at me, perplexed.

'You claimed that Mr. Doherty was the sender of these messages.'

I nod, leaning forward. 'Look, I was wrong, okay? But I'm showing you this to prove I wasn't lying, and also to ask for your help.'

Her face flattens in understanding.

'You want me to find out who's sending this stuff to you.'

'Yes. My feeling is that they are somehow related.'

'That whoever is harassing you is responsible for the death?'

'That message was sent to me just after the piece on Finn's death aired. That can't be a coincidence, surely?'

Kirkby thinks about this for a moment, then gets to her feet.

'Back in a sec,' she tells me, taking the phone with her.

A sec turns out to be twenty minutes. I'm jiggling my crossed legs against the cold that's taken over my body.

I'm uneasy, left alone in this room. When the door opens and she walks back in, I nearly jump up with gratitude.

She puts the phone on the table and slides it over to me.

'It's unlisted,' she announces in her deadpan tone. 'A pay-as-you-go number.'

'So, you don't know who it is?'

'Afraid not.'

Despite myself, I feel the bitter taste of disappointment. I had come here hoping for answers, and instead cold water has been poured upon my hopes.

DC Kirkby sits down again. She's looking at me carefully, as if waiting.

'Is there anything else?' she asks, and there's a softness to her tone that's unexpected.

'No. I don't think so.'

'Anything else that's come to mind since you were last here, about Mr Doherty, about what you saw?'

I shake my head. 'No. Nothing.'

She sighs. I can feel the push of frustration behind it. I notice, now, that she's brought a brown paper folder with her, and she opens it, leafing through the gathered documents until she finds what she's looking for and pushes it forward for my attention.

'Ring any bells?' she asks.

I look at the picture. It's a still from CCTV footage, grainy and distant, showing a slight figure, half-turned away from the camera. A young woman or a teenage boy – it's hard to tell, as they have a hood pulled up to cover their head, and it's too far away anyway.

'I'm sorry. I don't recognize this person.'

'It's a crap shot,' Kirkby admits despondently.

'You can't even tell the gender,' I offer.

But she's quick to refute that. 'It's a woman.'

Amy's face flashes across my thoughts.

'Really?'

'Look,' she says, 'I know that you and the deceased were having a relationship, but do you know – did you ever suspect that he might be having a relationship with someone else?'

I look at her. There's something behind her eyes – something she's not telling me.

'I don't know. He might have been.' I look down at the image again, try to discern her features through the monochrome haze. Amy didn't know Finn. They never met. Besides, I can't imagine the two of them together. I discount my suspicion, realizing it doesn't stack up. 'Who is she?'

'We haven't identified her yet. Although we have samples.'

'Samples?'

'Skin, hair, bodily fluids.'

I narrow my gaze sharply and she sees it.

'Forensics found evidence of bodily fluids in Mr Doherty's bedsheets – apart from his own, of course. We think that he had sexual intercourse not long before his death.'

I am so astonished, I can only stare at her as she explains how these were checked against the blood samples I'd given them, before I was discounted. The room's dimensions alter as my thoughts surge and retreat, the image looming queasily into focus and then drifting out again.

'Are you alright?' Kirkby asks.

I grip the table.

'It's just the shock,' I say, my voice a croak.

She waits for me to recover, and when I do I reaffirm that I know nothing of any other sexual relationship Finn might have been having. It was over between us. He was free to sleep with whoever he chose. I state all this mechanically, as if reciting by rote. Then I get to my feet, suddenly anxious to be outside in the fresh air. I've spent far too long in this police station, and am eager to get away.

'If there's anything else,' Kirkby begins, and I nod.

'I'll let you know.'

'In the meantime, do yourself a favour,' she advises, her voice tired but kindly, 'block that number from your phone. They'll soon get fed up, start bothering someone else, eh?'

A heavy rain is falling as I leave the station, pedestrians with umbrellas staggering beneath the weight of them. I pull up the collar of my jacket and fold my arms over my chest, tucking my hands into my armpits, keeping my head down as I hurry to the Tube. I need to pick up groceries for dinner, as well as laundry detergent – there's a mountain of dirty clothes waiting for me at home. But I'm on edge, and keep glancing behind me as I walk from the train station. In the underpass, I have the distinct sensation that I'm being followed, but when I turn and look, there's no one there. I need to get home, lock the door behind me, sit somewhere warm and quiet where I can gather my thoughts, try to see this thing clearly. Everything has become muddy and opaque.

As I walk, I think about the person in the photo Kirkby showed me. A woman, she said – a woman Finn had slept with before his death. I try to picture him with this shadowy hooded figure. Who is she? Does she know about me? What might he have done to her to provoke such an attack?

The apartment block feels quiet. The mass exodus to offices and banks and hospitals has taken place, and it feels like I'm the only person in the building. I am barely in the door, when I hear my phone ping with an incoming text and a plunge of doubt goes through me. Despite Kirkby's advice, I have not yet blocked the number from my phone and my reason for this is, despite wanting desperately for the harassment to stop, I equally need to know who is responsible. The chances that these anonymous messages are unrelated to Finn's death seem vanishingly small, and it is for that reason alone – the crazy hope that they might inadvertently or purposefully reveal their identity – that I keep the line of communication open.

I know who it will be before I even check the message. Gut instinct. Intuition. Call it what you will.

This is between you and me. No need to get the police involved. OK? YCF x

I read it quickly, then stuff the phone back in my bag and carry it into my room – Olivia's room – where I've set myself up in exile. My heart is banging away in my chest as I slam the door behind me, the swish of chiffon scarves that hang from the back of the door billowing briefly in the draught. I try to breathe, try to focus. *How do they know?* I feel watched. A prickling of nerves races along the back of my neck, bristling over my arms and raising the hairs there. I have my eyes closed, still leaning back against the door, when I realize that my limbs are shaking. Deep in my bag, my phone pings again, and it pushes my fear to one side, stirring a sudden anger to life inside me.

'Just fuck off!' I shout, flinging my bag across the room.

The bag slams against the wardrobe door, then falls on the floor with a loud thump. This is chased by a smaller, lighter-sounding bump, as something dislodged from my bag by the impact ricochets off the floor. I can hear the slide of it along the floorboards, before it comes to rest.

I put a hand to my face, pinch the bridge of my nose. There is pain there – the start of a headache. There's para-cetamol in my bag, and wearily I push myself away from the wall, cross the room and bend to retrieve my belong-ings. The bag is zipped shut, which raises the question in my head of how something managed to escape. Not a serious question, but it's what causes me to peer beneath the bed, and then behind the chest of drawers. I see some-thing small and dark there on the floor, and reach in, drawing it out. It's a small black wedge of plastic, almost like the key fob for a car. Turning it over in the palm of my hand, I try to work out what it is – some kind of bat-tery? Some part of the bag's inner design? I have no clue.

I look behind the chest of drawers again, as if to find another component part that I have overlooked. Feeling around, my fingers alight on something card-like, sharp at the edges, and when I draw it out, I see that it is a strip of photographs, the kind you take in a passport photo booth. Two girls – teenagers – posing and pulling silly faces. At first glance, I assume it is Olivia and a friend – this is her room, after all. But then I look closer. The older girl has braces on her teeth, long auburn hair that looks carefully brushed. I examine the younger girl and it takes a moment for recognition to kick in. She looks so much younger – not just the slight pudge in her cheeks, the childish haircut, but the unadorned glee in her face as she smiles. A show of unselfconscious happiness. There is nothing guarded about this face, not like the Amy that I remember. On the back of the strip, in blue biro, the words:

Me and C, November 2004.

Connie.

Amy's account of their friendship comes back to me. The girl had had an accident, and they had lost touch. I wonder if Amy has gone back to the States to find her. Whether she has felt the urge to fall back on that friendship, to take some comfort there.

I look at the strip of photographs for just a moment before unzipping my bag and throwing it inside.

In the kitchen, I fix myself a coffee and think about calling DC Kirkby to tell her about the latest text I've received. My interview with her has left me feeling itchy for information and so I sit at the table and flip my laptop open. Thoughts of Finn's death are colonizing my mind. I open the browser and start a fresh search for details, looking to see if there are any updates in the newsfeeds, any more titbits on the tabloid sites. It's depressing and frustrating, and I know I shouldn't do it, but the urge is compulsive and I can't resist.

Deep in my bag, my phone buzzes.

I look at the bag, uncertain. After a moment's pause, I open it, check the message.

This time there is no signature. No kiss.

Let the dead rest.

And I realize, with a cold chill of fear, that whoever it is that's sending me these messages – these threats – they know exactly what I am doing. It's like they can see my actions. Instinctively, I drop the phone and turn my eyes to the laptop. At the top of my MacBook, a little eye watches me from above the screen. I stare at the dot while fear backs up inside me. *Who are you?* I think, feeling the dark heaviness of its gaze. *What do you want from me?*

It is strange, walking back into Wogan House. I've only been gone a week, but so much has happened in the intervening time to make it feel like months, a year even. I don't want to go upstairs and risk seeing my colleagues, my boss. I am still suspended, but more than that, I am not yet ready for the prurience of their gaze, the fleeting looks of curiosity, the frisson that would accompany my walk through that space, all of them wondering: *Did she do it?*

I call Mark, and tell him I am downstairs in the lobby and then I wait, the security guard giving me an odd look as I take my seat, a sort of frown, like he's not sure why I don't go up.

I don't know Mark very well. He's only been with the corporation a few months, and in that time, I've only dealt with him a couple of times, the most recent being my email humiliation. It's a long shot, asking him for help. But when he comes out of the lifts and crosses to the bank of chairs, and I see the friendliness in his face, his stride, I feel more hopeful. When he asks if I want to come up to his office, I decline, and he is gracious enough not to ask why.

I take my laptop from my bag and hand it to him.

'I think someone might be watching me,' I explain. 'I know it sounds mad, but earlier today, I was googling for information, and I got this message from an anonymous source, and . . . Well, there's no other way of saying this, but it felt like that person knew what I was doing on my laptop, at that very moment.'

Mark frowns and takes the laptop from me, flips it open.

'Do you use the webcam?'

'Not much. Skype a few times. I haven't taken any steps to disable it.'

'No real way to disable it that you can't hack around,' Mark intones. 'Best to just stick some insulating tape over it.'

He asks for my password, and I jot it down on a Post-it which he sticks to the closed lid.

'There's also this,' I venture, taking out the plastic fob. 'I've no idea if you can help me with this or not. I found it in my bag. It might be nothing.'

He takes it, turns it over, peers at the serial number engraved on one side, then closes it in his fist.

'I'll check it out.'

He stands, puts the laptop under his arm and asks for my number.

'I'll give you a call later,' he tells me. Then, putting his phone in his shirt pocket along with the black fob I've given him, he shoots me a smile that is oddly reassuring. It carries me on an unexpected wave of hope out into the damp afternoon.

*

I feel better now that I'm doing something. Restive from days of being cooped up, it feels good to be proactive. Both my conversation with Mark and my interview with DC Kirkby combine to create the impression in my mind that things are beginning to swing in my favour. There's a lift in my step now as I hurry to the nursery to collect Mabel, and when we get home I pull out the Magimix and we spend a happy afternoon baking brownies and fairy cakes before she curls up on the couch to watch *Big Hero 6* while I clean up the kitchen and get to work on dinner.

'This is unexpected,' Jeff remarks that night, not unkindly, when we sit down to confit of duck and chips, a bottle of Sancerre. I have even lit candles in a gesture of optimism.

It's a small reciprocation – this comment of his – but I am grateful for it. Taken with this new energy, I am determined to turn things around between us. A fighting spirit has been reawakened within me, like I've only just shaken off this stupor I've been in since finding Finn's body.

We finish the Sancerre after Mabel goes to bed. Our conversation steers clear of recent difficult events, instead focusing on the imminent house move, a topic we have both been circling, reluctant to land on, but now, in the spirit of optimism, we start discussing ideas on redecorating once we've moved in, our talk fuelled by hopefulness for once, rather than wariness or distrust.

It's a surprise to both of us – this lifting of hostilities. We're not quite back in those early heady days when I was greedy for his company, longing for each exchange to go on and on. But still, it's a start. And somehow or other, instead of retiring to Olivia's room as I've done every night for the past week, I follow him upstairs where we lie together, not speaking, not touching. But there's comfort in knowing that he has forgiven me enough to allow my return to his side in the marital bed. For now, that is enough.

I wake the next morning to the smell of coffee brewing, the sound of eggs spitting in the pan. Stretching luxuriously, I see the grainy light creeping through the early-morning sky, and feel a wave of joy. We have turned a corner. A night of good sleep has awoken a sense of optimism within me. For the first time since this whole nightmare began, I believe that Finn's death can be solved, and that these hateful little text messages will peter out. The past few weeks can be put behind us and Jeff and I will find our way back to what we once shared.

Sitting up now, I hear his footfall on the stairs, and seconds later, he comes in bearing a breakfast tray and a smile.

'Thought you could do with a lie-in,' he says, leaning forward to place the tray down on my lap.

He is already dressed, I note, and Mabel trails in behind him in her uniform, hair inexpertly done in plaits.

'I'm taking her to school,' he says.

'Thank you,' I tell him, my voice soft, and I reach up and draw his face towards mine. Our lips meet and I hold him there, drawing out the kiss, feeling my own longing mingling with gratitude, and I hope that it conveys how much he means to me and how badly I want to make things up to him.

He draws back and looks at me, and we both laugh a little, made shy by the sudden strength of feeling between us.

'What?' Mabel asks, feeling left out of the joke.

'Nothing, sweetheart,' I tell her, and it feels like a perfect moment, the warmth and closeness I feel for both of them.

'I'm sorry,' I tell him, and it seems from the way his eyes pass over my face that this time he accepts it. He reaches forward and kisses me again, and I feel forgiveness in that kiss.

Then, remembering, he retrieves my iPhone from his back pocket as he straightens up, saying, 'You missed a call. Here.'

I listen to them as they gather their belongings and depart, and then there is silence, a silence that reverberates with the ghosts of their happy voices, and echoes my own inner calm.

I take a sip of tea and look at the missed call. It's a number I don't recognize. When I listen to the voicemail message, it's Mark's voice I hear.

He answers on the second ring.

'I'm sorry I didn't call you yesterday –' he begins.

Straight away I cut in, 'No, look, I'm the one who's sorry. I don't know what came over me yesterday. I feel kind of stupid about it now.' And it's true, I do feel foolish. Looking back on my behaviour of the previous day, it seems paranoid, those outlandish claims. 'I'm so sorry for wasting your time –'

But he interrupts me. 'Hang on a second. Look, I know you were worried about the webcam, but there's something else. I found something. A software program running in the background.'

'What kind of program?'

333

'It's called Zlob or Zlob Trojan. It's a type of spyware that reports information back to a control server.'

I sit up straight. 'Spyware?'

'Right. The information it sends back to the server includes search history, websites visited, even keystrokes.'

'I don't understand – how did this get on my laptop?'

'That's the thing. Someone must have downloaded it on to your laptop.'

A cold thump in my chest. I put down my tea, push the tray aside.

'How long have you had the laptop?' Mark asks.

'I don't know. Three years, maybe.'

'Did anyone own it before you?'

'No. It was brand new. It was a present from my husband . . .' My words trail off.

'I can wipe the software for you,' Mark explains. 'In fact, I'd recommend wiping everything and then reinstalling whatever applications you need, and starting afresh.'

I'm barely listening, too caught up in the dark tangle of my thoughts.

'But the thing is, Cara,' he says, 'that plastic key you gave me? I checked it out. It's a voice-activated audio recorder.'

'A what?'

'A bug. You can buy them from any surveillance shop or website, even on Amazon. They record and store audio which transfers to a computer. This one is battery operated, so someone must have had access to it, in order to recharge it . . .' He pauses, then asks, 'Are you still there?'

'I'm here,' I say, my voice low and calm, my thoughts slowing right down, homing in on my suspicion.

'You say you found this in your bag?' he asks, and when

I say yes, he makes a noise like a sharp release of breath. 'I don't mean to alarm you,' he goes on, not realizing the alarm is right there inside me, screaming like a siren in my head. 'But the spyware and this audio device – these aren't remote-access items installed by some hostile government in a scattergun approach. This is targeted and personal and would require physical access to install and to hide. Do you understand what I'm saying?'

I make a sound of acknowledgement but he doesn't hear it.

'Someone close to you has done this,' he tells me. 'Someone near you, someone you trust, is spying on you.'

24.

Cara

Jeff closes the door to his study and comes into the kitchen shortly after eleven. I am at the sink, rinsing out the milk frother in anticipation. He is breaking for coffee. I know his routine well enough, even if there are other things I don't know.

'Good news,' he announces, crossing the room and joining me at the sink where he pushes up his sleeves and takes over the hot tap, rinsing his hands. 'The estate agent just rang to confirm. We get the keys next week.'

I look at the cords of his veins rising along his fore-arms.

'Oh,' I say, and he glances across. The lack of any real feeling in my voice alerts him.

'Wednesday,' he goes on. 'Aren't you excited?'

'Of course.'

I dry the frother, return it to its stand, then cross to the fridge to get the milk.

'I've contacted a few different movers for estimates. One of them came back and said they could fit us in next week. It's more expensive than the others but it's worth it, don't you think?'

'I'm surprised you were able to get anyone to move us at such short notice.' I'm careful to keep my voice neutral, my movements steady as I insert a pod into the Nespresso machine, turn it on.

'Just lucky, I guess.'

I can hear him opening the cupboard where we keep the treats and rummaging for biscuits. I keep my back turned, my attention trained on the coffee filling the cup. I don't want him to see my face, the furious calculations going on inside my head.

'We'll need to get a move on with the packing,' he tells me.

I hand him his coffee, then turn back to release the used pod from the machine and insert a new one.

'I've ordered some boxes. Do you think you could take care of most of it? I'll help of course,' he adds quickly, no doubt reading the stiffening in my back as annoyance. 'It's just that I've to head back to Berlin to do the handover. Do you think you could manage on your own?'

I take my coffee from the machine, turn and lean back against the counter. I try to feel the reassuring press of the wooden surface against my lower back, the warmth of the mug in my hands. Some part of me strains to find again the warmth and affection of this morning, but I can't. A cold film of ice has formed over my heart after hearing Mark's words of warning.

'Sure,' I say.

'Great.'

'But you'll have to give me a phone number for the company,' I say casually. I take a sip of my coffee, then add, 'I hate sending emails with my phone, and there's something up with my laptop. I'm having someone in the IT department at work take a look at it for me.'

I'm watching him now, trying to gauge his reaction.

'Oh? Yes, no problem. I'll text you the details so you'll have them on your phone.'

'You didn't notice anything wrong with my laptop?' I intended to be subtle about asking, but the knot of nerves in my stomach causes the words to be blurted out somehow. I watch him carefully, catch the brief narrowing of his eyes, the ghost of a frown crossing his brow.

'No-o-o.' He draws the word out slowly, questioningly.

I say quickly, 'It's just I thought you used it a few weeks ago. When you were booking flights.'

'That's right.' The guarded look remains on his face, as he tells me, 'I didn't notice anything, though. Can it be fixed?'

'I hope so.'

'Well. Good.'

He pops a biscuit whole into his mouth, and stands there for a moment, chewing. Neither of us speak. He swallows and looks up at me with a brightening glance.

'I'm getting excited about it now – the new house. The new *old* house,' he corrects himself with amusement.

And then he crosses the kitchen towards me and, still holding his mug in one hand, he wraps his free arm around me and draws me into an embrace. I am so shocked by this sudden display of affection that I can't react. The proximity of his flesh, the musky smell of his aftershave, the slightly gritty sweep of his cheek against mine, all feel like an assault on my senses. Slowly, tentatively, my free arm snakes around his back, so that I am returning the hug, barely.

'It's going to be good for us,' he tells me, words said softly into my ear. 'I can feel it.'

And then he draws back and for a horrified instant, I'm

sure he's going to kiss me. But he just smiles and turns, taking his coffee with him.

A few seconds later, the door to his study closes. The breath slowly releases from my lungs. I throw the dregs of my coffee down the plughole, and lean against the sink.

He is in the flat all the time. When I return from the school run, he is already at his desk, tying up loose ends before he goes to Berlin, before the move. I busy myself with packing, attempting ruthlessness when it comes to throwing things out, but it's hard. My brain is preoccupied, skittering over the past few weeks, parsing previous conversations for evidence, some hidden clue, scouring for a memory that will reveal his culpability.

One thing keeps surfacing. Our conversation after my night in the police station. When he told me he wouldn't countenance a paternity test.

Mabel is mine, and I won't allow that to be corrupted by the ravings of some creep who is now, thankfully, deceased.

The way he had spoken those words – there was acid in his tone, a cold poison I had not heard before.

As I work through the contents of these rooms with bubble wrap and tape, I think of the text messages I have received since Finn's death. I am desperately trying to remember where Jeff was when each text came through. All that time, he knew about the affair and didn't tell me. Suspicion worms through my brain like a virus. For I cannot remember an occasion when he was there with me, blameless, innocent.

When did it start, this feeling of distrust? Part of me despises myself for the suspicions creeping around my mind, but I cannot seem to escape them. I try to recall if the distrust was there, the night I went out and got caught up in an act of terrorism. The things I told Amy – were they fuelled by that same distrust? I know that when I married him, I believed I could tell him anything. I just can't be sure when this rot set in.

I wrap and pack and label and sort, going through the motions mechanically. I am, I suppose, grateful for a distraction, an occupation. But the one thing I cannot do is imagine unwrapping these things in our new home. I cannot picture myself in that house, finding new places for our belongings, hanging pictures, arranging furniture, choosing paint colours. I cannot imagine anything normal happening between us. I cannot imagine living with him under the shadow of this growing distrust.

It is Sunday night. I am in bed before he is. I lie on my side with the duvet pulled up to my chin and my eyes closed, listening to him moving from wardrobe to bathroom and back again. He is packing his bag for his final journey to Berlin before finishing up on the project. I have been counting down the days, and it has been difficult playing at normality, trying to suppress my desire for his absence.

He zips up his suitcase and rolls it over to the top of the stairs. A minute later, I feel the mattress sag beneath his weight as he draws back the covers and climbs into bed next to me. The light goes off and he lies still and sighs. Silence enters the space around us. He seems to be waiting. He knows I am not asleep.

'Hey,' he says, half-whispering. 'Has Olivia been in touch?'

'No.' I don't elaborate.

He's well aware of his daughter's continuing sulk with me, no doubt exacerbated by my recent brush with notoriety.

'I'll email her,' he says in a mollifying tone, as if trying to make up for all those occasions he took her side over mine. 'Tell her if she hasn't come for her stuff by the time I'm back from Berlin, we're throwing it out.'

'Okay.'

He's half-turned to me – I've got my back to him but I can feel him watching me. It's weeks since we've had sex, and since the night of my confession we have hardly had any physical contact at all. This lacuna in our relationship becomes amplified now in the dark and silence of our bedroom, his departure the next morning pressing the matter.

'Did you get your laptop back?' he asks.

My eyes open. It was said so casually, but I feel how loaded the question is.

'No. Not yet.' I am whispering too. I can hear the blood in my ears pounding into the pillow.

'We'll have to FaceTime through your phone, then,' he says softly. 'While I'm away.'

And then I feel his hand on my hip. It sits there, poised for my reaction. In my head, I am scrambling for a response. He is my husband. We have a child together – a life. His hand on my hip is moving slowly now, tracing a line up into the dip of my waist, ascending now to my ribcage. This tentative approach of his is something I should be welcoming. After the dreadful wound I have inflicted with my infidelity, I should be rising to his touch – I should be spinning around and flattening my lips against his, thinking: *Thank God! Thank God, he forgives me!* But all I can think of is the bugging device. The spyware on my laptop. The suspicion has jumped to life inside me – my husband is spying on me.

His hand moves down to find the hem of my T-shirt, and then I feel his touch directly on my skin, stroking my belly, his body moving in so close that I can feel the brush of his erection against my thigh, and a wave of anxiety surges up through me.

'I'm sorry,' I say, my voice a mumble that masks my panic.

He pauses, his hand suspended somewhere near my breast.

'What is it?' he asks, and I half-turn my head, enough so I can see his face caught in the meagre moonlight thrown through the gap in the curtains.

'I'm just so tired. All that packing.'

It's a pathetic excuse – nowhere near enough to explain my rebuff of him, not now, after all I've done. He waits, neither of us moving, and I can feel the cogs of his brain working, confusion and suspicion dancing inside his head. His mouth is open as if to say something, but I can see his hesitation hardening into withdrawal. He moves his hand away, retreats to his side of the bed. Disappointment rises from him like a bad odour, the tension thickening the air. Of course, I could be wrong to suspect him, and that bothers me too. A big part of me hates myself right now.

'I'm sorry, Jeff.'

'That's okay,' he says, gamely mustering a tone of nonchalance.

He turns over so that we lie with our backs to each

other, both of us mulling over our own troubled thoughts, a dark unseen river of distrust and suspicion running between us, bisecting our bed.

Jeff leaves the next morning shortly after dropping Mabel at school. I don't offer to walk him to the Tube, even though I have nothing better to do. He pecks me on the lips, the strain of his hurt and disappointment from the previous night tacit within that dismissive goodbye kiss. And then the apartment door closes and I hear, from beyond it, the ping of the elevator, followed by the gentle whoosh of the doors closing. Only then do I breathe a heavy sigh of relief.

Peace comes over me, even though it's only temporary. The blessing of silence, that sense of finally being alone. I stand here, breathing it in, feeling the tightness in my temples begin to abate, and I think: *Now I can do it*. Now I can achieve some clarity, properly investigate my suspicions.

Most of the contents of our sitting room have been packed into boxes – bookshelves denuded, walls laid bare. Mabel's toys and clothes have been edited back to a few chosen gems. In our bedroom, we have emptied our wardrobes of those clothes we don't often wear; the kitchen has been hulled to the bare essentials. The only rooms that remain as yet untouched are Olivia's bedroom and Jeff's study.

I pause at the entrance and stare at his desk. An old partners' desk anchoring the rest of the room to it, a quiet shambles of paperwork, a few towers of books, a shelf of potted plants all lush and green and well tended. A patriarchal space, some might call it – the desk, the masculine palate, the hushed, cloistered atmosphere. But it has been part of our deal, this space, an unwritten clause in our marriage contract. He has taken on the role of principal carer, electing to stay at home, and this space has been his retreat. Somewhere the continuum of his work can endure, even at a low level during the early hectic years of parenting. And now it is flourishing again. This contract in Berlin has given rise to a new vigour within him, and it has caused him to spend increasing amounts of time in this room.

It's there, at the front of my mind, the pulse of suspicion, pushing me further into the room. I sit at the chair, swish gently from side to side for a moment, before I lean forward and turn on his computer. I look briefly through a stack of opened mail while I wait for the computer to power up. Correctly guessing his password – Mabel2012 – I gain access and double-click on the Internet icon. I search the browser history, not really sure what it is I hope to find. When I type 'spyware' into the search engine it throws up hits before I've even typed past *spy*.

I sit back for a moment, chewing my lip.

Next, I click on Google Calendar, trawling back through dates and times, trying to mentally match up any gaps and spaces with the occasions when I received a text over the past few weeks. When I track down the morning of 13th November – the morning Finn was murdered – there's a blank in the diary. I know Jeff flew in from Berlin at the weekend but I cannot for the life of me remember when.

Next, I begin looking through the drawers, not sure what it is that I hope to find. Or what I fear I'll discover. The top drawer contains stationery, as well as some opened letters, bills mainly. The second drawer yields more of the same. In the bottom drawer, I come across photographs of Jeff and Claire together. Albums that chart the progress of their lives from the initial meeting at university, right through their courtship to marriage on the lawn behind Claire's family home in Kent – pictures of a smiling, youthful bride and groom caught in the eternal sunshine of that day. There's something about the hopefulness of their expressions that pulls at my heart, neither of them knowing the pain of illness and death that was to come far too soon.

I put the album back in the drawer, heaviness bearing down on my conscience. I can't help feeling sad. For the past few days I have eyed my husband with suspicion, thinking the very worst of him, believing him to be capable of spying on me. Believing him to be capable of far, far worse. I rest my elbows on the desk and close my eyes, tiredness washing over me in a heavy wave. When I open them again, they fall on the corner of a scrap of paper half-hidden beneath the base of the lamp. Instinctively, my fingers reach out.

A phone number. My eyes pass over the digits scribbled on the small white slip. Instantly, it calls to mind Jeff's words: *She'd been down in the basement, doing some laundry, and a slip of paper had fallen out from the clothes. It had a phone number on it.*

Suspicion stirs again, but this time it's different. I take out my own phone, carefully type in the digits. No sooner have I typed in the last number, then those three familiar letters appear. My hand is clammy as I press 'call' and put it to my ear.

It rings. The pain is back in my temples as I wait.

It rings twice, three times and then the ringtone stops

and someone picks up. I hold my breath. All this time, whenever I have dialled this number, it has never been answered. Each time, it has rung out until the line goes dead. But now I find I am listening to street noises, the distant sound of voices, none of them discernible, bustling footsteps and music. I hold myself very still, hardly daring to breathe. And there, very faintly, comes the sound of someone breathing.

My heart is beating hard and fast. I'm so close now to the person who has been watching me from the shadows, the person who may have killed Finn.

'Hello?' I whisper, and I am leaning forward now, elbows on the desk.

I feel the intensity in the silence, the strangeness of knowing there is someone at the other end listening, someone who doesn't wish to be heard. And I don't know what instinct prompts me, what propels the thought into my head, but I say:

'Amy?'

It feels like my breath has grown small and is buried deep down inside me. Everything within me is straining for the answer.

'What the hell are you doing?'

I drop the phone in fright.

Jeff stands in the doorway, his face leeched of colour. He's in his heavy overcoat, and there's a look of perplexed anger on his face.

'I . . . I was going to . . .' I begin.

He takes a step forward into the room, casts his eyes past me to the computer awake on the desk, all the drawers open.

'You're snooping? You're spying on me?'

I open my mouth to say something, but then I stop. When he came into the room and startled me, I had instantly sprung to my feet. But now, knowing how badly in the wrong I am, I slump wearily back against the desk and close my mouth, defeated by it all.

There is pain in the depths of his eyes, a profound disappointment. The silence that follows ripples with unspoken arguments and accusations because there's no point to them any more. My betrayal of him is complete.

He steps past me, around to the side of the desk. His hand goes to the slide of papers, and after a brief shuffle there, he finds what it is he has come home for.

'My passport,' he declares in a broken tone, and I close my eyes briefly, hearing the tremor of quiet fury in his voice.

I don't say I'm sorry. It seems that I have apologized repeatedly for my behaviour, my indiscretions and failures, over the past few weeks until I have worn the word out. It no longer holds any meaning for us.

He stands there, and when I open my eyes, I look at the passport and see that his hand is shaking. I think he's going to demand an explanation from me, but he doesn't. He simply slips the passport inside his jacket pocket and then silently walks past me, the front door clicking shut seconds later. Besides, I have no explanations any more. I have allowed my life to spiral so far out of control that explanations can no longer be relied upon or trusted. Slippery as fish, they evade me, and I have worn myself out from chasing them.

25.

Amy

The girl says, 'Staying for Christmas?'

I look up from the cash I've just counted out for her – a disorderly pile of tens and fives, the notes weighted down by a fat two-pound coin.

'It's just that we're taking bookings already for the holidays,' she explains. 'So, if you want to reserve a bed, we'll need a deposit.'

She's not much older than me, a diamond stud winking from the side of her nose and a bored expression on her face as she watches me trying to make up my mind. There's a loud clunk as someone makes a purchase from the vending machine. Two girls with backpacks wait for me to conclude my business, indiscreetly shuffling their feet and letting out impatient sighs.

'Okay,' I say. 'I'll get it to you later in the week.'

'Today, if you don't mind,' she corrects. 'We're filling up fast.'

I sign my name on the form and she slides my passport back to me. I take it, shove it in the front pocket of my bag, mumble, 'You'll get it tonight.'

She blinks, flicks her chewing gum over to the other side of her mouth. There's a thread of curiosity lacing through the boredom of her look. But then she turns her eyes to the girls with their backpacks – new guests, new forms, same old drill. Besides, she's seen plenty like me pass through here. Girls with few options, and little money. Lost girls with nowhere to go.

I buy a coffee in a Leon, sit at a table on my own and open my laptop. I check, and then check again, but there's nothing there – still no activity. No browsing, no emailing. It's been five days now of this nothing. When will it come – the sign I've been waiting for? I feel like she's cut me off, abandoned me again. I hit 'refresh', but when nothing comes a sob of frustration bursts out of me. Two builders in high-vis vests at the next table look over.

'You alright?' one of them asks.

But I just wipe my face on the back of my sleeve and snap my laptop shut. The music's too loud anyway, all that fucking good cheer, chasing me back out into the streets where there's a paltry greyish show of snow.

I walk the pavement, eyes down, hunched into a jacket too flimsy for the season. Somewhere along the way, I lost most of my stuff. I can't even remember when or how. There are blanks in my memory, days and weeks blurring into a mutable cloud of events. I spend my days listlessly, waiting for a sign, tramping through museums and art galleries – anywhere that's free and warm. In the British Museum, I curl up on a bench and sleep until they come and wake me and tell me to leave. Everywhere, there are people. Even back in the hostel, there's always a door slamming, the inane chatter of girls doing their make-up or planning their sightseeing, FaceTiming their boyfriends back home.

I drift through a department store, just to get the

feeling back into my toes. I'm tempted to take my shoes off, walk barefoot over the thick-pile carpet, feel the plush give of it beneath my jaded skin.

I'm so tired. So goddamned exhausted. It feels like I haven't slept properly in weeks. One thought chases another, running around and around in my head, never letting up. There's Christmas music oozing through hidden speakers – the Rat Pack smarming their way through the oldies with brass and bass and crooning backing vocals. A week ago, I came back from the shower and found my iPhone earbuds had been lifted. Without them, I'm powerless to avoid this muzak – it invades my ears amid the baubles and the garlands and the twinkly lights. I'm just about ready to scream when the phone rings and I answer.

'Amy?' she says.

My heart pumps hard and fast, like it's going to burst out of my chest.

I hold the phone to my ear and listen, biting down on the tears that have surfaced, trying to get my breathing under control.

The line goes dead, but it's enough. Finally, after all these weeks adrift, waiting for a sign, she has reached out to me as I knew she would.

I buy a ticket and ride the Tube. The sprinkly pattern in the blue upholstered seats imprints on my retinas so that when I close my eyes, that's all I see: orange and red jags. I hear the clickety-clack of the tracks, the rumble of the tunnel.

And then Connie's voice cutting through it, saying: *What are you doing?*

A smudge in my memory, her voice. I keep returning to

it – or rather, it keeps coming back for me. Pressing, kneading, silently pleading. I do my best to resist it.

But sometimes, in idle moments, like when the tiredness has laid me low, and the lull of the rocking train helps me to believe that I am safe enough, far enough removed, I allow myself to be drawn back there. My eyes are closed, my head lolling back against the window, so I look like I'm asleep. But I'm not.

What are you doing? Connie asks, a rising curl of horror in her voice.

I keep my head in the pillow so I can't see the look on her face.

She's out of the bed now, spitting words at me – *dyke, pervert* – my heart a tight fist in my chest. I can hear her dressing quickly, her breathing laboured with disgust, hopping around on one foot as she pulls her boot on. Thoughts zip and chase around my head – how to calm the situation, how to undo what has been done. But part of me doesn't want it undone. The love in my heart for her is natural and true, even though the strength of feeling I have slams up against the cold wall of her revulsion. The covers are pulled up over my chin, my face pushed deep into the pillow. And as she pulls on her other boot and grabs her bag from the bureau, I can feel her standing over me, hissing the words at me, her voice so close and intent, it's like I can feel the heat on her breath.

Stay away from me, you skank. D'you hear? Her voice is low and deadly. *I don't ever want to see you again.*

And then the door bangs shut behind her, followed by the thud-thud-thud of her angry footfall on the stairs, and I'm alone in that room with nothing but an empty silence.

Dark thoughts flood in to fill it. Shameful memories. I relive the base animal desires that swept through me, only this time they draw a croak of embarrassment from my throat. The memory of me pawing at her breast, the way she recoiled from me, her voice weighty with loathing, makes me want to curl up so small I might disappear. But I can't make myself disappear, just like I can't blot out what I've done. Humiliation courses through my blood, swamps my brain. It itches and writhes within until I just can't stand it.

It's still dark outside, my breath clouding in the cold air. I'm shivering as I take my seat in Elaine's Pinto, my hand shaking so hard it takes several attempts to slot the key in the ignition. The chill of the night air fills my chest, turns my heart to stone. The tears dry on my cheeks. By the time I've caught up with her, I'm so numb inside, it's like all of this is happening to someone else.

She turns when she hears the engine and I slow the car, but when she sees it's me, she faces the road again, hunches deeper into her jacket and quickens her pace. Anger, contempt, dismissal – all of it there in her thin back, hands shoved into pockets, the scrape of her boots along the dirt track as she hurries away from me. Something breaks inside me. A shattering of the past and all that was precious to me. I hardly feel it when I press my foot to the accelerator, feel the old car lumber into action, the slam of the fender into her warm body, hear the high note of her scream cutting through the early-morning air. I have to break her in order to silence her. And she must be silenced; she cannot be allowed to contaminate our shared past with her revulsion, her sneering contempt. I cannot allow her to do that. I reverse the Pinto, the twitching body caught in the beams, and then I slam it again, the wheel rolling over her and landing on the hard earth beyond. I don't know how many times I go over and back, over and back, before finally pulling away, only the red tail lights watching her fade in the dust.

I don't cry while I drive. I hardly feel anything at all. Instead, I think of a time we were walking into town, along a little side track by the woods, so busy talking that I didn't notice the dead rat on the path until I stepped on it. I remember Connie's face screwing up into an expression of revolted amusement, both of us screeching and clinging to each other as we laughed and hurried away. But most of all, I remember the feel of that rat underfoot, the soft give of its body beneath the sole of my shoe, the nauseous thrill when I realized what it was, and how the thought of it kept returning to me hours afterwards in little secret surges of pleasure.

Now, the train lurches to a stop and I get off. I do this automatically, like I take this journey every day and am programmed to disembark here. And in a way, I know that this is where I always intended ending up. That the last two weeks have been a series of evasions and fillers, killing time until I would wind up back here, past Lidl and Lavender Gardens, turning the corner on to Dorothy Road.

She has given me the sign.

The snow has turned to sleet. It pelts against my face, causing my skin to sting, but I don't care. Connie's voice is silent now; Finn's was never there to start with. There is joy in my heart coming back here, the gut-scrape of desire increasing with each step. And when I turn the corner and see the apartment block lit up against the night like an Advent calendar, all the little flaps thrown open, all my anxiety fades away. A dreamy smile on my face, I look up and find her window, the drapes open, light shining from hidden sconces, and caught up once more in the slipstream of her love, I move towards the door.

26.

Cara

Night has fallen. The sky, though dark, has a strange pinkish hue – the promise of more snow while the city sleeps. I draw the curtain and go to check on the bath. Mabel sits on the toilet, grasping her knees, her small feet bare and dangling. She grins up at me, showing off the new gap where her tooth has fallen out. It came home from school in a twist of tissue paper, guarded and precious.

'Will the tooth fairy come?' she asks.

I hunker down, and test the temperature of the bath water, turning the cold tap for more flow.

'I'm sure she will,' I tell her, managing a smile, even though I am exhausted, more tired than I have felt in months.

I sit on the edge of the bath and help her undress. Tying her hair up into a topknot and then turning off the taps, I lift her into the water.

She splashes away happily with her bath toys as I leave her to play and cross into the kitchen. My bag is on the table and I check my wallet for tooth fairy coins, but there's nothing there save a couple of ten-pence pieces. I put down the wallet and dig around in my bag for loose change, and that's when my fingers alight on the strip of photographs. I had forgotten they were there.

I draw them out and hold them up to the light. Amy

and Connie. I think of the stories Amy has told me about this girl, and examine her image again: the mischief in her smile coupled with a languid sexuality in the curl of her lashes, the intense gaze at the camera – unapologetically suggestive. Amy's words return to me:

You remind me of her, in a way.

I try to read something of myself in this girl with her russet hair and seductive leer, but I cannot, for the life of me, see anything. It triggers something inside me, though. A push of curiosity.

My laptop is still in Wogan House with Mark, so, instead, I wander down the hall and into Jeff's study. Sitting at his desk, I try to push from my mind the events of this morning – the horrible scene that took place in this very room. Instead, I fire up the computer.

Miller. That was the name Amy mentioned. The Millers – Connie and Elaine. I open the browser, and google *Constance Miller, Pennsylvania*. The first hit throws up listings for 23 people named Constance Miller in the state of Pennsylvania. Spokeo has 53 records, and Been-Verified 73. Further down there are listings on Facebook and Craigslist, but before that, there are three obituary listings. In the first and second, the deceased are both septuagenarians, but the third one makes me stop.

Constance (Connie) Miller of Scranton, Pennsylvania, passed suddenly after a tragic accident Thursday, 14 February 2014. She was 26. Connie, as she was affectionately known, was the beloved and cherished daughter of Elaine Miller. Lost but forever in our hearts.

It occurs first in my heart, which begins banging away with uncertain beats. An accident. But didn't Amy tell me Connie had survived? *A concussion. Some broken ribs.*

Into the browser, I quickly type her name again along with her home town, adding the word 'accident' and the date.

Immediately, it throws up listings from newspaper stories. I open the first one from *U.S. News*. Quickly now, my eyes scour the article.

Valentine's Tragedy As Local Woman Killed In Brutal Hit-And-Run

Authorities say that a local woman was walking along the road towards her boyfriend's house, planning to surprise him for Valentine's Day, when she was brutally slain by a hit-and-run driver. The dead woman has been named locally as Connie Miller, aged 26. The death occurred on a rural highway outside Scranton, Pennsylvania, just a kilometer from the victim's mother's house.

State police said the accident happened around 5 a.m. Thursday on the westbound side of a minor road that links a few rural houses to the main highway. The woman was pronounced dead at the scene.

Initial reports say the killing was of a particularly brutal nature, with unconfirmed reports that the driver may have repeatedly slammed the body with the car. The body shows multiple injuries consistent with severe trauma. Although details have yet to be released, it's thought the killer may have been known to the victim. Police say they are following a definite line of enquiry.

I'm so focused on these words, I almost jump when my phone buzzes.

I'm coming.

357

That's all it says.

Fear rushes at me.

Distantly, I hear the swoosh and ping of the elevator doors opening.

I am out of the study and halfway across the hall when I hear the key slot into the lock, the turn and click of it opening, and I freeze.

My heart stops cold as the door opens, a rush of panicked thoughts coming at me.

And then she comes in, closes the door behind her and discards her bag on the hall table. The look she throws me is sulky and disdainful.

'Is my dad here?' she asks, running a hand through her hair as she looks about at the stacked boxes, the empty rooms.

'Olivia?' My mind is flickering with confusion.

'You've been busy,' she remarks, with something close to contempt, and then walks past me to her bedroom. I hear her flicking on the light in there, the loud creak of the wardrobe door.

Slowly, I follow her to the door, my thoughts jumping all over the place.

'Did you just text me?' I ask.

She is plucking hangers from the rail, pulling clothes off them which she tosses on to the bed.

Her answer is a bored, 'No,' released on a sigh.

'Are you sure?' My heart is thumping with fright.

'Of course I'm sure,' she snaps. Then, turning to hold me with her hostile gaze, she says, 'I'm just here to pack up my stuff, okay? I don't need you hovering over me, watching.'

I could turn away from her now, return to the bathroom and attend to my child, and perhaps I should. But I am frightened by that text, the possibility that my anonymous correspondent might be here at any moment, not knowing what it is that they intend. It feels like I'm on the brink of a precipice, a great chasm opening out in front of me that sends me scuttling towards last-gasp chances and risks.

I step forward into the room. Olivia is flinging clothes about with pent-up fury, and even though the history between us is full of misgivings and doubts, I need an ally and right now she's all I've got. Besides, over the past few days I've started to think that maybe I was wrong about Olivia. That perhaps I was too swift to judge.

'Would it help if I said I'm sorry?' I ask.

She rips a blouse from a hanger, throws it on to the growing pile.

'Not really.'

'Even if it's true?'

She gives a derisive snort, but it's half-hearted and I sense the slightest yield within her.

'We never got off to the right start, did we?' I say. 'That's my fault.'

Her eyes shoot in my direction, and she lets out a breezy, 'Yes, I know.'

'It was too soon for you. Too soon after your mother. Our timing was lousy.'

'You could say that.'

I sit down on the bed, look at the pile of clothes amassed there, the tangle of sleeves and legs in an orgy of cotton and silk and wool. This room has been hers since childhood. It was in this room she cried and grieved for her mother, an experience I am all too familiar with. It was to this room she would storm off in those early days when she first railed against my presence. A lot of unhappy memories, but I can tell from the brittleness of her tone, the downward turn to her mouth, that behind the bravado of her scorn and derision lies a tender spot. This has been her home since childhood, and we are tearing it away from her. The new house will have a room for her to stay but it will never be home, not like here.

'You'll miss this place,' I say gently.

I am trying to give her an opening, but I have misjudged her mood. She shoots me a look of pure venom and all the constraint inside her collapses. She flings the hanger in her hand across the room, it ricochets off the chest of drawers and clatters to the ground.

'This hasn't been my home since the day you stepped in the door!' she screeches.

Turning, she pulls hanger after hanger from the rail, sending them slamming to the bottom of the wardrobe, spilling out on to the floor, across the room. Tears burst hotly from her, and I watch in amazement as she shudders with emotion, realizing that I am witnessing an outpouring of unresolved grief. She turns away from me, draws the heel of her hand up to wipe at her nose, as if suddenly overcome with embarrassment, and it is this gesture that finally rends my heart.

I get up from the bed and go to her, say her name gently. I put my hand to her shoulder, braced for her rejection, fully expecting her to angrily shrug me off. That is why it is so surprising when she turns into me, allows herself to be taken into my arms, her face resting on my shoulder; her sobs are quieter now, but still I feel them quaking through her. In all the crazy tempest of recent days and weeks, what an unexpected blessing this is. But perhaps it is because of what's happened, the danger I have felt from some unknown outside source, that I find myself softening towards her, needing to reach out and connect. For the first time in our difficult history, I feel the warmth of a maternal link with her. A bridge crossed, a pattern broken, a difficult battle nearing a weary truce, both of us glad of it, relieved.

'It's going to be okay,' I whisper to her.

I feel her sucking in her breath in a bid to check her emotions, get herself under control. I draw back and she swipes at her face and offers me a watery smile.

'Leave the packing,' I say gently. 'Why don't you pour us both a glass of wine while I get Mabel out of the bath? What do you say?'

She nods, wipes a tear away with her index finger, and looks up. Her eyes flicker past me. The watery smile dies. The expression on her face is a complicated mixture of surprise and withdrawal. I turn to follow her gaze and my heart constricts in my chest.

I am coming, the message said.

Amy is standing in the doorway.

27.

Amy

'Look who's back,' the girl says, a huff of scorn in her voice. Her china doll features are all glassy and strange beneath the severe fringe.

I'm standing at the door staring at them, trying to make sense of it, my hands numb from the cold outside. The leap in me when I came into the apartment – all that hopeful momentum – is draining away. I'm confused by this scene: *What is going on? What is that girl doing here? Why is Cara holding her?* Angry questions are buzzing in my brain like a nest of wasps. And then I realize that the questions are not in my head – that I have actually said them out loud, for the girl turns angry.

'It's none of your business! This is my home. What the hell are *you* doing here?' she says.

I hate this girl. And I can make her pay, like I did before. Doesn't she realize? Doesn't she know that?

'Amy,' Cara says.

Oh God, my name in her mouth. It lifts the sudden gloom that has descended on me, and I turn to her, feeling the foolish grin breaking out all over my face, for there is everything in her voice – all that promise, all that hopeful love – and I don't care if the girl is watching. She will be gotten rid of and then there will be just the two of us, no more interruptions, no more misunder-standings.

'How did you get in here?'

The question confuses me, the hesitancy in her tone, like she's nervous or something.

I laugh, to put her at ease. 'With a key, of course!'

'But you left your keys.'

'Oh, I had spare ones made. In case.'

'In case what?' A crease has appeared between her brows. It throws me a little. Why is she getting hung up on this?

'For when you needed me. For when you gave me the sign.'

I see her and the girl exchanging a glance, and the hopefulness inside me teeters.

Cara takes a step towards me, her hand held out in front of her, and she says in a hard voice, 'You need to give me those keys, Amy. And then you need to go.'

'But you gave me the sign,' I say, my voice faltering.

The girl laughs. 'You are barking,' she tells me.

Something mean and pinched inside me awakens. 'Shut up,' I tell her, keeping my voice low, controlled.

'Amy, the keys,' Cara says sharply, drawing my attention back to her.

And even though a part of me is still thrilling to be back here with her, after our long separation, I'm confused by her approach. Her eyes have gone all small. She's sending me a message, I know it, so that the girl won't see, but the signals are all messed up and I can't read it.

'No,' I say, clarity descending as I realize that it's some kind of test. Pushing my resolve in front of Olivia, to see if I will cave. 'No, I won't give them to you.'

I'm shaking my head determinedly, but I've broken away from her gaze. I don't like the coldness of it, even if it's only a front for the girl's benefit, and later we'll laugh about it, just the two of us. For now, I feel the ice-burn of it.

'Get out of our fucking house, you freak,' the girl says, her screeching voice scraping my brain.

'Olivia,' Cara says quietly, warning her.

That settles my nerves a little, reassuring me that she's on my side in all this. We are together.

'I heard the sign,' I tell her, and this time I smile up at her, a beam of love and joy, re-establishing the connection between us.

'What sign? What do you mean?' There's a clipped note of impatience in her voice.

My mind is fizzing all over the place. This look she's giving me throws me off-balance. I'm still in my coat and it's so hot in here. My gloveless hands are stinging as the heat draws blood back into them.

'You *know* what I mean,' I tell her, but my voice falters. She's harder to reach than usual, like this hard, shiny layer has sprung up around her.

The girl is looking from one of us to the other, silent now, a grave expression on her face. But I'm not focused on her. I'm looking at Cara, scouring her reaction for something – anything – that will shore up my confidence. But everything seems rearranged in a fashion I don't understand. This whole place – the boxes in the hall, the blank walls still shadowed by the outline of frames that no longer hang there, the shocked and aggrieved look on Cara's face – all of it overwhelming me.

'Go, Amy. Get out now, before I call the police.'

I'm vaguely aware of the sharp turn of the girl's head, but I'm still catching up with my thoughts.

'But you gave me the sign . . .' I hear the crack coming into my voice, confusion giving way to a surge of alarm at the mention of the police.

And then the girl shoots past me into the hall, and all the panic in me rises to the surface, heat like a rash over my skin.

She's almost at the door when I catch up with her and I see at once what she's going for – her bag on the hall table, the phone tucked inside it. She doesn't even hear me approach, it's the stark shout of her name from Cara that alerts her so she's half-turning when I slam her against the wall. Her shock is momentary before she scrambles towards the door. I grab a swatch of her hair and yank it back, letting the hall table – a glass and iron affair, all angles and hard surfaces – break her fall.

28.

Cara

For a moment, that's all there is: the hard crack of Olivia's head glancing off the sharp edge of the table. It shouts and reverberates through me, like a struck tuning fork blurring out of focus.

And then clarity comes rushing in – Olivia on the floor, the blood, Amy advancing towards me, eyes black with fury. I back away towards the bedroom door, my mind skittering.

'Give me your phone,' she demands, and when I shake my head slightly, the terror clutching in my chest, she shouts it in my face. 'Give me your phone!'

It's in the back pocket of my jeans. I have both hands splayed and held behind me against the door. Her eyes dart over me, landing on my hips, and then she lunges forward and I cry out, the two of us struggling against each other. The phone is somehow in my hand now, and she is trying to prise it from my fingers. I know I can't let go of it. Olivia is slumped on the floor, unmoving, and behind me, Mabel is alone in the bath – I don't know if Amy knows this or cares. She's intent on her own dark purpose, and as she lowers her mouth and I feel her teeth sink into the flesh of my hand, the pain sears through me and I cry out in hurt and frustration, for I have dropped the phone.

She moves quickly now. Back to the hall table where I see, with a measure of temporary relief, Olivia shrinking from her, curled into a ball by the table leg. But Amy is no longer interested in Olivia. At the front door, she turns the key in the mortise, double-locking it, slots the chain in place and slams the bolt. Then she draws my keys from the lock, takes Olivia's bag from the table, and into it she throws my keys and my phone. I'm slack against the bathroom door, clutching my hand which is bleeding from the bite-mark, as she yanks the house phone from the wall and it too goes into the bag. Then she moves into the sitting room and I see too late what she intends.

'No!' I shout, rushing after her. But the window is already open, the bag flying through the air. With despair, I watch the arc of it before it disappears into darkness, imagine the impact with the ground, its contents scattered.

She slams the window shut and turns to me, her eyes lit up with triumph.

'I had to do that,' she explains, breathless and smiling, like she's just run a race. 'Don't you see? It's the only way we could talk.' And then she lets out a happy sigh and raises her eyebrows, as if to say, *How about that then?*

It's all such a parody, a horrible farce, I can't believe it is happening.

'Amy, you have to let us go. Look at Olivia – she needs help.'

'Oh, she'll be alright,' she says breezily, turning from me and walking back through the hall – past Olivia, who lies prone, unmoving – and then into the kitchen.

I can hear her in there banging cupboard doors, the clink of glassware. I hurry over to Olivia, crouch down beside her, whisper her name. Up close, I can see the seriousness of the head wound. Blood continues to rush from the gash in her temple, her eyelids fluttering closed.

'You must try and stay awake,' I hiss. 'Do you hear me? It's very important you stay awake.' And then, as I hear Amy approach, I lower my head so my mouth is right next to Olivia's ear and whisper, 'I'll get us out of here. I promise.'

'Now then!'

I look up and Amy is standing over me, a glass of red wine in each hand, her perfect hostess's smile splashed over her face. She gestures with her head for me to get up, which I do, slowly.

'Amy, she's bleeding heavily. I need to get her to a hospital.'

'No. She'll be alright, just leave her.'

'I can't leave her –'

With a huff of impatience, she puts the glasses down on the hall table, then turns on her heel back to the kitchen. Half a minute later she is back with a tea towel which she flings on the floor beside Olivia. I fold it carefully and press it to the wound, a low moan coming from deep in the girl's throat.

'That's enough,' Amy says.

I feel a jolt of anger going through me at her autocratic tone. 'It's not.'

'Get up!'

She grabs me by the arms and hauls me to my feet, and I feel the anger in the clutch of her fingers, the menace in her voice. As soon as a wine glass is thrust in my hand, she changes, the menace falling away.

She says in that overly bright tone, 'Come on then!'

Her hand grabs my elbow once more, and I allow myself to be drawn stiffly through into the living room. I choose the seat by the fireplace, nearest the door, but she frowns and shakes her head.

'No. Over there,' she orders, her tone becoming sharp as she indicates the couch.

'I'm fine here,' I say coldly.

She squeezes her eyes shut for just a second and then comes towards me quickly and hits me, an open-handed slap – my cheek flares with sudden pain.

'Over there,' she orders again, her voice at the same pitch, hardly betraying any rise in emotion at the sudden violence.

And it comes to me now that she has done this before. My legs are trembling. I do as she asks.

The couch sags beneath me as I lower myself, keeping my glass steady on my knee. She takes a deep slurp of her wine, as if needing to calm her nerves, and then sits down next to me. A musky feral smell rises from her, like she hasn't washed in days – weeks, maybe. The cuffs of her jeans are encrusted with muck, her trainers worn and threadbare. Her hair, which has grown longer now, scraggly ends skirting the collar of her jacket, is greasy and limp. Dark shadows linger in the hollows of her face. Her eyes are wide open and glittering with their own glassy light, and her mouth is animated – a twitching line that can't keep still. She is an accumulation of tics and twitches, some manic energy pulsing through her, making her dangerous and unpredictable.

'Here we are again,' she says, smiling effusively, 'back together, alone in a room. Just like the beginning.'

I don't say anything. In my mind, I am furiously playing

through the various paths available for me to take. She is slight and not much taller than me, but there is a wiry strength to her. Whether to call her bluff, take the chance that her violent unpredictability won't cause her to lash out again, or whether it's better to appease her, calm her down, lull her into dropping her guard and then seize the opportunity to escape. But the front door is locked and the only key is snugly fitted inside her jeans pocket. A door from the kitchen leads on to a fire escape but even if I could make a run for it, I cannot leave without Mabel or Olivia.

'You're not drinking,' she remarks.

My eyes flick to the glass in my hand. 'I'm not thirsty,' I say stiffly.

She reaches out and pushes the glass towards me. 'Come on. This is a celebration. Drink it.'

I hear the threat implicit in her tone, and warily raise the glass to my mouth. She watches me carefully as I sip and swallow, sip and swallow, the wine bitter-tasting, sediment lurking in the depths. After a couple of sips, I put the glass down.

'It feels like fate, doesn't it?' she asks, beaming at me with a maddening smile.

'What does?'

'Us!' she laughs, like I'm stupidly missing the point. 'That we should be together. Even our names point to it!'

'Our names?'

'Beloved,' she says, and there's a tremor of emotion as she says it. 'Amy. Cara. They both mean beloved.'

It's frightening, how intent she is, powered by this irrepressible belief.

'You're mistaken —'

'I'm not! They both mean –'

'No. Cara means beloved in Latin. But my name is the Irish version.'

Consternation clouds her face. 'So what does it mean?'

'Friend.'

She thinks about this for a moment, her face darkened with disappointment or irritation. Her eyes flicker about as if seeking somewhere to land her gaze.

'Oh no,' she exclaims suddenly, raising my alarm as she seizes hold of my hand, stricken. 'You're bleeding!'

I can feel myself recoiling even though my hand is firmly in her grip. She stares in horror at the bite-mark, as if it has nothing to do with her. Putting down her wine glass, she holds my hand in both of hers and I feel the clammy heat of her skin wrapped around my cold paw, all the blood having fled my extremities with shock.

'You shouldn't have made me do that,' she says in a softly admonishing tone, her thumbs stroking the puncture marks in my skin caused by her teeth. And then she does something that repulses me. She lowers her mouth to my hand and gently kisses the wound. I feel the wet warmth of her tongue against my skin, her eyes closing with reverence.

All of this has an air of unreality. My hand held in her lap, her head bent, face turned so that her cheek rests against my fingers, her eyes fixed on mine with a beatific gaze. In the hall Olivia is slumped and bleeding. My child is alone in the bath.

'Amy,' I begin gently, and she looks at me dreamily. 'I'm worried about Olivia. If we leave her there, it's only going to get more serious. You're going to be in a lot of trouble,' I say softly, careful to keep the threat from my voice, 'but if we take her to the hospital now, we can tell them it was just an accident. That she slipped and fell. The problem is, if we leave her . . . if she continues to bleed like that . . . she might die. And how will we explain it then? How will the police react when they learn she was bleeding profusely and we didn't help her?'

She lifts her head, stares down at the ottoman, chewing her thumbnail while turning the thought over in her head. Then, to my dismay, she shrugs and smiles and says, matter-of-factly, 'People die. Shit happens.'

Seeing the horror in my expression, she laughs and reaches for my hand once more.

'Don't worry! It won't matter! Not when we're alone. Not when we're together without any distractions.'

'How can you say that? Of course it would matter!' My voice rises and I pull my hand away from her.

She rolls her eyes, nudged by annoyance. 'That's not the way it works, Cara. You'll see. That's not how it happens.'

I know that she is talking of Connie. A cold shard enters my thoughts: *If she can kill her best friend, what else is she capable of?*

She throws the contents of her glass to the back of her throat and stands up quickly, shaking the glass in her hand distractedly. There's a jumpiness to her, like she can't stay still.

'We need more wine,' she declares. 'Come on. Finish up.'

I sip a little more and then hand back my glass.

'Stay here,' she instructs.

I wait until I can hear her in the kitchen, and then quietly I hurry back to the hall and crouch down over Olivia. Her breathing has slowed, her eyes are closed. I hiss her name in her ear, shake her arm gently, alarm fluttering inside me, but she is not entirely unconscious. Her eyelids partially open, and they fix me with a teary stare. I squeeze her arm to reassure her, for I know what I have to do. The only thing I can do to get us out.

All the contents of the hall have been cleared, packed away in boxes. The only thing that remains – the only object at my disposal – is the lamp. A rounded terracotta base with a linen shade. Not ideal, but heavy enough for my purposes. I unplug it quickly from the wall, wrap the flex around my hand and remove the shade. It's bulky and awkward, but I can just about hold it in one hand. Olivia watches through half-closed eyes, as I tiptoe towards the kitchen door, then pause, waiting.

From within, I can hear the pop of a cork being sprung from a bottle, the scrape of the bottle being dragged from the table. Her footsteps are light but her trainers squeak on the tiled floor. My heart beats high and fast in my chest. I hold my breath and raise my hand, the lamp poised, ready to smash down on her head. I can hear her coming.

'Mummy?'

My head whips around.

'I'm cold.'

Mabel stands there by the open bathroom door, a red towel slipping off her shoulders, the ends of her hair damp and dripping.

The blood still pounding in my ears, and with a feeling sweeping through me that may be disappointment or relief – I honestly can't tell – I put the lamp down, just as Amy emerges from the kitchen, rushing towards my little girl and sweeping her up in her arms.

29.

Amy

I hold her for a long moment. Feel the soft flesh in my arms, the smell of her, all pinky-clean and sweet from her bath – I burrow my nose into the crook of her short little neck and inhale.

'Hey there, little one. I missed you,' I croon.

She's trapped inside the towel so she can't wrap her arms around me and return the embrace, but that's okay. I draw back and beam at her, at the serious look on her sensible little face.

'Give her to me.'

I look around. Cara is there, with her arms out for the child. Her face is kind of stretched-looking, and I don't like her tone. I keep a hold of Mabel and walk into her bedroom, swinging from side to side, singing a little tune to her.

'Mummy,' she says again, sharply this time.

I break off my lullaby to whisper and hush. The door closes firmly behind all three of us.

'What's wrong with Olivia?' the little girl asks.

I say, 'There, there. She's just sleeping, that's all.'

'Give her to me now,' Cara says again.

This time I relinquish the child. My arms are tired from holding her, and that tiredness seems to communicate itself to my other limbs, my back, the creaking stretch of my shoulders. This room is softly lit, the bed made up in cloudy-white sheets, and I feel a yearning for it now – the need to lie down and drift away.

'Why is Olivia asleep on the floor?' Mabel asks, snapping me from my thoughts.

Cara murmurs something to her that I don't catch, and then she carries the child to the bed and sits down, holding Mabel on her lap and rubbing her with the towel. She's whispering something to her that I can't hear, and the sight of them there together – a loving mother tending to her sweet child – it redoubles my desire for her, making it luminous.

I come and sit by them, so Cara and I are shoulder to shoulder, and when I reach out and tenderly touch Mabel's hair, Cara lifts the little girl from her lap, holding her away from me, and puts her on the bed.

'Into pjs,' she softly commands.

Mabel sits solemn-faced, her two eyes like pebbles watching me as she raises her arms and allows her mother to slip her nightie down over her.

'Why are you back here?' the child asks.

Her voice is low and serious and it makes me pause. But then I laugh, and lean forward on the bed, grasping her little ankles, and say, 'Because I missed you, sweet pea! I missed my Maybelline!'

Cara's back is to me, and I see it stiffen. There's a gap between her T-shirt and the waistband of her jeans. I let go of one of Mabel's legs, and my hand trails across, tentatively strokes the pale band of exposed skin.

'I missed your mommy too,' I say softly.

Cara gets up quickly.

'Stop it!' she hisses, shooting me a fierce look that leaves me stunned.

She's holding up the duvet and shooing Mabel under the covers.

'Don't worry, my love,' she says. 'Amy is going now.'

'No, I'm not.' Injury in my voice. Why is she saying that? Lying to her own child?

'Yes. You are.'

She is tucking in the blankets now, something urgent and cross in her exertions, almost pushing me off the bed as she rounds the corner to tuck in the blanket there.

'Why would you say that? I came back here for you. So that the three of us could be together.'

'Don't be ridiculous,' she snaps, still fussing around the bed, picking up toys and putting away books.

'I'm not ridiculous. You're the one who's lying.'

'Mummy?'

'It's alright, sweetheart.' She brushes hair from the little girl's forehead and kisses her tenderly. Again, she murmurs something that I can't hear and the girl nods her head.

A chill comes over me, suspicion hovering like a bad smell.

'What are you saying to her?' I ask, but she ignores me, keeps on whispering, and the suspicion stirs up into anger. 'What are you saying?'

Without looking back, her gaze trained on the little girl, she tells me, 'We're sharing our secrets with each other. Telling each other the truth.'

And the little girl smiles at her, but there's something closed and conspiratorial about it that I don't like. A smile that pushes me out, seals them off from me. Mabel has spilled the beans – told Cara what I did, my various disciplinary methods. I can sense it. It sends me past the point of nervous excitement into a kind of blunt unease. The room which had felt so welcoming just a few minutes ago now seems to thrum with an energy that I don't understand. The bedside lamp casts shadows that can't be trusted. And reflected in the mirror, I see Connie's face, pale and gory. Her lips draw back into a smile. One of her front teeth is missing, blood in her mouth.

Don't you know when you're not wanted? she says, shaking her head and laughing at me, threads of blood strung between her teeth.

The whispering goes on and on, indiscernible and echoey in the chambers of my head. Everything in this room is clean and laundered. It makes me feel soiled and dirty. Filthy. Like the grime on my skin is so deeply ingrained I won't ever get clean.

I look down at my fingernails, see the blackened crescents, the stained and ragged cuticles. My hands are trembling. I'm so tired. So goddamned tired. And Connie won't shut up laughing. All I want is some peace.

I back out of the room. Leave them to their whispering. 'Don't be too long, okay?' I say.

But they don't even look my way, like I'm nothing to them, and I can't be sure I even said the words out loud.

I pull the door closed, lean my forehead against it for a moment. There's a pain in my chest, a sudden feeling of loss that is somehow tied up with memories of my own mother. It's the tenderness between them that's done it. Right now, in this place, the cold coming back into my bones, exhausted and unsure, I need something to hang on to. Some fleeting memory of warmth and belonging, some scrap of hope from loving words spoken. But inside is a blank, a vacuum, filling up now with this awful black pain.

Tears come and I shake them away, swallow them down.

'Stupid bitch,' I say, a little sob of self-pity surfacing, and I slap my face quickly. No more of this blubbing. I need to focus. To remember my goal.

I turn around and look at the empty hall. My eyes strain under the too-bright lights, trying to gauge what they are seeing. The blank floor – the space where the girl had been. In my mind's eye, there's a fixed memory of her curled around the leg of the table. But now I'm staring at the table and there's nothing there. It's almost as if I imagined it. Only the dark smear of blood on the floorboards betrays her recent presence.

The slump I've fallen into fades quickly, replaced by an urgency powered by my fast-beating heart. Bloodstains on the floor – sticky smears of it like drag-marks along the hall and past the kitchen – lead me on. The door to Jeff's study lies open.

She hasn't gotten far. But somehow, she has managed to crawl here, a bloody handprint on the white paint of the door where she pushed it open. Another bloody fingerprint on the switch of the computer which is fired up now. She's kneeling on the floor in front of the desk, half-slumped against the chair, one hand resting there, while the other manoeuvres the mouse. From where I'm standing I can see that she is barely able to keep her head up. She's just clicking on Skype when I come up behind her, a leather-bound periodical the weapon I choose.

The surprised look on her face, the 'o' of her mouth as I smash her head with the book, hear the snap of her neck flying back, and then she is slithering down the chair, on to the floor, like some rapidly wilting flower, the cursor on the screen poised and waiting, and Connie is shrieking with laughter behind me.

30.

Cara

'Is she dead?'

At the sound of my voice, Amy turns around. I'm standing in the doorway, rigid with shock and fear. I can hardly believe how calm my voice sounds when inside I feel liquid, molten. My head heavy with it all.

There is a look in her eye – a fleeting expression of wild disbelief, at what she has done, at what she is capable of – it lasts but a second or two and then it's washed away by that pitying smile she gives me, like I'm a child who's just lost her mother, who needs comfort and sympathy and love. Endless enveloping, smothering love.

'It had to be done,' she says softly, kindly. 'You know that. There was no other way.'

She casts a quick glance back at Olivia, unmoving on the floor, blood pooling around her head, matting her hair. It's a glance that's almost tender.

A gasp comes from me, like I've been holding it in until now. She turns to me with a quizzical expression, as if she cannot fathom why I'm so upset.

'You didn't even like her,' she remarks, almost bemused by my distress.

'She was innocent.'

'Oh, please!'

I have to hold it together. I cannot fall apart, not now. Not with Mabel waiting in her bedroom. Above all else, I must get her out of here safely. I realize that I am holding on to the door frame, leaning against it for support. I try to quell the shaking in my legs, try to will some strength back into my body. But I feel strangely weighted, like my limbs are filling up with water.

'Amy, whatever you think has happened between us – this love affair you keep alluding to – it doesn't exist. It's only in your mind.'

'Don't say that,' she chides, but she's still smiling, her head turned coquettishly to one side. She doesn't believe me.

'I was grateful for your help at the time, but then . . . You got so clingy, and manipulative. You took advantage of me . . .'

She's shaking her head, laughing lightly, as if I've made some self-effacing joke.

'Remember what you said to me? On the night we met?' she asks brightly, her face lighting up at the memory. 'You told me that you couldn't be sure you had met the love of your life yet.'

'No, I –'

'You said that you didn't love your husband –'

'I never –'

'You did, Cara,' she says, gently and firmly, and I have the sense again that she is talking to me like I'm a child, and it suits her to infantilize me like this. Make me helpless. Make me dependent. I'm shaking my head from side to side, but I feel the effort of it, like it's difficult to even hold my head up.

She goes on, 'You told me that when that terrorist came

towards you and you thought you were going to die, it wasn't Jeff's face that flashed in front of your eyes. It was Finn's.'

I close my eyes, as if that will erase the regret, the terrible folly of openly confessing such a thing. That night, I had been so grateful for her help. I thought she was rescuing me. What I hadn't banked on was the possibility that she could be every bit as dangerous as the killers on the street. My lids are so heavy, it's a struggle to open my eyes, to focus on what she's telling me now.

'You said you had been questioning your marriage anyway, that it had never really felt right, always overshadowed by the dead wife. You told me that the only thing holding your marriage together was your daughter, the irony of that being you couldn't be sure she was actually his.'

What does any of this matter any more? Finn is dead. And now Olivia. I can hardly bring myself to look at her body lying there on the floor. I catch a glimpse into the future, a moment when I will have to break the news to Jeff about the loss of his precious girl. It's almost too much to bear. And I think about how we stood here together, in this very room, by this old desk, only this morning, the current of animosity that zipped between us. What was it all for? What on earth had been achieved?

That's when I remember the phone call.

The scrap of paper. The number dialled. Someone had answered but no words were spoken, and struck by an impulse I couldn't explain, I had uttered her name.

'A sign,' she had told me. I had given her a sign.

'It was you,' I say, my tone tinged with amazement. 'I thought it was Finn, but all along it was you.'

The look she gives me is quizzical, and it suddenly infuriates me.

'Your Closest Friend,' I say, my voice dripping with scorn. 'What a joke.'

She grimaces – a disavowal there.

'Not the name I would have chosen,' she remarks blithely. 'And I think it's laughable that he thought so highly of himself as to pick that name for his little alter-ego.'

'What?'

'Oh, it *was* him, at first. Those pathetic little messages.' She laughs, a horrible mocking burst of it.

I shake my head, baffled. 'I don't understand.'

My confusion registers with her, and she explains.

'I caught him here one day, sniffing around for you. He was a mess,' she says, before continuing. 'Poured his heart out to me. Told me all about the little game he had going, posing as some kind of secret admirer. Pathetic. So I took the phone from him. It was for the best.'

'And the spyware on my laptop? The bug in my handbag?'

'Necessary measures,' she says primly.

I think of that naked picture. The audio file of Finn and me together.

'All that time, you were spying on me. Listening to my most private conversations.'

'I had to know so that I could protect you!' She laughs again but it is shrill, a manic jag in it.

'You sent those images to my workplace. That audio-clip of me and Finn. How was that protecting me?'

'I was saving you from yourself,' she declares.

Her conviction sets new alarm bells ringing in my head.

'You were so in thrall to him, you couldn't see how

dangerous he was. I had to drive a wedge between the two of you – something so bad you would never be able to forgive him. I knew that if you thought those things were done by Your Closest Friend – if you believed he was behind it – then it would kill off any last feelings you had for him. You would be free!'

'My God, Amy. What did you do?'

Her eyes are lit up, but her mouth is twitching like it can't settle on an expression.

'I had to stop him, don't you see?' she says, her voice brittle and loud. 'He was dangerous. Who knows what he might have done?'

'The night that he died – you were there?'

'Of course! You know that,' she says.

The quizzical look is back on her face and it sends a shiver of horror through me. There is a lack of remorse, a kind of perverse pride in her crime.

'It was you. You were seen going into his house. You had sex with him.'

'Oh!' She bursts out laughing, then claps a hand over her mouth to suppress it.

Laughter in this room, with Olivia not yet cold, is obscene, a perversion.

'Oh, Cara. Oh, my love. No – it wasn't like that. I had to, you see? Even after all that whiskey, and the sleeping pills, it was the only way I could be sure he would sleep. It wasn't . . . I wasn't being unfaithful to you. It was a necessary act. He had to be asleep for me to . . . You know.'

She can't bring herself to say it, wrinkling her nose in distaste, skipping around the subject, unable to land.

'For you to kill him.'

She seems to flinch at the word. Then recovers herself.

'It had to be done,' she says again, her tone flat and calm, no nerves, no conscience.

'Why?' I whisper, straining hard to keep my emotions in check, part of me back there in that bedroom, his blood vessels open and spilt on to the bed, the floor, the life gone from him.

'Because he was a pest. He was never going to leave us alone, Cara. And, like all pests, he had to be exterminated.'

There it is. The audible squeak of pure craziness.

'And Connie?' I ask, pushed by that same instinct. 'Did you kill her too?'

Something closes down in her face at the mention of the name, a fidgety inward recalculation.

'It wasn't the same,' she says. 'That was . . . personal. But this,' she moves on, brightly animated again, lit up by the gleam of madness inside, 'this was for you.'

'Me?'

'All of it. I've only ever done it for you. To bring us closer together.'

'Your Closest Friend,' I say, and I cannot keep the sourness from my voice, the heavy disdain.

She mops a hand over her brow, as if to wipe the sudden display of emotion away. She shakes her head, trying to come back to herself. Then she looks at me, and there is pain and love and wistfulness in that gaze.

'I love you, Cara. From the first night we met. It felt fated, that we should have been thrown together like that. Something beautiful coming out of all that terror.'

She is moving towards me now, and I back away, towards

the bookshelves, that waterlogged feeling in my limbs and in my head. She is almost upon me, and I can feel the ridge of the shelf cutting across my shoulder blades, my hands behind me touching the dust of the books, when I remember the wine. The sediment. The way she had urged me to drink. My thoughts are swampy and heavy – they press down on the panic that rises now I realize that she has drugged me, just as she drugged Finn.

'All of it will be forgotten,' she whispers, 'all the bad things that happened so that we could be together. You'll see.'

She's so close to me now, I can feel the heat of her breath on my face, a sour taste of fear coming into my mouth. She lifts a hand, tentatively touches my face. I'm holding myself still, pushing back so the shelf is cutting a line into my back. I feel the chill of her fingertips passing over my cheek, my chin, my mouth. The salty, acrid smell of her hands. The cool dryness of her touch as it lingers in the hollows under my eyes, everything inside me straining away from her.

'You look so tired,' she says, pityingly.

Working hard to keep my voice steady, I say, 'I need to lie down and sleep.'

Her eyes flicker over me.

'And so do you,' I say.

I hold her gaze, see the bloom of hope in it, the yearning, and when her mouth pushes against mine, I clench my hands into fists, steadying myself, preparing. Our lips part and her face draws back, her gaze containing infinite and mysterious tensions.

'Shall we go up?' I ask, my voice a hoarse whisper.

I go first. It's such an effort to climb the stairs. My heart is beating slow and hard now as we enter the bedroom. Darkness fills the space and we don't turn on the lights. Darkness is what's required for what must come next.

I lie back slowly and she perches on the mattress next to me. One half of her face is visible by the paltry light coming through the window, the other half in shadow. There's a stillness about her now that we're up here, the two of us, alone. Sitting there, looking down at me, she seems to be deep in contemplation. My eyelids are closing. I fight to stay awake, just a little longer. But I'm so tired, so weary. And then I feel her hands at my waistband. Slowly, she unbuttons my jeans. I don't fight her as she slides them from me, and I hear the dull drop of them on the ground. My hands are by my sides, my arms weighted to the bed. I breathe in and out, keep myself steady, waiting, wanting this to be done with. For it all to be over.

She gets up and rounds the other side of the bed. Quickly, she unzips her sweatshirt and shrugs it off, then rips off her T-shirt, steps out of her jeans. In the moonlight, she's thinner than ever, her ribcage protruding, bra straps tracing lines over the ridges of her clavicles, depleted arms hanging limply by her sides. She is staring down at me, composing herself, and I feel a corresponding steadying of nerves within myself. Distantly I remember the bruising on my thighs, the shadowy threat of her from that night.

She slips under the covers and I wait for her to come to me. The touch of her hands on my flesh, the creep of her fingers, tentatively exploring, becoming bolder. And then she is hovering over me and I can feel the weight of her, the unbearably intimate invasion of her skin on mine. My heart thunders in my ribcage.

'You know I love you, don't you?' she whispers, her hand in my hair, her face drawing close now, close enough to see the light of mad love in her gaze.

This isn't love. This is survival.

I clench my fist tighter, feel the steel warm from the hot clutch of my sweaty hand, taken from the shelf in Jeff's study, secreted up here, hidden in the dark.

She lowers herself, her face on my face, her beating heart covering mine. I gather whatever scraps of strength I have left, grip the letter opener, and with a hard thrust, plunge it between her ribs. I feel the burst of skin and the sickening give of flesh. She rears back instantly, and for a held breath she seems suspended, the light catching the strain of tendons in her neck, the wild pulse throbbing in her jugular. And then a sound like a sigh of pain or disappointment escapes her. And I will remember this sound, and later I will wonder whether the thought went through her – the realization of the irony? For as the blood leaps out of her and she collapses forward, her fantasy is made real. Her flesh meets mine, skin to skin, finally, here at the end of things, our bodies entwine.

31.

Cara

Four months later

It is evening, and I am alone in our apartment for what will be the last time.

I stand at the window, listening to familiar noises: the rumble of traffic on the high street, the whoosh and ping of the elevator doors, a truck downshifting at the corner on to Kathleen Road, children playing in the gardens along Amies Street. But here, inside the place I have called home, everything feels different. The rooms echo with a new emptiness. The sale, held up for weeks because of some financial error – although Jeff and I both believe the real reason lay in the buyer's last-minute wobble over making their home upon the site of such a well-publicized crime – is finally going through. Everything has been cleared out and scrubbed clean. There is no trace of blood on the floorboards in the hall. The rug under the desk has been rolled up and discarded, the desk now installed in the new house in Dulwich. The kitchen seems vast without the table and chairs. A few last boxes sit on the worktops.

The buyers have offered to purchase the L-shaped sofa that fits snugly in the corner of the living room. It is the sole remaining item of furniture.

It is April, and the sky retains a quality of brittle blue brightness even though it is after six. From where I am standing, I can see the shiver of a breeze ruffling the petals on the cherry blossom trees that line the courtyard. In a week or two, the trees will be denuded of their flowers, and drifts of confetti-like petals will amass in corners and drains, growing dirty and trodden underfoot. But I will not be here to see it. I look down at them shimmering with hopeful beauty – the promise of summer to come. I turn away from the window, and pad softly over the bare floor towards the kitchen.

I am not supposed to be here. I should be sitting in a dentist's chair in Fulham, my problematic molar being tended to. But just after leaving the office, on my way to catch the train, I received an apologetic call from the surgery, explaining that Dr Nichol had an emergency to attend to and would have to reschedule. It could not be helped, they said. I did not mind. Perhaps that was apathy born of the fact that I had swallowed my last temazepam an hour beforehand in preparation for my dental treatment. The sedative was already taking effect, so that I didn't mind my appointment being bumped – I didn't much mind anything. The decision to come back here to The Village rather than heading home to the new house was made then. I was starting to feel muggy and vague, and not quite up to the longer journey home. Besides, part of me wanted – needed – to come back here one last time. Alone. To feel a different energy in these rooms than I had felt that last night, when all was chaos and fear and violence and bloodshed. Like an exorcism, I needed to leave this place behind me, cleansed of those memories.

I had tried explaining as much to Jeff on the phone just

now, and though he said all the right things – Was I sure? Did I want company? Offering to come over with Mabel – still, I heard the bafflement in his tone. He doesn't know what to make of me lately. I catch him, sometimes, out of the corner of my eye, looking at me with an unguarded expression of watchfulness and uncertainty.

In the kitchen, I poke around the empty cupboards, check the contents of the cardboard boxes. In one of them, along with some jars of pickles and various packages of flour and baking powder and a grimy plastic gallon of cooking oil, I find an old bottle of Marsala I used for cooking. There's still some left, and I pour a generous measure into a chipped cup that's also in the box, and carry it into the living room.

My limbs feel heavy, and the Marsala slides down my throat, warming and reassuring as I half-recline on the sofa, the cup clutched to my chest, staring out at the darkening sky beyond the window, alone and weary, but grateful too. Grateful for this chance to be here without the pressure of watchful eyes, of nervy solicitousness. I am tired of being treated like a patient or a victim, or even a survivor. Here, at last, there is privacy, a respite from all those prying eyes and good intentions. I have been so concerned with getting on with it, reclaiming my life, re-establishing and strengthening all those bonds and attachments I came so close to breaking, that I have had little opportunity to properly reflect on that night and all that led up to it.

I finish the Marsala, and put the cup down on the sofa next to me. Somewhere outside a car alarm goes off. My eyelids lower. My thoughts grow long and heavy. Silence in the room surrounds me. I allow myself to drift.

Perhaps it is inevitable that I fall asleep, under the influence of the wine and temazepam in my bloodstream, and when I do, I dream of Amy. She visits me a lot in my dreams, for that is the only way she can get in. During my waking hours, I push back hard against any thoughts of her. That is how I cope. But at night, the barriers are down and she drifts on through, a vague, troubling presence, the ghost of her laughter, the persistent glint of her fierce gaze still with me when I wake in the mornings, sweating and breathless.

But the dream that I have now is different. It feels like déjà vu, though I don't remember anything like this ever taking place between us. But the dream is so vivid and real and full of colour that I can almost be persuaded that Amy is right there with me, and I am sharing my secrets once more.

I did not kill Amy that night. But I wounded her seriously. So seriously that she spent the next few weeks under armed guard, first in Intensive Care and then later in a military hospital. They patched her up enough to remand her in custody in Holloway Prison until her trial, a date for which has not yet been set. They are still putting together the charges. Murder, grievous bodily harm, false imprisonment, to name but a few. It's quite the shopping list.

I have been told that a warrant for her extradition back to the United States is also being prepared. For Connie's murder. But also for an aggravated assault on a young woman in Philadelphia, whose name I had never heard mention of before. It makes me wonder whether there are more victims, more grisly crimes lurking in her past history, yet to be discovered. Sometimes, when I think on it too long or too deeply, I become overwhelmed at the knowledge of how close I came to disaster. How a brush with terror on a London street led me up a stairwell and into her head, her heart, her dark obsession. An obsession that led her to intimidate and frighten my daughter, to tear apart my marriage, to almost bludgeon to death my stepdaughter, to murder my lover. All because of her own twisted attachment, her dangerous need to love and be loved.

When I wake now, the apartment is in darkness. There's a chill in the air, the heating off, and despite my earlier confidence, I feel on edge, intimidated by the nudge of that disturbing dream. The sedative is wearing off, and I feel the need to get out of here, to be among those I love, kept safe by their reassuring presence.

The last look I take around the apartment is scant and half-seeing. I don't go upstairs. My old bedroom is the one room I won't check. And when I lock the front door and back away, I try to feel some sense of closure – an ending of sorts. But what I feel instead is disappointment. As if the missing piece is out there but I can't see it. It's beyond my reach. Instead, I come away without answers, just a frustrating lack of completion. A blank space, like the square tattoo on Amy's inner arm – dark and mean-ingless, an empty box.

The days pass and at the end of the week, Olivia finally comes home. We have prepared her room for her – the rear bedroom on the return, with a view of the garden which is coming into bloom. The walls have been painted the gentlest shade of green that I could find – a calming colour after all the trauma she has suffered. I have bought new bedlinen and made the room as pretty and welcoming as I can, and Jeff has installed a comfortable armchair pulled up to the window so she can sit there and look at the apple trees and pear trees, the laburnum readying itself to burst into colour, and feel her wounds start to heal.

Her hair has started growing back, a nasty jagged scar lurking beneath the new growth. One side of her head had been shaved for surgery in the hours following the attack. A skull fracture and a life-threatening subdural haematoma meant she had to be operated upon almost immediately, followed by three weeks in a coma. In that time, I watched my husband grow thin and gaunt and as wraith-like as his beloved daughter lying unconscious in the hospital bed. His vigil was almost constant and, in a strange way, I feel this helped to save our marriage. Neither of us had the energy for anything other than focusing on Olivia and her recovery, scouring the doctor's words for hidden meanings, researching online and through friends the various follow-up treatments to deal with the long-term effect of brain injuries. It meant that we didn't delve too deeply into the problems in our own marriage that led to that disastrous night. It was, I suppose, just sweeping those problems under the carpet, but it meant that when we did come to confront them – in the softly lit rooms of a marriage guidance counsellor – we were both ready, our thoughts more composed. We'd had time to mull things over separately before voicing them aloud.

It feels, at times, artificial, the way we are managing.

We carry on with our routines – work, school, home – altered as they are to accommodate Olivia's recovery and all the necessary medical attention she requires. We try our best to make our home a calm and peaceful environment for her, and for Mabel too. Jeff and I are at pains to be kind to each other, to be loving. We kiss each other hello and goodbye, we hug and embrace and compliment each other. All our resentments and grievances are stored up for those sessions with our counsellor where they are released, sometimes with vitriol, other times with reservations, and then picked over and examined like scientific specimens. It is exhausting but worthwhile, and I feel the dividends when we are alone together, preparing a meal or deciding where to put up bookshelves, some simple domestic task or decision undertaken together, a hum of pleasure running along beneath it.

We talk more now than we ever did, making time and space for each other, both of us, consciously trying to be open and honest. When he asks me about Finn, I answer as truthfully as I can – that I loved him once, but I had been wrong – foolish and reckless – to think that I could maintain something of that bond while being married to Jeff. Sometimes, he asks me about Amy, about whether I had any inkling of her obsession. For some reason, my mind always tracks back to that first night, when we were leaving the storeroom, nerves and fear colliding inside me at the prospect of facing the terrorists on the street, and I remember the clutch of her hand around mine – there was an urgency about it that, even in the heightened state of fear, was notable. I had no idea then of the murderous tendencies lurking inside her. But it had still made me uneasy.

I don't tell Jeff about my dream of her. It is unusually vivid, and unlike other dreams, whose narratives and images fade quickly with time, this one lingers and survives, announcing itself at odd moments – in a break between recording, in the lull of a train journey, that moment of the evening when the light is fading and night starts coming on.

I don't tell Jeff or any of our friends about it. But I do tell Dr Nichol.

It takes me over a month to reschedule my dental appointment, so that by the time I return to the surgery, the pain in my mouth has become unbearable. Dr Nichol is brisk and efficient but gentle too – almost tender. She has had her baby – a picture of a wide-eyed newborn with a shock of black hair sits proudly next to the monitor of her computer. She looks trim and tired, the familiar smudged shadows beneath the eyes of a new mother showing above her mask as she peers into my mouth.

After it is done, and I have rinsed and spat, rinsed and spat, I swing my legs around so my feet touch the ground and sit for a minute while she snaps off her gloves and slips down her mask.

'So?' she asks. 'How was that?'

'Fine. It was fine,' I say, my voice holding a note of surprise.

'You were able to control your fear?'

'Yes.'

'Good,' she says, sounding genuinely pleased.

I had decided to undertake the surgery without a sedative.

'What caused you to change your mind?' she asks, her head cocked to one side, interested.

'I don't know. I just thought I should try without it.'

She nods and keeps holding my gaze, like the answer I've given is not sufficient. Which it's not.

'Actually,' I say, 'the truth is, I was a little wary of taking temazepam again.'

'Oh?'

'The first time I took it – for the hygienist – was okay. But the last two occasions I've taken it, I've felt a little odd.'

'Two occasions?' Her eyes narrow, a slight frown mark appearing over the bridge of her nose. 'There was the last time, when I had to cancel your appointment. But the other time . . . ?'

Inwardly, I squirm a little, then decide it's best just to confess. So I tell her about the night I took the sedative not for imminent dental treatment but to calm my nerves. I don't mention anything about waking up the next morning alongside Amy, the bruising, the disaster that ensued.

'I was going through a bit of a personal crisis,' I explain, and even now, when I think about those difficult days – the photographs of me sent to my colleagues, Finn's threats over Mabel – it brings a shudder of fear or anger. 'And on this particular night, I was upset, and I took the drug to calm me down.'

'I see,' she says, keeping any note of judgement or disapproval from her tone. 'So, what happened? What kind of oddness did you experience?'

'On both occasions, there was a kind of blankness – like I'd blacked out, or something.'

'Was there alcohol involved?'

'A little. More so the first time. Definitely, yes, the first time – I was drinking a lot that night.' A flash, then, of Amy cupping her hands around mine, pushing the vodka to my lips and urging me to drink. 'The second night, not so much – a little Marsala, that's all. But I had the weirdest dream.'

'The second time?'

'Right. A really vivid dream. But the thing is, I was dreaming about the first night – the night I blacked out. A lot of the same details, the same circumstances, but then all this crazy stuff as well that didn't happen. And the thing I find strange is that I keep thinking about this dream. Most dreams, you forget, right? But this one keeps coming back to me.'

'Are you sure it was a dream?' she asks quietly.

The air between us changes – it pulses with the sense of imminent threat.

'Of course. Why, what do you mean?'

She gives the slightest raise of her eyebrows, a careful smile that does nothing to assuage the panic that has jumped alive inside me.

'Might it have been a recovered memory instead of a dream?'

'No . . . I . . . No, that's not possible . . .'

I look to the side, trying to remember. Outside the window, the sun is beaming down on the street. Fretful thoughts clamber and squirm inside me. *It's not possible*, I think. *It couldn't be.*

'Temazepam interferes with the consolidation of memories,' she explains. 'Events that happen while under the influence of the drug often don't enter the long-term memory and so will not be recalled subsequently. The potent amnesiac effects of these drugs complement the sedative effects. And of course, the effect of all of these drugs is enhanced by alcohol intake. You've heard of the drug Rohypnol?'

The spectre of bruising on my thigh rears up suddenly. 'The date-rape drug?'

'Exactly. It is a benzodiazepine drug, like temazepam.'

I'm struggling to take all of this in, and perhaps she sees the confusion in my face, for she adopts a less academic tone.

'Memory is a strange thing, Cara. Some studies have indicated that memory lost while under the influence of a drug like temazepam might be recovered when you take another dose.'

Sweat forms and rolls along my spine. My mouth, still partially numb, is beginning to tingle. I feel assaulted by this information, like my thoughts are scrambling to get away from it, while at the same time needing to understand.

'Memories that have been repressed for any reason,' Dr Nichol continues, 'are more likely to be recalled from long-term memory when the person is exposed to the same or a similar situation. It acts as a powerful cue.'

'So, if something had happened to me while under the influence of temazepam and alcohol, but I had repressed the memory, you're saying I could remember it if I took the same drug, coupled with alcohol, in the same place –'

'Yes. It's a possibility.'

'Jesus.'

'Are you alright?'

Both my hands have come up to my face, my fingers pressed against my mouth.

'Cara?'

'I just —'

'It's a theory, dear, that's all,' she says kindly, and I can see the concern in her gaze, perhaps a slight push of regret. 'Perhaps, whatever it is you thought you dreamed was just that — a dream.'

'But how can I know?'

I hear the desperate edge in my own voice, see her suck in her lower lip and shake her head. In this matter, she cannot help me. No one can.

I turn the key in the lock and push the door. The numbness in my mouth has worn off, a tenderness there instead. I test the filled tooth cautiously but obsessively with the tip of my tongue. A wave of warm air comes to meet me, voices from outside alerting me to a presence in the back garden. The day has bloomed into an unseasonably hot afternoon, the kind that occurs in high summer, not a Saturday in May. I go into the kitchen, put my bag down on the table and look out the window behind the sink.

All three of them are there. Jeff, keeping to his promise, is standing on a stepladder fastening a rope swing to the largest tree in the garden. Mabel is jumping up and down with excitement below him, trying to contain her impatience for the swing to be ready. In a deckchair nearby, Olivia sits watching. The chair faces away from me, so I can only see the wide-brimmed hat she wears, and one stalk-like arm raised as if to hold the hat in place.

It is a perfect scene. An idyllic snapshot of family life. I want so badly to go out there and join them, to kick my shoes off and feel the spring grass beneath my bare feet, to push my little girl on her new swing and hear her squeal with delight, to stand back with my husband and observe with silent gratitude all we have, all that has been saved.

But I don't. I can't. I am held back by a memory. Not a dream.

Just a theory, Dr Nichol had said.

But I felt the hum of truth in it, the unmistakable feeling of authenticity.

'Tell me what's wrong?' she says.

We are sitting together on the couch. It is the middle of the night, and there is that quality of stillness that accompanies the hour, like everything said or done is veiled in darkness and secrecy. Outside, a car alarm is going off. I feel oppressed by all that has happened – the way Finn has turned on me, sending that photograph to my colleagues, his threats over Mabel. My hands are wrapped around a glass of vodka and Amy urges me to drink. I can feel the burn of it in my throat, feel it wending its way through my bloodstream, dancing and twisting with the sedative, filling my limbs and my head with a welcome heaviness – the promise of obliteration.

We have talked and drunk and somehow ended up on the floor, my arms around her. She is sobbing after her account of Connie, the accident. Tears roll wetly down her cheeks – they seep into the cotton of my T-shirt, making little dark marks of their own.

'Poor Amy,' I say. 'Poor, poor girl.' The words feel foreign in my mouth.

I don't feel afraid. I don't feel threatened or violated. I feel perfectly at peace.

She is stroking my hair, and it makes me think of my mother, and it's like I'm a little girl again and my mother has momentarily left aside her own dark thoughts to focus on mine.

'What is it?' she asks. 'What's wrong?'

And I realize that I am crying too. I am sobbing hard, gulping for air, so great is the emotion that has built inside me.

'Cara, sweetheart, what? Tell me. Angel, what's wrong?'

The crisis that's working its way up through me is urgent and overwhelming – I feel like I can't breathe. Mabel – my daughter. Finn is going to take her from me. Suddenly, I am sure of it.

'He's never going to leave me alone,' I tell her. 'I won't ever get free of him.'

'Who?'

'Finn.'

I'm shaking now, little nervy spasms shooting through my limbs. I can feel her crouched beside me, the closeness of her body to mine, the heat of her skin, her breath. And I know that it is not my mother. It is Amy.

'He's dangerous to you,' she says. 'It scares me, thinking of what he might do.'

'God, I wish someone would just . . .'

She puts her hand to my face, smooths the hair back from it. I close my eyes, surrendering to her touch.

'It should just be the two of us,' she says. 'No one else to interfere. No one to stand in our way.' Her body quivers with fear or excitement, and I can feel her holding herself back, as if afraid of releasing the held breath between us.

'Let me help you,' she says, her voice coming close to my ear. 'Let me get rid of him for you.'

Even though the word is not uttered, it is there between us. I know, somehow, that for her killing is a possibility. I know that she will do it because she loves me; loves me to the point of obsession.

'It's the only way,' she whispers.

In that moment, we are closer to each other than we have ever been to another living soul. Both of us exposed, vulnerable, dependent, needing to trust the other.

I open my eyes and look at her. See the expectation in her face.

She has seen my darkest thoughts, my most wicked desires.

'Will you?' I ask and, slowly, I smile at her.

Her eyes pass quickly over my face. They light up in understanding.

'Yes,' she says as she closes in, as her lips meet mine.

For why should I not rely upon her help? Why should I not ask?

She is, after all, my closest friend.

Acknowledgements

To borrow a phrase from my friend Tana French, this book has gone from brain to shelf in just under a year. It's been a wild ride that would not have been possible without the skilful steering of my wonderful agent, Jonathan Lloyd. I'm indebted to him for his wit, wisdom and careful guidance, and I hope he will forgive me for the challenges of this last year! I owe thanks to the fantastic team at Curtis Brown, particularly to Melissa Pimentel and Luke Speed, for their stellar work in handling foreign rights, and film and television rights, respectively.

I'm deeply grateful for the continued support of my publisher Penguin Random House, and the amazing team at Michael Joseph. Maxine Hitchcock has been championing the Karen Perry cause for some years now, and I cannot think of a better person to have in my corner. I'm hugely thankful for her tireless support, her inventiveness and wise counsel, and indeed, her friendship. Matilda McDonald worked closely with me while I wrote this book, lending her sharp editorial skills and astute insights, and making me feel like each deadline was achievable – I couldn't have done it without her. Thanks also to Penguin Ireland, in particular Cliona Lewis, for bringing this novel to the attention of readers in my home country.

Good fortune allowed my path to cross with that of Professor David Harris in the autumn of 2017. I thank him for his generosity in sharing with me his knowledge of conscious sedation during dental surgery, in particular the effects of Benzodiazepine drugs on memory. I have taken some artistic licence with the facts he provided, and I hope he will forgive me for this. I claim full responsibility for any mistakes made.

I was lucky enough to have Alice O'Sullivan at RTE show me around behind the scenes of Ireland's national broadcaster's radio studios. I thank her for so generously sharing her time and experience with me, and for giving me a fascinating insight into the world of live broadcasting and the working life of a radio producer.

Part of this book was written at the Tyrone Guthrie Centre at Annaghmakerrig – a place I have returned to again and again over the years, always finding inspiration and peace there. I thank them for continuing to have me back. I'm also grateful to my wonderful parents-in-law, Catherine and Paul Sweeney, for allowing me to escape to their beautiful house in Donegal to work on this book when I was particularly panicked (and for feeding my husband and children in my absence!).

So many of my friends have provided encouragement and support in various forms over the past year. I must thank especially Tana French, Rowena Walsh, Rachel Conway, and the ladies of the Exclusive EU Book Club.

As ever, the support and love of my mother, my extended family and my in-laws make my writing life possible. My beautiful girls who almost always reacted with patience and grace when told to 'leave Mummy alone, she's working on the book' – thank you, and sorry. And last, but never least, Conor Sweeney, for his love, his endless supply of coffee, and for keeping me going with his infectious optimism.

A deeply atmospheric and masterfully crafted tale of love and loss that will chill you to the bone . . .

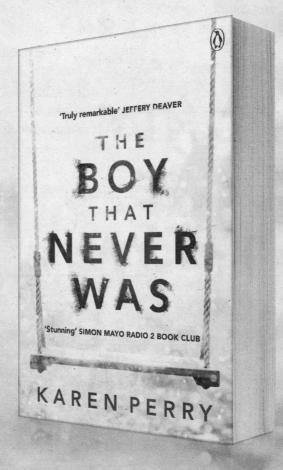

'Truly remarkable' JEFFERY DEAVER

THE
BOY
THAT
NEVER
WAS

'Stunning' SIMON MAYO RADIO 2 BOOK CLUB

KAREN PERRY

Available to buy now

He just wanted a decent book to read ...

Not too much to ask, is it? It was in 1935 when Allen Lane, Managing Director of Bodley Head Publishers, stood on a platform at Exeter railway station looking for something good to read on his journey back to London. His choice was limited to popular magazines and poor-quality paperbacks – the same choice faced every day by the vast majority of readers, few of whom could afford hardbacks. Lane's disappointment and subsequent anger at the range of books generally available led him to found a company – and change the world.

'We believed in the existence in this country of a vast reading public for intelligent books at a low price, and staked everything on it'
Sir Allen Lane, 1902–1970, founder of Penguin Books

The quality paperback had arrived – and not just in bookshops. Lane was adamant that his Penguins should appear in chain stores and tobacconists, and should cost no more than a packet of cigarettes.

Reading habits (and cigarette prices) have changed since 1935, but Penguin still believes in publishing the best books for everybody to enjoy. We still believe that good design costs no more than bad design, and we still believe that quality books published passionately and responsibly make the world a better place.

So wherever you see the little bird – whether it's on a piece of prize-winning literary fiction or a celebrity autobiography, political tour de force or historical masterpiece, a serial-killer thriller, reference book, world classic or a piece of pure escapism – you can bet that it represents the very best that the genre has to offer.

Whatever you like to read – trust Penguin.